RYANN FLETCHER

A Recipe for Regret

To all the ones that got away.

Contents

Chapter 1	1
Chapter 2	10
Chapter 3	16
Chapter 4	25
Chapter 5	32
Chapter 6	43
Chapter 7	49
Chapter 8	59
Chapter 9	66
Chapter 10	74
Chapter 11	83
Chapter 12	91
Chapter 13	98
Chapter 14	111
Chapter 15	115
Chapter 16	125
Chapter 17	133
Chapter 18	148
Chapter 19	152
Chapter 20	163
Chapter 21	171
Chapter 22	185
Chapter 23	193
Chapter 24	201
Chapter 25	209
Chapter 26	219

Chapter 27   222
Chapter 28   224
Chapter 29   232
Chapter 30   242
Chapter 31   254
Chapter 32   262
Chapter 33   274
Chapter 34   287
Chapter 35   299
Chapter 36   307
Chapter 37   319
Chapter 38   328
Chapter 39   342
Chapter 40   348
Chapter 41   361
Chapter 42   377
Chapter 43   388
Chapter 44   409
Chapter 45   425
Chapter 46   432
Chapter 47   441
Epilogue   457
End of Book 5   462
Unbound Oath preview   463
About the Author   466
Also by Ryann Fletcher   467

Chapter 1

The day had already dragged on for far too long when the Overseer's voice rang out into the corridor. "Ms. Dodson!" echoed off the metal-walled corridor and rang like a broken chime.

Delia cringed. That woman's voice was like gears grinding in a poorly maintained ship. At least back on Gamma-3, gods, even in Skelm, she could escape it for a while. Here at the Outer Rim, there was no getting away from her. "Yes?" she answered in her usual bright, obedient tone. "What can I do for you, Overseer?"

"I need you to draft an announcement for tomorrow morning's broadcast."

"I thought you already signed off—"

"The situation has changed."

"I'll be right in," Delia said, swallowing back an aggrieved sigh. What she wouldn't give for a moment's peace. She slid off the rickety stool and made sure that her shirt was tucked in. The overseer's lectures on presentation were unbearable.

"Bring a pad of paper with you."

"Of course!" Rolling her eyes to the bare, unfinished ceiling, she mouthed a swear and tucked a pen behind her ear. She knocked on the adjacent doorway and poked her head in. "Are you ready for me?"

"I've been waiting for what feels like several days. Yes, I am ready."

"Alright, what did you want to add to the broadcast?"

"Sit. We need to rework the entire thing."

Clawing her eyes out was preferable to another session with Allemande, but still, she sat down in the high-backed chair opposite her. "Okay."

"First of all, we need to scrap the story about nutritional needs here at the station. As it happens, one of the laborers has been writing home, telling them all about the appalling food here. We have now instituted censoring on wires home, but the damage has been done." The overseer glared at the paper in her hand. "Now, we've had to hire a cook for at least the higher ups here on site. We can still use this piece once we can prove that any communications suggesting otherwise are nothing more than exaggerations."

"Mhmm. Understood."

"Ms. Dodson, if I may ask, what is your opinion of the nutritional offerings here?"

"Er—perfectly adequate, ma'am."

"If only every worker here was like you, we wouldn't have to trouble ourselves with this trivial nonsense!"

"Yes, ma'am. Thank you." It was easier to agree with her. The food, if you could even call it that, on the station was nothing short of disgusting, and Delia had been living almost entirely off the stash of illicit imported chocolate in her cramped quarters. "And what of the progress report regarding construction here? Are we going to scrap that from the broadcast as well?"

"Move that to the evening. We will have additional information to add concerning the ventilation systems here, as well as proposed improvements to crew quarters. While I find it entirely preposterous, it is proving a challenge to recruit skilled laborers to work out here. Other stations get by just fine using indentured workers, but this place has sensitive information. We just can't risk it."

"Mm," Delia agreed. Maybe if the Coalition agreed to pay laborers more than a pittance, they'd have an easier time obtaining craftspeople. "What did you want to replace the rest of the morning broadcast with, then?"

"Have you spoken to Mr. Cross?"

"No, I haven't seen Thomas all day." She'd spent half the afternoon looking for him, too. How the hell was she supposed to deliver the evening broadcast without an operator?

"I'm afraid I have some grave news, Ms. Dodson."

"What happened? Is he alright?"

"We made the unfortunate discovery that Mr. Cross had been passing information to The Scattered."

Every muscle in Delia's body tensed. Thomas? A spy? "Gods," she managed to squeak. "How did you find that out?"

"An anonymous member of the work crew tipped off General Fineglass last week. She said that she had seen him scavenging through the shredded document discards, trying to piece together papers. We laid a cunning trap, and he eagerly stepped directly into it."

"I can't believe it," she breathed, and it was the first true thing she'd said to Allemande in days. "To think, I'd worked alongside him for years, and never knew."

"Yes, I'd have thought a dedicated reporter like yourself would have noticed that something was awry with him, or at least suspect." The overseer arched an eyebrow. "You didn't, did you?"

"No, of course not."

"Then I am very disappointed in you. I expect my staff to be observant, keenly so. To think that a traitor loomed under your nose for years, undetected!"

"They are getting more sophisticated lately."

Allemande frowned. "Yes, I suppose that is true, after all. In any case, General Fineglass has already seen to his punishment. I appreciate that you are now in need of a new operator—"

"Punishment?"

"Yes, of course, Ms. Dodson. Thomas Cross was a traitor."

Was. The word hung in the air, heavy and inescapable. "I just thought, a trial—"

"We don't have time for trials out here, you know better than that."

"Of course." She blinked furiously, desperate to keep the tears from pooling in her eyes. Dangerous to show any affection for a traitor, and even more fraught to show weakness this far from Gamma-3.

"Do not cry for him," Allemande scolded. "He was an enemy. A treasonous snake. He wanted nothing more than to see us all suffocate. The paperwork he was stealing from the incineration pile concerned the ventilators on this station, and we can only assume that he was passing that information to The Scattered to give them an edge over us."

"Did he already pass the information on?"

"Don't be ridiculous. The information was planted. Fabricated. General Fineglass is no fool, and no stranger to the activities of miscreants."

Delia nodded. "It is good that he didn't put the station in danger." She'd find whoever ratted him out, and push them out of the airlock herself. Thomas was a good man, a friend. She hadn't even known that they shared an alliance beyond broadcasting, though she should have guessed when he didn't intervene when she'd reworded scripts back in Skelm. Some reporter she was, missing the obvious.

"Quite right. As it stands, we have to get out in front of this mess before word gets out. I've already informed the workers that communications off the station will be limited going forward due to cost analysis and staffing shortages, but someone will notice that he is missing."

"Missing."

"We can't have people knowing that The Scattered were so close to infiltrating us, Ms. Dodson. It will only encourage them."

"Yes."

"I propose a statement about the hazards of mind-altering substances. Poor Mr. Cross, having smuggled illegal spirits onto the station, became rather inebriated, and decided to go for an unsupervised space jump. Tragically, he did so without a protective suit."

"Understood."

"Offer your personal condolences. After all, you knew him best of anyone on the station." Overseer Allemande glared at her over the smooth, polished desk. "Do you swear that you didn't know about his proclivities?"

"Of course, ma'am."

"Hmm. Very well then, I suppose. You will be assigned a new operator, some volunteer from the new crew arrivals. She has assured the general that she has experience with broadcasting, but I am sure you will need to guide her along in the beginning."

"Yes, ma'am."

"If she is not suitable, we will have to send for someone, but it would be at least a month before we could get someone out here, you understand."

"I'm sure the new operator will be just fine." Her heart squeezed in her chest. Thomas, gone, just like that. Her own demise felt even more inevitable than usual. She couldn't keep this up forever, certainly not with a new operator who would be quick to snitch to Allemande. "Did you want any other changes for tomorrow morning? Or evening?"

"No, that will be all. Work up a draft and bring it back in twenty minutes for approval."

"I'll be as quick as I can."

"And Ms. Dodson, if you see my daughter, please tell her that I need to speak with her urgently."

"If I see Emeline, I will send her here."

"You are dismissed."

Delia nodded, pushing herself up out of her chair, her limbs heavy, her chest tight. Without Thomas, she really was alone out here, all by herself, in the crushing, endless darkness of space.

* * *

"Good morning, I'm Delia Dodson. Overseer Allemande and General Fineglass wish to remind the good citizens of the Coalition of the dangers of illegal substances." The words felt like ash in her mouth. She swallowed hard and continued. "Thomas Cross, my broadcast operator for many years, smuggled contraband onto Turas-Mara Station in the way of strong, unfiltered alcohol. He was tempted to indulge, and despite the strict access controls, he attempted to go on an unauthorized space jump without a protective suit."

Tears welled in her eyes. "Goddamnit, Thomas, why couldn't you at least tell me? I could have tried to protect you, or - or..." she trailed off, leaning her forehead against the cool glass of the mirror in her bathroom, the dark blond ringlets that had escaped their pins, hanging down over her shoulders. "How in all the gods' names am I supposed to get through this tomorrow?"

She sighed and watched the fog expand across the mirror, and then contract, obscuring her gentle curves and wide hazel eyes. She'd only seen him that morning after the broadcast. He was making some joke about how disgusting breakfast was. She'd been ready to kill him when he hadn't showed up for the evening broadcast, leaving her to rush from room to room preparing all the equipment.

And now he was gone, just like that. No doubt Fineglass had probably gotten some sick sense of achievement out of shoving poor Thomas out an airlock. Sadist. Monster. Gods be damned, if only she'd known! They could have protected each other, could have... well. Maybe that's what he'd been doing all along. Protecting her.

Bending, she turned the bronze tap and waited for water to flow, the newly constructed pipes creaking and groaning. Unless that new aquifer got built soon, no doubt they'd start seeing water rations. She splashed the cool water against her face in a bid to slow her heart rate. Mammalian diving impulse, it was called. It helped, if only a little.

How long could she keep all this up, really? She didn't even know if her messages since arriving at the Outer Rim were reaching the rebels, or if they were of any use. She hadn't had contact with a member of The Scattered since Skelm. Poor Lawrence Tripp. His idea to let the storms destroy the city was rash... too rash, in her opinion. But it didn't matter. He was dead now, too.

The door to her quarters slammed, and she stiffened. Was Fineglass going to throw her out an airlock, too?

"Dee?"

She jerked away from the sink. "William?" Drying her face, she stumbled out into her cramped quarters. "Will! What in all the gods' names are you doing here?"

"Isn't a husband allowed to visit his wife?"

"Of course, I just… it's an awfully long way to travel just to say hello."

"What would you say if I told you I was here for a potential business investment?"

She grimaced. "I'd say to be careful."

"What's wrong?" he asked gently, his brow furrowed.

"They… Thomas is gone."

"Gone?"

"Dead." The word didn't feel real.

"Gods! What happened!"

She searched his face, chewing the inside of her cheek. "He smuggled some booze onto the station. Got drunk, stumbled out an airlock."

"That doesn't sound like Thomas."

"No, it doesn't. I don't think I ever saw that man take a drink in all the years I knew him."

Thomas reached out for her, drawing her into a warm embrace. "I worry about you being out here, you know. This kind of darkness can do strange things to people."

"I'm alright."

"I'm sure Thomas was, too, until he wasn't. How did he even get that stuff on board? They all but turned all my things inside out before I was even allowed to board the transport from Nox Beacon."

"I don't know, I—William, what were you doing at Nox Beacon?"

He grinned amiably. "Coming to see you, of course. And to look into this investment, as I said."

"If I find out that you were—"

"Don't worry, Dee, I am behaving myself. I made you a promise, and I intend to keep it."

She pulled away, cuffing the sleeves of her shirt. "I hope that's true."

"When have I ever lied to you?"

Raising an eyebrow, she gave a small tut. "Do you want a list, Will?"

"Alright, alright, you've made your point. On my word as a good-for-nothing husband, I was only there to transfer transports."

"How did you hear about this *opportunity*, anyway?"

"An old friend."

"Am I to assume—"

"Yes, but he's on the straight and narrow now. Just like me. He's solid, and the recommendation looks to be promising. I'm just here to verify a few things, check up on some of what he said, and I'll be out of your hair. Barely enough room in here for one person, much less two."

"If this old friend is so solid, how come you have to come all the way out here to verify it?"

"You're the one who wants me to be more careful," he huffed. "Damned if I do, damned—"

"You've made your point," she said with a sigh. "I do appreciate your dedication. How long will you be here?"

"A few days, a week, maybe."

"I'll have to move some things out of the closet for your suits."

"No, no, I'll do it," he said, setting his old, worn leather case on the bed. "I'm the interloper here. I won't need much space, just enough for a couple of hangers."

She nodded. "Sure."

"So..." he mumbled, unpacking the neatly folded suit pieces. "What can I move from the closet? I don't want to ruin your system."

"That's why I said I'd do it." She opened the small wardrobe and pulled a few hangers out, folding the clothes over the back of the desk chair in the corner. "There, should be plenty of room."

"Thank you, Dearest." The hangers rattled gently as he hung his suits, admiring them before closing the door. "Are you sure you're alright? Losing Thomas, that must be hard. When did you find out?"

"About an hour ago."

"Dee!" he gasped, rushing to fold her into his arms again. "Gods, you must still be in shock! Why didn't you say?"

"I don't really know what to say, Will. What can I say? I have to deliver the report in the morning, and I'm afraid I'll just break down and cry. No doubt that would send me packing. Overseer Allemande..."

"Yes, I've heard. How can I help? Do you need food? Sleep? Practice, or—"

"I appreciate the offer, I do, I just…" she sighed again, rubbing her forehead. "I think I just need a bath and then some sleep. Tomorrow won't be any easier if I'm dead tired." Dead. Thomas was dead. Tears welled in her eyes again, and she sank into Will's arms. "I am glad to see you, Will. I feel more alone than ever now."

"Shall I sleep on the floor tonight?" he asked. "Or—"

"No," she replied. "On top of the covers is fine. Just don't drool on me. It will be nice to have a friend by my side, at least for tonight."

Chapter 2

"Hey!" The military police officer shouted. "Where do you think you're going?"

"The kitchens?" Rosie replied, waving her hand vaguely down the hall. "I was just pulled in from Nox Beacon to be the new cook."

"Oh! Oh, hey!" the guard said, smiling. "It's about time we got some decent grub around here, we—"

"I'm told it's for management only."

"Figures. Fine, let me scan your chip."

Rosie held out her arm obediently and waited for the grumbled chirp of the scanner. "Thank you," she said, when the military police officer released his grip on her.

"Kitchen's that way," he said, nodding his head at the corridor. "First door on the left. Hope you're not expecting miracles."

Turas-Mara Station was still small, duty-built for the small exploration team that first inhabited it. Now that she was inside, it was obvious just how cramped everything really was. Low ceilings, metal walls and flooring, none of the opulence that usually signified the Coalition's architecture. Out here, things were different.

The heels of her boots clacked noisily against the grates beneath her feet. There was no way to sneak around here, not with the painful metallic echoes. She swung into the first door on the left, and immediately, her heart sank.

"Gods below," she whispered aloud. "What the hell am I supposed to do with this?"

The word 'small' didn't come close to describing her new workspace. 'Minuscule' was more like it, or, perhaps, 'infinitesimal.' There was one bare counter, crumbs strewn across it. Two small heating elements in the corner, and one oven that pulled heat from the boilers.

The cupboards were bare, except for a few dented cans of spinach. If there were more than a handful of management, she was going to have a very hard time keeping up, much less having extra time to cook for the rest of the staff. Rosie heaved a sigh, regret sinking into her chest. She should have stayed where she was, making gallons of broth a day for the MPOs. Boring work, but at least she wasn't squeezed into a box the size of a goldfish bowl.

"Ms. Gordon, I presume?"

"Er—yes, that's me," she replied. The woman was dressed sharply, despite the grim setting of the station, down to the top hat perched atop her head. There was something about her that made Rosie feel on edge.

"I am Overseer Allemande. I am who sent for you."

"Nice to meet you, ma'am."

"Thank you for coming so quickly. It would seem that much of the management was growing to resent the efficiency of the protein blocks."

Rosie resisted the urge to make a face. Gods, how long had these people been eating that crap? "My pleasure. I'm excited to get started, it's just—"

"We have a limited staff here. We cannot be reassigning workers to do your job for you. The food shipment is in the cargo bay. We get shipments weekly. You can request ingredients a month ahead of time, as that's how long the cargo ships take to get out here."

"Understood."

"The management will be expecting two meals a day, breakfast and dinner. They will fend for themselves for lunch, as most will not have the time to leave their posts. The mess hall is on the other side of that wall. As you can see, the station is currently undergoing a major overhaul, in order to prepare it for the expanded crew that will be arriving in approximately six months. We cannot endure any inefficiency out here. To be inefficient is to die."

"Yes, ma'am."

"You may start immediately. The management will be expecting breakfast in the morning."

"Is there anything you would like to request, Overseer?"

Allemande's lip curled in disgust. "No, certainly not. Some of us are quite happy with protein blocks. Your quarters are across the hall. We don't have maintenance staff, so unless something is entirely non-functional, you will have to deal with it yourself for now." She smiled now, a cold, emotionless expression that didn't reach her eyes. "We are glad to have you on board, Ms. Gordon. If your work is efficient, and management commends you, then I expect you could be promoted in six months' time, when the expanded kitchens and mess hall are completed."

"Oh! Yes, ma'am, that sounds wonderful."

"You'll want to get right to work, I imagine. If you have questions, I'm sure you're smart enough to answer them yourself."

Rosie nodded, and the overseer swept out of the room with a definitive swish from the tails of her long jacket. She could put up with this for six months if it meant she could really start to climb the ranks. After all, Allemande was hugely influential, and not just in her own sector. The same could be said for the fabled General Fineglass, despite having been hermetic as of late.

Maybe Turas-Mara was her shot at climbing out of the gutters, of making her family proud for once.

* * *

Rosie squinted at the map taped to the wall. She'd spent more time lost than unpacking the kitchen, and now she was going in circles trying to find the cargo bay. Two lefts, a right, and the stairs. These maps were already inaccurate with all the construction going on, which is how she'd found herself in this service corridor, surrounded by boxes of spare filters and light bulbs.

Groaning, she set off again, repeating the instructions in her head. One left led her down a dark hallway, lined with broom cupboards and spare ladders. The second left looked familiar, but then, everything on this damned station looked familiar. Stairs! Thank the gods. She descended the steps down into the cargo bay, and found the pallet marked "kitchens," surrounded by MPOs pulling cans out.

"Hey!" she shouted. "What do you think you're doing?"

"Who the hell are you?" one of them demanded. "No civilians in the cargo bay!"

"I'm not a civilian, I'm the cook!"

"Oh, shit," another one said, placing one of their cans back into a wooden crate. "We didn't know. Please don't tell the general. We've had nothing but those damned protein things for weeks."

Rosie softened. "You can't be stealing food. They'll find out sooner or later. Just... okay, let's make a deal. You put back all that food, and I'll see if I can get you something."

"Fuck that," the first one spat. "Abara said you're only cooking for the management. That true?"

"Yes, but—"

"Then forget it. You have no proof of what we took."

"Put it back!" Rosie shouted, her arms crossed. "I'll cross check it with the order list, I'll—"

"Piss off, chef. We've left you plenty for the management. There's another shipment coming in a week, anyway."

"Wait." She raised an eyebrow, her jaw set firm. She'd dealt with meaner assholes than these. "Do you really want to be eating, what is that, canned carrots? Maybe some canned corn?"

The guard shifted his weight from foot to foot. "Better than protein blocks."

"Still though, it's hardly a nice stew, is it? Put the cans back, and I'll bring you leftovers."

"How do we know you're not lying?"

"This isn't a large station, it's not as though you don't know where the kitchens are to come find me if I am. Listen, I get it. The food out this way is garbage. But if you trust me, we can all win, here."

"What's in it for you?"

"Knowing my shipments will be safe from pilfering."

"Fine," the guard said nonchalantly, tossing the can back into the wooden crate with a heavy thud. "But I'll believe it when I see it. If you screw us over, chef, next time I'll take double." He nodded to the others. "Put it back. All of it. We have to give cheffy here a chance to make good on her promise."

One by one, the cans landed in the box. "Thank you," Rosie said sweetly, grabbing the handles of the crate. "Tomorrow, after supper, I'll sneak some down here for you."

They grumbled amongst themselves as she left, carrying the heavy crate back up the stairs. She'd end up with calves of steel in no time with this job. Up the stairs, a left, and two rights brought her back to the kitchen. So far, so good. Maybe in a year she'd know her way around without having to memorize directions.

By the gods, they'd given her a lot of crap to work with. Who the hell had even placed this order? Someone who never eats actual food? Nothing but cans, some of them dented, at least two bulging, the result of improper canning methods. Rosie puffed out her cheeks with a sigh and began to categorize them. Most of it was canned vegetables, which she could at least use in soups. Not even any flour to be had, though, so that ruled out any kinds of bread or pasta.

Stacking cans in the cupboard, she tapped her fingertips against her temples, drumming up ideas. Stews she could do. There were a few cans of soybeans. A whole pile of canned citrus fruits - no scurvy on this station, at least.

Leaning over the counter, examining the amounts, she scratched out a tentative menu on a pad of paper she'd found in a drawer, the soft graphite of the pencil whispering across the page. It would be slim pickings until they got some better ingredients. She'd at least need flour to start making things interesting, and that should be easy to get out here. No harder than cans, anyway.

Breakfasts would be canned fruits, that was unavoidable. Without anything else, what could she even offer? Dinners, soups, for the most part. If she could coax the soybeans into a soft tofu, maybe a mousse, for dessert. There wasn't enough for a main course.

This was going to be harder than she had anticipated. Unbuckling her suitcase, she placed her cast iron pan atop the heating element. Given that the only pans stored in there were warped or cracked, she was once again grateful that she'd brought it along.

Closing the kitchen door behind her, the latch clicked. She frowned at it, wondering if she should request a padlock. Those MPOs might sneak in and steal food otherwise. Her own quarters were even more cramped than her tiny room back home had been. Enough space for a bed, a desk, and a chair. The bathroom was similar, with a half-sized bathtub she'd be lucky if she fit a third of herself into, and a dirty, water-stained mirror over the sink. The toilet was strangely low to the floor, but at least it was only hers.

She set her suitcase on the bed and began to unpack, hanging her Coalition-issued yellow and purple apron on the hook next to the door, placing her stationery on the desk. Even if she wrote them a letter tonight, it would be months before her family received it. She couldn't afford to send a wire, not yet. Sending them from this distance would cost a fortune in credits.

Sitting down in the uncomfortable chair, the arms biting into her hips, she began to write.

"Dearest family, I am writing to you from the Outer Rim. Please don't be angry."

Chapter 3

Delia swallowed the last bite of the tasteless protein block and opened the door to the recording booth. She didn't want to do this. It felt wrong. Poor Thomas, her one friend out here. Will would be gone in a few days, but... well, that was just complicated. They'd never had a normal kind of relationship.

"Good morning!" A woman chirped, her grin broad and irritatingly welcoming. She leaned against the doorway at her wide hips, her dark curls tumbling over her shoulders.

"Morning," Delia grumbled in reply. "You the new operator?"

"That indeed! I wanted to go over some checks with you before we got started."

"What kind of checks?"

"Oh, just routine, that sort of thing. I don't want to cramp the style of the great Delia Dodson!"

Delia blinked at her. "You've listened to my broadcasts?"

"Oh, every evening! I've followed you from when you had those traffic reports back on Gamma-3."

"Right." Why the hell would someone follow her traffic reports? Hardly riveting. "Thomas used to..." she stopped and took a deep breath. "The previous operator ran checks five minutes before broadcast. We have this booth to ourselves, so we don't have to worry about other people changing settings and such."

"Great!"

"And my scripts have to be signed off on by either the overseer or the general. We aren't allowed to deviate." It was making things much harder to sneak past the desk, with Allemande going over everything with her meticulous eagle eyes.

"I understand."

"I can run things myself, but I prefer not to. Usually means dead air as I run from the other room into here."

"I'm happy to help."

"If you could just stay out of my way, I'm sure we'll be fine." It had come out more harshly than she'd intended. "I'm sorry, I just - Thomas was my operator for years. We were..." She didn't want to say that they'd been friends, even though they had. She didn't need any more scrutiny. "We worked well together."

"I'm not here to impede your work," the woman said, the bright canary yellow of her dress oddly dim under the light of the bare bulb that hung overhead. "I'm here to help."

"Yeah." Her mere presence was irritating. Delia missed Thomas already, missed their morning jokes as they set up, his gentle chastisement of her almost-lateness. It was like a hole in her chest. It felt wrong, like a dream, or a nightmare. This woman was an interloper.

"Mic level seems fine for you in here. I've checked the connections already, we should—"

"The connections are fine. Thomas just checked them last week."

"Fine for now, yes, but a couple of the wires are beginning to fray. We should—"

"I'm sure he didn't miss anything."

"Ms. Dodson—Delia, if I may? I don't mean to question your friend's work. I just want to be sure that your broadcasts are never impeded or interrupted."

"He wasn't my—never mind. Fine. Do whatever you want."

"It's natural to be upset. It's not even been a day."

"Who even are you, anyway? For all I know, you could be the crew worker who ratted him out."

The woman's brow furrowed. "What? But I thought—"

"Just do the checks." Delia held a breath and exhaled slowly. She had to be more careful. She was losing grip on the situation, and this place was too dangerous for that. "What is your name?"

"Carmen." She tapped the microphone and made a note in the margins of the page she was writing on. "I arrived on last night's transport."

"Convenient timing."

"I was selected to be Ms. Allemande's tutor while they are away from their sector. It just happens that I have some broadcasting experience."

"Where?"

"A small settlement on Delta-4. You wouldn't know it."

"Try me."

The woman frowned. "Quorrik Settlement. You can check my references if you wish, but I can assure you that General Fineglass has already done so."

"That won't be necessary. This booth is so rudimentary, most schools have similar equipment. We're hardly a high-tech production here. For now, anyway."

"I will be assisting Ms. Allemande during the day, when I am not queuing up the waves for you. The general made it very clear that I will have no part in the script-writing. I think she was keen to make sure I wouldn't step on your toes."

"Mm." Far more likely that Fineglass wanted to make sure nothing got onto the air without the overseer's express permission, more like. "Live in five, Carmen. Are we about ready?"

"Yes, I'll just head over to the next room to get you set up."

"Fan-gods-damned-tastic," Delia muttered under her breath as she pulled on the headphones.

* * *

"Your broadcast was excellent," Will said, tipping his grey top hat.

"Thomas deserved a better tribute than that," Delia answered, her throat thick with emotion. "But it was the best I could do. Couldn't get much else past Overseer Censor."

"I'm headed back to Gamma-3 when I leave, if you want me to take anything to his parents. I'll drop it off to them in the Capital myself. Would be faster than the cargo ships, in any case."

"I'll see what General Fineglass will let me take from his possessions. No doubt they've already sent half his things to the incinerator." She flinched at the thought of going through his things. They were friends, but he never would have expected that she'd be the one going through his private effects, and not his parents, or his betrothed back on Gamma-3. Gods, she was supposed to come out for a visit next month. Now she'd be seeing nothing more than a few old letters Thomas had kept.

"I'll do whatever I can. I know you care about him."

"It's difficult not to grow attached to someone you work with every day for years."

William tilted his head. "Sometimes I think you preferred his company to mine."

"Don't."

"What's on the docket for this evening's broadcast?" he asked, abruptly changing the subject.

"Construction updates mostly. Allemande already signed off on the script. It's nothing special."

"Do you have time for a walk, then?"

Delia tucked a curl back behind her ear. "Don't you have research to do?"

"Nothing that can't be done without some pleasant conversation." He leaned in closer, his voice low. "Not to press, Dearest, but it never hurts for higher ups to see us together."

"You're right. Where to, the corridor on the left, or the corridor on the right?"

"The left, I think. You know," he said, loudly now, "Turas-Mara Station is really going to be something when construction is complete."

"That's at least six months from now."

"Yes, but imagine, Delia! Wider corridors, more storage, recreation spaces, a big, beautiful eating area! It's going to be the gateway to the rest of the universe!"

"Okay, tone it down," she whispered, stifling a snort. "You sound like a snake-oil salesperson."

"Imagine, once we've established settlements beyond the rim, tourists will come through here, the possibilities for expansion are endless."

"True enough, I suppose."

"I am very glad to see you," he said earnestly. "It's been months, Dee."

"I can hardly come for a weekend visit, can I?"

He took her arm as they walked slowly down a dark, depressing corridor. "No, of course not. Doesn't mean I don't miss you."

"It's for the best," she said, repeating what they always told each other. "We do what we must."

"For the glory of the Coalition," he continued. "I am glad to make personal sacrifices for our advancement."

"The mess hall is on the right. Protein blocks morning and night, supplements at midday. I heard they're getting a cook for management."

"They did," a voice said from the other side of the closed serving hatch. When it opened, Delia's heart shot into her throat. No. It couldn't be. After all this time?

"Rose? Rosie? Gods, I haven't seen you in—"

"Delia Forrest? Gods, Delia." Rosie stared, her blue eyes wide and sparkling. "I just got here yesterday, I had no idea—"

"It's Dodson now," Delia said automatically. Emotions were crashing into Delia like waves during a hurricane. Of all the places to find her again, it was all the way at the edge of the galaxy. She looked the same as the day Delia had left, all curves, her hair tied up the same way she always had, that subtle hint of a dimple in her cheeks.

"Oh, you know my wife!" William said cheerfully. "I've been so terribly worried about her all by herself out here at the Rim, it's wonderful to see that she has an old friend! What a beautiful coincidence, don't you think, Dee?"

"Mhmm," she agreed, her heart fluttering.

"Your... wife?" Rosie asked, blinking. "That's... unexpected."

All at once, reality slammed into Delia. "It's not what you—I mean, it is, but—Rosie, gods above, I missed you."

"Yeah, I uh..." Rosie shook her head. "*Married*, Delia?"

"You can't have expected me to—"

"Enjoy your stay, Mr. Dodson. I'm afraid I have plenty of work to occupy me."

Delia grabbed the edge of the serving hatch as Rosie tried to close it. "Hold on, wait!"

"What do you want, Delia?"

"To talk to you!"

Rosie released the window. "Talk, then." Her eyes flicked back to William. "I'd be very interested to hear how this happened."

"You didn't know I was here? The broadcast—"

"I'm not one for radio, Dee, and besides, I knew you as Forrest, not Dodson."

Delia let her hands fall to her sides. "Of course." She was silly to think that Rosie had come all the way to the Outer Rim for her after all this time.

"So, what, then? Everything you told me was a lie? Or..." Rosie tightened her apron strings. "Or... or nothing. We were children, then. People can change. Learn more about themselves. I don't blame you, Delia. I'm glad that you found happiness."

"Rosie... there's so much I need to tell you, so much—"

William cleared his throat loudly. "Something you want to tell me, dearest?"

"Rosie is an old... friend, from school."

"Yes, I gathered that much." William glanced from Delia to Rosie and back, searching her face. "I've just remembered, I left my pocket watch in our quarters. I had better go and retrieve it before my meeting with General Fineglass later this afternoon - and if memory serves, you have some work to do in the booth."

"Sure. I mean, yes." Delia burned to vault over the counter and whisk Rosie away. Fate was impotent in the modern times, too many avenues and pathways for someone to travel down, but this... this certainly felt like destiny. A dangerous destiny. She pulled back from the serving hatch and fussed with the cufflinks at her wrists. "I'll see you around, maybe."

William offered his arm, and she took it. "So," he said simply, prompting.

She was quiet until they turned down the next corridor. "It's a long story." Long, and hers. She didn't want to share it.

"Perhaps we should be rather quieter about our stories in places like these." His voice dropped low to a whisper now. "Given the precariousness of our relationship, I don't think it is wise to draw attention to it."

"I know."

"Delia, this feels dangerous."

"Maybe we should talk in our quarters."

He shook his head. "No. Now, more than ever, we have to present as a solid husband and wife team. United in goals and ambition. Good to be seen together."

"You didn't tell me you had a meeting with Fineglass," she accused.

"A meeting is a generous description. I've heard tell that she's grown skittish, even her own corporals hardly ever see her. She's working on something secret, Dee, and I want to know what it is."

"Why? What does that have to do with you?"

"This way," he said, pulling her into a dingy alcove. "I've heard talk she might be working on something top secret. Something even Allemande doesn't know," he whispered, barely audible.

"And who gave you that information, Will?"

"It doesn't matter."

"It does matter, or it's nothing more than meaningless speculation. You said this was a sure thing, that you just had to verify. Now you're telling me that you don't even know what the project is, or if there even is one?" She shook her head. "I thought we were past all this."

"Delia, dearest, the supply contract is a sure thing. That much is one-hundred percent solid as an asteroid. If I can put in a good show, I can convince Fineglass to let me be the middleman for some rare parts. This other thing, it's just a hunch. A supposition. One that could be worth a hell of a lot of credits if we pull it off."

"I should have known this was some scheme."

"I don't think you have any room to be critical when you were ready to spill everything to that cook."

Delia tightened her jaw. "No, I wasn't," she said, but it was a lie.

"I know it's a small station, but you should stay away from her." She rolled her eyes and started to walk away, but he gently took her elbow. "Dee, I mean it. One slip could unravel everything we've—*you've* worked so hard to build."

"Fine."

"Don't be angry with me. It was *you* who said you wanted this at any cost."

"I'm not angry!" she huffed.

His eyes searched her face, and she turned away. "It's her, isn't it?" he asked gently. "She's not just some friend from school, and she's not just some old flame." He sighed. "She's the one."

Tears started to gather in her eyes, and she hated herself for it. "Yes."

"This complicates matters."

"I'll be fine I... I just won't eat, or I'll ask the new operator to grab me my rations before broadcasts. I stay in my room most of the time anyway, unless I'm working, it's not as though this piece of shit station has anything resembling recreation."

"I'll send you food parcels. How about that?"

"I get protein blocks—"

"That's hardly food, dearest. Might it not be easier to avoid the mess hall if you had your own private stash of tasty treats?"

"You'd do that for me?"

He wrapped her in a warm embrace. "Of course I would. We're in this together. We made a promise. If I can send you some of your favorites—canned, of course, fresh won't survive the journey—then I'll do it with a smile. I know this will be immeasurably difficult."

"Thank you, William."

"We're so close now, we can't let things fall apart."

She nodded. "I know."

"I really did leave my pocket watch in your quarters. What time is it?"

"Half past," she said, checking her own. "When are you supposed to meet the general?"

"Twenty minutes, assuming she shows up."

"Do you have your projections, all that?"

"In my briefcase. This could be a good one for us, Dee."

"Shall I have a look before you go?" she asked, reaching for his case.

He pulled away. "You don't trust me, do you?"

"Of course I trust you!"

"Not everything I've done has been a disaster, you know. How about those artifacts from last year?"

She grimaced. "Those were fake, Will."

"Sure, okay, but those other ones were real."

"We still lost money on them."

"I can do this, Dee. It's a solid proposal, and with my new connection, I can get those parts for a third of the price. It's a tidy profit, excellent margins."

"I hope your new connection isn't another con artist."

"Of course he isn't. I had him vetted! He's Coalition through and through, spent decades on trading vessels!"

"Alright, alright," she relented, straightening his cravat. "I trust you."

Chapter 4

Delia. Married. To a *man.*

Maybe she'd changed, maybe... maybe she'd found the one man in the entire galaxy who could turn her head. He was handsome enough, and polite. She could have done worse. He could have been some muscled brute, or an MPO, or worse, a politician.

Every muscle in her body, every neuron in her brain was screaming for her to leave. To get off Turas-Mara, never look back. Pretend she'd never seen Delia Forrest—well, Delia Dodson, now. Not a day had gone by she hadn't thought of her. They were something like soulmates, once.

Could she even bear to see her all loved up with someone else?

Rosie noisily rustled through supper's ingredients. Fucking gods, how could she be expected to concentrate after *that*? Stew. Soup, rather, with nothing hearty to put into it. Still, better than a protein block. She'd eaten one for breakfast and nearly spat it out. It tasted of nothing, and the texture was like a tough aspic. No wonder the MPOs were desperate, even for canned carrots.

Carrots, right. She punctured the lid, drained the can into a pot to use later. She couldn't afford to waste anything here, not even the canning liquid. Corn. Celery hearts. Fucking gods below. What was Delia even doing here? Tomatoes. More tomatoes. She'd request a bumper shipment of these. They'd be very useful.

Salt, pepper. Not much else in the kitchen, unfortunately. She adjusted the heating element and stirred the enormous pot, letting the canned vegetables dry out a little before adding the stock. Her stomach was churning painfully. Her dream of finding Delia again had turned into a nightmare.

"What is for supper?" someone asked from the other side of the serving hatch.

"Vegetable soup," Rosie answered, leaving the hatch closed. She wasn't in the mood to answer questions, not even from management. "It will be awhile yet. Supper isn't for a few hours."

"Is that it?"

"Yes, that's it, unless you have a cache of ingredients you'd like to donate."

"I don't appreciate your tone."

Shit. Rosie slid open the hatch, a wide smile plastered across her face. "General Fineglass, my apologies."

The general stood tall in her charcoal military uniform, her hands clasped behind her back. "You don't have any, I don't know, potatoes?" she asked, towering over Rosie.

"No, unfortunately, there wasn't much in the cargo hold. Mostly vegetables and citrus fruit, all canned."

"What about next week?"

"I don't know what's coming next week, I only arrived on the station last night. Whatever order I give to Overseer Allemande won't arrive for at least a month, barring any pirate attacks."

The general grimaced. "You can give your order requests to me directly. I'll handle them."

"But the overseer—"

"Is not in charge of this station. I am. As such, I think someone who has a more vested interest in keeping her subordinates happy should be the one to make those decisions." She straightened, her hands clasped behind her back. "Are we clear on that matter?"

"Yes, ma'am."

"Do you have your first order ready? The sooner we place it, the sooner it arrives. I, for one, am not thrilled with the idea of vegetable soup for weeks on end."

"I do." Rosie handed over a slip of paper. "More of the canned ingredients, plus sacks of rice and flour, which should be easy enough for the long transport."

Fineglass nodded. "This should all be acceptable."

"Arrowroot or flaxseed, if you can. I know we won't be getting anything like fresh eggs out here."

"Certainly not," the general agreed. "I've requested some supplies from Nox Beacon, but I'm not sure they'll oblige us. That's where you're from, isn't it?"

Rosie nodded. "It is. Their supply lines are so disrupted now, I'm not sure they could give you supplies even if they wanted to. Lots of pirate attacks happening between there and the midway point, from what I've heard."

"Lousy, cretinous whelps. We have more security on transports out this way than any other in the galaxy, and it's still not enough. Damned pirates know that we're bringing high-value materials out here for the new station."

"It will be beautiful when it's completed," Rosie offered. "A real achievement, and the first step in colonizing past the Rim."

"We have a long road ahead of us. We'll get there, though." She sighed. "We have to."

"Are there any dishes you might request, General?"

"Steak and potatoes."

Rosie blinked. Not even lab-created meat would last the journey out here, and almost no one ate the real thing anymore. The farms had all collapsed decades ago. "General?"

"I know, I know. Just anything that tastes better than soggy vegetables in broth. Reminds me too much of training camp." She shuddered. "I know you will do your best with what you have. You came very highly recommended."

"Thank you, ma'am."

"That's why we poached you from Nox Beacon. So don't let me down."

"I'll try not to."

General Fineglass slipped the supplies request into her breast pocket, sweeping aside her long, auburn braid. "Best not to mention this to the overseer, for now."

"Understood."

"I look forward to supper, even if it's not my favorite. It has to be better than those damnable protein bricks."

"I hope so, ma'am." Rosie started to turn back towards the soup. "Oh! General! Would it be possible to get a padlock for the kitchen door and the serving hatch window?"

The general's brow furrowed. "A padlock? What for? There are no pirates on the station, Ms. Gordon."

"No, it's just..." If she got the MPOs into trouble, there's no way she'd be able to keep them out of her shipments. "Nothing. You're right. Old habits from Nox Beacon."

"Understandable. Not every station has our kind of discipline. Plenty of corporals using half-measures with their troops, it leads to disarray and disorder."

"Yes, ma'am."

"At ease, Ms. Gordon. And welcome aboard."

* * *

The letter she'd written sat on her desk, neatly folded into an envelope. There was no point in sealing it, not when the MPOs down in the cargo bay would be ripping it open to check for sensitive information, to run through it with thick, black ink. She'd been careful not to give many details, but it wouldn't matter to the guards.

It would take at least a month, probably longer, to reach them, so why hadn't she sent it yet? Rosie rubbed her temples, her eyes squeezed shut. She hadn't anticipated that Delila would waltz back into her life, and on the arm of a husband, no less. An unnecessary complication, and yet, her heart had jumped when she saw Delia's face after all this time. How long had it been? Over a decade?

She grumbled at the letter, shoving it into the drawer. It's not like it would make it off the station before tomorrow's cargo pickup, anyway.

There was a soft, hesitant knock at the door.

"Delia?" Rosie asked, her pulse racing.

"ER—no."

The door creaked open, the hinges rusty from disuse. Before the announcement to turn Turas-Mara Station into the 'Gateway to the Beyond,' it had run with a skeleton crew.

"Can I help you?"

A girl with long blond hair pinned up stood in her doorway, the long fabric of her green skirts hitched in one hand. "Hello, Ms. Gordon. I'm—"

"Oh. You're the overseer's daughter. Emeline."

"I am."

"What can I help you with? Has she sent for me?"

"No, nothing like that. I was hoping you could make me something."

"Like what?"

"Cornbread?"

Rosie shook her head sadly. "I'm afraid the supplies I was given to work with aren't much. No flour or grains of any kind."

"Oh." Emeline's face fell, and she dropped her hands to clasp in front of her. "No problem at all then, I understand. If you could just keep this between us—"

"I might be able to whip you up an orange mousse." This poor girl, all the way out here at the Rim. No one her own age for at least five hundred thousand kilometers, no recreation.

"I don't want to trouble you, ma'am, Ms. Gordon."

"No trouble. I can't sleep, anyhow. Can never sleep the first few nights I'm in a new place."

"Me neither."

Rosie closed her own door and pushed open the kitchen. "How long have you been out here?"

"About a month."

"Do you like it?"

There was a moment of pensive silence before the girl answered, "It is where I need to be right now."

"Very diplomatic."

"And you?" she asked. "Do you like it here?"

"Too soon to tell, I think. It's only been one full day. Things will get easier once the new supplies arrive." Rose looked sideways at her. "Cornmeal is on the list already, if you're curious."

"If only shipments didn't take so long to get out here."

"I'm sure it will get faster as more trading beacons crop up, and flight paths become standardized. For now, though, yes, it feels impossibly long to wait for some flour and rice."

"My mother, the overseer, has some unpopular opinions about the importance of food."

"Mm," Rosie said, aware that this girl could be reporting everything back. "Don't tell her I said that."

"My lips are sealed."

Emeline sat atop one of the stools in the corner, rickety and unused. "So how do you plan to make a mousse without dairy?"

"Soybeans. I hope you have a strong arm, because we'll be mixing until they're as smooth as the butter we'll never get out here." She poured cans of tinned soybeans into a large bowl and handed it to Emeline. "Smush them down. I'll start juicing some lemons."

"How long have you been a cook?"

"Depends what you mean. If you mean, how long have I been cooking food, well, then, almost all my life. My grandfather taught me almost everything I know. If you mean how long have I been cooking for other people to earn credits, then the answer is twelve years."

"Do you like it?"

"Some parts more than others, I suppose. What about you? What do you do for fun?"

Emeline looked up from the bowl. "Fun?"

"Yes, fun. Like painting, or embroidery, or..." she trailed off. "Or archery. Something like that."

"Not much room for archery on a station like this."

"I meant before you got here."

"Oh. I used to like going for walks with my sis—I mean, I used to like walking."

Rosie strained the juices from a can of tinned lemons. There was a slight and unpleasant metallic smell to them. "Your sister?"

"No, I don't have any sisters. I misspoke, I'm just tired." Emeline set the bowl on the counter. "I'm terribly sorry, Ms. Gordon, suddenly I'm very tired. I hope you don't mind if I turn in."

"Not at all."

"Thank you for being kind to me. I hope I haven't left you with a terrible mess."

"Nothing I can't fix in a snap. Good night, Ms. Allemande."

Chapter 5

"Good morning, I'm Delia Dodson with your report from the Outer Rim. The expansion project continues apace, making record time in the overhaul and restoration of Turas-Mara Station, preparing it for adventurous merchants, explorers, and pioneers. Whatever lies beyond the rim will someday stand as a monument to Coalition strength and ingenuity."

Carmen waved at her through the window. What the hell was she even doing? Why wasn't she in her booth?

"Er—conditions here at the Rim remain pleasant and steady thanks to the efforts of all the hard-working people pushing us into a bright, new tomorrow. If you're looking for a world of excitement, register with your local Coalition recruiter and tick the box to have a chance to be assigned here."

Gods, it was all such horseshit.

"Soon, the Turas-Mara loading bay will have space for multiple vessels. In a few months' time, we'll be one of the busiest places in all the Near Systems. The views from out here are nothing short of breathtaking."

As if she could see anything but endless black nothingness out of the tiny porthole in her quarters.

"In other news, negotiations continue with sectors across the galaxy who all want to be part of the next chapter of Coalition history. With all the opportunities afforded from exploring what was previously beyond our reach, it's no wonder that people are flooding in from all corners, desperate to have a taste of the freedom that 'The Gateway to the Beyond' can give."

She wished she'd never come up with that slogan. Meaningless. Gods below, why in all their hells was Carmen still at the window? Delia turned away from the glass, shooing Carmen with her hand.

"The military has stepped up security on all routes within the Near Systems to combat against the piracy that makes costs rise for all of us. A hearty and well-earned thanks to all MPOs who make travel safe for the rest of us. Before long, we will together stamp out the remains of the old world."

Now Carmen was tapping at the window. Had she lost whatever meager sense she had?

"I'm Delia Dodson, thank you for listening. Join us this evening for another news update, and an exclusive interview with Emeline Allemande, first civilian at the Rim."

When she heard the disconnection click, Delia tore off her headphones and marched into the next room. "What do you think you're doing?" she demanded. "An operator is supposed to, you know, operate! Not gawk at me through the booth window!"

"I'm sorry, Ms. Dodson," Carmen replied evenly. "I was only trying to tell you that your signal had been blocked."

"Blocked? By who?"

"I'm not sure, but we were overridden by the military."

"What did they say?"

"I don't know that either, because your signal was still being broadcast here on the station, blocking *them* out."

"How the hell did that happen? Why didn't you tell me?"

"I tried."

Delia shoved her hands into the pockets of her trousers. "You should have opened the door!"

"Would that not have alarmed the rest of the station's residents?"

"Yes," Delia sighed. "You're right. Setting off a panic here would be terrible. Not enough shuttles. Only two, really. How can we find out what they said?"

"I'll check frequencies to see if there was anything. Maybe someone will be repeating it now on their broadcast."

"I should tell the general and the overseer."

"Yes. For all we know, it could be something important. Why else would a military vessel be all the way out here, overriding our frequencies?"

"Right." Delia strode out of the room and down the corridor to Allemande's office, where the door was open. She gave two cursory knocks and opened it. "Overseer, we—oh, Emeline. I didn't expect to find you in here. Rifling through your mother's desk?"

"She asked me to find something for her." Emeline held up a file, triumphant. "And here it is!"

"Where is the overseer? We have an urgent—"

"She is in a meeting with General Fineglass."

"Even better, I should speak to them both at once."

Emeline brushed past her. "She was very clear that she didn't want to be disturbed, unless, and I quote, 'the station is on fire or flooding.' I'll tell them that you need to speak with them."

"I outrank you, Emeline," Delia said firmly.

The girl smiled prettily at her as she closed the door and locked it, pocketing the key. "Do you, though?"

Delia narrowed her eyes, but knew that she had been beaten. "Please tell them it's urgent."

"Of course."

As she strode down the hallway, file in hand, Carmen poked her head out of the booth. "What's that file?"

"No idea, but apparently it's more important than our broadcast getting overridden. Any luck?"

"No, we're so far out from other broadcast beacons to hear anything. Usually they take ours and amplify, they've got better tech there. Better than a pissy little booth, that is."

"This doesn't feel right to me, Carmen. I feel like something is up."

Carmen nodded. "It definitely feels that way."

"What now? It's not like I can go burst into their meeting unannounced."

"Why not? Wouldn't this constitute an emergency?"

Delia tapped her fingers against the door frame. "You haven't been here long enough, you don't know Allemande. She doesn't like being interrupted."

"No, but I've heard stories."

"Stories? From who?"

"Oh, you know," Carmen said with a shrug. "Around." She ran another frequency scan, twisting knobs and pulling at levers much faster than Delia could. "I still think she should be notified. Who knows how long they'll be in there."

"How long who will be in where?" Allemande asked from behind.

"Overseer!" Delia shouted, nearly tripping over her own feet. "I thought you were in a meeting, I—never mind."

"Spit it out, Ms. Dodson. I don't have all day."

"The military overrode our broadcast."

"And?"

"And we're not sure why."

Allemande stared coolly. "You know as well as I do that they take precedent."

"Of course, it's just—"

"Do you think that your little news report should supersede military operations?"

"No, of course not! I was worried there might be an emergency."

"You thought there would be an emergency out here, at Turas-Mara Station, that General Fineglass was not privy to?"

Delia tugged at the cuffs of her shirt. "No, I just mean, what if it was... a pirate attack or something?"

"There are no *pirates* out here, Ms. Dodson." Allemande's glare narrowed. "It's the best part of being at the Outer Rim, wouldn't you agree?"

"Sure, I just thought, with the increase in piracy along the transport route—"

"That has already been dealt with."

"Of course, my mistake. So, what was the broadcast, then? We can't catch any repeats out this far."

"Nothing important, nothing that should concern you."

"Yet important enough to override our broadcast?"

"Ms. Dodson, is that all, or do you have more meaningless and tiring questions for me? I've said it's of no concern, yet you question me."

"Apologies, ma'am. It's just new out here, that's all."

"Very good. There is no need for an evening script, as we can use this morning's."

"Oh," Delia said, a tiny pinprick of hope for an afternoon off. "I suppose I will see you—"

"In which case, you have time to rewrite the interview with Emeline. I won't have you asking her inane questions about her past. You know how troublesome that was for her when I first pulled her from the tenements in Skelm."

"Of course, Overseer."

"Instead, I want you to focus on her academic achievements and how much time she has out here to study. You will also make a point of guiding her to talk about her commitment to the Coalition's expansion and the role that she has personally chosen to take on."

Delia nodded. "Yes, ma'am."

"I have meetings scheduled until late this evening, so you may slide the revised outline under my office door. Be at the booth early tomorrow morning to discuss any last-minute changes. I will make sure that Emeline is ready then as well."

As the overseer closed her office door, Carmen let out a long, slow breath of air. "Still seems suspect to me, you know,"

"Of course it's damned *suspect*," Delia grumbled. "But you can bet your ass we're never going to hear about it."

"Should I keep scanning?"

"No, there's no point. Whatever they said, everyone else is keeping tight-lipped about the whole thing. Probably some military exercise, or some warning about a test mission." Delia buttoned her cuffs again. "In fact, I'd be surprised if that wasn't the case. Test missions that go out past the Outer Rim get quite the fanfare around here."

Carmen nodded. "Mm."

"Well, you heard the woman, plenty to keep us busy. Don't you have some tutoring to get to?"

"I do. Emeline is so bright that most days she doesn't even need me. To be honest, I get bored sometimes."

"Don't tell the overseer that, or she'll have you scrubbing the floors with a nail brush to pass the time."

"I just hope Emeline doesn't rat me out."

Delia snorted. "Better start giving her harder work, then. Keep up the illusion."

"I do that, and she's liable to surpass me entirely, and then where will I be? Scrubbing those floors, probably!" Carmen grinned as she turned out the lights in the booth. "See you this evening, then."

"Yeah."

"I hope that rewrite doesn't take you too long."

"Me, too," Delia mumbled, heading back to her quarters. She might as well take advantage of being able to work in privacy, without Allemande standing over her shoulder. Lost in thought, she stumbled into William, who was exiting one of the newly built corridors, his hat askew.

"Will?" she asked. "What were you doing down there?"

"Research, Dearest, of course. It's what I came here for."

She tilted her head, straightening his cravat. "Why are you out of breath?"

"No reason. Fitness. Don't want my muscles to atrophy, you know."

"In full artificial gravity?"

"Delia, my love, my darling flower—"

"What did you do?"

"Nothing!" he spluttered. "I was only doing some business reconnaissance. To think you would accuse me—"

"Please, I know you better than that now. You're..." she trailed off, and lowered her voice, "up to something."

"Nothing untoward, I assure you. Merely a meeting of the minds down in the cargo bay to discuss shipping schedules."

"Will..."

He took her hands and kissed them. "I promise."

"If you say so," she said with a sigh. "I just don't have time to be cleaning up any messes right now."

"And you won't have to."

"I hope so. First Rosie, now this weird broadcast anomaly, the interview... it's a lot to handle."

"I will hold up my pillar, to run business, and stay out of trouble, as I vowed."

"Good." She rubbed her neck, feeling a headache coming on. "How was your meeting with the general? You came back to my quarters so late last night, I didn't get a chance to ask."

He nodded. "Good. As expected."

"That's it? Good?"

"The plan can continue apace." He began to walk down the corridor, and she followed. "I'll be leaving tomorrow or the next day, then. As soon as they have room for me on the cargo transport."

"That's so soon! I thought you'd be here a week."

"In fairness, my darling, I said *perhaps* a week. I've seen what I needed to see. I've convinced the general to sign on the dotted line, and now I have to get to work sourcing what I promised."

"Most people don't sell things they don't already have in their possession."

"Without risk—"

"Aren't we already taking enough risks?" She sighed. "I'm tired of risks. Sick of everything being an uphill battle."

"But we're almost there, Dee. Look around you! Opportunity lurks around every corner. Soon, we'll have everything we dreamed of when we started out on this path. What was it, nearly ten years now?"

"Feels like a damned century."

"Is being around me that much of a trial for you?"

"No, it's not that. It's just... it's getting dangerous, Will."

"We always knew that it would."

"Yes, but now that we're here, it's all rather more perilous than I'd imagined. Razor-sharp edges around the corners where all those opportunities are hiding."

"Good thing you're the most armored woman I know."

She laughed. "Send me some chain mail when you get back to the Capital, eh? By the looks of things, I'm going to need it."

"Things not working out with the new operator?"

"No, she's fine. She's not Thomas, but she's... adequate. For now, anyway." Delia leaned against the wall, tightening the clasp on her suspenders. "I have a feeling that things are going to get worse before they get better."

"Twas ever thus."

"I need to keep..." she trailed off, before continuing, "*her* off my back. At least until I can get some kind of breakthrough."

"Any chance of that happening?"

"Zero, unfortunately."

"Dearest, if anyone can manage it, it's you."

"You always say that."

He gave her a half smile. "Because it's true."

"You just butter me up so that I'll stick around."

"Yes."

"Not even going to deny that?"

"Why should I? It's true. Without you, I'd just be a washed-up failure, probably hunched over in some underground casino in the Capital, gambling away my last credits."

"Probably."

"It's going to work this time. I can feel it. We're so close to grasping that future."

Sometimes, she felt deeply guilty that he only knew half the truth. "We are." He couldn't be trusted with secrets, though. He was handsome, kind, and charming, but information fell out of his mouth like a sieve. "We'd better pack your things so that you're ready when the transport leaves."

* * *

Delia leaned back in her chair, her boots up on the desk. Working in her room felt like a forbidden treat in comparison to writing with Allemande all but standing over her.

She chewed at the end of her pencil. What did teenage girls really want to talk about? She barely knew Emeline. The poor thing was locked away in her room most of the day with Carmen as her tutor. Did she do *anything* other than schooling? Gods, even she was bored all the way out here, she could only imagine how small and claustrophobic it would feel for a girl of Emeline's age.

"What do teenagers think about?" she asked.

"Depends. Food. Staying out too late. Boys," William said, waggling his eyebrows.

Delia snorted. "You might have thought of boys. I certainly didn't."

"Oh, I definitely did."

"That's not a secret."

"No. Not from you, anyway."

She twisted in her chair. "Do you ever regret it? Getting married?"

"Do you?"

"Answer the question."

"No. It had to be done. For both our sakes. I regret that neither of us had another viable option, though. The gods know *I* wouldn't want to be tied to me."

"Oh, stop."

"Do you?" he repeated. "Regret it?"

More now than before, but she couldn't say that part aloud. "Not really. You needed money. I needed a name. We'd both have been sunk, otherwise. No futures that didn't end in a work camp."

"I do love you, in a way."

"I know."

He threw a sock at her. "And you care about me, too."

"I do." She stuck her tongue out at the sock. "Keep your stinky socks away from me, sir."

"I don't thank you enough for what you did for me."

"No, you don't."

"Thank you."

"Shut up."

"I mean it!"

She tossed the sock across the small room, and it landed neatly inside his suitcase. "I know you do. Stop being so mushy. What's gotten into you?"

"It's lonely in the Capital all alone."

"You knew I'd have to start traveling for work."

"Yes, Dee, but I didn't think you'd never be home, ever. Gods above, you were in Skelm for a year, then the Capital, now you're all the way at the edge of the known galaxy. I didn't quite anticipate that."

"I'm sure you'll find a way to occupy yourself."

"Not in the way I'd like."

"At least you're not trapped on a station the size of a tin can with the love of your wasted life."

He snapped the case closed, concern clouding his face. "We have to be careful, Delia."

"Yes, I know," she snapped. "*You* don't get to lecture *me* about being cautious."

"Is she going to be... a problem for you?"

"No. I told you, I'll be fine. I'll just keep away. It will be like she wasn't even here."

"I could always request a reassignment for you. I know someone in—"

"*No.*"

"We can't falter now."

She turned back to her desk to hide the scowl on her face. "No one is faltering, William."

"I'm just saying it won't be easy."

"Of course it won't be fucking easy," she hissed. "But it's what has to be done. I get reassigned now, and that's falling back down the ladder. The Capital might have been the place, once, but now... out here, that's where people are going to be. We're at the precipice—"

"Of a new age, yes," he finished. "I know. I helped you write that speech.

Don't be angry with me, Dee, I was just trying to help."

"I'm not angry."

"Tell that to your face."

She allowed herself to crack a smile. "Better?"

"If you change your mind, that would be okay. If you wanted to, as you said, fall back down the ladder, it wouldn't be the end of things, you know. We'd climb back up."

"While I appreciate your enthusiasm and faith, I'm not so sure. Maybe once, but the sands are shifting too fast. Someone who's on the up and up today could find themselves in a work camp tomorrow. One wrong move, that's all it takes. It doesn't matter if everyone in the damn Capital knew you, drank in your tavern." She rolled the pencil across the desk. "Any news about Marina?"

"Nothing yet. I'd heard a rumor they were keeping her in the Capital, but I'm not so sure of that."

"No, I don't think they'd keep her there," Delia whispered. The walls might be thick, but you never knew who might be lurking on the other side. "We can't let that happen to us."

"We won't."

"So long as we're careful. That means no fucking around when you're back on Gamma-3."

"How did this suddenly become about me again?"

"Oh, William. It was always about you."

Chapter 6

Another week, another shipment of garbage. Her order couldn't get to Turas-Mara fast enough. If she didn't start giving the MPOs something better, she wouldn't be able to keep them out of the food stores. They were already grumbling about the vegetable soup as it was.

"Anything good?" Officer Abara asked hopefully.

"Same as last week, I'm afraid," Rosie answered.

"Fucked gods," they replied, spitting onto the floor of the cargo bay. "Did you know that the team here before was getting at least one hearty square a day? Not this protein brick bullcrap, or watery vegetable soup."

"I'm doing the best I can with what I'm given. I told you, in a few weeks—"

"I hate it out here."

Rosie flinched at their candid honesty. "Yeah."

"They promised us more, you know."

She nodded. "I'll try to get you something better."

"It's not your fault, you're just the chef."

"Not a chef, just a cook."

"Does it really matter?"

"No." She hefted the crate up into her arms. "Once my order comes in…"

"We're looking forward to it. Shit's grim out here. Barely even a pack of cards."

"It will be better once the expansion is done."

"As if they'll let us have access to any of the good stuff. Management only, I'll bet."

She shifted the weight of the crate onto her hip. "We can hope, I guess."

"Sure," they replied, but half-heartedly. They didn't even look up when she turned to leave the loading bay, climbing the three flights of stairs back up to the small, cramped kitchen. She hadn't seen the girl, Emeline, for almost a fortnight. She hadn't seen Delia, either.

Even knowing that she was somewhere on the ship was like a knife in her side, festering, an ever-present ache that only grew with every passing day. She thought she'd gotten over it. She'd been a fool.

With a heavy sigh, she unpacked the crate, the same as the weeks before. And, just like each time before, she organized, and planned, and wrote the menu on the chalkboard in the mess hall. Not that the same thing they'd been eating for weeks was much of a menu. Even she was getting sick to death of vegetable gods-forsaken soup.

She wasn't sure she could face another tin of oranges. One more week before her order arrived, and then things would be good. They could handle one more week of protein bricks for lunch. Maybe.

Strange to know that she'd be giving the general her next order before she'd even seen the first one. Even stranger that she'd been dodging the overseer. At least she forgot about the kitchen more often than she remembered.

"Ms. Gordon," Fineglass said from the door, and it made her jump. "A rather unfortunate last name."

Rosie's shoulders tightened. "I'm afraid I didn't choose it myself, General."

"I'll need your next order in just a few days."

"Yes."

"I look forward to reading what the menu has in store for us."

"I hope it will be more to your liking, ma'am."

"You know, before... we had a cook."

"Oh?"

The general's broad frame took up almost the entire doorway. "He was excellent."

"I have some large boots to fill, then." When Fineglass lingered, Rosie continued, "Did you need something, ma'am?"

"No. Thank you." She hesitated. "I heard you were giving food to some of the MPOs down in the cargo bay."

Rosie froze. "Oh?" she asked nervously.

"You shouldn't let them push you around like that. They know better. You're just... fresh meat."

"I was just using the best way I know how to keep them on my side. Life is easier without having to fight them for every can."

"Some would call that efficient."

"I—"

"But others on this ship would say that it's the antithesis of efficiency, so you'd better tell them to be more careful about where they leave their dishes, or their caravan of free food will dry up faster than a keg in a trading beacon."

"Oh. Of course, ma'am."

"I'd tell them myself, but that would be admitting that I know what's going on, and I don't. In fact, we never had this conversation, did we?"

"No. In fact, I haven't seen you all day."

"As I thought." The general sniffed hopefully. "It might only be vegetable soup, but it's better than a damned protein brick."

The click of the general's boots faded down the narrow corridor, and Rosie breathed a long sigh of relief. Why did everything out here feel like it was a secret? It was just soup! Hardly illegal swill, or tobacco. Just watery cans of corn and carrots. Gods, she was tired of corn and carrots.

"Rosie."

No. She couldn't do it. Turning her back to the door, she stiffened, bracing for the inevitable impact of long-buried emotions. "I'm busy."

"I just wanted to—"

"To what? Remind me of how *married* you are?"

"No!"

"What, then?"

"I..." Delia trailed off, her boots squeaking softly as she dragged the soles across the textured metal flooring. "I don't know."

"Supper is over. You'll have to wait until breakfast."

"I don't get that anyway, I'm not management."

Rosie continued to put away the tins, refusing to make eye contact. If she met Delia's eyes, she might die. "I don't know what you're doing in my kitchen, then."

"Your food was always amazing. I always expected you to be in some fancy restaurant in the Capital, not all the way out here."

"Things don't always work out the way we imagined." She shut the cabinet door a little too forcefully. "Especially if we aren't willing to sell ourselves out."

"That's not fair."

"Neither is being stationed here with you." When Delia didn't respond, Rosie sighed. "You're the one who left. Looks like you got what you were looking for."

"I didn't leave, I—"

"So you didn't pack up all your things in the middle of the night? I didn't wake up alone in that tiny apartment? I imagined all that then, did I?"

"It's more complicated than that!"

If only she'd get sucked out into space, they wouldn't have to continue this conversation. "It's always more complicated than that."

"Rosie, I..."

"Don't."

"I missed you."

"You're not allowed to say that to me. What makes you think you can just—just glide in here, and pretend like ten years haven't gone by? Ten gods-forsaken *lonely* years, Delia. You decided to go and chase your dreams somewhere else. I wasn't... I wasn't good enough to boost you up that ladder."

"It's not just that!"

"I don't want to hear it, Dee. Being all the way out here at the ass-end of nowhere is hard enough without... whatever this is."

"I didn't have a choice, you know."

"Of course you had a choice. We all make choices. You made yours. And now look, here you are, top of your field, probably poised to squeak into management, aren't you? You're damn good, I'll give you that. Never been one for radio, but you make this place sound like a wonderland, not the cramped shit hole that it is." Rosie gripped the edges of the cabinet doors, still staring at the cans that lined the interior. "If this was anywhere else, I'd have been on the first transport out of here the second I saw your face."

"Why don't you?" Delia asked softly.

"Because you're not the only one trying to build a career, not that you'd know it."

"Maybe I could—"

"We both know that's not going to happen, so don't even bother floating it as an option. We're both here, and we just have to deal with that."

"I just wanted to say... that I'm sorry."

"Yeah," Rosie agreed. "I'm sorry as hell, too. What we had was real. But it's gone now. You're all loved up and married, and I'm..." she trailed off, tears springing to her eyes against her will. "Forget it."

"You don't have someone back home?"

"No. Unlike you, I don't leave people hanging, Delia."

"Was there ever anyone?"

"Gods, do you even hear yourself? What makes you think you have the right to know that, after all this time? For ten years I mourned you, the loss of us, what could have been. Yes, there were others. No, it's none of your business."

"I'm sorry, I just... I'm sorry. Truly. For everything."

"Yeah."

"I don't want things to be awkward or upsetting for you. It's a small station."

"Both those bridges have already been crossed, Dee. I'm just trying to do my job."

"Do you want me to leave?"

No. "Yes."

"Then I will. If you change your mind, you know where to find me."

"Mhmm."

The sound of Delia's boots echoed down the corridor, and then disappeared, and it was like she was leaving her all over again.

Chapter 7

Delia drummed the tips of her fingers against the broadcast desk. Gods, she needed a distraction. Spending all her time fixating on that awful conversation with Rosie wasn't getting her anywhere. She stared down at the blank page that sat waiting for ink.

These broadcasts were tiresome. Nothing but construction updates and appeals for crew, and the overseer kept pushing back the interview with Emeline. "She's not ready yet," Allemande kept saying. "This interview is too important to rush."

So Delia was relegated to chipper propaganda again. The Coalition had never been big on hard-hitting journalism that wasn't about how morally corrupt pirates were, but still. She was hungry for something, anything more. Her brain was starting to rot in her skull from inactivity.

Six months, maybe another year here, and she'd have enough clout to pull for her own team. This station would get its own broadcast beacon, and for once, Delia would be in control. Will thought it was just about power, about credits and an easy life, but she'd have so much more ability to drop information to The Scattered once her scripts were in her own hands.

She huffed angrily and dragged her boots across the scuffed wood of the desk. Some days, it didn't feel like life meant anything. Just the same routine over and over, until they all died of starvation or got blown up by rebels.

"Ms. Dodson!"

Great. "Yes?"

"Come in here, please. I have something I wish to discuss with you."

"Be right in," she said, mouthing curses silently. It wouldn't be a day too soon when she never had to hear that woman's voice again.

The door to the overseer's office was open, and Allemande sat behind her desk, hands folded primly. "Close the door, please. This is of a more sensitive nature."

Delia nodded as the door clicked closed. "What can I do for you, ma'am?"

"Have a seat. I want to talk about the interview again."

It took every ounce of willpower to not roll her eyes. "Of course."

"I am worried about my daughter."

"Oh."

"Emeline stays in her chambers all hours of the day, working on her studies long after her tutor has completed teaching her the assigned modules."

"Surely studying is a... good thing?"

"Don't be silly," Allemande said, her voice tinged with irritation. "Of course I want her to excel academically. She is a gifted mind, a keen talent for political maneuvering, that is why I wanted to adopt her, to make sure that she had every opportunity possible to make the Coalition more efficient, more flexible, with prowess that easily evades any of this rebellion nonsense."

"Then what is the problem, exactly? Ma'am?"

"She won't come out, even for supper. Her door stays closed. She says that she is studying."

"Perhaps she is."

"I don't understand where this sudden change is coming from. Emeline's reticence to participate in agreed-upon activities, like the interview, is concerning."

Delia stifled a smirk. "Not to be rude, or too forward, Overseer, but that is a normal thing that teenagers do. Hardly a cause for alarm."

"I suppose you're right." Allemande tucked a silver pen into her breast pocket. "I did wonder if it was the right decision, bringing her all the way out here, but I couldn't bear to see her in a standard boarding school. There are certain... influences there that might corrupt a young mind."

"Understandable."

"She's already been through hell with that... well. Her origins are meek and troubled, to say the least."

"Turas-Mara can be hard on people, even grown adults. I've even heard some of the MPOs talk about how they can't wait for the recreation room to open up, once the construction is finished."

The overseer's face twisted like she had smelled something foul. "I don't see the need for such an inefficient use of space. Surely, if they are bored, there's always more work to be done."

"I suppose most people want to spend at least some of their waking hours doing things other than work," Delia offered cautiously.

"And what about you, Ms. Dodson? Are you awaiting recreation with bated breath?"

"No, I've always enjoyed my work."

"That's why I've always liked you."

"I appreciate that, ma'am." She hadn't realized that Allemande liked *anyone*, and was slightly horrified that she was somehow the chosen one.

"Maybe you could talk to my daughter. Ask her to do the interview. Maybe if she feels she's had input, she will agree to leave her room for once."

"I can try."

"As for this evening's broadcast, I want to highlight the barracks going in at the back end of the station."

"Dormitories?"

"Yes, for most of the crew. Management will have quad quarters until the upgrades are completed, and then those will be converted into civilian lodgings as we venture further out past the rim."

"How about teasing some of the discoveries that have been made?"

The overseer shook her head. "That information is classified."

"We don't have to talk about anything important, just—"

"The answer is no, Ms. Dodson."

Gods be damned, she just wanted a reason to research something other than blueprints. "Understood."

"Perhaps once the first settlement locations are identified, we can begin the process of messaging that to potential pioneers."

"I imagine that many are already eager to see the gateway to the universe."

"We can't let them see it like this," Allemande said, frowning. "Building is close to slipping behind schedule, which we cannot afford. The longer we're out here without proper outposts, the more vulnerable we are."

"Surely pirates wouldn't dare venture out this far?"

"It isn't a risk we can take. Not with the more dangerous crews."

"Still, a whole station, it seems—"

"Do not underestimate these miscreants, Ms. Dodson. I have seen things that would shock and disappoint you about the state of the Coalition's control over the Near Systems. My fear is that the disgusting thieves and brigands will use the expansion to their advantage." She shook her head. "No, we mustn't lower our guard until we have appropriate posts and patrols."

"I didn't think most pirates even had ships that could make it out this far without fuel reserves."

"As I said, it's unwise to underestimate those motivated by chaos and greed. They'd steal from their own mothers if it meant a few extra credits to ply themselves with swill."

"Are there any pirates you know of that you find particularly disconcerting?" Delia poised the pen over the paper hopefully.

"Even if I did, that certainly wouldn't be for broadcast, Delia. The last thing we need out here are pirates."

"It might make average citizens more vigilant, if they knew the danger."

"Absolutely not, and that is my final word on the matter."

"Understood."

The overseer smoothed imaginary wrinkles from the papers on her desk. "When you have seen what I have seen, you know that any temptation towards rebellion or piracy must be immediately quashed. Otherwise, what do you have? In the place of a vibrant, forward-thinking society, you have chaos."

Delia nodded, but remained silent.

"How long have you been working for me now?"

"Since Skelm. Almost two years."

"You are a valuable person to have on staff, Ms. Dodson. As such, perhaps you should be trusted with more... authority."

Resisting the urge to lean forward in excitement, Delia merely smiled plainly, her hands folded in her lap. "What kind of authority?"

"For one thing, I remain unconvinced by your new operator. Her records seem... incomplete."

"Oh?"

"Keep an eye on her."

"Yes, ma'am."

"I also want you to befriend my Emeline, if you can."

"Of course."

"Make sure that Carmen isn't filling her head with any nonsense. I want my cunning girl back. I have no use for surly, uncooperative teenagers."

"I'll do my best."

Allemande stared silently. It was unnerving. "I worry that she might be... tempted."

"Tempted?"

"The allure of rebellion once sparked in her. She knows better now that she has been properly educated, but this change in her behavior is disconcerting."

"Ah." Worried that Emeline would want to escape back to her birth family, no doubt. She had been a powerful force back in Skelm, a force that disrupted the entire city.

"I do care for her, Delia."

She blinked, and then nodded. "Of course you do."

"And as such, I want the best for her. She could grow into a fine young woman, she could have the entire universe at her feet someday, but not if she is swayed into ignoring her true calling. The rebels don't deserve her."

"No," Delia agreed, still shaken at the sudden turn of candor.

"I know too well what rebellion leads to."

"Chaos?"

"Bloodshed." The overseer looked away now, casting her steely glare over the low ceilings of her office. "When I was young, my parents were stationed in Rakam on Gamma-3. They were weapons analysts, and we lived remotely. One day, some rebels showed up, then more, until there were droves of them streaming across the landscape. They took my parents and they ransacked their laboratory. I had to hide in a cupboard."

"Gods," Delia whispered.

"I vowed then that I would do everything in my power to rid the Near Systems of the rebels' rot. And so, I have, and will continue to do so."

"Was it... The Scattered?"

"Likely. I will never know for sure."

"Have you told Emeline that?"

"Of course not. It is unseemly for a parent to project their own past onto their children."

Delia sat back in her chair. "Oh."

"You will understand someday, if you are ever a parent." The overseer cleared her throat and stacked the pages neatly on her desk. "I assume you and William will want children soon?"

"Oh, I..." she trailed off. "We haven't decided." Not much to decide in their situation, really.

"Plenty of time for all that, I suppose."

"Yes."

"Do check in on Emeline. I've told her to expect you."

* * *

Delia knocked on Emeline's door. "Hello in there, anyone home?" She'd never been any good with kids. "Your mother sent me to check on you."

"I'm fine."

"Can you open the door?"

"No, thank you."

"She wanted me to discuss—"

"I am not interested in talking about the interview."

Delia squeezed her eyes shut. Why the hell were teenagers so difficult? Surely she'd never been this irritating. "Is there anything you *are* interested in talking about?"

"Not with you."

"If you could just open the door a crack, I can tell her that I did my best."

"That's not my problem."

"What if I had some sweets I could share?"

The door opened. "Where are they?"

"Here, in my pocket."

Emeline squinted at her. "You'd better not be lying."

"Never," Delia promised, making the shape of an x over her chest. "Cross my heart." She reached into her pant pocket and produced a chocolate bar, delicately wrapped in silver foil.

"What does she want? For me to do the interview?"

"Mostly."

"What else?"

Delia shrugged. "She seems worried about you. She said you won't come out of your quarters."

"It's not as though there's much else to do on this fucking station."

Ah. So that was it. "Pretty boring out here at the Rim, isn't it?"

"Don't try to relate to me as though I am a child. I am nearly nineteen."

"I'd never suggest that someone with your impressive knowledge and experience was childish," Delia said lightly, despite the fact that the girl was, in fact, acting childish.

"Back in the Capital, I was responsible for researching contracts, for setting up meetings between my mother and other overseers or governors. Did you know that I facilitated the deal that put Skelm back on the map after half the city was destroyed?"

"I had heard something about that, yes."

"And out here?" Emeline gestured down the empty corridor. "All we do is wait. Wait for shipments, wait for projects to be completed, wait for the next transport to arrive. Gods, the most excitement I get is going down to the loading bay to count through shipments of parts.”

“Don’t the MPOs do that?”

“My mother likes it to be done twice. Less risk of human error.”

“Right.”

“Was there anything else, Ms. Dodson?”

“You can call me Delia,” she offered.

“That won’t be necessary.”

“She’s just going to keep sending me back here, you know. Until you agree to the interview.”

“I’ll agree to the interview when I get a say in what’s included.”

At last, something to work with. Delia grinned. “What do you want included?”

“The economic recovery of Skelm, reporting on the efforts there to supply us here with what we need to expand the station. Everyone wants to talk about ‘The Gateway to the Universe’ yet the ones making that possible are ignored, forgotten.”

“I can work on some additional questions for you that might highlight the struggle there.”

“I am not unreasonable, Ms. Dodson. I know you see me as just a girl, but I know in my heart what’s right.” Emeline sighed, widening the gap between the door and the frame. “You can come in, if you wish.” She narrowed her eyes. “Chocolate first.”

“Of course,” Delia said, handing over the treat.

“I’m not usually so easily bribed, but...”

Delia stepped into the room and closed the door. “The food out here isn’t exactly anything to write home about.”

“Home.”

“Where’s home for you, now? The Capital?”

“I suppose, yes.”

“Do you miss Skelm?”

Emeline tore at a corner of the chocolate bar, snapping off a square. “I was brought there when I was very young. I was raised there. It’s difficult not to hold sentimentality.” She handed Delia a piece. “Where are you from, Ms. Dodson?"

"A very small settlement on Gamma-3."

"How odd, then, that you should end up all the way out here."

Delia let the chocolate melt on her tongue before answering. "I could say the same for you."

"The Coalition offers many opportunities."

"Sure."

"Do you hold sentimentality for where you were raised, Ms. Dodson?"

"I suppose. I haven't been back since I left. I can hardly remember more than my home, the school I attended when I was little. We—my father and I, that is—left when my mother and sister died."

"I'm sorry to hear that."

"It was a very long time ago. I was younger than you are now."

Emeline, having eaten her square, wrapped the chocolate back up and stored it in the drawer of her desk. "How did they die?"

"A fire." The memory of it was still almost too sharp to bear. "I don't like to talk about it." She cleared her throat and took a small pad of paper from her breast pocket. "So, to answer your question, yes, I have some sentimentality for where I grew up, but I don't have any desire to return there."

"Understandable." Emeline tucked a hair back into her braid. "If you are taking notes, then you should include that Skelm's recovery has far surpassed even my own hopes. The factories have all been repaired, and are now providing eighty percent of the materials we use out here, but that's not enough."

"And why is that?"

"The housing shortage there is only getting worse. Workers are left to sleep in factory basements if they are lucky, and in the streets if they aren't. It's beginning to impact efficiency."

"What would you do to fix this problem?"

"It's a simple answer, Ms. Dodson. Investment in Skelm's infrastructure. It must be done. Now that the city is growing, becoming ever-more important in the Coalition's aims, it is attracting more merchants and traders who wish to follow the lure of credits. If there is no housing, if efficiency continues to fall, then another sector may well swoop in when the initial contract expires next year."

"It is rare for a contract like that to be so brief, is it not?"

Emeline shook her head. "Not really, not for a project of this size and scope."

"And you wish you could be back there? To oversee that investment?"

"In a word, yes. But my responsibility and commitment right now is here at the Rim, at least until the initial expansion has been completed." She sighed, a tiny, prim exhalation of breath. "It's only a few more months. They say that the recreation room is nearly completed."

"I haven't been down there to look, have you?"

"No, of course not. It's out of bounds." Emeline smoothed her skirts, the same gesture that the overseer made with papers on her desk. "But if I had gone down to look, I'd be able to tell you that the new billiards table has been assembled."

"Oh?"

"I'd also be able to tell you that they installed several card tables, and that my mother is furious about it. No doubt it will lead to gambling."

"But you haven't been down there."

"Definitely not."

"Have you also not seen the new atrium? So much glass!"

"No, I haven't seen it, and it's beautiful, isn't it?"

Delia snorted. "It really is."

"Ms. Dodson, I'll happily do your interview, so long as we give Skelm its due." She smiled and gestured to the door. "And if you have any more chocolate, I'd gladly take it off your hands."

Chapter 8

Rosie sighed happily, covered in dough almost up to her elbows. She'd been baking bread all morning, but it was worth it for the deep, yeasty smell coming from the oven. Finally, she had flour, and rice, and dried lentils, along with sacks of beans. She hadn't even had to pull the crates up from the cargo bay herself; the MPOs were so excited for a little treat that they did it for her.

Four loaves down, six to go. They'd have enough for toast in the morning, and she'd managed to make marmalade from some of the canned oranges. Her mouth watered just thinking about it, after weeks of bland vegetable soup and protein bricks for lunch.

"Hi."

Rosie looked up. "Hello. Carmen, right?"

"That's me. And you're Ms. Gordon?"

"Rosie. I'd shake your hand but..." she waved her arms in the air. "You're Emeline's tutor, aren't you?"

"And the broadcast operator."

Just the thought of the broadcast, or Delia, tied her stomach into knots. At least the bread had distracted her for a little while, anyway. "Ah."

"I just stopped by to..." Carmen trailed off.

"To see if there is any extra food? You can save your breath, because there isn't."

"It's certainly different out here at The Rim."

Rosie sighed. "Is there something else I can help you with?"

"Don't worry, I don't want to get in your way." Carmen leaned on the counter. "I'll leave, if you want me to."

"No, it's fine. The company is nice, I guess. It can feel isolating this far from anything else."

"Miss your family?"

Another topic Rosie didn't want to discuss, especially not with a stranger. "Sure, who wouldn't?"

"True. I suppose everyone on this station misses someone." Carmen wrinkled her nose. "Except maybe the overseer."

"What's it like working in close proximity to her?"

"Challenging."

Rosie couldn't help but laugh, her shoulders shaking as she kneaded the dough. "An understatement, I'd wager."

"Seems we were both thrown into this, weren't we? I mean, I was already headed here to be Emeline's tutor, but the booth operations was a surprise."

"I jumped at the chance to come out here."

"How come?"

"Tired of being a prep grunt. Tired of... people, I guess. Wanted some peace and quiet."

Carmen grimaced. "Gods, and here I am, chattering away, ruining your silence."

"As it turns out, silence gets old pretty fast. I don't miss Nox Beacon, but at least there you had some semblance of being social, even if it was only ever the chef shouting at you to chop the produce smaller."

"Have to make it all go as far as you can out here."

"I'd give my right eyeball for a greenhouse. Gods, even a couple of herbs would make a world of difference," Rosie said, smoothing the dough. It was light and elastic now, perfectly round. "My grandfather always said that a little flavor sets the universe in spin."

"Did your grandfather teach you how to cook?"

"He did. Best cook I know. The man's peach cobbler is to die for."

"And what about your grandmother?" Carmen asked. "What was she like?"

"Oh, you know," Rosie replied evasively, "like most other grandmothers. Judgmental but loved us all the same."

"Don't I know it. Mine spent my entire childhood telling me off for scraping my knees and putting holes in my dresses. Though, I can't really blame her, seeing as she was the one patching them."

"Spent a few years climbing trees, did you?"

Carmen chuckled. "More than a few, truth be told. It's a wonder that woman never ran out of thread."

"Grandmothers are like that."

"They are indeed."

A strange silence fell over the small kitchen, and Rosie's skin burned under Carmen's searching gaze. "So, any plans for when you rotate off this block of metal?"

"I rarely make plans. Even when I do, it seems like fate, or whatever it is, has other ideas for me. No, I'll just settle into my duties, and when the time comes, I'll see what lies ahead."

"That sounds wise."

"And you?"

Rosie dug her hands into a fresh mound of dough, the sticky mixture coating her fingers. "I'll stay here as long as I can, and then maybe look for jobs back in the Capital," she lied.

"Wow, from one extreme to the other, eh? Dark space to the bustling chaos of the city."

"Might make a nice change of pace."

"At least you'd be able to get decent fruit there. I'm not so sure about all this canned citrus," Carmen said, eyeing the stack of tins on the counter.

"It does the job, at least."

"Emphasis on *least.*"

"Better now that we have flour. I was starting to wither away from the lack of bread and pasta."

"Do you ever wonder what's beyond the Rim?" Carmen asked abruptly.

"Er—I guess... who doesn't? Not as though there's much else to ponder out here."

"I mean, what if there were extraterrestrials?"

Rosie laughed. "I think we'd know by now."

"Or secret settlements?"

"No one could survive this far out without being detected." Rosie's shoulder blades tensed. "Besides, what would be the point of that? Pirates already have their settlements dotted around the Near Systems. No reason to set up shop beyond the Rim."

"You never know."

"I guess not." Rosie glanced at the clock hanging on the wall. "Isn't it almost time for Emeline's lesson?"

Carmen searched her face again for a moment. "I suppose it is. Thank you for the chat, Ms. Gordon."

"And you."

* * *

Rosie almost didn't see the note that had been shoved beneath her door when she stumbled through it that night, exhausted but finally able to be proud of her cooking on Turas-Mara. She picked it up, the smooth parchment scrawled with an unfamiliar hand. It wasn't Abara, who usually left notes to let her know if there was a shipment, and Carmen didn't seem like a suspect, either - she had been with Emeline all day, and then in the broadcast booth, which was where she still was.

She squinted at the writing, almost illegible. Didn't anyone take the time to practice handwriting anymore? By the gods, it looked like it had been written by a toddler, or a severely drunk adult. Was it a prank? Some feeble attempt at a joke from one of the officers?

Rosie switched on the small radio on the desk with an aggrieved huff. She hated Delia, but she also couldn't resist tuning in for every morning and evening broadcast. Even hearing her voice made Rosie's stomach ache.

"Good evening, I'm Delia Dodson."

Dodson. Fuck. A permanent reminder that she'd run off and married someone else.

"Broadcasting all the way from the Outer Rim from Turas-Mara Station, we're proud to announce that the expansion project is running smoothly, in part thanks to the hard work of the workers in Skelm. Every job, and every person is important for furthering the goal of the Coalition, the expansion into the unknown."

Ugh.

"The Coalition workforce may begin requesting transfers to the Outer Rim, which will be processed by your managers, and your applications sent on, if you are one of the highly anticipated additions to the team here. Civilians may begin booking transports to arrive at the start of next year."

The radio crackled and snapped. What the hell was that?

"—is important—thank—"

A low hum emanated from the small speaker. Rosie smacked the side of it, the same way she did to the one back home. Still, nothing but static.

"—night."

Her radio must be on the fritz. Maybe it was for the best. At least she wouldn't be tempted, or obligated, to listen to Delia's voice twice a day. It was hard enough knowing that she was on the same station, and seeing glimpses of her in the halls made Rosie's heart pound. Of all the damnable stations, they both had to end up on this one. It was a cruel joke.

The note was beginning to crumple in her hands, the creases in the paper making it even more of a challenge to read. Honestly, who wrote like this? Rosie stared at it, twisting it one way, and then another, until the letters she could make out began to swirl together, unintelligible. She squinted, willing the words to reveal themselves.

Ah, Fineglass, that was one of the words. Was it *from* the general? No, it seemed to be talking about her. Rosie sighed heavily and took out a piece of paper to try to trace the letters. Maybe that way she'd be able to figure out what they were. She started at the end.

Twin.

"What?" she muttered aloud, tracing more letters against the page, her fingers stained with ink as it smeared across her skin. Being left-handed was a damned trial, sometimes. She'd be scrubbing that ink from her hands for days.

Fineglass has a sister who could be her twin.

Rosie frowned at the note. It hadn't been meant for her, surely—what was she supposed to do with this information, and why was it even important? Plenty of people had siblings, even if Rosie didn't, and in some families, the resemblance was strong.

She crumpled the note and tossed it into the trash basket under her desk, but she continued to stare. It was too odd to ignore, even if it was obvious she wasn't the intended recipient. Should she report it to the general? To the overseer? Or pretend she'd never seen it at all?

If she was back home, she'd ask her family for their advice. Her mother would know what to do, she always did, whether it was a scraped knee or a nasty breakup. And if her mother didn't know, then her grandfather would. He'd spent years working in camp kitchens in settlements early in their development, and knew everything from herbal remedies for stress to hammering out an accord with a problematic crew member.

But she wasn't home. She was all the way out at the Rim, and her family didn't even know she was here. They might never speak to her again if they knew she was. "Too dangerous," her grandfather had said when she floated the idea two years ago, "and why would you want to be working in some kitchen, anyhow?" Things were different now than before. Opportunities for people like them were scarce. Almost everyone she'd known in school were all in work camps now, or worse.

The letter she'd written them still sat in her desk drawer. She'd send it. She would. Eventually, when the time was right, and it wasn't right yet. It wasn't right because she wasn't ready for the reply she'd likely get—if she even got a reply at all.

Did General Fineglass miss her family, too? Was she spending all that time in her quarters, aching with the loneliness? Was her sister back on Gamma-3?

She pulled the note out of the garbage and smoothed it out across her desk, examining it once more. Maybe she'd missed something, like a name, or a reason she'd found it under her door, but the crumpled page revealed no such thing. Rosie slid it into her desk drawer to lay next to the letter she was definitely going to send. Eventually.

Chapter 9

"I can't believe the damned broadcast was overridden again last night," Delia griped, sitting at her desk in the broadcasting booth.

"I checked all the frequencies, I couldn't hear anything," Carmen replied. "If we were being overridden, we should have been able to grasp their signal, but we weren't."

Delia chewed at the end of her pencil. "You don't think it's... pirates, do you?"

"No."

"How do you know for sure?"

"I just know."

"You just *know*? What does that even mean?"

"It means that their signals usually have specific defining characteristics," Carmen explained. "And this had none of that."

"And not the military? They have vessels—"

"No, I told you, it wasn't. There were no additional calls after that."

"What the hell was it, then?"

Carmen shrugged. "I wish I knew."

"This is horseshit."

"I didn't think you cared that much about the structural updates."

"Of course I care," Delia shot back, scowling. "It's my job to care. Besides, if we can't keep this from happening again, the overseer will take great pleasure in replacing us."

"I'll have another look, but I don't think I'm going to find anything."

"The wiring? You said the wiring was damaged, what if Thomas…" she fell silent, her heart still aching at his loss. "What if the last operator spliced something together in a haphazard way?"

"Could be, but I think I'd have noticed in one of the last two dozen checks you've had me do."

"This doesn't just happen, Carmen."

"Of course not, but arguing with me isn't going to change that."

"I'm not arguing with you."

"Certainly feels like it," Carmen mumbled, crawling under the desk again to check the wiring. "Ever since I got here, you've been barely anything but openly hostile to me."

Delia sighed. "I'm sorry. It takes me a little time to get used to new people."

"That much has been made crystal clear."

"I think it *was* the military," Delia announced again. "It's the only explanation that makes any damned sense. No one else out here has that kind of broadcasting range."

"Could be a civilian trying to have a laugh about it. There have been more ships around the station, looking for a scoop."

"They're not going to get one, not so long as I'm still around."

"If it was the military, why wouldn't we be getting secondary calls from them to fill us in?"

"Maybe we are, but we're not privy to it."

Carmen sat back on her haunches, the crisp canary yellow wool of her dress gently brushing the metal floor. "That's possible." She folded her arms. "More than possible, if you ask me. Likely."

"What would they be hiding from the rest of the crew?"

"Who knows? Could be anything. Probably something unimportant."

"Or," Delia said, rising to examine the corkboard on the wall with a map pinned to it, "it could be something about the ship's structural integrity. With all the renovations going on, they're bound to uncover something."

"What about asking Allemande again?"

"No, she wasn't in a rush to explain things the last time. I imagine she's in even less of a frame of mind for that now."

"Because of Emeline?"

"Something like that." Delia sat back in her chair, looking up at the low, water-stained ceiling. "Does she seem alright to you?"

"I've heard she can be... rather harsh. I try not to get in her way."

"No, not the overseer, her daughter!"

"Oh." Carmen straightened and leaned against the thin wooden desk. "She doesn't eat much, not that I blame her. Protein bricks are pretty disgusting."

"Anything else?"

"Nothing I would consider alarming. She's a teenage girl. After all, moodiness is to be expected."

"Hmm." Delia nodded. "I suppose you're right."

"You worried about the interview?"

"Yes, especially if our signal keeps getting knocked out. I had to bribe that kid with the last of my chocolate. I'd hate for it to go to waste. She's so popular in the mainstream newspapers, too, especially back on Gamma-3."

"A wonder child, plucked from the tenements by a benevolent governor. It's a good story."

"Of course it's a good story, it's heart-warming, and she's whip-smart, too." Delia sighed. "Too smart. She'll probably outsmart us all." She snorted. "Maybe she's the one sabotaging the broadcasts, just to get out of doing the interview. Teenage girls have done more to get out of less."

"Unless you gave her your keys for the booth, there's no way anyone but us, the overseer, or Fineglass could get in here, and I doubt either of them are messing with the controls."

"I was joking, Carmen."

"Could have been a working theory if it wasn't for the padlocks on the doors."

"Either way, we need to figure out what the hell is going on. I can't let some loose military frequency tank my career in broadcasting."

"The gods forbid you miss out on a promotion," Carmen chirped. "That would just be the end of civilization as we know it."

"Excuse me, I—"

Carmen winked. "It was a joke, Delia."

"Ms. Dodson, have you spoken with my daughter yet?" Overseer Allemande was standing in the corridor, her arms filled with files.

"Yes, she's agreed, but—"

"Excellent, let's do it tomorrow."

"She had a few... alterations she wanted to make."

"If this is about Skelm, I don't want to hear it."

"I thought she made some good points, ma'am, and—"

"Emeline is far too preoccupied with that city. It isn't healthy for a girl of her age to obsess about something like that. It holds too much trauma for her, and I am trying to encourage other interests for her." Allemande straightened the files in her hands, shuffling them around until they were in size order. "She will do the interview as planned, and I don't want to hear any more about Skelm. It may be a focal point of manufacturing in my sector, especially with the expansion here, but it's far from the largest settlement. We need to focus our efforts there and not get overly sentimental."

"Understood, ma'am."

Allemande softened for a moment, worry clouding her face. "I don't say this to be cruel to her, you know that, don't you? I care for Emeline. She's a bright young mind with boundless potential. I just don't want her getting bogged down in the petty affairs of some backwater."

"Of course."

"She won't see it that way, of course. I'm trusting you to make that clear to her, Ms. Dodson. Don't let me down. Emeline's future depends on this interview."

* * *

"No. I made my position clear to you, Ms. Dodson."

The gods save her from the wrath of a teenager. "I understand that, Emeline, but your mother is very insistent that we not discuss Skelm in the interview."

"Then we won't do the interview."

"You're making this very difficult for me."

"I fail to see how that is my problem specifically."

"I gave you the last of my sweets!" Delia spluttered. "I thought—"

"You thought you could buy me off with some chocolate, like a child?" Emeline crossed her arms over her chest, standing in her doorway.

"No, I thought we had an accord!"

"And we did until you knocked on my door ten minutes ago to explain why my requested revisions were all thrown out of the script."

"It wasn't my choice."

"I realize that, but it doesn't mean that my position on the matter has changed."

"Emeline—"

"I'm not going to change my mind on this."

"The people love to hear from you, the newspapers all line up to report on your speeches, this interview—"

"Then they can report on the fact that there is no interview to be had."

"You're wasting your influence," Delia spat. "This stubborn behavior is only going to make things more difficult. We don't always get our way. We have to give a little to get some in return."

"Wasting my influence? What good is influence if you're not allowed to use it in a way that has any meaning? The next people that will show up here at the Rim will be transports packed with MPOs, ready to scout out settlements. After that, it will be the monied merchants and traders, they'll be tended to and treated like royalty. What of the workers, Delia? What do they get?"

"I don't disagree with you, but your mother is adamant that Skelm be left out of the equation. What about doing a focus on some other settlement?"

"Because it's Skelm that is providing the materials for the expansion! To focus elsewhere would be pointless." Emeline's expression became even stonier. "You don't know anything about what that kind of life is like."

Delia swallowed back the barbed response she wanted to spit back at her.

She was hardly about to tell the overseer's daughter all the things she'd seen. "Emeline," she began softly, making a concerted effort to quiet the curses on the tip of her tongue, "we don't have much of an option here. Neither of us do."

"I will continue to refuse the interview until my terms have been agreed upon."

"And there's nothing at all I can do that might change your mind?"

"No."

"What if I spoke to her about doing a separate feature on Skelm once I'm back there?"

Emeline shook her head. "That's much too far in the future, and I'd have no way of holding you to that. I'm not so foolish as to throw away my one bargaining chip."

"Okay. What if we do a feature from here? A special broadcast, all about the workers that are making the Outer Rim project a reality?"

"You know she'll never agree to that."

"She might if I ask her, and she doesn't know it's coming from you."

"Please, she's no fool. She would know in an instant that it was coming from me."

Delia sighed heavily. Cajoling interviewees wasn't one of her strengths. "Emeline, I am begging you to please help me out with this, and do the interview. I promise, upon my heart of hearts, I will do everything I can to get Skelm into the spotlight."

"That's just not good enough."

"Gods be damned, Emeline, can't you just work with me?"

"Get away from my door," she replied, her gaze steely and unblinking. "Don't come back until you're ready to meet my terms."

* * *

"*Dear William,*" she wrote, her loopy handwriting small and compact, the same way she'd been taught at school. Paper might be plentiful now, but that hadn't always been the case. "*I hope that your trading is moving along well. I trust that you will remember to be cautious, even when you are sure that things are steady and settled.*"

She put the pen back in the inkwell and leaned back in her chair, letting the front two legs hover in the air. Will hadn't written to her yet, at least, not as far as she knew. Letters would take weeks to get back to Gamma-3, but it had been almost a month since he had left, and nothing.

This assignment wasn't only dangerous because it was at the Outer Rim, but because it left William to his own devices. He was a good man, but an easy mark for con artists. She'd lost count of how many credits he'd lost on bad bets and useless crap. He'd promised, though. Promised that he'd do better, follow her instructions on how to vet someone, not be impulsive.

Still, he hadn't written, and that was a bad sign. Tempted as she was to send a wire, they were prohibitively expensive, and there was still a chance that he had written, but the post was delayed, or he didn't send it right away. Or, and this was her fear, he had completely forgotten what she'd said the second he boarded the transport back home, and was busy spending every credit they'd managed to save up on forged artifacts and card games with cheats.

She picked up the pen again, letting the excess ink drip back into the well. "*I hope to hear from you soon. It is lonely out here, in spite of everything.*" At least he'd know that she'd stuck to her word to stay as far away from Rosie as she could.

It was the kind of challenge she'd never wanted, and found herself wandering past the kitchen door late at night, hoping to run into her. An excuse to see her pretty face, a chance to make her smile, not that she'd been able to do that for years. Rosie all but hated her now. At least that made avoiding her all the easier.

Some nights, Delia lay awake in her quarters, staring up at the empty ceiling, playing out scenarios in her head. If she hadn't left. If she hadn't married William. If she'd accepted some other kind of fate other than the one she'd built forcibly out of nothing.

"*I love you.*" She signed her name simply, without a flourish. She did love him, that was true, just not in the way that married couples should.

A best friend, perhaps, albeit one with the power to drag her career down into the mud, if he wanted to. If he ever stopped needing her. The thought had crossed her mind more than once.

As much as she hated it, Will held her future in his hands.

Chapter 10

Burying her hands in her pockets, Rosie breathed deep, revitalized from her walk through the dark observatory. It was off-limits to workers like her, but she'd started to feel like a caged animal. Still, it wasn't smart. A small infraction was enough to get dismissed. She couldn't go home empty-handed. Not now.

"Rosie!" Delia shouted, hurtling down the corridor so fast that it was almost a sprint.

"Shh! What do you want?"

"I was just... out for a walk."

"Erm, yeah. Me, too." All the peace of the quiet, starlit observatory drained away, leaving her with nothing more than irritation. "I should get to bed."

"Wait!" Delia reached for her, but Rosie pulled her hand away.

"What is it, Forrest?" Even as she said it, she flinched. "What do you want?"

"I just thought we could talk, maybe, or—"

Rosie turned away, fixing her stare on the empty metal of the wall. "I don't think that's a good idea."

"The overseer wants me to do a short series with you," Delia blurted out. "As part of the recruitment program, to show potential crew what it's like to live at the Rim."

"You going to find a replacement for me?"

"No! No, it's for additional workers. I don't actually have any say over—"

"It was a joke, Dee."

"Oh. Very funny! As I was saying, Overseer Allemande is hoping that a positive account might help drum up some new blood for the reserves."

"And you wandered around the ship in the middle of the night to tell me this?" Rosie turned back to her, raising an eyebrow.

"I would have told you tomorrow, it's just, we're both here now, and..." Delia looked away, a hand wrapped around the back of her neck. She always did that when she was nervous about something, ever since they had been children.

"Right. Well, I should get to sleep. Big day tomorrow," Rosie said with an exaggerated yawn. She just wanted to be alone, to recover the carefully cultivated peace of the observatory.

"What's on the menu?"

"Pasta."

"I love pasta."

"I know."

Delia looked back at her, squeezing her eyes shut. "Rose, I—"

"You should get to bed, too, you know. Don't want to be late for that morning broadcast."

"You listen?"

"I do." Rosie's stare fixed on the gently flickering overhead light, casting dancing shadows past their silhouettes.

"I didn't think you were much for radio."

"I'm not." Before Delia could reply, she added, "But it's not like there's anything else to do out here."

"Do you want help with morning prep? I could measure ingredients, or stir, or keep you company," Delia suggested.

"That's not a good idea."

"Why not?"

"How many times do we have to go over this, Dee?" Rosie sighed, brushing her hands against the rough wool of her skirts. "This is hard enough as it is."

Delia blinked, and even in the dark corridor, the tears nestled into the corners of her eyes sparkled. "I miss you."

It took every ounce of willpower to not reach out and wrap her in an embrace. Gods below, why couldn't Delia just stay in her own quarters? It was enough of a challenge to pretend they weren't on the same damned station, much less having to push her away, time and again, when all she wanted was to give into her heart. "Yeah."

"Maybe some other time, then." She turned to walk away, arms at her sides.

Rosie caught her by the hand, and the brush of fingertips against wrist threatened to undo her, unwinding every nerve into a puddle on the metal grate of the floor, dripping down into the ship where she'd rust into nothing and it would be only her own fault. "We could get a head start on the pasta for tomorrow. If you want." She prayed Delia would say no. She prayed she would say yes.

"Of course, you know I'd do anything for you." Delia gave a sad smile. "*Anything*."

"Straighten up then, sous-chef. We've got work to do. Come on, the kitchen is open. I was thinking a nice, fat noodle, thick enough to hold a chunky sauce." Rosie pushed open the metal door, already regretting inviting Delia. "I know that's your favorite."

"Put me to work!"

"First, you'll need an apron. There's a spare one in that cabinet, under the towels." Rosie tied her own around her waist, double-knotting, the same way she always did, and scrubbed her hands beneath scalding water. "I wouldn't want your fancy clothes to get covered in flour."

"Hardly fancy, Rosie."

"Fancier than anything I ever saw you in before." The small kitchen, usually claustrophobic in size, suddenly had a dangerous familiarity with Delia by her side. Rosie took a breath, trying to ignore the pull from years before.

"We were at school! Uniforms aren't anything to write home about."

"You forget, we spent a lot of time together outside school, too."

Delia pinned a stray curl up into her loose updo. "Of course I haven't forgotten. I won't ever forget."

"Get the semolina flour. It's on the third shelf. And wash your hands."

"No eggs?"

"Do you really think they'd let me have eggs out here? Gods below, I can barely get food that doesn't taste like tin." How was it that they were sliding so easily back into their old patter, the convention of their routines, moving around each other like they'd never spent a day apart. It pulled at Rosie's heart, fraught and maybe fatal.

"Too bad, I bet chickens would love roosting in Allemande's office."

Rosie snorted. "Don't give me any ideas, I'm a desperate woman." Gods, all these years, and it felt like no time had passed at all. Rosie laughed again, filling a steel measuring cup with water. "As much as the general would probably appreciate fresh eggs, I don't think she will sign off on overtaking the overseer's office with a gaggle of hens."

"A gaggle is for geese, isn't it? More like a flock of chickens. Or a brood of hens."

"Given how aggressive they were back home, I'm surprised it's not a murder of hens, rather than of crows. I bet they'd eat you alive if they had the chance."

Delia pushed the bag of flour across the counter, her hand brushing gently against Rosie's. It was enough to make her gasp softly, but she forced a cough to cover it. "Right," Rosie said, "make a little well in the middle for the water. This is a sticky dough, so I hope you haven't grown too precious to get your hands dirty."

"I'm a radio broadcaster, Rosie, not a princess."

"Looks the same from where I'm standing," Rosie said with a wry smile. Delia glowed, somehow, even in dark space, even beneath the harsh yellow light of the bulbs that hung from the ceiling.

"Oh, please, don't be so dramatic."

"We need three batches," Rosie continued. "Usually I would make one batch, but we don't have enough space, and you run the risk of not kneading it thoroughly enough."

"And why would that be bad?"

"Because then you'd have disgusting pasta, and I'm not trying to get fired."

"They'd never fire you, Rosie Posy, you're too good."

The outmoded, affectionate name threatened to turn words to ash in Rosie's mouth. "Don't... call me that."

"You used to like it."

"Things were different then, Delia. *We* were different."

"It doesn't have to be so different. You're still you, and I'm still me."

"For the third time, you're *married*."

Delia chewed on her lip. "It doesn't mean we can't be friends."

"Maybe this was a bad idea."

"No! Don't send me away again, Rose. I know this is difficult and... and strange, but I don't want to spend all my time on this gods-forsaken station alone."

"Fine. Stay. But if you don't start mixing that flour better, you're fired as my assistant." Rosie handed her a tarnished fork. "Try this."

"I've heard that some of the MPOs have been getting extra rations."

"They aren't getting extra rations."

"But I heard—"

"Gods be damned, Delia, do you always have to wheedle for information?"

"I'm not! I'm just trying to make some conversation!"

Rosie snorted. "Sure."

"You don't have to be so suspicious, you know."

"It's not so easy for those of us without *connections*, Dee. We don't all have a rich husband with a good name that we can fall back on." Rosie's hands were covered in wet dough, but she placed one on her hip all the same.

"He's not—you know what, maybe you were right. Maybe this was a mistake. I'm sorry I even came in here." She wiped away a tear before it fell into the pasta. "I'm sorry I even thought I could try to repair what I've broken, I'm sorry I wandered the corridors almost every gods-forsaken night hoping to see you, I—"

Rosie shook her head in disbelief. "You were creeping around the ship hoping to see me?"

"I wasn't creeping!"

"You know where my quarters are, Delia, I live across the hall."

"I didn't think you would want to see me. You've made it very clear that you resent my presence here on the ship."

"I don't... *resent* you. If I did, I wouldn't have invited you to make pasta with me." The tension had wedged between them, an uncomfortable departure from what they were.

"What, then?" Delia asked quietly.

"Don't make me go there. Don't make me say the words, I just... I can't, alright? Let's just make pasta. You can't leave now, we've already mixed half the ingredients."

"Okay," Delia whispered, wiping away another tear with her forearm. "I will try not to cry into your pasta dough."

"You'd better not, you'll over salt it."

"I'd make a terrible sous-chef."

"Yes, you would, but lucky for you, the competition here is pretty scarce." Rosie leaned across the counter to add more flour to Delia's dough. "Too sticky." She sprinkled it over the mixture, a silent falling snow that reminded her of times long gone. Places they could never return to, not like they were. Maybe too much had changed. Maybe all of this was a huge mistake, maybe—

"Are you going to make that red sauce I like?"

Rosie nodded. "As good as I can. Not like there are many fresh herbs out here."

"Shame I'm not management."

"I could probably save you a portion if you keep your big mouth shut."

"I shall only open my mouth to eat pasta. It will remain closed otherwise on the subject." Delia closed her eyes, and for a moment, she looked just like they had when they were teenagers. "I might actually kill someone for a slice of strawberry shortcake."

"That I definitely can't do. Inefficient, according to the overseer."

"How long do we knead this for?" Delia asked, scraping wet dough off her fingers. "My arms are getting tired."

"We've only just started, you fool. At least fifteen more minutes."

"Gods, how do you do this every day?"

"I enjoy it. Peace and quiet." Rosie gave Delia a wry smile. "Usually."

A silent moment passed between them before Delia changed the subject. "What was it like on Nox Beacon?"

"Boring. Same thing day in and day out. Opened so many tin cans, I could probably do it in my sleep."

"What, you weren't the head chef over there?"

Rosie leaned into the dough, stretching and kneading it into smoothness. "No. I was just another grunt in the kitchen. I'm lucky I got this gig."

"Nah, this *station* is lucky. I think everyone was getting really sick and tired of protein bricks."

"It's a challenge to scale things up at the start of a project. They went from a skeleton crew of ten to, what, nearly fifty now? With more arriving soon?"

Delia nodded. "Yeah, once the barracks are completed."

"That new kitchen can't come fast enough. It's going to be a hell of a challenge to keep up."

"They should get you an assistant or something. Or, and don't say no—"

"No."

"You didn't even hear what my idea was!"

Rosie sighed. "You can't be my assistant, Dee. You have enough to worry about with the broadcasts."

"Sure, but when I'm not—"

"You know Overseer Allemande would never go for it."

"No," Delia agreed, her shoulders slumped. "I guess not."

"To be honest, I don't think that she'd sign off on an assistant at all. From what I can understand, she barely wanted to hire me in the first place." Rosie buried her palms deep in the dough once more, developing the elasticity it needed. She dusted her hands in flour once more, sprinkling the excess over the counter.

"If she hadn't, there'd have been a mutiny on her hands."

"Yeah, with General Fineglass first in line."

Delia raised an eyebrow. "Oh? Why's that?"

"You know," Rosie said nonchalantly, "Fineglass likes her food, whereas Allemande seems pretty nonplussed." She smiled, digging into the dough ball again. Even if it was just Delia, she was a reporter now. Anything Rosie said could wind up on a broadcast, and she couldn't risk losing this job.

"Hm. Yeah."

"What about you, Dee? You've been all over the Near Systems by now. What was Skelm like?"

"Polluted."

"That's it?" Rosie asked.

"It's a manufacturing settlement, it's a backwater."

"Still, you were there for the storms!"

Delia grimaced. "Yeah."

"That must have been exciting!"

"I thought I was going to die. Those lightning strikes went on for so long."

Rosie focused on the dough, smoothing the edges to test if it was ready. "I'm glad you didn't."

"Me, too. I much preferred the Capital, at least the food there is better."

The dough was growing firm under Rosie's hands, and she set it aside to start on the next batch. "I bet the chefs there have amazing kitchens."

Delia smirked at her. "And plenty of assistants."

"Maybe someday I'll see the inside of one, if I prove myself out here. If I keep my nose clean."

"I can't imagine you'd ever get tied up in something you shouldn't. You were always such a rule-follower, Rosie."

"Gods, you make me sound so boring."

"Not boring... dependable, maybe. Steadfast."

Rosie groaned. "Somehow, that's worse."

"Some people *like* steadfast!"

"Not enough, apparently." She hadn't meant to say it out loud, yet she had. Now the only sounds were the soft squelches of wet dough against the counter top, and the vague hum of the station's boilers, somewhere far below on another deck.

"Rosie…"

"Your dough looks good. Here, you can start rolling it out and cutting it into strips. Thick, but not too thick."

"People might cry tears of joy when they see pasta on the menu."

"They'd better. Not easy all the way out here to create dishes that taste like home."

"You're an excellent cook. They couldn't have gotten anyone better than you for this job." Delia leaned her weight into the rolling pin, smoothing the dough into a wide, flat sheet. "I'm glad that you're here."

It was too much, having her in the kitchen. A million different emotions bubbled up just below Rosie's calm, collected surface. Love. Jealousy. The deep, inexorable yearning to go back to before Delia left. It was impossible. "If you stack the sheets of dough with a little flour between, you can cut twice as much at once," Rosie said, her eyes trained on her own dough. She didn't dare look anywhere else.

"Are you going to save some for me?"

"Of course."

"Do you get to eat the food, or do they have you on protein bricks?"

"I'm supposed to be on the bricks."

Delia wiggled her eyebrows. "Ah, okay, I see. Maybe you're not such a rule follower after all."

"Shh. Don't give me away. I think I'd jump out of the airlock myself if I had to eat those things." Rosie laughed, but sobered when she saw Delia's face. "Oh. Your friend. I'm sorry, Dee."

"I think I should head to bed. It looks like you won't be much longer, anyway."

"Wait—"

"Night, Rose." Delia folded up the apron and placed it back on the shelf she'd pulled it from. "See you around." The kitchen door closed, and Rosie bent over the counter, her tears dripping down onto her apron.

Chapter 11

"Did the overseer sign off on tomorrow morning's broadcast?" Carmen asked, draped against the door frame.

Delia laid her pen down on the desk. "No, not yet. She's been in meetings all afternoon with new management they brought on board to start preparing the station for investors."

"Seems premature."

"Especially when the barracks aren't even completed yet. What exactly are they going to be showing the investors? A tiny station crammed with people?"

"Delia, I was wondering if we shouldn't include some information about which routes are safe from piracy. You know, where the new Coalition military patrols are stationed? Might make people feel better about making the trip out here."

"It's a good idea, but I'll have to run it past Allemande."

"You should make the case for it. I got a letter from home yesterday, and from what I can tell, most people won't even consider setting foot near the rim unless they're sure that they'll get here safely."

Delia nodded. "Makes sense."

"So, including information about which routes have those additional patrols might be prudent."

"Sure," she responded, making a note in the margins of the page. "I'll see what I can do." Announcing that would also let any rebels listening know which flight paths to avoid. If she could get it into the script, it would be a damn miracle—but Allemande was able to sniff out any whiff of useful information, and scrub it from the broadcast. Hells, given all the problems with the signals lately, it was possible that no one in The Scattered was even listening.

"Did you get some of that pasta last night?" Carmen whispered.

"No, I was busy."

"*Busy?* On this station? What, did you have a hot date with a protein brick?"

"I was in the middle of working on something."

"*Oh,*" Carmen said, fluttering her eyelashes. "*I see.*"

"There isn't anything to see, Ms. Rojas."

"Mhmm. And hearing you in the kitchen with the cook the night before last has nothing to do with anything, I suppose?"

Fuck. Who else had heard them? "I was just trying to help out. Many hands make light work, as they say?"

"Oh yes, I'm sure the overseer would be absolutely *thrilled* with your dedication to efficiency."

"Please don't say anything. To anyone. We're old friends, that's all. I had no idea she'd—"

Carmen extended her hand. "I promise, on my honor. It's none of my business. I'll even shake on it."

"That's very..." Delia shook her hand, searching Carmen's face. "Honorable of you."

"It's not like close friends are barred from working together at the same station, is it? That rule is only for previously undisclosed *romantic* entanglements."

Delia coughed. "Yeah."

"Stranger things have happened on a work assignment."

"Can we stop talking about this now?"

"I met a lovely man on an assignment once. Roger. So kind, and sweet, and *very* attentive—"

"I wouldn't be spreading that around if I were you. Even if you're no longer on that assignment, you can get into trouble."

Carmen shrugged. "It was before I joined the Coalition."

"Oh? What were you doing, then?"

"You know, this and that, here and there. Nothing important. Certainly nothing as absolutely essential as what you do."

Delia chewed on her lip. There was something almost suspicious about Carmen, but the amount of checks and paperwork required to come out here would definitely have uncovered anything untoward. "It's just a radio broadcast."

"Sure, but people rely on them to know what's going on. How else would anyone know of all the impressive work being done out here at the Rim?"

"What *were* you doing, though?" Delia asked. "Before you joined the Coalition."

"I told you, I ran a small broadcast—"

"About what, though? Where?"

"Listen," Carmen said, her voice dropping to a whisper. "We've all got secrets. I can't let mine get out."

"What did you do, kill someone? Join a pirate crew?"

Something like recognition, or fear, flashed across Carmen's face. "No. Definitely not."

"You know my secret. It's only fair I should know yours."

"Alright, alright!" Carmen said, stepping into the booth and closing the door. "You have to promise you won't say anything."

"Of course."

"I might have... plumped up my employment history."

"What?"

"I was never a private teacher for the diplomatic families on Delta-4. That's how I got this job here, teaching Emeline."

"How did you pull that off?"

"Being very careful."

"What *did* you do, then?"

Carmen leaned against the desk. "I was more of a casual private tutor."

"I'm amazed you got that past the recruitment desk."

"The oldest is all grown up now. He was my reference."

"You'd better hope he doesn't squeal on you."

"Oh, he won't. We have an... understanding."

Delia snorted. "You have dirt on him."

"Of a sort."

"Blackmail and lying, what else have you gotten up to? Here I thought you were just some up-jumped tutor trying to horn in on my broadcast, but really, you have a sordid history!"

"Hardly sordid."

"For all I know, you could be a *spy*!"

Carmen clamped a hand over Delia's mouth. "I'm not a spy."

"I was kidding," Delia answered, her voice muffled through Carmen's palm.

"Don't even joke about that. I've seen people gunned down for less."

"What?"

A sharp knock at the door interrupted their conversation. "Ms. Dodson! Are you in there?"

"Er—Yes, Overseer, Carmen and I were running some checks on the equipment."

Allemande pushed the door open, her eyes flitting from Delia to Carmen, and back again. "I should hope you two aren't wasting time with needless chatter."

"No, ma'am, as I said, just checking on that wiring."

"Very good. Is your script for the morning ready?"

"It's on your desk already."

"You went into my office?"

"No, Emeline took it in."

"Emeline." The overseer blinked. "Yes, of course."

Delia stood, edging past Carmen. "I did have a possible addition, ma'am, about civilian travel out here to the Rim. With the uptick in piracy around some of the travel beacons that head out this way, maybe we should reiterate how safe the approved flight paths are."

"Come sit in my office. We'll discuss it." She turned to Carmen. "Shouldn't you be with my daughter for her evening tutoring session?"

Carmen nodded. "Yes, of course, was just finishing up here."

"I'm sure Ms. Dodson is more than capable of completing the checks. You are dismissed."

"I'll see you in the morning," Delia added.

The overseer's office was pristine, as usual, the desk cleared except for the script, the shelves neatly filled with books and wide file folders labeled across the spines.

"I have reservations about these additions you've requested, Ms. Dodson."

"I anticipated that. If I could just—"

"We have to be very vigilant about what kind of information we are disseminating here. One wrong word and we could find that we've inadvertently been helping pirates, or worse, rebels."

"I would never want that," Delia lied.

"What brought you to this idea?"

"I've heard from... some of the crew members, that letters from home have suggested a great resistance to traveling out here for fear of pirate attacks. I know that one of our main goals is to attract not only investors, but laborers. If they are assured that their journey will be safe and secure, then perhaps it will have a positive impact on recruitment for both categories."

"Hmm." Allemande scanned the script. "You do have a point." She set it down on the desk again. "I should perhaps check with General Fineglass before I sign off." The overseer scowled. "She is, after all, the final say of what goes on around here, despite our partnership."

"I can run the amended script over to her," Delia offered, careful to stifle her excitement.

"Yes, do. If she agrees, then I'll approve it."

Delia stood, taking the script. "I'll do that right now."

"Ms. Dodson," Allemande said, "I would be careful about whispering behind closed doors. Some that are stricter than I might make incorrect assumptions about what a married woman was doing with the new operator."

* * *

"This has been Delia Dodson from the Outer Rim. Tune in for our evening broadcast, in which we will interview one of the architects of the Turas-Mara Station expansion."

"We're clear," Carmen shouted from the other side of the wall.

Delia grinned, setting the headphones on the small table. It was such a small win to broadcast the patrol locations, but it was better than no win at all. "Thanks, Carmen."

"Did you get breakfast yet?"

"Protein bricks for me today."

"Eugh. Gods, Dodson, you should at least try to grab some scraps. It's better than whatever's in that crap."

"I'm fine."

Carmen leaned into the room. "Lover's tiff?" she whispered.

"No. Shut up."

"Alright, alright. I could grab you some, if you want."

It was tempting, but if word got back to Rosie... "No, thank you," Delia said. "I'm not that fond of fresh baked bread and strawberry jam."

"Are you sure? Because your eyes went a little dreamy, there."

"I'm... sure." Damn Rosie for making strawberry jam. She knew strawberries were her weakness. The thought of biting into a piece of that bread was making her mouth water.

"Okay then, more for me." Carmen fluffed her skirts, swishing the fabric against her legs. "Good broadcast, Delia. I think we really had a win including that information about the patrols."

"Yes." Their eyes met for a moment, and Delia squinted. "Is there something you're not telling me?"

"No. You already know all of my secrets."

"Mm."

"Last chance on that bread, Dodson. You know the cargo crew is going to get in there and clear it all out."

Delia sighed. "I'm sure."

"Your loss, then."

"Yup."

Carmen leaned in closer. "You know, if there was something going on with the cook, you could tell me. I'm like a vault for secrets."

"I thought you said I already knew all your secrets."

"Yeah, *mine*, not everyone else's."

"There's nothing going on with Rosie."

"So much not going on that you're on a first-name basis?"

Delia huffed. "I told you, we're old friends. We went to school together a long time ago."

"Sure."

"It's the truth!"

"Relax, Dodson. I'm just saying, if I had the opportunity for some bread and jam, nothing in the universe would keep me from it. Especially not when we're on brick rations otherwise."

"Gods, they're disgusting."

Carmen laughed. "They could at least put some flavoring in them. They taste like... I don't even know. Gelatinous pond water."

"Don't, you'll make me heave. I still have to eat mine."

"Be nice if we could convince Allemande to extend kitchen meals to the rest of the crew, wouldn't it?"

"That will never happen. Besides, the kitchen isn't big enough, especially with more MPOs and researchers showing up in a couple of weeks. There's no way anyone could keep up with that, not without help."

"Pity. I'm going to go, before the wildebeest clean the kitchen out of breakfast."

"Have fun," Delia said, her stomach rumbling.

* * *

Thank the gods, Allemande had meetings all morning. Delia heaved a sigh

89

of relief and sat down on her bed, kicking her boots off. Still no mail from William. No doubt he was busy getting mired in more trouble. No, she shouldn't think like that. He'd promised it would be different this time. They were so close to having more influence, more power... though *his* main interest was in having a fat credit account.

She looked at the protein brick that had been slid under her door, wrapped in paper, the same as every morning. Some days, she'd rather go hungry than eat it. If she had declined the overseer's offer to come out to the Rim, if she had stayed in the Capital, she'd be eating well every meal. Instead, she got this crap.

With a heavy sigh, Delia picked it up off the floor, placing it on the desk to unwrap.

Instead of a protein brick, though, it was two thick slices of fresh bread, slathered in strawberry jam. When Delia started to cry, it wasn't only at the relief that she'd been spared a protein brick. It was knowing that deep down, somewhere, Rosie still cared for her, and that maybe everything hadn't been ruined forever.

Chapter 12

Rosie shoveled porridge into bowls as they appeared at the service window. One after another, the wet noise of the oats plopping against the steel dishes. She'd barely slept. Her eyes were dry from exhaustion, and all she wanted to do was curl up under the rolling cart and sleep for a week.

"Thanks," the station manager said. She was still new, not yet accustomed to ignoring anyone who wasn't pulling in the same kind of credits, or who didn't have the kind of power that management had.

"You're welcome," Rosie mumbled in reply. "Additions on the table, there." It wasn't much, mostly canned fruit, but it was better than nothing. They were lucky to be getting oats at all.

"I think I'm the last one. Everyone else is clearing out."

"Already?"

"It's the same time as normal."

Rosie checked her pocket watch and blinked. "So it is." There were a few stragglers, but most had already finished. The tables were littered with dishes, as always. She sighed and went through the side door, which opened out from the wall. Sticky porridge fell in wet splodges on the floor as she carried the dirty bowls back to the kitchen to wash.

"Psst. Hey, Cook," Officer Miller said from the kitchen doorway. "You got any left?"

"I told you lot, I'll bring whatever's left down to the loading bay. You can't be up here. It's a dead giveaway."

"I know, but I'm hungry."

"Go on, get out of here. I'll bring whatever's left in a little while. There's not much, but you can divvy it up amongst yourselves. I know Abara isn't big on oats, maybe you can have their share."

"Nah. They've been trading theirs for... never mind."

"Trading theirs for what?"

"I can't tell you," Miller said.

Rosie sighed, the exasperation leaking from the sound. "You really shouldn't be up here. If the others catch wind, they'll think you're getting extra."

"What if I said I'd tell the general that you're giving away scraps? You'd get into trouble. Maybe you should give me a bigger portion, and I'll keep quiet."

"I'm in no mood for this." Rosie dropped the bowls into the sink of hot, sudsy water. "Besides, I think you'll find that the general and I already have an understanding."

Miller stared with a frown that slowly spread into a smirk. "Okay, then I'll tell the overseer. I bet she wouldn't appreciate the inefficiency."

"You know what? Go ahead. Tell the overseer. I'll make damn sure every single MPO on this gods-forsaken station knows it was you who overturned the gravy train."

"Alright, gods," Miller grumbled. "You don't know what it's like to live on protein bricks."

"I do, *actually*, which is why I agreed to help you folks out in the first place. Don't make me change my mind. I have enough problems as it is." It was a hell of a focus of willpower to not physically shove this little worm back into the corridor. "Get out of my kitchen."

"Hey, I'm sorry! I just—"

"Don't dare come into my workspace and threaten me, when all I've done is go out of my way to help you. I'm up here making extra food, altering the quantities on orders to make sure there's enough, and you have the audacity to try to back me into a corner." She waved her spoon at him, threatening. "Leave."

"Please don't tell Abara—"

"I'm going to give them a full account of this if you're not out of my sight in three seconds."

"Shit!"

"And close the door on your way out!"

The latch slammed closed, and she fished the dishrag out of the sink. First Delia, then strange, mysterious notes, now this. Didn't she have enough to deal with? Now she was running behind. So much for having a few minutes spare to check out that note again.

She washed the bowls, cringing at the wet slop of porridge collecting at the bottom of the sink. What she wouldn't give for kitchen staff—even though once the renovations were complete, she anticipated being relegated back to being kitchen staff herself. No doubt the high-profile investors would be expecting a gourmet chef from the Capital.

The dirty dishwater disappeared down the drain, the sucking noise muffled by the globs of waterlogged oats. Grimacing, Rosie reached in and scooped them out with her bare hands, swallowing back a retch. Her love of cooking was balanced by an inverse revulsion for cleaning strangers' dishes.

Blinking back the tiredness, she swung the serving hatch closed and locked it with the slide latch. It didn't matter that General Fineglass said her MPOs were disciplined enough to keep out. After that irritating interaction, she couldn't take chances anymore. She'd find her own padlock if she had to, there was no way she'd be leaving the kitchen open from now on.

What the hell was on the menu for dinner again? Rice and... something? Dumplings? She squinted at the chalkboard that hung on the far wall. Yes, that seemed right. She needed to get started on the dough, she was already running late. Usually she'd start preparing a meal like that in the morning, as management all filed into the mess hall, but that morning, she was so tired that she had three cups of coffee instead. They hadn't helped.

With a heavy yawn, she measured out the dry ingredients, dumping them onto the counter. She added the requisite water and began to mix it into a firm dough. The hypnotic, soothing rhythm of kneading almost led her to sleep on her feet, her head lolling down into a shallow drowse.

"I don't give one single fuck why you think this is necessary, Amaranth. I've told you time and time again, this station still has to function as a military outpost!"

Rosie shrank down in the kitchen, crouching behind the counter. Whatever the general and the overseer were arguing about, they wouldn't like knowing she'd overheard even a snippet of it.

"*Language*, Wilhemina, *please,*" the overseer chided. "There is no need for that kind of coarse behavior, no matter how... *enraged* you've become."

"How am I supposed to do my job out here with you flitting around, second-guessing my every decision? You may be an overseer, but you're still a damned civilian. You're not in the military anymore. You have no idea what kind of importance this station holds regarding the potential for expansion."

"Pardon me, but I know very well the razor-edge we're all standing on out here. If it wasn't for me, this little pet project of yours would still be nothing more than a backwater with little funding."

"And if it wasn't for my *pet project*, as you put it, your half-empty sector would still be the least important in the eyes of the High Council. Like it or not, you need me." The general sighed heavily. "And this station needs the positive public relations you've provided. I will admit to that."

"Skelm is the jewel of—"

"You don't need to give me the advertisement spiel, I've heard it a hundred times from you."

"Need I remind you of your dirty little secret? One slip of the tongue and you'd be buried in inquiries for the rest of time."

"Oh, please. As if you wouldn't get dragged into those inquiries alongside me. You're the one who made the deal with her."

"Me? I'm nothing but innocent! How was *I* to know that the great Wilhemina Fineglass had some sort of doppelganger?"

"I'm not so sure the judge would agree. Especially not if she became acutely aware of some of the other deals you've struck to elevate yourself."

"*Myself*? All I do, I do for the good of the Coalition."

Fineglass snorted, filling her mug with coffee from the carafe. "Sure."

"I'm not being unreasonable. All I ask is to be kept in the know of what's happening on this station. You agreed, long before I even arrived out here, yet every time I turn around, you're making decisions without me, sneaking around sending updates back to your superiors without telling me."

"It doesn't concern you, Amaranth!"

"Everything that happens out here concerns me!" Allemande cleared her throat lightly. "I don't know what you think you're getting away with, but it stops now. I will not be party to any schemes that undermine the efficiency and progress of the Coalition."

"Sending reports back to the Capital is hardly a scheme."

"Call it what you will, but you know as well as I do that these delays are only costing more and more. The Council isn't going to be impressed with how slowly the station build is coming along, and it only takes one bad mood, one ill whim, and we're all shut down out here. Everything we have worked for will have been for naught. I don't want that, do you?"

"Of course not," the general grumbled.

"We need to present as a united front, especially to the laborers. They are under the impression that I have no power on this station. I trust you will disabuse them of that fallacy?"

"Fine."

"I didn't move my daughter to the Outer Rim just to allow all her potential to be crushed. She deserves better than that, wouldn't you agree?"

"Amaranth, just stay out of my way."

"It's rather a challenge to be in your way when you're rarely even seen outside of meetings. Your officers are running wild across the entire station. Did you know that one of them was caught *gambling* last week?"

"Oh *no*, not *gambling*!"

"Are you mocking me?"

"You're a brilliantly smart political strategist, but you have no idea how to manage teams of people way out here. In a city, they'll take their day off and visit a speakeasy, a brothel, an underground casino. Blow off some steam, come back to work all the ready to put the time in."

"My employees were never doing any of those activities."

"I sincerely doubt that."

"Wilhemina, I thought we were on the same page with this. Alcohol? Cards? We worked together to bring that speakeasy in the Capital down—"

"And I guarantee its place has already been filled by another. They were an easy scapegoat. We had to do something to get the heat off. People were getting suspicious. Neither of us would be out here if the Council had found out."

"I didn't realize you ran your station like a lawless rebel settlement."

"Come find me if you catch one of my MPOs shifting supplies to pirates, then we'll talk. But gambling for a few credits, maybe a candy bar? It's hardly the crime of the century. We have bigger, more important things we're working on, here."

"I vehemently disagree. Any deviation from legality is a departure from efficiency. It's only a matter of time before they start showing up to their shifts inebriated. How long until we crash into an asteroid, because one of the flight crew passed out on the control deck?"

"Don't be so dramatic. If anyone's even managed to smuggle alcohol aboard, it won't be enough for whole swathes to be getting blackout drunk. You have to let them think they're having some semblance of control, or before you know it we'll have a damned mutiny on our hands."

"Preposterous. No good ever came of lax policy."

"You've barely been out here three months. Things don't start getting hard until half a year sets in, and the transports aren't running every day. That's when they'll start dreaming up ways to throw us both out of an airlock if we don't give them something to hold on to."

"From my perspective, you're looking for ways to excuse bad behavior."

"And from mine, you're going to end up alienating half the crew if you don't stop interfering."

Allemande huffed. "I am not concerned with my popularity."

"That much is painfully obvious."

"And what is that supposed to mean?"

"Listen," Fineglass said, exhaling slowly, "it is unfortunate that we both need each other out here to keep this place humming along. You manage your staff, and I will manage my crew. I will run my reports by you before they get sent back to Gamma-3. Happy?"

"Definitely not. But I don't see the point in arguing any further, given your reckless attitude."

"I will make a concerted effort to show my face outside of meetings. And I'll make sure no one is drinking. I can't keep them from gambling, not without round-the-clock surveillance."

"Then I shall put in a request for more surveillance tools."

"They'll turn on you, Amaranth."

"They can try. But at the end of the day, we'll see who's still standing, and I guarantee that it will be the two of us. Just wait, Wilhemina. Let me whip this crew into shape, and efficiency will shoot through the roof of this place. We'll get back on track and have investors here inside a month."

"Whatever you say."

The mess hall door clicked closed, and Rosie finally breathed out, her heart pounding in her chest. The note was all the more dangerous now.

Chapter 13

"*My dearest Delia, I write to you with excellent news. The trade deal with the parts supplier continues apace. We are set with excellent margins, and by the time this letter reaches you, they will begin arriving on Turas-Mara within days.*"

She tucked a loose curl back into the clip at the nape of her neck. At least she'd finally gotten a letter, and surprisingly, it was good news. Maybe William was finally growing into the family business, even if his family had cut him off a long time ago.

"*I know that you will be lonely there, assuming that what you promised remains true. I also know that I promised you a parcel; unfortunately, in my haste to secure this agreement, I missed the cutoff for the civilian transport. I will send it along as soon as I am able.*"

Typical. No wonder there were no packages for her in the cargo bay. If she had to eat one more protein brick, she might start devouring her boots instead.

"*I hope that your trust in me continues. I am keeping my vows close and true, and rest assured I will not abandon them. I will write again, and soon. Yours, Will.*"

Delia frowned at the brief note, the creases blurring the words in the center of the page. Will's letters were usually much longer and offered more than just a cursory glimpse of home. When she was in Skelm, he'd almost written her a novel by the time she arrived back at their apartment months later. Something was distracting him, and she could only hope that it was the deal, and not the Banríon tables.

He'd promised, though, and she trusted him to keep his word.

She shook her head vigorously, turning loose another lock of hair that now hung down the side of her face. Annoyed, she pinned it back again, toying with the clip in her hands. There was too much going on, too much that she couldn't explain. Never one for mysteries, the lack of information scraped against her like sand, rubbing at her day and night.

The clock on her nightstand chimed quietly, announcing the late hour. She should be in bed already. Her sleeping pattern was already tattered as it was, and staying up all night was only going to make things worse. A walk would help. That's what she always did back home.

Her fingers found the laces of her boots and lazily tucked them inside the soft canvas, pulling her socks up before locking the door to her quarters. It didn't seem like anyone else on the station bothered with locks, but the broadcasts getting interrupted had made her uneasy, suspicious. Besides, she didn't want anyone going through her things. There was nothing to find, not really, but it would be a violation, nonetheless.

The station was quiet at that time of night. Most of the crew was sleeping, with only a skeleton assembly, most of them in the control center on the other end, far from where the living quarters were located. She'd spent time on a good number of stations in her time, for work mostly, but never one that had been purpose built for military use.

She avoided the kitchen. It was too dangerous, the temptation pulled at her day and night, inescapable. Inexorable. Everything about Rosie was a risk that could bring everything in Delia's life toppling down around her, and she had enough problems to deal with, from grouchy teenage girls, to broken broadcasting equipment, to upholding the elaborate charade that was her marriage. That last one was definitely the most challenging.

"Evening," one of the night watch military police officers mumbled as she walked by, his dove grey uniform matching the drab metal walls, except for the yellow and purple trim that adorned the shoulders and pockets.

"Hello," she responded, nodding.

"Your laces are untied."

"I know."

"I heard the kitchen has leftovers," the MPO whispered. "If the rest of us didn't get to them first."

"Thanks for the tip." She edged past, the corridor too narrow at that point for two adults to walk next to each other. Her stomach rumbled hopefully, but she swallowed back the bile from the empty retches that followed.

She found herself wandering down towards that end of the station, passing the entrance for the newly completed atrium, where the stars sparkled past the thick glass, past the new recreation room which sounded almost lively, even at that time of night. Gambling, most likely, it's not as though the MPOs had much else to do off-duty. She grimaced, knowing that Will had picked up the habit during his years of service, too.

Her hand hovered at the door to the kitchen for a moment before she tried to ease it open. It wouldn't budge. She pushed harder, but still nothing. The bronze knob was cold in the palm of her hand the third time she tried, this time turning and shoving with her shoulder.

"What are you doing?"

Delia spun around. "Nothing."

"It looks to me like you're trying to break into my kitchen."

"Not break into, just... an MPO said there were leftovers."

"Yes, there *were*, four hours ago. The night shift cleared me out."

"Oh."

Rosie tilted her head. "Are you okay?"

"Yes."

"I might be able to get you a can of peaches—"

"No, thanks though."

"Leftovers always go fast when it's dumplings. Or pasta."

"Of course they do. You're an excellent chef."

"I'm a cook, but I appreciate the sentiment."

Delia released the doorknob. "Someday you'll be serving the High Council in the Capital."

"Maybe."

"Sorry I bothered you. I was just out for a late walk around the station."

"Not much of a walk, is it?"

"No, but it's the best we've got. For now, anyway."

Rosie reached out but pulled her hand back, letting it fall to her side. "Do you... want company?"

"That feels like a complicated question."

"It's not."

"I don't know how to answer. Everything feels wrong." Delia fidgeted with the clasp of her suspenders. "Thank you for the bread, by the way. I know it was you who sent it."

"I'd hoped you would come by the kitchens after that, so I could apologize in person. You didn't, though."

"No."

"I'm sorry for what happened to Thomas. I shouldn't have said what I said."

"You didn't mean it."

"Yeah, you know me, though. A big mouth." Rosie smoothed back the stray hairs framing her face. "This isn't easy."

"I wouldn't have come here if—"

"Yeah. Me neither."

Delia chewed at her lip. "So, that company you offered...?"

"I could show you something. Something... secret."

"You, keeping secrets? That's not the Rosie I remember."

"People do change, Dee."

"What is it, a bottle of whiskey?"

Rosie laughed. "No. Can't handle that stuff, never could."

"I guess people don't change *that* much."

"Do you want to see, or not?"

"Yes!"

"Follow me. But be quiet. Sometimes the night patrols wander up this way."

"What, trying to make sure the sacks of flour don't run off with the canned peas?" Delia stepped back as Rosie closed the door to her quarters and motioned for her to follow.

"No, for the same reason you're standing in this hallway. To see if there're leftovers."

"You're very nice to save them some. I bet most cooks wouldn't do that."

"Most cooks have staff, or at least the ability to keep them out of the shipments. They're getting braver, though. Just today, one showed up in my kitchen threatening to blackmail me."

"Did you tell Fineglass?"

"No. Not yet, anyway. If Allemande would just back off the efficiency stuff, we could feed more of them. Would make my life easier."

"Who'd have thought the idea of making *more* food would be *easier*?"

"If it keeps them the hell out of my raw ingredients, then yes, I would call that easier." Rosie nodded down a dark corridor. "This way."

Delia shook her head. "This hall doesn't go anywhere. It dead ends with the meeting room."

"That was true until last week. They finished the access panel."

"That's not authorized, I—"

Rosie raised an eyebrow. "Delia Forrest, not willing to break one tiny rule? My, it seems people really do change." She grimaced, almost imperceptibly. "Delia Dodson now, though, I suppose."

"It's just a name."

"As it turns out, a few letters on a page really can make a difference."

"Show me this access panel."

"It's through here," Rosie whispered, nudging a loose panel in the wall. It gave way to reveal an additional corridor, lined with beautifully framed photographs of the Capital. "It's for the investors, when they show up. So they don't have to mingle with us commoners."

"Where does it lead?" Delia asked. With any luck, it would lead somewhere secret, where they could talk in absolute, guaranteed privacy. She had to tell Rosie the truth about it all, before she lost her forever.

"The observatory."

"Why not just take the main hall that leads up to the atrium, and—"

"Will you just trust me for once, please?"

"Of course, I just—"

Rosie replaced the makeshift door behind them, leaving them alone in the small corridor, the opulence strangely juxtaposed with the dingy metal flooring that matched the rest of the station. "We'll bypass any night security this way."

"Where the hell are we going? Some secret tavern? Got a whole bar set up, making credits hand over first from the bored MPOs?" Delia joked.

"Please, I can barely keep them out of my kitchen, prying open cans of corn. You think I could keep them from a stash of bootleg swill? Gods, that one from earlier would probably kill me in my sleep for it."

"Shame, I could use a drink. Shit else to do on this station, eh, Rose?"

"If I was going to make hooch, you can bet I wouldn't be advertising that."

"Wait so... you could make it?"

Rosie shrugged. "It wouldn't be the fancy crap you're used to, but yes, technically. Easy enough to ferment fruit with some yeast and a dark cupboard. Would probably taste like garbage, though."

"Still, they'd pay for it."

"Overseer Allemande would throw me off this station so fast, it would change the laws of physics."

"Yes, she would," Delia said with a laugh.

"What's it like, working for her?"

"Challenging."

"Is that a good thing or a bad thing?"

"It is what it is. I chose to work with her because it would... never mind. It's a long story."

Rosie looked over her shoulder with a smirk. "Sounds like I'm not the only one with secrets."

"Not secrets so much as difficult choices that were made. In any case, it's been good for my broadcasting career. I've got real fans now, I'll have you know."

"It doesn't surprise me that people would enjoy waking up to your voice every day," Rosie said, and then stopped to clear her throat. "I just mean—"

"I know."

"What's she like with her daughter, anyway? That girl, Emeline."

"She cares for her a lot. Maybe too much."

"Emeline came by the kitchen once, asking for cornbread or some such. I felt bad. I didn't have it—it was before the first real shipment showed up. She got upset, mentioned some sisters or something."

Delia stopped. "She mentioned her sisters?"

"Only briefly. She left right after."

"What did she say?"

"Nothing much, just something about going on walks together. I hadn't realized that the overseer had any other children."

"She doesn't."

A flash of surprise streaked across Rosie's face. "I knew she was adopted... are her sisters... gone?"

"They very much are not." Delia had tracked the older sister, Georgie, as well as she could, before she disappeared. Emeline's birth mother and other sister had vanished from the city months earlier. "As far as I know."

"Gods."

"We shouldn't even be talking about this. The overseer is very... sensitive about Emeline's origins."

"Obviously. I'm not a fool, Delia."

"I know you're not a fool, this place, it just... feels..."

"Dangerous. Like you're always on the edge of a cliff."

Delia nodded. "Yeah."

"Prepare to be amazed," Rosie said, nudging another panel out of place. "The observatory."

They stepped out of the small, cramped corridor into a wide space with a domed glass ceiling, distant starlight twinkling down out of dark space, on scaffolding that hadn't yet been removed. "Gods," Delia breathed. "It's so beautiful."

"I've been spending a lot of time here lately," Rosie said, and looked sideways at Delia. "Thinking."

"I didn't even realize we were up this high."

"There's a slight incline in that corridor we were just in. Slopes up to here. I heard that next week they'll take down this scaffolding once the permanent balcony is in place."

"Getting friendly with the builders?"

Rosie shrugged. "Beats being alone all the time."

"You're not alone right now."

"No, I guess not."

"So," Delia said, sitting down to let her legs dangle over the sides, "what else are they going to put up here?"

"No one seems to know for sure, but if I was guessing, maybe a telescope. The first expedition team is due to arrive next week."

"The barracks aren't done yet."

"Hope they enjoy sleeping on the deck of the cargo bay," Rosie joked. "I'll bet no one told them about that before they signed on to come out here."

"I don't think you understand what they're trying to do out here," Delia said. "There's a reason they're calling this place 'The Gateway to the Universe,' and it's not because they want to send research teams to small settlements. I think they'll be on the search for rhodium, and lots of it."

"You can't expand the Near Systems on mining alone."

"They can try. Lots of credits in mining, these days."

"Faster ships, shorter transport times. Is that all we can hope for?" Rosie asked with a sigh. "What about art, and music, and..."

"And food?" Delia finished.

"Everyone needs to eat, and those bricks aren't giving anyone a reason to get out of bed in the morning."

"You're such a romantic." She'd meant it as a joke, but the way Rosie had flinched turned her thoughts to the past again. Flowers, stolen from a garden. Long walks in the woods outside the school grounds. The way Rosie's dark eyelashes looked when she was sleeping.

"How am I supposed to be this close and not touch you?" Rosie whispered. "Gods, I thought it was hard then, but now..."

Delia inched her hand closer and brushed against Rosie's fingers with her own. "You can still touch me."

"It's too much," Rosie replied, her eyes squeezed shut.

"I can't... lose this again. Lose *you*, again."

"So what do you see for us, Dee? Sneaking around the station, pretending that we don't have the history that we do? Acting like we didn't spend those years in love?"

"I'll do whatever you want me to do. If you want me to go, I'll go."

"Of course I don't want you to go." Rosie's hand found Delia's, their fingers interlaced. "I don't want to think about that now. I just want to enjoy the view."

"It certainly is unparalleled."

For a moment, both of them were silent, sitting, hand in hand, gazing out at the vast expanse of possibility and unknown. The station lilted again, adjusting its position, drawing the stars in streaks.

Rosie shifted. "I have something else. Something that I think I might need your help with."

"Alright," Delia said, a piqued tone in her voice. "What do you need my help with, then?"

Rosie reached into her pocket and produced a crumpled piece of paper. "This."

"Fineglass has a secret sister?" Delia snorted. "Looks like some silly prank to me."

"I thought so too, until I got another one." Rosie handed her a second note.

"Allemande has a secret file in her office?" Delia shook her head. "I've been around long enough to know that this is probably some rite of initiation, directed by the older MPOs on board."

"Carmen seemed to think they might be legitimate."

"If they are, then you should get rid of these. Burn them in the oven, throw them down the trash chute."

"You just said it was a joke."

Delia chewed on her lip. "I have a feeling there's something about Carmen... never mind." She took Rosie's hands again. "It's likely just nonsense, but if it isn't, then I'm almost positive that someone is trying to get you to do something stupid."

"Like what?"

"Break into the overseer's office, maybe."

Rosie laughed. "I'd never do that. Besides, why would someone want to get me into trouble?"

"In my experience, it's usually because someone wants your job."

"I'm just the cook."

"Just the cook? You have access to the only nutrition that's not gelatinous protein bricks. That's valuable. I bet there are plenty of builders or officers that would sell their own mothers to a fence if it meant they could get better food on board."

"I guess."

"Don't fall for whatever this is, Rosie. I've seen good people go down for less. Burn the notes, and any others you might get."

"You used to love a mystery."

"That was when mysteries didn't have high stakes."

"You're not curious at *all*?"

Delia huffed. "Of course I'm curious, but I'm not willing to risk my life—or yours—to figure it out. Besides, even if Fineglass did have a sister, what does that prove? Even if Allemande did have a secret file, it could be on anything! It could be about her daughter, for all the gods' sakes!"

"Why keep it a secret?"

"Maybe it's none of our business. Why does *anyone* keep secrets? It's not like the note said she had a secret file about you, or this station, or..." she trailed off. "Or, I don't know, anything that even directly concerns us."

"Ms. Harvis' file at school didn't concern us, either, but that didn't keep you from picking the lock to her office and reading it front to back."

"That's different!" Delia protested. "She was our principal. The odds were much higher that it was about the students. I was young and reckless then, and you know it."

"Put you on the path to who you are today, though."

"I don't know about that." She grimaced, turning away from Rosie. What had started as a deep, burning need to uncover the truth had morphed into nothing more than canned propaganda for the Coalition. "It was a long time ago."

"Still, if you hadn't stolen that file, we never would have learned that she was getting kickbacks for every kid that ended up there."

"She took care of us. There were much worse places than that to end up. We were lucky, Rosie."

"That doesn't make it right."

"Are you going to let this go?"

"Fine, I'll let it go. I should get to bed, anyway. Morning always comes sooner than I'd like."

"Do you want me to walk you to your quarters?"

Rosie stood, smoothing her dress over her wide hips. "I don't need an escort, Delia."

"Maybe I want to come with you."

"I'm not going to stop you." Delia followed her back through the panel in the wall, setting it back into place. It would be a doorway next week, if the builders got back on schedule. "I still think you should get rid of those notes. They're dangerous in a place like this."

"I almost thought you'd been the one to send them."

"*Me?*"

"You've done stranger things to get my attention. Like hanging all those streamers in the tree outside my window at school, for example." She looked at Delia sideways. "Or skulking around my quarters at night, hoping I'll open my door."

"I told you, I was hungry."

"Okay, Dee."

"I wouldn't be leaving weird, cryptic notes under your door. It's just not my style." Delia smirked. "I'd at least make a joke, or a riddle."

"I'd rather get potentially incriminating information in a note than one of your crappy riddles."

"Crappy! How dare you?"

"If I never see another riddle for the rest of my life, it will be too soon."

"Harsh."

"Carmen told me not to ask you. She said we should keep it between us. Don't tell her I told you."

"Oh, so you want me to lie for you now, too?"

"Delia," Rosie said in a warning tone. "I'm serious."

"What does she know about these notes, anyway?"

"Just that they could be dangerous."

"She's right, they could be. There's no doubt about that. Are you sure she didn't write them?"

Rosie nodded. "I'm sure. One of them arrived when she was with Emeline."

"How can you be sure?"

"I'm sure. Just trust me."

"She could have handed it off to someone else to slip under your door," Delia suggested.

"To what end?"

"Like I said, someone might want your job. Maybe it's *Carmen*."

"She said she's a bad cook."

Delia shrugged. "Could be a lie."

"Or it could be the truth, and it really was you who sent them in a desperate bid to catch my attention."

"If that was the case, then... I don't know. But I'm *not* lying. I had nothing to do with it."

"Whatever you say," Rosie said, pushing open the gap in the wall. "Whoever it is, I doubt they're going to stop unless I figure out who it is."

"Maybe it's that MPO who threatened to blackmail you. What better blackmail than if you were found with strange notes in your room, or folded in your pocket?"

"Hmm. You might have a point."

Delia flashed her a smug smile. "Of course I'm right. When have you ever known me to be wrong?"

"Many, *many* times."

"I'd bet a stash of chocolate bars that I'm not wrong about this."

"Sweets?" Rosie asked, eyeing her suspiciously. "Where did you get those from?"

"I'm expecting them any day now, a package from... home."

Rosie's eyes flicked away, but her tone remained light. "I could make some nice mousse with that."

"What do I get if I win?" Delia asked.

"What do you want?"

"If I prove that the MPO is behind it, then... you owe me a pan of cornbread."

"You're on."

Chapter 14

Rosie kneaded the dough quietly, straining to listen to the empty corridor. Whoever was leaving the notes was doing it when she wasn't in her quarters. It wouldn't be hard for people to assume her schedule, being the station's cook, but it still left her feeling unnerved.

In the early morning, though, she was one of the only ones awake and working, aside from the night patrol, who would be swapping over with the day shift in another hour or so. Wet dough stuck to the surface, and automatically, she dusted it with flour, working it in, developing the gluten. Gods below, she should have done this last night—but then, she'd been distracted.

Maybe it still was Delia who'd left the notes. Maybe she had lied. It wouldn't have been the first time that happened. Rosie turned another batch of dough onto the counter, kneading her frustrations into what would soon be a steaming loaf of bread.

The station shuddered gently with the arrival of a cargo vessel locking into the loading bay. It was early, even for that. Rosie scraped the dough off her fingers and checked her pocket watch, just to be sure. She was right on schedule, but the shipment wasn't. Better to be early than late, she supposed, digging her palms into the dough once more.

It wasn't a food shipment day, so she didn't rush down to collect her pallet of goods. With the recent influx of MPOs and researchers, they were getting anxious about leftover supply. Someone had already tried to pick the padlock, leaving deep scratches all around the keyhole.

Another loaf, ready for proving. She set the four finished lumps of dough on the counter, covered with light towels to keep out the draft. Maybe once the kitchen was renovated, she'd get a real proving drawer for the bread. For now, she had to work hard to make sure that the dough didn't get too cold. No one wanted flat, dense, under proved bread, least of all her.

Flour. Yeast. Salt. Sugar. Water. Sparkling granules and fluffy, powdery clouds. They didn't mean anything without the other. She mixed ingredients, again, thinking too much about how she'd have to portion the slices to make sure there was enough for everyone. Overseer Allemande didn't realize how important food was to people. You can't just feed them tasteless protein bricks three meals a day and not expect people to push back against that.

Quiet footsteps in the corridor outside the kitchen lingered, shuffling gently against the metal flooring. Rosie wrenched open the kitchen door with force, leaving globs of dough on the knob, expecting to see whoever had been slipping her those notes.

"General Fineglass!" Rosie choked out.

"Everything okay?"

"Yes, of course, sorry ma'am."

"You opened that door like you were about to raid a rebel settlement," the general said, smirking.

"Just a little too enthusiastic in the mornings."

"I'll say. I think you'd have had some real talent in the infantry."

Rosie wiped her hands on her apron. "I've never been much for fighting, ma'am. I'm afraid I'd be entirely useless in that scenario."

"If you can knock heads like you nearly tore this door off its hinges, I'd say you could hold your own."

"Is there something I can help you with, General?"

"Yes, I just wanted to know whether you'd had time to put together the next shipment list."

"I have it mostly ironed out. I can have it to you before lunch today. I thought your deadline for placing the order wasn't until tomorrow evening?"

"It is, but I wanted time to look it over. It seems as though Overseer Alle-mande is concerned that certain amounts of ingredients are... unaccounted for."

"Oh?" Rosie asked, feeling hot shame and fear crawl up her neck.

"She is concerned that the kitchen isn't yet running at maximum efficiency. What would you say to that?"

"Er..." she trailed off. A rock and a gods-damned hard place. "I'd have to see those calculations, I suppose. There is always a little bit of wastage, flour left on the counter after kneading, rice that sticks to the bottom of the pot..."

"Are you feeding the MPOs, Ms. Gordon? Still?"

"What?"

"Now listen, I've told you that I don't mind scraps going to them, but we can't be preparing full or even half portions for everyone on the ship. It just isn't feasible with the current supply chain."

"I was going to ask to speak to you—or to the overseer, in fact—but I would request that we did."

"That isn't possible, nor is it necessary. My troops, and the researchers, knew what they were getting into when they volunteered for the Rim."

"I understand that, ma'am, but in my experience at least, the stark reality of a situation is sometimes far worse than the idea of it. We aren't always the best at judging in advance what we can take."

"Given the current production schedule, we can't fit in any additional food shipments. I'm sorry, but you're going to have to stop making so much extra food. It's gone far beyond what I can explain away to the overseer, and one of her duties out here is to maximize efficiency here."

"I haven't needed any additional shipments, I can—"

"We will also be reducing the amounts in the weekly nutritional supply shipments, in order to allow for more protein bricks to be sent up. As the station grows, so too do our nutritional needs, but we don't have the space in those cargo ships to be adding anything else that isn't absolutely necessary. We're at the weight limit as it is, with all of the materials being shipped up here."

"Not to overstep, ma'am, but I've seen mutinies before, and they aren't pretty."

"My troops would never mutiny, not with me on board. They have to undergo assessments to even be allowed this far from the nearest beacon. I promise you, they will be fine. Some might try to bully you into giving them food, but you just stand firm."

Rosie sighed. "I understand."

"I have faith in you, Ms. Gordon, don't let me down."

"I'll do my best."

"While I'm here, was there anything else you wanted to discuss? Anything... unusual?"

"No, ma'am." Rosie mushed a blob of dough between her fingers. "Just waiting on a letter from home. I've been worried about my sister." Rosie didn't have a sister. She just wanted to see what the general's reaction would be. "Do you ever find yourself worrying about family back home? Siblings?"

Fineglass' face hardened. "No. I'm an only child."

"Lucky you," Rosie said hastily. "Mine keeps me up worrying, some nights."

"I must be going now, Ms. Gordon. Get me that list by lunch and I'll go over the amounts." The general turned on her heel and marched down the corridor, towards the stairs that led to the cargo bay. Before her footsteps faded, though, the alarm began to sound.

Chapter 15

What in the gods-damned hell? Delia awoke to the station's alarm blaring in her room, the red glow of the warning lamps creeping under her door. Was it a drill? She stumbled out of bed, pulling on the same clothes she'd worn the day before. Whatever it was, she was going to find out. Pulling her boots on, she didn't even stop to tighten the laces. She grabbed a pad of paper and a pencil from her desk and leaped out into the corridor.

It was chaos. Half-asleep managers standing around, looking bewildered, most of them still in their pajamas. Delia squinted against the harsh light of the lamps and pushed back a group of newly arrived researchers that were still wired from the journey.

"Hey!" one of them shouted. "What's going on? Is this a drill?"

"I don't know," Delia responded. "I'm going to go find out."

"To hell with this. I'm going back to bed. I have a double shift starting in a few hours," another said. "Gods-damned alarms, you'd think we'd at least have some answers by now."

Everywhere she went, no one knew what was going on. There had been no announcements, but then, she'd be the one to make them, and she had no idea what the commotion was.

"Overseer?" she called through the door to Allemande's private quarters. "Ma'am?" There was no answer. Of course she wouldn't still be in there, she'd be wherever the problem was. She knocked on the next door. "Emeline? Are you in there?"

"What's going on?" the girl asked from inside.

"I don't know. Have you spoken to your mother?"

"She told me to stay in my room, but I don't know why!"

"Alright, I'll go find out. Probably best you do stay in your room, it's chaotic in the corridors. I'll make an announcement when I find out."

"If you see Carmen, can you ask her to come stay with me? She bunks with other people in the old barracks."

"If I see her, I'll tell her."

"Thanks."

Delia sped up one corridor and down another, shoving past groups of bewildered workers and merchant traders, only stopping to ask a few builders if it could be an equipment malfunction.

"I don't think so," one of the builders responded. "There are different protocols for that." He paused. "Could be something wrong down in the cargo bay, though."

Of course! Without even replying, she ran to the far stairs, using the handrails to balance as she swung down several at a time. She hadn't felt this kind of rush for years, not since she was chasing down that informant on Delta-4. At the base of the stairs, she halted at the sound of angry, unfamiliar voices.

"This is going to go exactly as we say that it will. You got me?" a woman asked.

Delia crept towards the doorway, peering around the frame into the cargo bay. The woman and others stood around the MPOs assigned to the loading area. They had guns, and they were pointed.

"What's your name?" the woman—pirate—asked one of the MPOs.

"Miller."

"Do you want to live, Miller?"

"Y—yes."

"That's what I thought. Now, load all these crates into our ship, and hurry up." When Abara hesitated to give the order, the woman fired a shot in the air, her loose, blond waves bouncing from the recoil. "I said now!"

The MPOs bustled about, stacking cargo crates and wheeling them onto the ship, which, at least from the angle Delia was at, looked identical to a

Coalition transport vessel. How the hell had a bunch of pirates gotten hold of that?

"We don't have much time before someone gets down here," the pirate said to her crew. "Help these fools load us up."

"But Josie—" one of them protested.

"If you don't want to land yourself a public execution, you'll get your asses in gear. These people don't mess around, and one of these weasels already sounded the alarm!"

One by one, crates got loaded onto the empty cargo transport. Delia didn't dare intervene, not without a weapon. The pirates had guns in their hands and extras slung across their hips in makeshift holsters tied from black scarves.

"Hold it right there!" Allemande bellowed, holding a revolver of her own. She must have come in from the stairs at the opposite end of the bay. "Unload those crates immediately, and I might allow you a quick death."

"You think you can beat us with one gun?"

"Of course not." Allemande nodded her head, and a squad of MPOs streamed in from behind her, guns at the ready.

"I thought you said that they had a skeleton crew up here!" Josie hissed at one of her pirates, who was already holding his hands up in surrender.

"They did!"

"Clearly not!"

The overseer pulled back the hammer of her revolver. "Enough! Tell me where Evie Anderson is!"

Josie laughed. "She's not one of mine."

"Tell me where she is!"

"I don't have a damned clue where the hell she is."

Allemande adjusted her aim. "Tell me, or I will shoot your second in command."

"Can't tell you something I don't know." Josie fired her pistol, and Allemande crumpled.

Shots rang out from both sides, the deafening echo disorienting. Delia crouched in the corner, her hands over her ears, watching, terrified. One fell, then another. There was no way to tell who was dead and who was injured; it was the most blood she'd seen since the aftermath of the storms in Skelm. She wanted to look away, to hide her eyes, but her body wouldn't listen to her commands.

Delia's heart pounded with a threatening rhythm, and a vise closed in around her lungs. The loading bay was filling with smoke, and she squinted against the stinging air to see what was happening. Miller tackled Josie at the knees, knocking the gun from her hands and kicking it away.

More MPOs streamed in from the far stairs, along with another squad from behind Delia.

"Move!" one barked.

Delia moved aside, and they flooded the cargo bay. The huge ship was already pulling out of the station, scraping against the walls as it went, flying lopsidedly out into dark space.

"Someone get into a shuttle and follow them!" General Fineglass shouted, bursting into the bay. "Right now!"

"Ma'am, they disabled our shuttles," Miller said, now having handcuffed Josie to an exposed supply pipe.

"Fuck!" Fineglass holstered her gun angrily. "Someone get medical down here. Looks like the overseer got hit. Did we lose anyone?"

"Two," Miller replied. "Not as many as we got."

"Small fucking mercies. What the hell were you clowns doing down here? How did a pirate vessel even get clearance to fly in the restricted zone, much less pull into the damnable station?"

"It was a Coalition vessel, ma'am. They knew all the clearance codes."

"Get the rest of this filth locked up in the brig immediately. I'll see to them later. As for the rest of you, I hope you realize that your gross negligence caused the death of two of your fellow officers. Expect demotions in the morning." When the MPOs left looked at each other, Fineglass roared, "MOVE!"

Delia rushed to Allemande's side once the rest of the pirates were secured, their guns confiscated. "Ma'am! Are you alright?"

"Of course I'm alright, they only got me in the leg. Where's my daughter?"

"Safe in her room."

The overseer's shoulders slumped in relief. "Good. I'd hate the thought of her getting mixed up in all this."

"I did tell her that I would send out a station-wide announcement when I found out what—"

"Don't even think about it. Can you even imagine? It would cause mass panic. We'd have an impossibly long list of officers, researchers, and builders, all desperate to get reassigned off this station. Make the announcement. Tell everyone it was a drill."

"They'll surely hear that something is wrong, from the others who were here in the loading bay when it happened."

"Those involved will be sworn to secrecy on pain of being dragged in front of the judge for treason." Allemande grimaced, holding pressure against her leg. "It's a damned good thing that pirate is a terrible shot."

"Can I get you anything?"

"No, medical will be here soon enough. The shot hit the plate in my leg, courtesy of another band of brigands. Go! Make the announcement. Check on Emeline after. Don't tell her I was hurt. I wouldn't want her to worry."

"I will."

"Tell her to clear my schedule. I know that I'd had some trade meetings lined up, but I will have more pressing things to deal with first, namely keeping this news off the broadcasts."

Delia nodded. "Understood."

"And then I will have to interrogate some of these sniveling leeches, find out who sent them, and how they managed to get that ship." Allemande winced again, the dark red blood barely visible as it soaked through the black wool of her skirts. "Fineglass!"

"I've already called medical, Amaranth."

"You need better security protocols down here. I didn't realize that when you were in charge, anyone with a half-decent ship could park up in our station and pillage our supplies."

"These aren't average pirates. They got around three separate checks."

"Clearly, it's not good enough."

"Yes, and *clearly*, I'm already working on improving that."

"Too little, too late."

The general scowled. "Easy to say when you're—you know what, never mind. Let the doctor sew you up before you start giving any orders. Anyone actively bleeding is obviously insufficient in defending themselves."

"Wilhemina, you come back here!" Allemande hissed. "Ms. Dodson, what are you still doing here? Get out of my sight!"

* * *

"Attention, all Turas-Mara Station residents: we apologize for the disruption. The alarm was triggered by an automatically scheduled drill as part of the training for the cargo workers. Please continue with your duties as normal. I repeat, the alarm was a drill."

"So, what really happened down there?" Carmen asked.

"I can't say."

"What? Why not?"

"Because I don't want to end up charged with treason."

"*What?*"

"I have to go check on Emeline now. She asked me to grab you if I saw you. I think she's scared."

"Hell, we were all scared."

Delia rubbed her eyes. "Yeah. Hell of a wake-up call."

"Is everyone... okay?"

"No."

"Gods," Carmen breathed. "Should we be doing anything to help?"

"I think the best idea for both of us right now is to keep our heads down, do as we're told, and stop asking questions."

"What the hell, Dodson?"

"Carmen... I can't talk about it. Not right now, anyway."

"Was it pirates?"

Their eyes locked, and Delia didn't even blink. She allowed herself to nod, almost imperceptibly. "No. It was just a drill."

"No wonder. Okay, let's go check on Emeline."

Locking the door to the broadcast booth, Delia pushed past a lingering pair of researchers in the hall. "Was it really a drill?" a woman in a lab coat asked.

"I know as much as you do," Delia lied, not even bothering to turn her head to look at them. "Best get back to work."

Carmen knocked on Emeline's door. "Em? It's me, Carmen." There was no answer. She rapped harder this time. "Emeline!"

"Of course she didn't stay in her quarters. Why would she? *I'm* the one who asked her to," Delia grumbled. "We need to find this girl before the overseer is out of medical, or she'll have both our heads on platters."

"*Me?* What did *I* do?"

"Just shut up and help me find her. There's enough chaos on this damned station right now. We can't have a missing overseer's daughter, too."

"The station isn't that big. Where would she go?"

"You are seriously underestimating her ability to find trouble. You should have seen her back in Skelm."

"Why? What happened in Skelm?"

"Never mind. We should split up, we'll cover more ground. Meet back at the broadcasting booth. If you find her, I'll loop back every thirty minutes."

"I'll search the cargo—"

Delia huffed an aggravated sigh. "No, I'd better be the one to look there. It's going to be on lockdown for hours."

"In that case, I'll hit the atrium and the kitchen. Unless... *you* want to head to the kitchen."

"No, you go ahead. Maybe Rosie saw her. I'll head to the cargo bay first." Delia turned on the heel of her boot and almost tripped over the loose laces. She bent to shove them back under the tongue, and a sick feeling settled in her stomach. Emeline going missing right now was the last thing she needed... and if her fear was true, then the overseer would throw her off the station, and probably have her barred from broadcasting. Not to mention the danger Emeline could be in.

She ducked under a sign on a rope at the stairwell advising people not to enter. There was blood splattered across the steps down to the cargo bay, and despite her usual iron constitution, Delia nearly heaved up the acidic contents of her empty stomach. Bile burned at the back of her throat.

"Hey!" Miller shouted. "You can't be down here. It's locked down for the... for the drill."

"I was already down here when it happened, remember?"

"General's orders. No exceptions."

She couldn't very well admit that she'd lost the overseer's daughter. All the gods' hells would break loose on the station. "Well, I'm here on Allemande's orders."

"The general outranks her."

"Do you want to be the one to tell her that, or shall I?"

Miller rolled her eyes. "Fine, go down there. But it's not pretty. They found another one of those pirates hiding in a crate. Fineglass blew his head off."

"Gods."

"Yeah. Don't say I didn't warn you. I know people like you don't tend to have strong stomachs for this."

"I'm fine, thank you."

"If anyone catches you down there, you'd better not mention my name. I'll catch a demerit if the general finds out, she's in a foul mood."

"I can imagine."

"Mind the blood on the third step from the bottom, yeah? Someone's already stepped in it, tracked it halfway across the station. Given this was officially nothing more than a drill, we should try to avoid bloody footprints."

"Er—thanks." She edged around the officer, descending the rest of the stairs, being sure to skirt the pool of thick, arterial blood. "Emeline?" she hissed, not wanting anyone to hear her. "Emeline, if you're down here—"

Delia was stopped short by the sight of a corpse propped against the wall. Hells below. Miller hadn't exaggerated. Her stomach catapulted into her throat, plummeting back down to her knees in a split second.

"Emeline?" she called softly, stepping over the body. "Your mother is worried."

As she had expected, there was no reply. Few officers were left in the cargo bay now, having been redeployed to the rest of the station to check every tiny hiding place for pirates. If they'd found one, there could be others. What if one, or more, had escaped the loading bay during the chaos?

Peering into an open crate, her guts lurched again. Grisly. They'd been fools to try to brigade a station like this. It might have worked months ago, before all the extra squads of MPOs had shown up. But now, mired in extra artillery and security measures? It was a death sentence.

"Emeline!" Delia said again, only slightly louder this time. "If you're in here, come out!"

The shuttles were all in place in their bays, disabled. Still, Delia checked each one, pressing her forehead against the darkly tinted glass to see if Emeline was in the back seat. They were small transport vessels, only meant for two, maybe three at a time. Any more, and they'd lose too much speed.

The utility closets hidden in the corners of the loading bay were empty, too, as was the one lavatory on this level. The bodies of the dead MPOs had already been removed, and other than the faint streak of blood on the floor, there was no evidence that they'd ever been there at all. No doubt they'd cover up their deaths the same way that they'd done to Thomas. Bastards.

She hid behind a wide pillar as a patrol pair passed by. She didn't need any extra questions, especially not about this.

"Abara said we lost two."

"Two? I heard three."

"Guess we'll find out at the next squad meeting."

"If they don't rotate a bunch of us out first. You know what happened last time."

"Yeah."

Delia shook her head in confusion. Last time? When had this happened before? It was the first time the alarm had been triggered. Were they talking about Thomas? Did they know what had happened to him?

"Looks all clear down here. We should double back to the atrium, meet up with the others for evening assignments."

"Yeah. You can bet your ass the general isn't going to let us sleep for the next damned week. We'll be pulling triple shifts pulling this whole damn station apart to make sure one of them didn't get past us."

"I wish I'd never volunteered to come out here."

"Aw, but then you wouldn't have met me!"

"Shut up."

When the soft, metallic clatter of their footsteps had faded, Delia picked through another crate. This one did not contain a corpse, thankfully, just burlap sacks of nuts and bolts for the builders. What had the pirates stolen?

Delia chewed on her lip. Carmen must have found Emeline by now, surely. There was no way that she was... off the station. Even with her history, she wouldn't be so reckless as to escape with pirates, would she?

Chapter 16

"Rosie!" Delia shouted, careening into the kitchen. "Rosie, have you seen Emeline?"

"What's wrong? What happened with that alarm, everyone—"

"Have you seen her, or not?"

Rosie shook her head. "No."

"Can you tell me if you do, right away?"

"Dee, what's wrong?"

"Did Carmen already swing by and ask?"

Rosie shook her head again. "No, I haven't seen her."

"Gods be damned!"

"What's *wrong*?" Rosie asked for the third time.

"Nothing. Everything." Delia sighed and slumped against the door frame. "Days like today, I want nothing more than to take a shuttle and be anywhere but here."

"Do you... want to talk about it?"

"No. I don't have time. Listen, Rose, can you just tell me if you see Emeline? Or Carmen, for that matter, I... it's a long story. I can't tell you right now."

"Yes, I will tell you if I see either of them."

"Thanks." Delia swept back out, closing the kitchen door behind her.

Rosie rolled up the sleeves of her dress, preparing to slice the hot, steamy loaf of bread for the managers' breakfasts. "You can come out now," she whispered.

"Is she gone?"

"She's gone."

Emeline emerged from the small pantry, smoothing the creases in her skirts. "Thank you."

"Any particular reason you're hiding from Ms. Dodson?"

"She annoys me."

Rosie snorted a laugh. "Me, too. Is that the only reason?"

"She's going to want to drag me back to my quarters and keep me there, and I want to know what happened. People are entitled to know why that alarm went off."

"I'm not so sure your mother will agree."

"So?" Emeline said with a shrug. "She'll get over it. I'm tired of being left out of conversations on this station. I'm not a child."

"None of us know what happened yet. At least, no one who wasn't wherever it happened, whenever it happened."

"That's not good enough."

"Make yourself useful, slice this," Rose said, sliding a bread knife across the countertop. "Not too thick, or they won't toast evenly."

"Do you ever get tired of this?"

"No."

Emeline scrunched up her nose. "I'd be bored out of my mind."

"There's a certain calmness in the kitchen. It can be stressful too sometimes, but mostly, I enjoy the quiet seclusion of kneading dough, or slicing vegetables—well, opening tins, here. It gives you lots of time to think and analyze your own thoughts."

"I don't think I'd enjoy that."

"It's not for everyone. Hells, you don't see your mother, or the general in here, do you? People have different lives. In mine, I make food."

"When the coast is clear, I want to go down to the loading bay."

"Why?"

"Shipment was early today."

Rosie raised her eyebrows. "I noticed that, too. I didn't think anyone else would be awake at that time."

"I'll bet anything that had something to do with the alarm going off."

"The announcement said it was a drill—"

"Oh, please, Ms. Gordon," Emeline said, rolling her eyes. "You don't really *believe* that, do you?"

She didn't, in fact, but she shrugged anyway. "Hard to know."

"I'm going to find out."

"It was probably just a damaged proximity alarm, or something."

"Then why lie and say it was a drill? A damaged sensor is hardly going to incite mass panic across the station."

Rosie rubbed her temples. It was far too early in the morning for any of this. "Assuming you're right that it wasn't a drill or a malfunction, what could it have been?"

"Pirates."

"That seems very unli—"

"Or rebels."

"Turas-Mara is a foolish target. We've got loads of officers on board, not to mention the arsenal they've been stocking."

"What arsenal?"

"I don't know where it is on the station, but it's somewhere. The loading bay always smells like gunpowder when I'm down there collecting the food shipment."

"Maybe the rebels were trying to break into the weapons cache."

"Assuming there even *were* any rebels."

"Or it could have been pirates. The amount of raw materials coming here for the expansion project would fetch a small fortune in scrap. Maybe they're scrappers."

"Or it could have been nothing at all like that."

"My mother hasn't come for me. If nothing was wrong, she'd already have me back at my lessons with Carmen. I'd be knee-deep in my literature work by now." Emeline dragged the knife through the loaf again, letting a slice fall to the side against the worn wooden cutting board. "That's how I know something is wrong."

"Maybe she's looking for you, too."

"Do you really think she wouldn't mobilize half the forces on this ship to find me? Or make an all-station announcement?"

"No, I suppose you're right," Rosie admitted.

"And the general hasn't been anywhere to be found, either."

"To be fair, Em, that's hardly out of the normal state of things for her. I go entire weeks here without seeing her, just shoving my order list under the door of her office."

"True, yes, but to not see her after a station-wide alarm? That's not just unusual, that's against protocol. You'd think the head in command would want to be easing people's fears, making the rounds."

"Or she's fixing whatever the problem was."

"They don't hire generals to do the work, Ms. Gordon. Generals wind up in power because they're good at delegating, and because they play well to the crowds."

"Very observant of you."

Emeline shrugged. "After growing up in Skelm, and then living in the Capital a while, and now here, some things become too obvious to ignore. Half the generals I've met couldn't even manage to screw in a light bulb, much less anything else."

"Don't let Fineglass hear you say that."

"I'm not afraid of her."

"I am," Rosie said with a laugh. "She has the power to send me away, replace me, change the way I do things with just a word. I do my best to stay out of her way."

"My mother also has the power to do those things."

"Yeah, and I'm afraid of her, too."

"Are you afraid of me?" Emeline asked this in a cold, flat tone.

Rosie swallowed hard, turning back to the tray of cans that needed to be opened. "Do you want me to say yes?"

"I want you to be honest."

"I am aware that you could ask your mother to do any of those things."

"Do you like working on this station, Ms. Gordon?"

"I do."

"Why is that?"

"This is the first time I have been trusted to run a kitchen. I've worked as a cook for a long time, but always under someone else, usually some angry chef bent on making everyone else miserable."

"Is that the only reason?"

"Should there be another reason?" Rosie asked airily, despite the growing pit in her stomach. What did Emeline know, or think she knew?

"For many out here, they're running from something."

"Ah."

Emeline stacked the slices of bread on a plate. "Are you running from something?"

"Are *you*?" Rosie shot back, and instantly regretted it.

"I'm here because my mother has important business on this station. Surely if I was running from something, I'd be a long way away."

"Of course. My apologies."

"I've heard that they will start more proactive psychological screening on recruits for the Rim. Rigid, thorough background checks."

"Are you trying to imply something?"

"No," Emeline answered with a shrug. "Just mentioning it in passing. Making polite conversation is all."

Rosie resisted the urge to grumble. "Mm," she answered, turning away again. "Rest assured, Ms. Allemande, I am as boring as they come. The worst they'll find on me is some silly school hijinks."

"I'm sure."

"And to answer your other question, no, I am not running from anything." Rosie tipped another tin of peaches into a bowl, trying not to think about the letter that had gone unanswered. "Sometimes, people are just not attached to where they're from."

"I find that hard to believe. Everyone has attachments."

Rosie shrugged. "Sure. But not always to places."

"You have no affinity for where you're from? Where are you from, anyway?"

"A small place on Gamma-3. I left there to attend a boarding school when

I was fourteen. That's where I met Delia." Rosie mouthed a curse word. This damn girl was putting her off balance.

"I didn't know that you knew Ms. Dodson."

"It was a long time ago. We didn't stay in touch," Rosie said. That much, at least, was true.

"Were you friends?"

"Sort of."

"I bet you were happy to see her here on the station when you arrived. Did you know that she would be here?"

"No, I knew her under a different name, then. Besides, our lives have grown in two very different directions."

"Not that different, if you both ended up here."

"We don't have anything in common anymore."

Emeline nodded sagely. "I understand. There are people I used to care about that I doubt I will ever see or hear from again."

"That must be very hard for you."

"It's for the best. We all have to do the best we can with the cards we are dealt. I was lucky enough to be given a hand up out of the tenements in Skelm, away from unsavory groups that wanted to use me."

"I'm sure your mother is very proud of who you've become in such a short time."

"Perhaps." Emeline reached for another loaf of bread and began to slice. "Is your family proud of you?"

"I don't know. It's been so long since I heard from them. It's very isolated at the Outer Rim."

"How long?"

"I don't know, almost a year now, I'd guess. I haven't gotten a letter from them since before I was at Nox Beacon."

"I hope you hear from them again soon."

"Yeah," Rosie agreed. "Me too." Thundering footsteps thudded down the corridor outside the door. "Quick, if you don't want to be found!"

Emeline stepped back into the pantry, closing the door in on herself.

"Rosie!" Carmen shouted, skidding through the door. "Rosie, you haven't seen Emeline, have you?"

"No."

"Delia's about to have a breakdown, and frankly, so am I."

"What the hell is going on?"

"We can't find Emeline."

"I gathered that much, Carmen. I mean, what happened that you're not just assuming that she's somewhere on the station?"

"I don't know what happened, but the overseer is in medical."

"Medical! Why?"

"I overheard one MPO say she got shot. Delia won't tell me any more than that, but it has to be serious stuff or she wouldn't be running across the whole damned station looking for her."

"She was in here a little while ago, and asked me to tell you she was looking for you. I think she wanted to see where you had checked."

"Gods, everywhere. I can't even think of another place to look."

"Yes, I'm sure you've looked everywhere you can," Rosie said, the words tumbling clumsily out of her mouth. "If she's not anywhere else, then maybe she's in the off-limits research area?"

Carmen paled. "Gods, that's even worse."

"You might have to involve Fineglass if—"

"No one even knows where in the damned hells she is, and besides, you know we're all in for it if she finds out. The gods help us if Emeline is still missing by the time the overseer gets out of medical."

"What about the atrium?"

"I checked there."

"The observatory?"

"She's not there, either."

Rosie shrugged nonchalantly. "I'm sure she'll turn up. It's not like there was any way for her to leave the station."

"Gods. The shuttles. What if—"

"I don't think Emeline knows how to pilot even a small vessel, does she?"

Carmen buried her head in her hands. "I... might have taught her a few tricks. She asked and was so curious! I thought it was harmless!"

"If I were you, I'd get down to the cargo deck and count them."

"It's all locked down."

"The longer you wait, the further away she might be getting."

"I never should have come to this damned station," Carmen grunted, backing out the door. "You'll let me know if you see her?"

"Sure." The kitchen door slammed shut once more.

"Why did you lie for me?" Emeline asked, exiting her hiding spot.

"I lied to Delia already. It would only blow my cover if I didn't keep up the charade."

"Thank you. I need to get to medical."

"They're not going to let you in, you know."

"You bet your ass they will. I'm Emeline Allemande."

"Suit yourself, but when Delia and Carmen inevitably find you, don't tell them you were in here."

Emeline gave her a cursory glance. "I won't." She snatched a slice of now-toasted bread from a plate and took a bite. "Ms. Gordon, I hope that you will keep quiet about this."

"Of course."

"Ms. Dodson has no right to know where I am, and neither does Ms. Rojas, for that matter." Emeline edged out the door and quietly latched the lock.

Rosie reached for another tin and sighed. As if she needed more people to follow orders from, now she had a teenager calling the shots, too.

Chapter 17

Delia leaned against the wall, her hands on her knees. She could barely breathe through the abject and crushing panic of losing Emeline. The girl could be halfway to anywhere by now, back to the Capital, or... or worse. She could be bunking up with pirates. They'd probably take her as a hostage, or they'd throw her out an airlock in punishment for what happened to the rest of their crew.

"No luck?" Carmen asked, rounding the corner at the end of the hallway.

"No."

"I sneaked down to the cargo deck."

"And?"

"All shuttles present and accounted for."

Delia sighed. "I could have told you that, I checked that right away."

"It's... a mess, down there."

"Yeah."

"What happened?"

"I really can't tell you, Carmen. Not now... not here, anyway."

"Shots fired?"

"Someone will hear you! Shut up!"

"You don't think she... got away with them, do you?"

"I have no idea."

Carmen pulled at a dark ringlet. "Would she do that? Something so... reckless?"

"She might. You know her better than I do. Did she have any fantasies of running away?"

"No more than any other teenager stranded at the Outer Rim."

"Allemande will actually kill us. You do realize that, don't you?" Delia buried her head in her hands. "Gods, how did it come to this?"

"We don't even know for sure that she's gone! She could be moving around, and that's why we haven't seen her."

"It's not a big station. We'd have found her by now."

"We haven't checked medical," Carmen said, giving her a hopeful smile. "Maybe she's in there."

"Why in all the gods' names would she be there?"

"I don't know. Why would she be anywhere?"

"They don't let anyone in there without authorization."

"She's the overseer's daughter. You really think some underpaid MPO is going to try their luck with that?"

"All we can do is check, I suppose. Come on, it's a left at the end of the corridor."

"You don't think she'd have... *really* run away, do you?"

"I think that Emeline is a very stubborn girl, and she'll do whatever it takes in order to get what she wants, even if that means putting herself in danger."

"Would she have tried to see her family?" Carmen whispered. "You know, her old—"

"Saying things like that is even more likely to get us killed than losing her in the first place. Don't you know how you got the job as my operator? Thomas committed treason, that's how."

"I thought he went out an airlock."

"You don't strike me as naïve, Carmen, so you can cut the act." Delia gestured towards the door on the left. "Medical."

"Hello in there," Carmen called cheerfully. "We just had a quick question."

The door opened a crack. "What do you want?" a grizzled, bored MPO asked. "This area is off-limits to everyone except medical staff and patients."

"We know, we just needed to know if Emeline Allemande was in there."

He narrowed his eyes. "Why?"

"Just... wanted to, uh... make sure? She... missed her literature lesson."

"This is a restricted area," he repeated. "Get lost."

"Listen, friend," Delia hissed. "I know that you don't get much to do in your day other than push people around and work on your scowl, but I work for the overseer."

"I know who you are, Dodson. Your screeching wakes me up every morning."

"Then you'll also know that I work very closely with her, and—"

"Let them in. They have some explaining to do." Overseer Allemande's voice was as steely as ever, unhampered by whatever pain killers she'd been given. The officer rolled his eyes and stood aside.

"Ma'am," Delia said, her heart pounding in her chest. Did she already know that her daughter was missing, probably on some pirate vessel having to barter information for passage to wherever they were going?

"Ms. Dodson, how good of you to come," Emeline said, nestled in the chair next to her mother's bed, a wide, threatening smile playing across her lips.

"Emeline! You're—you're here! In the medical bay!"

"Of course I am. Where *else* would I be?"

"I told you to stay in your room!"

"And then I heard the announcement that it was only a drill, and I went for a walk across the station." She smiled again, staring coldly. "I ran into Ms. Gordon in the kitchen."

"Rosie? But—"

"She lied to you and to Carmen because I asked her to. I overheard that my mother had been injured during the drill, so of course I had to come and see her."

"Of course."

The overseer was still prim and crisp, writing notes in a thick, brown file. "Ms. Rojas, am I to understand that you *lost* my daughter?"

"All due respect, ma'am, I'm not her nanny. I am her tutor. I showed up after the all-clear, at the time of our normally scheduled lesson, and she wasn't in her quarters."

"I find it difficult to trust incompetent people. Are you incompetent?"

"No, ma'am, I'm not."

"How much time have you wasted today, running about the station, when Emeline was here by my side the entire time?"

"Er—"

"Get out of my sight, both of you. I've had enough to deal with on this station today, I certainly don't need you two mumbling at me."

The heat of embarrassment crawled up Delia's neck. "Ma'am, we're very sorry about the inconvenience. Given what happened earlier, we thought it best to make sure that Emeline was safe. That is the only thing we wanted to do."

The overseer glared. "A routine drill is hardly cause for concern, now is it?"

"Of course," Delia said, staring. "I guess the error was ours."

"Ms. Dodson, I trust you will have the evening script ready for me shortly. There is no need to mention the drill, and in fact, I think that we should focus on the observatory. The viewing platform is nearly completed now."

"Yes, ma'am."

"It seems as though you're about to be late for your broadcast, are you not?"

"We'll head to the booth immediately."

"See that you do. I'll meet you in my office this afternoon to discuss script revisions. It's clear that you cannot be trusted to do anything independently, and I'll have to be far more scrutinizing of these little radio shows. Go on, now, if you're late for your broadcast, I may have to consider replacing the both of you. There's plenty of talent in the Capital desperate to be out here."

Delia straightened the strap of her suspender and nodded, the shame and humiliation taking root in her guts. "I look forward to our meeting later. We hope you make a quick recovery."

"I'm all but recovered already. Now get out of my sight."

As the door to the medical bay closed behind them, Carmen leaned over. "Do you think that today happened because of what we said in that broadcast? About the patrols?"

"Gods, I hadn't even thought of that," Delia admitted. "I suppose it's possible, I—I guess I never thought they'd come *here*."

"It's possible that they'd never heard you at all, but... well, it does make me wonder."

"We need to know for sure."

"Do you think the overseer made that connection?"

Delia sighed. "She's perpetually three steps ahead of me, so I imagine she already knows the truth." She shoved her hands into her pockets as they rounded the corner. "I just wanted to help people."

"I know."

"Sometimes, it feels difficult to know which end is up."

"They took some prisoners, didn't they?" Carmen whispered. "Maybe we could—"

"How did you know that?"

"What?"

"How did you know that there were prisoners taken? You weren't down there when it happened. Unless..."

"I was in the wings. I was there."

"Why didn't you say anything?"

"Because, honestly Delia, you're a hard woman to parse. I didn't want you to turn me in."

"I'm not going to turn you in!"

Carmen inhaled a deep breath and pulled her into a utility closet. "Do you promise?"

"What the hell are you doing? We have a broadcast to—"

"Do you promise not to tell anyone?"

"Yes."

"I'm a spy. I was sent by Intelligence to keep an eye on this station."

"*What?*"

"My assignment is to be sure that the expansion is continuing on schedule, and to keep an eye on certain residents here."

"Which ones?"

"That, I can't tell you. It would jeopardize the mission."

"It's not me, is it?"

Carmen shook her head. "No, not you."

"That explains your reluctance to talk about your past. A spy. Of *course* you're a damned spy." Delia was already replaying every conversation she'd ever had with Carmen. What had she picked up on? Did she know about her arrangement with William? Or, more seriously, her dalliances with The Scattered?

"I can't have you reporting this to the overseer or the general. This is for... the good of the Coalition, you realize."

"I understand."

"You also can't tell them that I was in the cargo bay today."

"I won't say anything, Carmen."

"Good. Now, come on, we have a morning broadcast to deliver."

* * *

"Ms. Dodson, in my office, please."

Delia swept a loose curl behind her ear and plastered a congenial smile across her face. "Overseer, it's good to see you up and around," she said, entering the office.

"Of course I'm up and around. Where else would I be? A minor injury, no need to laze about in bed."

"All the same, I am glad that you are well." Delia sat in the chair opposite. It hadn't looked like a minor injury when the overseer had crumpled to the ground. It looked like she was dead.

"I've taken a look at your draft for this evening's broadcast."

"Oh?"

"It needs to be re-written, I'm afraid. With today's... incident, we need to be more careful than ever about what information we are disseminating from this station."

"I understand."

"For example, I should not have allowed you to manipulate me on including that information about the safety patrols. Look what happened, Delia. Two officers' families are grieving today. Their loss is on your head."

Delia didn't respond. After all, Allemande was right.

"This part about the observatory glass needs to be stricken. Glass is a liability on a station, easily penetrated by missiles and the like. What do you think would happen if these pirates, or worse, rebels—decided to blast a hole in Turas-Mara Station?"

"We'd all die."

The overseer gave a wan smile. "Yes. We would all die."

"I'll remove that part."

"No, as I said, if you had bothered to listen for once, the entirety of the script needs to be re-written. The very notion of an observatory implies a material other than steel or iron. We should instead include an interview with one of the recently arrived researchers."

"But you said—"

"I said what?"

"About the observatory, this morning—"

"I said no such thing. In fact, I told you to prepare questions for an interview. Have you done that?"

"No, I—"

Allemande tutted softly. "You are skating on some very thin ice, Ms. Dodson."

"I can go prepare them right now."

"Yes, I think that is for the best."

"Was there anything else you needed, ma'am?"

"No."

Delia stood, gripping her notepad with such force that the corners bit into her palms. "I'll return as soon as I am finished."

"Make it quick. I'll need to go over your script with a fine-tooth comb."

"Was there any particular researcher you wanted me to—"

"That is *your* job, Ms. Dodson, not mine."

"Of course." Maybe if Delia was lucky, Allemande would get punched in the jaw and have to have it wired shut again. Anything for a few weeks of blissful peace, a respite from the constant barbed comments. Gods below, where was she even supposed to find a researcher to interview at such late notice? Most of them were on stringent shift work, especially at this time of day.

She struggled to calm the tightness in her chest, even with purposeful, slow, soft breathing. No amount of meditative mindfulness was enough to shake off the likes of the overseer. It was enough to make Delia doubt herself and what she'd heard that morning. Maybe she really was losing it, after all.

The research wing of the station had been the first area to undergo expansion, overseen by General Fineglass. It was night and day compared to everywhere else, with pristine tiled floors, sterile white walls and small, isolated labs lining the corridor. What they expected to find out here, she didn't know, but every room was stocked with equipment and hermetically sealed.

"You can't be in the research wing when they're running tests," a woman in goggles said, waving at her with a clipboard, the pages bent at the sides. She had one hand on her hip, her dark skin in sharp contrast with the crisp white lab coat.

"I was hoping to interview one of the new researchers."

"Oh. For what?"

"For this evening's broadcast."

"This *evening*?"

"The schedule... has been in flux today."

"What's the interview about? We can't share proprietary information. Our contracts forbid it."

"Obviously I'm not going to ask that live on air."

The scientist shrugged. "You never know with you reporter types."

"Mm," Delia mumbled, deciding to ignore that comment. "The interview would be about their experiences here, what it was like to volunteer and arrive, the average day, that sort of thing. To encourage more recruits."

"We don't need more recruits, the research division is full," the woman said defensively.

"To entertain the poor souls trapped on Gamma-3, then."

"Why are they trying to get more scientists? Do you know something we don't know? Are they... are they going to have a mass staff turnover?"

"Gods, no," Delia answered, already exasperated.

"That's the only reason they'd be trying to recruit new people. Oh, gods, I thought I was finally starting to climb the ladder, I thought the CSA—Coalition Science Academy—"

"I know what the CSA is."

"Well, we thought that they were on our side with this, but I guess not!"

"On your side with what?"

"Oh, don't pretend you don't know!"

Delia blinked. "I promise you, I have no idea what you're talking about."

"Sure, sure, and yesterday someone found a colony of goats living in dark space."

"Can you just direct me to a new recruit that might want to do an interview?"

"I'm new to Turas-Mara," she answered. Her face brightened. "Hey, you could make me look good, couldn't you?"

"Sure, I can make you look good." Delia resisted the urge to roll her eyes. These science types were always so *strange*.

"We can't talk about you-know-what, though."

"I can promise that we won't, because I don't even know what you-know-what is."

The woman winked at her. "Excellent. I'm Dr. Arteo."

"Delia, but you probably already knew that."

"We don't really listen to radio broadcasts down here."

"Right."

"So, what are these questions?" Dr. Arteo asked, grabbing at the notebook.

Delia snatched it back. "It's more a free-form interview, we'll see where things go." She gestured towards an empty lab. "Can we sit down?"

"Oh, you definitely don't want to sit in there. Microbiotic experiments."

"Sounds interesting?"

"Oh, you know," the scientist said airily, "nothing more than routine tests on samples brought back from some of the nearby asteroids. I'm sure your listeners wouldn't be interested in that. If you head back up the hall, though, there's a pair of benches."

"Great. Let's get started then, shall we? How did you decide to come to the Outer Rim?"

"That's classified."

"Okay, then... what is your specific field of research?"

"That's also classified."

"How long have you been a researcher?"

"That's—"

"Classified, yeah, I got it. Is there anything that *isn't* classified?"

"I could tell you why I became a scientist."

"That sounds good," Delia said, swinging a leg over the bench and reaching for her pencil. "People love that kind of thing. Human interest, you know."

"I blew up my parents' basement when I was nine."

"You—alright, we definitely can't air that."

"It was an accident!"

"I'm sure it was, but we try to refrain from advocating for explosives on public broadcasts."

"I could... lie?"

"Lying works."

Dr. Arteo straightened her lab coat. "When I was very young, I found the study of celestial bodies fascinating. I always vowed that I would one day leave Gamma-3 and live among the stars."

"Good answer. What else? Where did you grow up?"

"The Capital."

"What has been your favorite assignment in your career?"

"This one."

"Why?"

"The Outer Rim is the *gateway to the universe*, so I'm told," Dr. Arteo said with a smirk.

"I thought you didn't listen to the broadcasts."

"I'd have to be rather dense to miss the marketing campaign going on here."

"You don't agree with it?"

"Let's just say I think that research should remain the top priority for at least five more years." The scientist blinked. "You can't broadcast that. It's off the record."

"You usually have to say something is off the record beforehand for that to apply. But, no, we won't be broadcasting that." Delia scribbled some notes on the pad. "How about the food here?"

"It's fine."

"Just fine?"

"When you go from full catered breakfasts in the Capital to tinned oranges every damned morning, yes, it's fine."

"Do you think you could lie about that, too?"

"I suppose. For a fee."

"A fee? Aren't you researchers getting paid double credits to come out here?"

"Never hurts to get a few more."

"No, I'm not going to pay you for an interview. I'll find someone else who wants to suck up to management." Delia stood and turned to leave.

"Wait, wait! Okay. No fee. But you have to make me look *really* good. Avoid getting demoted good."

Delia sighed. "Sure."

"You have to work in how only the best are chosen to come out to the Rim, and that I am doing an excellent job in my role out here."

"I thought your field was classified."

Dr. Arteo shrugged. "I lied."

"Sure, *that* lie you'll tell for free."

"Let's just say plenty of us are suspicious of your type."

"My *type*?"

"Reporters have blown more than one major discovery in recent times."

"Those weren't public broadcast reporters. I am, and I can't record anything that could be used against the Coalition."

"Good."

"What do you look forward to at the Outer Rim?"

"The expansion being completed, and that part isn't a lie. Our quarters are triple bunked! Six of us in a room! Once the secondary barracks are done, we'll only have two. I still can't figure out why they let the MPOs have the upgrades first," she grumbled.

Delia squinted. "You can't say that last part."

"It's ridiculous! They're a bunch of up-jumped security guards with rocks for brains. Surely consideration should be given to the ones discovering new things and technological advancements first." Dr. Arteo tossed a fat blond braid over her shoulder. "Wouldn't you agree?"

"I have to admit that I don't have much of an opinion on the matter."

"Of course not, I bet you get a private quarters, seeing as you're the overseer's little pet and all."

"I do, but it's smaller than the bunked rooms."

"It's still yours."

Delia shifted uncomfortably. "I'm sure the barracks will be completed soon."

"Maybe you should interview one of the builders next, find out why they're so behind schedule."

"I feel like we've strayed from the original point here."

Dr. Arteo leaned in close. "What do you think of the rebels?"

"Excuse me?"

"Rumor has it we have sympathizers here on the station."

"What *rumors*?"

"Oh, you know. People talk."

"We really shouldn't be talking about this," Delia said firmly. "Can we please get back to—"

"So you're one of them, then?"

"No!" Delia nearly shouted. "Gods below, what's wrong with you?"

"Touchy, touchy. I was only making polite conversation."

"Are all researchers so odd?"

Dr Arteo snorted. "Probably."

"Whatever you've heard, I can all but guarantee that it's not true. Anyone coming out here has stringent background checks, you know that."

"That could be faked. Or maybe they just keep their cards close to their chest."

"Whoever you're talking about, it's only a matter of time before they're found out." Delia exhaled. That was exactly her biggest fear. "Now, if you don't mind—"

"Have you ever met a pirate?"

"What in all the gods' names is wrong with you?"

"I met a pirate once, in some tiny, disgusting tavern on Delta-4. He bought me a drink."

"Alcohol is illegal."

"I never said it was that kind of drink. He was very nice to me."

"I wouldn't be advertising that if I was you."

"Loads of people have," Dr. Arteo said with a shrug. "It's not like it's a big deal."

"I certainly have never met a pirate, nor do I want to."

"Do you ever miss home? Ever think about taking a shuttle and just flying away?"

Delia squeezed her eyes shut in frustration. "No."

"I do. I wouldn't, of course, but some days it's sure tempting."

"Maybe I should find someone else for this project. I don't have much time, and—"

"No. No! I'm sorry. Ask me something else."

"What was the journey out here like?"

"Long," Dr. Arteo answered. "I took many naps."

"So you'd say it was... restorative?"

"Sure."

"What do you miss most from home? Other than food and your own room."

"My family, I suppose. I won't see them until the civilian accommodations are finished in a few months."

"But you're looking forward to seeing them?"

"Sure."

Gods, this interview was like pulling teeth from a lion. As difficult as it was dangerous, with her random asides about rebels and pirates. "What else do you want me to say to make you look good, then?"

"Delia, do you ever wonder what life outside the Coalition would be like?"

"No." It was a lie. She thought about what kind of life that would be almost every moment of every day. A life uninhibited by stringent adherence to rules and protocols, the freedom to... be with Rosie. Or at least report something that wasn't canned propaganda.

"Yeah. Me neither." Dr. Arteo looked down at the floor. "Except for when I do."

"Without the Coalition, our society would have no structure, no basis of governance. It would be chaos."

"Do you really believe that?"

"Yes."

"I think that everyone has doubts sometimes."

Delia chewed on her lip for a moment before answering, "I don't."

"Why did you want to become a reporter?"

"Who's conducting the interview, here, me? Or you?"

"I was just asking," Dr. Arteo grumbled. "Seems unfair that you get to be the one with all the secrets and answers."

"I don't have any secrets."

"Everyone does."

"I don't." Delia sighed heavily. "I wanted to go into broadcasting because I think that kind of communication is paramount to a growing society. To progress as a whole."

"Even canned scripts like these?"

"Yes, it's still important to share what goes on around here. There are people on Gamma-3 who will never leave the planet in their entire lives, much less make it to the Outer Rim for a visit. Knowing that we're here, conquering the stars, well... for some people, that's a reason to live. To wake up every morning and go to their jobs, to put in the time to make the Coalition better than it's ever been before."

"That's complete bullshit," Dr. Arteo said with a smirk and a raised eyebrow. "Looks like I'm not the only one who lies."

Chapter 18

There was a soft knock on the kitchen door, almost hesitant.

"Come in," Rosie called, up to her elbows in disgusting, lukewarm dish water. There was something particularly revolting about tomato sauce in the sink, where the off-putting tinned smell became almost overwhelming. "Hi, Abara."

"A few of the others are waiting in the loading bay. Is everything okay?"

She should have told them. She should have been honest about the new protocols, but instead, she'd chosen to hide from them, instead. "They're locking me down. Tight restrictions on ordering to cut down on the amount of space in shipments, so they can fit more building materials on each transport."

"So...."

"So I can't be feeding all of you anymore. I've been found out. I couldn't account for that much of the raw ingredients to be missing."

"You should have tried harder to account for it, then!"

"I'm sorry, I did my best, I really did!"

"Yeah, I'll bet. I'm sure you really fought hard for us. Who was it? Allemande? I should have known, she's got a stick up her—"

"General Fineglass was the one who told me."

"Figures. Those two are thick as thieves. Did you know that before the overseer came out here, there were three squares a day?"

Rosie kept her eyes on the fading suds in the sink. She couldn't face Abara, she wouldn't be able to handle the shame of it. "The crew was much smaller, then, and they weren't in the middle of one of the most complicated expansion projects in recent memory."

"So, you don't have anything extra?"

"I'm sorry."

"I can't keep protecting you now. I won't be able to keep them out of the crates."

"Then I'll tell the general. I'm sure she'll be able to handle it."

"You'd do that to us?"

"I'm just trying to do my job out here," Rosie said with a sigh. "This isn't what I want. You have to know that, at least."

"Did you tell *them* that?"

"Yes."

"Hmph."

"I'm trying hard to advocate for you. If they start stealing rations out of the delivery crates, then it's going to get that much harder to prove."

"You'd better be down there the second the transports arrive, or the rest of them will be on those crates like a pack of starving wolves."

"I'll make sure that I am."

"We were counting on you, Rosie."

"And I did everything I could. I'm not a magician, I can't just make more supplies appear from thin air. What was I supposed to do?"

"I don't know. I'm not the chef. Skim a little off the managerial plates for us, or something."

"Do you really think someone like Fineglass wouldn't notice being shortchanged on dinner? Besides, that wouldn't be enough for everyone, even if I did."

"Better than nothing."

"You just... you have to give me time. I'm working on it. Maybe if you all wrote home how bad the protein bricks are, and it affected recruitment—"

"You know as well as I do that all that stuff gets censored before it even sees the inside of a post bag."

"Yeah."

Abara shifted in place. "I wish I'd never come here."

"Yeah, me too."

"Or maybe I just wish I'd chosen a different role. Must be nice to be the one in the kitchen."

"Oh, haven't you heard? I've been put on the bricks, too. The overseer has made it very clear that I am not management, and as such, I am not allowed any portions of cooked rations."

"Gods."

"I'm in the same boat as the rest of you. Don't make things any harder, or it's my head that will be on the chopping block, not yours. If they find out that you all started stealing supplies because I'd been feeding you, they'll say it was my own fault. You do know that, right?"

"Sure," Abara said, rolling their eyes.

"I'm doing my gods-damned best!" Rosie shouted, tears welling in her eyes. She hated this station, and she hated being here, and most of all, she hated what it was turning her into. "I didn't make these rules, I just have to abide by them, or lose my livelihood."

"I can't accept my squad not getting anything other than bricks every day."

"Take it up with the overseer, then. I don't have control over the situation."

"You have more control than you think you do."

"Horseshit."

"Imagine what would happen if you just stopped cooking for management until they agreed to full rations for all?"

"Are you dense? They'd haul my ass off the station and replace me in a heartbeat. And then I'd wind up before the judge charged with treason. And then what happens? The rest of you are still stuck here without any proper food, with a new cook even less sympathetic than me, while I rot away in a prison cell far from here."

"You've thought all this out, haven't you?" Abara asked in a barbed tone.

"I don't have much else to do when I'm spending all day alone, cooking twelve-hour tomato sauces that no one has any appreciation for. Then I get to eat another damned brick, maybe write a letter home, and call it a day before it all starts over in a few hours."

"Life in the barracks isn't much different."

"No, I imagine it would be quite the same. We're nobodies. Invisible." Rosie sighed. "Expendable."

"How do we make ourselves indispensable, then?"

"We don't. No one is truly irreplaceable." She laughed darkly. "We give our whole lives to the Coalition, and in return, it would throw our corpse into an open grave and have someone new within the day."

"Do you really believe that?"

"I don't know. I suppose. I'm just feeling a little overwhelmed lately."

"They're not going to be happy, you know."

"I assumed as much."

"Rosie—Ms. Gordon, that is—while I understand your predicament, I'm afraid the rest of the MPOs won't be so gracious."

"I don't know what you expect me to do. I already said I can't help you."

"Then whatever happens next, you'll at least have been warned."

"Great," she said, draining the sink. "You can leave now." She dried her hands on a towel. "Leave the door, I'm about to finish."

Rosie put away the freshly washed dishes and set out the ingredients for the next morning—porridge, again. They were out of bread flour until the next shipment.

She still hadn't heard from Carmen or Delia. No doubt they were angry that she'd lied, but what else could she have done? Emeline was the overseer's daughter. She had more power than any of them.

The padlock snapped closed, and Rosie pushed open her own door. She groaned with frustration—another damned note. Why the hell was she getting them, anyhow? Why did everyone think she was able to change any of this? She was a cook, not a spy, or an assassin, or a thief.

Dear Ms. Gordon, Have you found the file yet?

"No!" she shouted at the page, and threw it into the trash. As if she was going to break into the overseer's office and rifle through documents. It was foolhardy.

Chapter 19

Delia was still sitting at her desk when there was the sound of shuffling feet on the other side of the door. "Who's there?" she asked.

"It's me, Rosie! I have to talk to you!"

"Go away." She still hadn't forgiven her for lying about Emeline. If she had just let her know somehow, she wouldn't be in the mess she was in. The silly interview had gone terribly, with Dr. Arteo veering off-topic with every other sentence. No doubt the overseer would have her head on a platter in the morning.

"Please, it's important."

"You lied to me."

"I'm sorry. Let me in and I'll explain everything."

"No."

"Delia... I need you."

The words were enough to melt the block of ice around her heart, though she resented it. "Fine." She leaned over and flipped the latch. "It's open."

"I'm glad you're okay. I was worried when I heard the alarm this morning."

"Do you know what happened?"

Rosie closed the door. "A drill?"

"Sure," Delia said, laughing bitterly, "a drill."

"Is everything alright?"

"No, Rose, everything isn't alright. You lied to me and to Carmen about Emeline and now we're both up to our necks in shit."

"I... didn't know what else to do."

"Clearly."

"She seems lost, sometimes, and then other times..."

"A scheming little monster?"

Rosie smirked. "Yeah."

"As bad as she is, her mother is worse."

"So I've heard." Rosie sat at the edge of the bed, perching like a bird expecting to be shooed away. "Rations got cut again."

"Oh, good, I'm so glad we'll all be eating protein bricks day in, and day out, until we all go totally mad."

"Maybe this is a bad time. I should go."

Delia caught her by the arm. "I'm just upset. It's been the longest day from the deepest hell, and I'm not in a good frame of mind. You know me."

"I do know you."

"What's wrong, Rosie?"

"I... don't know if it's safe to talk here."

Delia laughed. "What's wrong? Did you sneak a peek at another restricted area?"

"No, it's..." Rosie hesitated before handing over several crumpled notes. "It's this."

"Gods," Delia breathed, resisting the urge to light them all on fire. "Another one? Who's sending you these?"

"I don't know."

"Is it that MPO?"

"No."

"Are you sure? Because—"

Rosie nodded. "Positive. They were sent on a research mission three days ago. One of the other MPOs told me."

"Shit. Whoever's sending these, they're very fixated on the idea of this file."

"I'm scared, Dee. I don't know what to do."

"The options are to try to find whoever is sending them, or look for this file, or continue to ignore the notes. After all, it could still be someone after your job."

"Fat lot of good it will do them. I'm on brick rations now, like everyone else."

"At least we know they're definitely for you now. It has your name on it."

"I wish it didn't."

"Someone must think you're very important."

"I'm not!" Rosie protested. "It's so strange to me that they would do this, single out the cook for some kind of covert nonsense, as if I didn't have enough to do already."

"What do you want to do about it, then?"

"Ignore it!"

"Rosie, if you had already made up your mind to do that, you wouldn't be in my quarters at almost half-past midnight to tell me about it."

"This is ridiculous. I'm going to bed."

"Something is telling you to look, isn't it? Some kind of pull that makes you want to unravel that mystery."

Rosie dropped her arms to her sides. "I guess."

"I used to get that, too, about stories I wanted to report on."

"You don't anymore?"

"Not usually, but... well, this is piquing that interest, don't you think?"

"We'll get caught."

Delia shrugged, lifting an eyebrow in a mischievous grin. "We might. Or we might not."

"Where the hell would we even begin to look for some secret file?"

"Her office?"

"No way. That's far too dangerous."

"Would you prefer breaking into her quarters in the middle of the day?"

"No," Rosie said with a huff. "Of course not."

"I think we should do it. If nothing else, it might give me some more insight, help me understand her, get inside of her head."

"From what I've heard, I don't know that I want to know what's in Allemande's head."

"True, but what if the secret file is about blackmail, or Emeline's family, or—or Fineglass?"

"I don't know, Dee, how would we even get in there without her knowing? It's not like we can casually break the lock without her noticing and putting the whole damned station on high alert."

Delia grinned. "Who said anything about a lock? Or a door, for that matter?"

"I don't know about you, but I haven't exactly mastered the art of morphing through solid objects yet. You have something you want to tell me?"

"Don't be silly. I'm talking about the ventilation shafts."

Rosie thought for a moment. "I guess that would work, if we knew where we were going."

"Lucky for you, I've spent the last three months reporting on the expansion project. Do you even listen to my broadcasts?"

"I do, but I haven't exactly memorized them."

"There's a shaft behind the broadcast desk, it's covered with a big iron grate. It's one of the main flow tunnels, leading everything back to the filtration area on the deck below. If we jump over the big drop, Allemande's office is right there."

"A big drop? I don't love the sound of that."

"Oh, come on Rosie, we've done worse."

"We were younger, then."

"Maybe so, but we're hardly decrepit. Come on, we can do it."

"Dee, this is... treason." Rosie whispered the last word so quietly, she barely made a sound at all, more of a resigned sigh passing over her lips.

"What's a little casual snooping between friends?"

"Still treason."

"She won't find out, I promise."

"You can't promise that."

Delia took Rosie's hands in her own. "If anything happens, make a run for it. I'll take the blame."

"What could be in that file?"

"I don't know. Weapons? Research developments? Come on, Rose, the longer we dither, the more likely we'll get caught. We should go now, before it gets any later." She checked her pocket watch. "Night patrol shift swap is in fifteen minutes. That would give us about thirty minutes before anyone will pass by the broadcast booth or her office again."

"How the hell do you know all that?"

"I'm observant. It's part of my charm."

"If you say so."

"Are we doing this, or not?"

Rosie pulled her hands away. "Fine. But if we get caught, or killed, I'll never forgive you."

"We won't get caught or killed."

"I'm warning you, Forrest, if I die, I will absolutely haunt the living daylights out of you."

"On my honor as a reporter, I will respectfully accept my ghostly haunting if I put you in danger." Delia stood, repinning a loose curl. "Besides, if anything happened to you, your mother would kill me herself."

"That is true. She probably would."

"Quiet in the corridors, now, I don't want to give anyone any reason to come back this way any earlier than anticipated." Delia eased open the door, just wide enough that it didn't creak, before closing it quietly behind them, the latch sliding into place with a definite click.

Rosie reached out for her hand, and Delia, out of instinct, took it. It was a small comfort in a day that had stripped away much of the reasons she'd even come out to the Rim in the first place. Soft and warm, their fingers interlaced as they crept up one hallway and across to another.

When they reached the broadcast booth, Delia unlocked it, pocketing the padlock. They hadn't seen any guards patrolling. An excellent sign.

"Help me move the desk," Delia whispered. "But be quiet. We should lift it, not drag it."

Rosie nodded, lifting her side up and over the lip of the rug. "How do we get the cover off?"

"With this." Delia pulled a butter knife from the desk's drawer and released each screw, falling softly onto the carpet below. "Grab the grate from that side, we'll prop it against the door so no one can get in."

"How long have you been planning this?"

"Plan? No, I didn't plan this."

"This is suspiciously organized, Delia."

"Are you accusing me of... *scheming*?"

"It wouldn't be the first time, now would it?"

"No need to bring up ancient history, Rose. Follow me, we're going to take a right immediately after we enter the shaft. Wait! Take your boots off. Less noise." Delia pulled off her own, placing them under the displaced desk. "Come on, Rosie Posy, let's find us a file."

"Gods, this is the stupidest thing I've done since I was at school."

"I could say the same, except it absolutely wouldn't be true."

"Oh, yeah? Do you make a habit of this?"

"I wouldn't say it's a habit. More of a hobby."

Rosie snorted. "You're just as wild as you ever were."

"I think you bring it out in me." Delia bent to enter the vent. "Okay, to the right." The vent was freezing cold, and the metal walls were covered in a gentle condensation that had long turned to frost.

"You could have told me to bring a jacket."

"Yes, and there's nothing suspicious about that at all, is there? 'Oh, sorry madam MPO, yes it's just a coincidence that I'm wearing a suspiciously thick piece of outerwear on our climate controlled ship.' You won't ice over in the few minutes we're in here."

"You don't always have to be so snarky."

"I know, but it's in my nature. I can't help it."

"It's a good thing that these vents are wide, or I'd never get my fat ass in here."

"I like your ass," Delia said, and was immediately grateful for the darkness, which hid the rapid blush spreading across her cheeks. Much to her appreciation, Rosie didn't respond to that. "And, if you look to the left," Delia announced, "you can see Overseer Allemande's very own office."

"Wow."

"We just have to get over that gap." She chewed her lip, staring at it. At least a meter wide, and a four meter drop that landed in a dead end.

"Am I supposed to jump over it?"

"Sure."

"Right," Rosie said, crouching like a cat ready to pounce. "Where will I end up if I don't make it to the other side?"

Delia shrugged. "I don't know. Probably the filter."

"And then what?"

"Filter particulates get pushed out into space. But don't worry, that hose isn't wide enough for a human."

"Oh, good, I'll just get my eyeballs sucked out with the loss of pressure."

"Fine, I'll go first," Delia said, and leaped across to the other side. "Now you."

"Why do I feel like you've done this before?"

"I haven't! Well, not here, anyway."

"If the gods weren't long dead, Delia, they'd strike you down."

"I like to think they'd be on my side. They got up to enough mischief before they left us all to fend for ourselves."

"Count me down, or something."

"On three, then. One, two—"

Rosie jumped across the chasm, landing lightly next to Delia. "Three."

"See, that wasn't so bad, was it?"

"Like being back in ballet class."

"You always were the more graceful one." Delia reached through the wide slats of the grate with the butter knife and fumbled until she found the screws, clumsily removing them one by one. "Help me push, but keep hold of it. We don't want to knock it over."

With the grate removed, Delia pulled herself up and crawled through first. "Where should we start to look?"

"I don't think she'd keep a secret file in the very obvious file cabinet, but I guess we could look there."

"You start there. I'll see if the desk has any hidden compartments."

"I wonder if we should tell Carmen, she—"

"Absolutely not. Don't tell her anything."

"What? Why?"

Delia tapped the side of the desk, listening to the wood. "I shouldn't repeat this, but she's Intelligence."

"No, she isn't. That's ridiculous."

"She told me herself."

"That's impossible."

"Is it?"

"Yes, she was…" Rosie trailed off. "Shit. Maybe she *is* Intelligence."

"Be careful what you say around her."

"I'll say." Rosie rifled through the first drawer and grumbled. "These are all just schematics."

"Keep looking."

"Medical records?"

"Potentially interesting, but not likely to be useful."

"Ooh, Allemande's medical records."

Delia grabbed the file from Rosie. "This isn't very ethical."

"Is breaking into someone's office to steal information *ever* ethical?"

"That depends on your moral code. No, we shouldn't read this." She held the folder out, and the pages spilled from within. "Oh, gods be damned."

"Looks like fate intervened."

"I didn't think you believed in fate."

Rosie bent to scoop up the pages. "We both ended up on the station at the ass-end of nowhere, didn't we? One hell of a coincidence."

"Yeah."

"Would these have been in chronological or alphabetical order?"

"I don't know, just pick one."

"Whoa, she had her jaw wired shut."

Delia handed her another page. "I heard about that. It was before I ended up in Skelm. Seems plenty of people there preferred her that way. To be hideously honest, I'd have to agree with them."

"She got pushed down an elevator shaft?"

"Broke a leg in four places. She's more metal than human there. It's why that shot today didn't do much damage."

"Shot? Delia, what happened?"

"Shh, I'll tell you later. Let's focus on this first."

"Next drawer down is background checks."

"No surprises there. Anyone with a dodgy history wouldn't have been allowed on the station."

Rosie pulled at another handle. "Last drawer in this cabinet is... eugh. Emeline's academic records."

"This file must be somewhere else. Help me check this desk."

"That drawer on the left looks deep. Might have a false bottom."

Delia raised an eyebrow. "And here I thought *I* was the observant one."

"What can I say? I learned from the best."

"Damnation. There's a false bottom under this paperwork, but it's locked."

"Move out of the way," Rosie said, shoving her gently to the side. "Don't they teach you anything in broadcasting school, or wherever it was you went?"

"You can't break the lock, she'll—"

"I'm not going to break the lock! Here, give me that butter knife."

"Be careful."

Rosie shoved the knife into the joint of the wood. "I'm always careful." With a soft pop, the bottom of the drawer came free from the sides. "Easy as laminating dough."

"That's not easy for anyone other than you. Come on, what's in there?"

"Razorblades. Tiny ones."

Delia shuddered. "I've heard stories about that. Let's just say we don't ever want to be on the receiving end. What else? Be careful, don't cut yourself."

"Oh, there is a file!"

"Open it!"

"What the hell is a Cricket?"

"A bug?"

Rosie leaned over. "No, it's got... more files inside of it. Almost like a crew, see? A name, no photo, rank. Here we have Violet Vear, captain. And here, Nedrick Beckett, navigator. Kady Riha, auxiliary pilot. Alice Green, mechanic. Some blank pages here, no names for the medical staff. Oh."

"Oh? Why oh?"

"I don't know who Evie Anderson is, but apparently she's the one responsible for Allemande's jaw. She's listed just as being part of the crew. And someone called Mabel Masterson. They're both suspected of murdering some governor in Skelm?"

"Ralph Baker. A real piece of work."

"There's another file here. It's labeled as accomplices."

Delia's stomach lurched. "Who's in it?"

"Three names, here. Henrietta Weaver, who was apparently a scientist. Roger Beauregard, her lab partner. And... Georgina Payne?"

"What else?"

"Someone named Bailey, but that name is crossed out. No photo, either."

"Rebels?"

Rosie shrugged. "Must be, though it seems strange that she would have that file in secret. No doubt that Intelligence and the bulk of the military is focused on rooting out any kind of rebellion, there's no need for hiding that."

"It must be something else, then. What do each of their papers say?"

"Weaver and Beauregard were both dismissed from their rotation in Skelm and barred from the CSA." Rosie looked up. "Unauthorized experiments, maybe?"

"Perhaps. Keep looking. She can't be this obsessed over a broken jaw."

"The Mabel Masterson file only has a jaywalking violation in it."

"Maybe that's enough to end up in secret files these days," Delia said with a snort. "Hardly a master assassin."

"Umm... oh, there's a note here that Evie Anderson is suspected to have involvement in helping this Bailey person escape."

"Strike two for Evie, then."

"Holy hells. Dee, it says Georgie Payne was... Emeline's sister?"

Delia nodded. "I'd wager that's one reason she's all the way out here at the Rim, Allemande wants her as far from Skelm as she can get. Emeline was trying to organize strike action with the help of her sister and some Scattered. The overseer—well, governor of Skelm, then—worked for weeks to track down what was left of the labor union. She almost did, too, at least, that's what the rumors were."

"You didn't know what was happening?"

"Snippets. Troop movements, where they were looking. I tried to—well, I didn't know why Allemande was so obsessed with finding them. They were just a small group. No weapons, no supplies. Sometimes they'd hit the shipments at the docks. Then they all blew up just about the entire city."

"I thought that was a terraformer malfunction."

"That's the official story, yes. Anyway, Allemande adopted Emeline right away, she even went to the judge to request it be expedited. Said that such a bright talent deserved better than the mud of the factories."

"Makes sense she'd want to keep tabs on the old family, then."

"Sure, but that doesn't explain the rest of all this."

Rosie frowned. "Also doesn't explain why the file would be secret."

"Maybe she doesn't want Emeline to know."

"Could she be afraid that Emeline would leave?"

"Hard to get anywhere from here," Delia said. "Although that might explain why she brought her out here to the Rim, instead of leaving her to run some things back in the Capital."

"She won't be able to keep her under lock and key forever. Emeline is all but grown."

"Allemande will have other ways to do that. Okay, let's put all this back. We can talk in my quarters. The guards will be making rounds soon."

The sound of a key in the lock turned Delia's lungs to ice. Rosie was shoving papers back into the drawer, ready to bolt back into the ventilation shaft, but it was too late. The door swung open with a wrathful creak.

Fineglass towered over them. "Well, this is an interesting development."

Chapter 20

Fuck. That was the only word expanding in Rosie's head. Fuck, fuck, fuck. This was it. This was going to be how she died, imprisoned on a station hundreds of millions of kilometers from home, and her family would never even know what had happened to her. Grandfather would shake his head sadly before he reminded everyone that he'd told her not to go.

"We were just, uh..." Delia tried.

The general smirked menacingly. "Just breaking into the overseer's office?"

"She asked us to find something for her."

"In the middle of the night? I suppose I'll just go and ask her, then, and she'll confirm all of that?"

Delia gripped the leg of the desk. "Yes?"

"I suppose she also instructed you to... tear apart her desk?"

"The, uh... lock was broken."

"You two have to be the clumsiest blockheads I've ever seen. At least we know for sure that you're not working for Intelligence. Or The Scattered, for that matter. Even those bastards have better form than to remove the lock from the broadcast booth. A dead giveaway, Ms. Dodson."

"I—uh—"

"Should I take you down to the brig right this second, or should I allow you another chance to explain yourselves? Could be entertaining to watch you flounder, if nothing else."

"It was all my idea," Delia said finally. "Rosie—er, Ms. Gordon—didn't

163

want to come. I forced her."

Fineglass laughed and leaned against the door frame. "She doesn't look forced to me."

"I... blackmailed her."

"Ms. Gordon, is that true? Did our intrepid little explorer threaten to expose you in some way? I can't imagine what kind of devious foolishness a cook could get into, but hey, try me. I love being surprised."

Rosie was frozen, rooted to the spot. She couldn't even get her mouth to move, much less articulate anything other than the soft squeak that emanated from her throat.

"What I can't seem to understand," the general continued, "is why you would risk everything you have to do... whatever it is that you're doing." She laid her hand on the gun holstered at her hip. "This is no less than treason. The judge will, I'm sure, agree to an expedited punishment in order to prevent any further expense to the Coalition. There's no sense ferrying you home, just for you to wind up in a pine box anyway, right?"

"I'm—we're sorry, ma'am, we—" Delia started.

Fineglass closed the door behind her. "Pick up those papers. Give them to me."

"But—"

"I said, hand them over, you little thief. I need to know what classified information you may have just been exposed to."

Delia did as she was told, taking the rest of the documents from Rosie's still-shaking hands. "We were trying to do our duty to the Near Systems."

"I'm sure." The corners of the general's mouth twitched upward. "Was there anything else in this file?"

"No."

"How about in the drawer that you just ripped apart?"

"There were some small blades, but that's all. If anything else is in there, we haven't seen it."

The general tilted her chin. "Look again."

"Ma'am?"

"I said, clean out that drawer, so you can put it back. I won't have the overseer coming into her office to find a disgusting mess that two little trolls made."

Rosie set the box of blades atop the desk's leather top and fished around in the drawer again. "It's empty," she said, and her voice was quivering like a baby bird.

"Put everything back."

She did that, too, before popping the bottom of the drawer back into place with a gentle scrape. "It's done."

"I'll bet you thought you were clever, Ms. Dodson, but if you were really smart, you would have taken everything back to your quarters, rather than risk being found here with it." Fineglass bent, examining the vent shaft. "We'll have to install new grates, won't we? Ones with locks. Or perhaps I can ask our friends in engineering to create spikes that shoot up through the vent when a certain pressure is applied?"

Rosie shuddered at the thought. They'd been so foolish. Reckless. Regret wasn't a strong enough word for the torrent of shame and nausea that flooded through her. "I'm sorry," she whispered. "I know that it's not enough, but—"

"I didn't expect this from you, Ms. Gordon, I have to admit. Though given your apparent dalliances with Dodson here in the past, I shouldn't have been surprised."

"How did you know about that?"

"I know everything that goes on around this station." Fineglass' stare burrowed beneath Rosie's skin. "*Everything.*"

"What are you going to do with us?"

"Throw you into the brig, of course. Then the overseer will want to question you—you'll regret having put those blades back, I can tell you that much—and a sentence will be passed."

"No," Delia said firmly. "This is all a big misunderstanding. Go get the overseer, she'll tell you."

The general narrowed her eyes. "Are you trying to call my bluff, Dodson? Because I will tell you, free of charge, that I never bluff."

"I am not trying to call your bluff. I am merely trying to smooth out what is obviously a miscommunication."

"I fail to see how this is a miscommunication."

Delia stood. "We know secrets."

"Secrets? What secrets?"

"General, someone on this ship is spilling classified information. We broke in here to see if the overseer had any leads. We thought that if she did, we could take matters into our own hands. For the sake of the Coalition."

"Delia, no—"

"Shh," Delia hissed.

Fineglass crossed her arms. "Give me an example of this classified information, then."

"Someone wrote me a note about Emeline's family."

"Hardly classified. You were in Skelm when much of that happened, Ms. Dodson. The note-writer could very well have been you."

Delia hesitated. "Another note said that you have a sister, General. One that looks like a twin."

At this, she laughed. "I am an only child, I assure you. There was nothing in that file about me or any supposed sister of mine."

"What if there are other files? Or, what if the letter-writer is intentionally trying to undermine your authority?" Delia added.

"Preposterous."

"If this wasn't all so ridiculous, you would have arrested us already."

"I can drag you down to the brig whenever I like. There's not much entertainment here, so this is all very amusing."

"Don't think I don't remember what went on in the Capital, General."

Fineglass crossed the room in two steps, grabbing Delia roughly by the arm. "You don't know shit about the Capital."

"I know that *something* happened, and you and Allemande covered it up. I'm no fool. There were whispers that you arrived in the city like another woman. Some thought you'd sustained a head injury and had amnesia, or that you weren't up to the task of managing this project anymore. You disappeared for weeks after those interviews."

"People always talk," Fineglass spat. "It's nothing more than conniving jealousy by those unfit to serve or to lead."

"Maybe so," Delia said coolly. "But I'll note that you still haven't arrested either of us."

"You think you're so smart, don't you? All you reporter, broadcaster, writer types do. You snoop around people's private lives, publish incendiary headlines, and for what? To sell a few newspapers? To elevate your own name?"

"If you're angry about what people said about you and your husband, I had no part in that."

Fineglass released her, shoving her arm away. "You're all the same."

"General, I helped you repair that damage. I think you'll find that you got away rather unscathed, given you were photographed in a utility closet with a woman while your husband was away on business."

"Strange how *he* was never photographed during any of his dalliances, isn't it? The man has been running around with countless women since the day we got married, yet I'm the one who ends up in the limelight for five minutes of indiscretion."

"It wasn't you, though, was it?"

The general's eyes narrowed. "Of course it was me. Who the hell else would it be?"

Delia shrugged. "It doesn't matter now, people are past caring about that indiscretion beyond tight-lipped gossiping. It would have been a convenient excuse to take, yet, you didn't. Why?"

"Because, Ms. Dodson, it sounds entirely ridiculous, not to mention it would undermine my position within the military. A doppelgänger who impersonated me for an entire week without detection? What does that say about our protocols, never mind my own ability to retain security clearances?"

"Of course," Delia said, nodding.

Rosie looked from one woman to the other. What in all the gods' names was going on?

"You can't prove that," the general said. "You can't prove any of what you think is true."

"No, I can't, you're right. But a slip of the tongue, one small whisper… it could carry across dark space, could it not? One mere suggestion, and it winds up on the desk of someone at the High Council. Or the Judge."

"You're a little beast."

"General, ma'am, I'm just trying not to wind up dead."

"You have a funny way of showing it, breaking into offices in the dead of night."

"Preventative measures."

Fineglass turned to Rosie. "And what about you, eh? How did you get all wrapped up in this?"

"I got the… notes, ma'am."

"Let's see them, then."

"I already destroyed them."

"Good." The general tapped the drawer which held the false bottom. "What do you make of what you found in here, Ms. Gordon?"

"I think that the overseer has a concern for her daughter. It's nothing that most mothers wouldn't do."

"What of the other names listed, then?"

"I don't know. Rebels, maybe pirates. I don't run in those circles, ma'am, I wouldn't know. I spend my time preparing food for management. If I'm lucky, I'll have time to write my family a letter once a week."

"Rebels. Pirates. You make it sound so inconsequential, Ms. Gordon, as though these people aren't a direct risk to our way of life. To progress, and innovation, and expansion past the Outer Rim into the stars beyond."

"With respect, ma'am, your MPOs rifling through my food shipments are of bigger risk and immediate concern to me right now than any pirates or rebels."

Fineglass turned her glare back to Delia. "You didn't tell her what happened this morning? My, but you can keep a secret."

"What—what happened in the loading bay this morning?" Rosie asked, feigning ignorance.

"Pirates, Gordon. They killed two of our own, though they got worse than they gave. More sophisticated and organized than ever, yet you're worried about sacks of flour. What I wouldn't give to live in your fantasy world."

"I—"

"I do wonder if formal punishment would teach you that all-important lesson. A few months in a work camp, I bet your concern for supply shipments arriving intact would lessen somewhat."

"No," she begged, her voice quivering. "Please."

"Lay off her, Fineglass, I told you it was my idea," Delia interrupted. "You want to send anyone away, make it me. Wouldn't that be a pretty feather in your cap, General? Uncovering some dastardly spy—actually, that's a thought. You *do* have a spy aboard, but it's neither of us."

"Excuse me?" the general spat. "Who?"

"Carmen Rojas."

Fineglass scoffed noisily. "The girl's tutor?"

"Yes," Delia answered, nodding. "She's from Intelligence, sent here to keep an eye on you and your friend Allemande. It looks like someone up the chain has their suspicions already."

"How do you know that? It's certainly not in her file that she's ever worked for Intelligence."

"Why would they put that in her personnel file, knowing you both would have access to it?"

"It isn't customary to send Intelligence to deal with a military inquiry. We have our own standards of conduct."

"Customary or not, those are the verifiable facts."

General Fineglass leaned against the door again. "Does the overseer know?"

"No."

"Good. Don't tell her."

Delia raised an eyebrow. "Excuse me?"

"She'll find out in her own time, don't you worry. As for you two... get back through that damned vent. Make sure not a single thing is even remotely out of place."

"So we're... *not* going to prison, then?"

"Not immediately, anyway. Don't think I'll forget about this little show of impulse, either—I'm going to have the both of you tailed, constantly, until the end of your days. And when the moment is right, I'll come for you when you least expect it."

Chapter 21

"We're clear," Carmen said from the next room. "Nice broadcast, Dodson."

"Mm." Delia, still shaken from the night before, had spent the rest of the night pacing in her room. She'd give her left arm for a strong cup of coffee.

Carmen poked her head into the broadcast booth. "What's on the docket for later?"

"Uh... another interview. One of the building crew, this time."

"I hope it's not as wild as that Dr. Arteo interview."

"Yeah, you and me both."

"Good morning to my favorite broadcasting team," General Fineglass said, grinning broadly. The sight of her gleaming teeth made Delia feel ill. "Ms. Rojas, I've heard good things about you."

"Have you?" Carmen asked, her brows furrowed in confusion. She didn't know that Delia had so easily sold her out. The cowardice of it made Delia's face burn with shame. She'd been so desperate for any leverage against the general, and she'd failed in every possible way.

"Oh, yes, I hear about everything that goes on here. I was so impressed by your dedication to the Coalition, your flexibility in jumping in to help poor Delia out here when Thomas so tragically lost his life, I decided to have you elevated to a management position."

Carmen coughed. "Excuse me?"

"I think it's only fair that someone who is working so hard gets access to better rations, no?"

"What will I be... the manager of?"

"The broadcast booth, of course. Oh, Ms. Dodson will still have to have her scripts cleared by the overseer. There's no way around that—but you'll be responsible for keeping the equipment running smoothly. How does that sound?"

"Thank you, ma'am. I appreciate that a lot."

The general leaned into the booth. "It's really just a title to get your hands on some real food," she added with a wink. "Gotta keep your strength up!"

"What about Delia?" Carmen asked, still bewildered.

"Oh, Ms. Dodson is well-accustomed to brick rations. She'll be fine as she is. After all, everyone can't be a manager, can they? Many aren't exactly management material."

Delia's jaw was firmly clamped shut, the pressure of it already building a headache at the base of her neck. She nodded wordlessly.

"In any case, Ms. Rojas, if you need anything aboard Turas-Mara Station, you can let me know personally and I'll see to it. I have a great passion for radio, you know."

"Thank you, ma'am."

Fineglass disappeared down the corridor, the percussive snap of her boots fading shortly after.

"What in hells was *that* all about?" Carmen asked.

"I guess she really does have a... fondness for broadcasting."

"No, something else is going on. People don't act like that unprompted."

Delia shrugged. "Maybe the general does."

"I don't believe that." Carmen sighed. "It's almost as though she's trying to leverage me for something."

"Mm."

"Delia, did you tell her that I'm Intelligence?"

"What? No, of course not!"

"So it *wasn't* you running around the station last night, sneaking into offices?"

"How did you know about that?"

"You forget, Dodson, I'm in a bunk in the barracks. I hear things. Some MPO was going on about how they got a dressing down by Fineglass for missing something. Said a management office was broken into and someone stole some food?"

"Something like that."

"It wasn't food, was it?"

"No."

"You going to tell me, or are you going to make me guess?"

Delia sighed. "It's a long story. I probably shouldn't—"

"You compromised my mission here, Dodson. I won't have much time left once people start to figure things out."

"What? Why?"

"I can hardly observe people who know they're being observed. I'm careful to stay under their radar, and you're just kicking doors in?"

"I didn't kick any doors in!" Delia hissed. "I—we—used the ventilation shafts."

"Very clever. Am I to assume you dragged Rosie into this, too?"

"*She* came to *me!*"

Carmen leaned against the door. "So she got another note? What did it say?"

"It asked if she'd found the secret file yet."

"And did you?"

Delia hesitated. "Maybe we should—"

"Did you find the file, Delia?"

"Was it you who sent her those notes? Get poor Rosie to do your dirty work for you?"

Carmen's face fell. "No. No, of course not, I—I'd never put a friend in danger like that."

"I didn't think Intelligence *had* friends."

"I'm a spy, not a robot. And whoever is sending those notes is being incredibly reckless. What I can't figure out is why."

"I thought it might be someone gunning for Rosie's job at first."

"You found a file, didn't you?"

"Yes," Delia whispered. "But I don't know what it means. Fineglass caught us. I thought she would kill us then and there. I told her she was being watched by Intelligence."

"I'm glad you're not dead, at least, but this complicates matters. She'll... well. Let's just say that we're all in for a storm of hell once they figure it out."

"Figure what out?"

"Things are about to get very dangerous, Delia. Your friend Thomas might have just been the first of many."

"I can't let that happen."

"Good, we're agreed on that count. What was in that file?"

"Something about a ship called the Cricket."

The color drained from Carmen's face. "What else?"

"Some names, only a few photos. There was a photo of Emeline's older sister—birth sister, that is, she used to work in Skelm, and some scientist woman with her lab partner, their dismissals from the CSA were in that file."

"I need the names."

"I... I don't remember them all. There was a captain... Violet. A navigator. A mechanic. There was no information on their medical staff. There were a couple of names associated with the killing of the old governor of Skelm, a Mabel Masterson and an Evie Anderson. In the loading bay yesterday, the overseer asked those pirates if they knew anything about her."

"We need to be very careful from here on out. You come to me before you do anything else foolish that could get us all killed."

Delia nodded. "I promise."

"I need you to do something for me, Dodson. The general is going to be following me closely if she thinks—er, now that she knows I'm submitting reports back to Intelligence. I was going to get down to the brig to question those pirates, but I can't do that now."

"You want me to do it? What do we need to know?"

"Do not let anyone see you go down there, especially not Fineglass or Allemande. Or Emeline, for that matter. I want to know why they're here. Why they chose Turas-Mara to try to rob."

"That's going to be a challenge, given Fineglass is going to be keeping a close eye on us now," Delia said. "It's going to be hard to slip past the MPOs on guard."

Carmen's brow furrowed as she flipped through a notebook. "The general has a meeting with Allemande, you could get down there then. You'll just need to get past the regular guards."

"That's it?"

"I also need you to... no, never mind. Not that, yet."

"I can do it, Carmen, just tell me."

"Ask Josie if she's a pilot."

"A pilot? Why?"

Carmen pulled at one of her dark ringlets. "If she's the pilot, then someone less experienced is flying that ship. Might make them easier to find."

"Of course, I didn't think of that."

"Do it today. When's your next meeting with the overseer?"

"In an hour for script revisions."

"Do you think Rosie would help you?"

Delia rubbed the back of her neck, still throbbing from clenching her jaw. "After last night, I don't know. She's... well, she's not accustomed to doing things like that. I talked her into it. I promised nothing would go wrong."

"You shouldn't make promises you can't keep, Dodson."

"I'm worried for her. Why was she chosen to send these notes to?"

"If I had to guess, I would say it's because she has more access than the builders, less outright supervision than the MPOs, and an inquisitive mind."

"How would they know that?"

"Perhaps we need to assume that whoever is sending them knows more about Ms. Gordon than we thought."

"That just makes me worry even more."

Carmen nodded. "Me, too."

* * *

"Rosie?" Delia called softly through her door. "Rosie, come on, open the door."

"Go away."

"Rosie Posy, just let me in for a minute."

There was a deep sigh from the other side of the door, and then the lock unlatched. "Fine."

"Are you okay?"

"Of course I'm not okay, we barely escaped with our lives," Rosie hissed. "For all you know, someone is following you right now."

"I wasn't followed."

"How do you know that?"

"I just do. Now listen, I need your help with something, I—"

"Absolutely not."

"It's for Carmen."

"What is it? Breaking into Fineglass' office this time?"

Delia reached for her hand. "I'm sorry. I shouldn't have pressed you into that last night."

"Do you ever think of consequences for anything past yourself?"

"Of course I do! I'm just worried about these notes you've been getting, and—"

"This is probably just for another scoop, isn't it? Ferret out some information so you can move to private sector broadcasting."

"What? No!"

"You'd get paid a hell of a lot more, for one thing, and—"

"Do you really think that the Coalition would let that kind of information out? Private sector or no, they'd have me killed before I even showed up for my first day of work."

Rosie fell silent and shook her head. "No. I guess not."

"Carmen knows that I sold her out. She said things might get... worse."

"How in hells can it be made worse?"

"I don't know, she wouldn't tell me. But she asked me to sneak into the brig, and—"

"Is she trying to get you killed?"

"She needs me to ask those pirates why they came here, and—"

Rosie shook her head. "This is asking for more trouble than we can handle. Aren't we in enough trouble as it is?"

"What else are we supposed to do, Rose? We're stuck here, and Fineglass knows that Carmen is Intelligence, not to mention she could turn *us* in at any moment."

"Gods below, I wish I'd never come to this forsaken station. Anonymous notes, secret files... I just came here to cook!"

"So you won't help me?"

"Of course I'll damned well help you," Rosie grumbled. "I'm not about to let you walk into the lion's den alone, am I?"

"No," Delia said, smiling, "that's not your style at all."

"What is it with you? How do you convince me to do this shit?"

"I have a knack for persuasive arguments?"

"You can say that again. Fine, let me get my boots."

Delia grinned at her. "You know I appreciate you, right?"

"Not enough."

"Don't be like that. You know I do."

"I'll be sure to treasure that appreciation when I'm being held in a prison cell for the rest of my life."

"I won't let that happen."

Rosie looked up as she tied the laces of her boots, tucking the excess neatly beneath the tongue. "We'll see about that. Last night certainly didn't inspire much confidence."

"A fluke."

"You'd better hope so, or our asses will be the next thing on the menu for management."

"I don't think the High Council approves of cannibalism on their stations."

"Desperate times, Dee."

"Guard shift change is in a few minutes. We should go now. The brig is on the bottom deck."

"Of course it is." Rosie locked the door behind them, dropping the small key into the pocket of her dress. "And what if I had said no?"

Delia shrugged. "I'd be going down there alone."

"And getting caught, most likely."

"It's not against the law to visit the brig. It's not off-limits... technically."

"Excellent, that can be my defense when I'm on trial," Rosie said with a snort. She looked at Delia. "Somehow I don't think that will save me if Allemande asks to have us tried for treason."

"Visiting a prisoner is hardly treason. Merely inadvisable."

"Even if the prisoner was captured trying to loot a Coalition station?"

"Those are just details."

"You're a reporter. I thought details were your whole thing."

"That's different. Anyway, you need to relax. This is all going to be fine!" Rosie shook her head. "And what if it's not?"

"Then we panic."

"Great, just the reassurance I needed."

"Oh, come on, I bet those smelly pirates won't even tell us anything interesting. Allemande can't take issue with us if we *don't* have classified information."

"Except, we do have that," Rosie whispered. "We stole it from her office."

"It doesn't even mean anything! So she has a fascination with Emeline's birth family. That's hardly abnormal."

"Pirates, though?"

"She was an inspector for years. I imagine she can't quite shake off those impulses." Delia nodded towards a dark stairwell. "This way, we'll take those stairs all the way down."

"For all your instincts, Dee, sometimes you miss the forest for the trees. It's obvious that something else is going on there, or she would have just asked that someone else look into this Cricket ship. It's not like she doesn't have the authority or the influence to do so." Rosie looked back at her. "It's some kind of obsession."

"You'd want to know where to find someone who broke your jaw, too."

"It's vengeance. Or something like it, anyway. Makes me wonder if she already requested that case be reopened and was denied. Why keep it secret otherwise?"

"Privacy?"

"It was hidden inside a concealed panel in her desk, Dee. That's not normal behavior."

"What about Allemande *is* normal?"

Rosie snorted a laugh, and then swallowed it at the sight of an MPO headed their way. "Quick, into the alcove," she said, pulling Delia by the hand. "I don't want to risk being seen anywhere near the damned brig."

"I like this. Working together, I mean," Delia whispered, pressed up against Rosie in the small, hidden area.

"I'd rather we weren't working together to end up in a work camp."

"Rosie, I—"

"Shh, he's coming."

Footsteps grew and then faded, and in that short space of time, Delia found herself melting at Rosie's proximity. Gods, how long it had been since she was so close to someone she wanted so much. "I think he's gone," she said finally.

"We should hurry," Rosie said, not moving. "In case he comes back."

"I wish you knew how much I've missed you," Delia whispered.

"Don't." Rosie took a deep breath. "It will only be that much harder when you leave again."

"What if I didn't leave?"

"Delia..."

"What if—"

"Let's just get this done. I don't think now is the right time to talk about that."

"Will it ever be?"

"Maybe. If you leave him."

Delia buried her face in Rosie's shoulder. "It's complicated." Old promises leaped into her throat, but Delia swallowed them back down. Rosie was right. It wasn't the time for this. Not now, but... she shook her head. Dangerous, tempting thoughts. She had to stay the course, and that meant fronting as William's wife until...

"Dee? We should go."

"Yeah. Sorry." She pulled away from Rosie and peered around the corner. "Coast is clear. I don't think there are any other prisoners in the brig, it shouldn't be hard to find them."

"How many are there?"

"Three, I think—but it's the captain that we need. She's the one who will have the answers we're looking for."

Rosie checked her pocket watch. "We should have about ten minutes before the next guard change. What's the plan if one of them finds us?"

"We got lost on the way to the atrium."

"No one is going to believe that, not even these fools."

"Then I'm here on an assignment from Allemande."

"What if they check back with her?"

Delia smirked. "They won't. They're too afraid of her, and besides, Fineglass is their superior."

"You're awfully confident, given we nearly wound up dead last night."

"A tiny complication. And anyway, we didn't wind up dead."

"Barely."

"Shut up and follow me in."

The brig felt even smaller than the rest of the station, with ceilings so low, they both had to crouch to get through the doorway. The light was dim, casting a yellow pallor over the empty cells along the wall.

"Gods, this is depressing," Rosie whispered. "See? This is why I don't want to end up in a place like this."

"Where could they be? It looks empty."

"I'm over here, numbskulls." Captain Josie stuck her arm out of a cell around the corner and waved it. "You here to rescue me?"

"I'm afraid not," Delia said. "I'm here to ask you a few questions."

"Haven't you assholes had enough information out of me?"

"Who have you been talking to?"

Josie snorted. "Well, if you don't know, I'm certainly not going to tell you."

"Right. I just need to know what made you want to attack this station."

"Yeah, you and every other two-bit inspector they send in here."

"I'm not an inspector, I'm a reporter. Maybe you've heard of me, I'm—"

"Darlin', I don't give a rat's ass who you are." Josie leaned into the light, her two black eyes still swollen from the day before. "Unless you're here to spring me from my cell."

"I can't do that."

"Then I don't have any interest in talking to either of you. Piss off."

"I could tell the guards—"

"You're not going to tell the guards shit, because the two of you came creeping in here like a dog looking to steal dinner from the kitchen. Now, I don't know why you're sneaking through the ship, but I can guarantee it won't mean anything good for me. Just more trouble, and as you can probably tell from the two shiners I've got, I have plenty of trouble already."

"Did someone send you here? If they did, then—"

"Do I seem like the kind of woman who gets ordered around?"

Delia blinked at her. "No."

"Damn right."

"How many of you did they—*we* capture?"

"You have working eyes. I invite you to use them to count how many cells have occupants."

"Three, then. And three dead."

Josie gripped the iron bars of the cell. "Get the fuck out of my face before I start screaming," she snarled.

"I'm sorry that you lost people."

"You're not sorry for a damned thing. I know this act. Butter me up, pretend like you're on my side, just to get information, and then bam—I'm right back in the shit."

"How could we prove that we are on your side?"

"Delia!" Rosie hissed.

"You could spring me from this cell, for starters. If you're not prepared to do that, then this conversation is over."

"I can't set you free."

"Then get out or I tell the guards all about this little tea party."

"We could get you food, though. I can't imagine that the rations down here are very good."

Josie laughed darkly. "One protein brick a day, how generous of our glorious Coalition." She leaned back from the bars, her fingers still curled around the metal. "Get me a seven course meal and I'll think about telling you why we came."

"You're being impossible!" Delia sighed angrily. "I'm trying to help!"

"I lost people. I know they were just pirates to you, but to me, they were family. I'm in no rush to give you any information that might lead you to the rest of them. I'd die first."

"Yeah, and you very well might! I don't think you realize—"

"Then I'll welcome my death with open arms. We won't sell them out."

"I'm not asking you to."

"I'm not a fool. Anything I say, you'll be poring over it. Chances are, they're a million kilometers away by now. You'll never catch them, and I won't help you."

"Come on, Dee, she's not going to tell us anything. She probably doesn't even know what the Cricket is," Rosie said, tugging gently at her arm. "We only have a few minutes until—"

"The Cricket?" Josie nearly shouted. "What do you know about that?"

"What do *you* know about that?" Delia questioned, an eyebrow raised in suspicion.

"If you think I'm ornery, then you've never met Captain Violet Vear. She's a real piece of work."

"Why?"

"Thinks she's a goddess. Very high opinion of herself."

"I take it you two aren't friends, then."

Josie smirked. "No. But if you free me and my friends, I can lead you right to them."

"You'd do that to another pirate crew?"

"Captain Violet killed my captain, once upon a time. We aren't exactly friends."

"What else do you know about them? What about Evie Anderson?"

"Anderson deserves better than to be stuck with that rag-tag bunch."

Delia reached for her notepad. "Why?"

"That's all you'll get out of me unless I see the other side of these bars. There, take that to your fucking general. Bitch with a mean right hook, and I've got the black eyes to prove it. Tell her I'll give them whatever they want on the Cricket, as soon as I'm free."

"Delia," Rosie repeated, pulling on her sleeve. "We have to go."

"Hang on."

"The guards are back, Dee!"

"Don't mention our visit to the guards," Delia threatened. "We're... we're Intelligence. They can't know. Neither can the general, or the overseer. We'll work on getting your release."

"Intelligence, eh? You must be the new recruits, because your methods are terrible. The guards are already on the steps, spies."

"We'll sneak around the back of the cells," Rosie whispered, leading the way. "Then we'll get upstairs while their backs are turned. Come on!"

Delia followed, crouched behind. Gods below, what in hells were they getting themselves mixed up in? "If they see us, I want you to run," she whispered.

"Shut up."

"But—"

Rosie reached behind and grabbed Delia's hand. "Shh."

"Fuckin' gods-damned bricks," one of the guards muttered. "I never should have left the Capital."

"At least the pay here is better."

"Is it, though? We'll probably be dead before we see any bonuses."

"When do you think they'll let us rotate out?"

"When all the hells freeze over."

Delia crept around the corner of a cell, putting her finger to her lips when they passed one of the other pirates' cells. They'd have heard everything. Did they resent Josie for getting them caught and thrown into the brig? No doubt they'd be shipped off to a work camp as soon as an inmate transport arrived. But out here, that could take weeks.

"If I have to eat one more of those bricks, I'm going to waltz out of the airlock myself," the first guard said. "I think we should raid the kitchen."

"The general would let that cook serve *us* for dinner if we did that."

The last cell in the row should have been empty. After all, the only prisoners that were supposed to be on the station were Josie and her crew. There shouldn't have been any more prisoners, yet, there was.

Thomas.

Chapter 22

Rosie pulled at Delia's sleeve again, but she was frozen in place.

"Thomas," Delia whispered. "What have they done to you?"

He didn't speak. His eyes were swollen shut, his arms covered in bandages. He only mouthed one word: "Go."

Panic swelling inside her chest, Rosie tugged again. "We have to go," she whispered into Delia's ear. They all but leaped up the steps, running back down the corridor they'd come from. They ran all the way back to Rosie's quarters.

She unlocked the door, gently pushing Delia inside. There was no one in the hall, thank the gods. No one had seen them leave the brig.

"Thomas..." was all Delia said.

"I thought he was dead."

"They must have had him down there for months. Months!"

"Why?"

"He must have gotten himself mixed up in something, or... or I don't know. We have to get him out of there, Rose."

"How? This isn't the Capital, Dee, it's not like we can just pack him onto a janitorial cart."

"No, but we might be able to get him into a cargo transport."

Rosie shook her head. "Have you completely lost your senses? They'll throw us in there with him if we're not careful."

"They'll kill him if they keep him in there. Did you see? He's emaciated."

"Anyone would be, only getting one ration brick a day."

"Even if he had committed some kind of crime, why wouldn't they send him out on a prison transport? Why keep him here? To what end?"

"I don't know."

"Everything feels upside down."

"You can say that again."

Delia perched at the end of the bed, hands on her knees. "I can't just... leave him there. He was—is—my friend."

"I know."

"The longer I'm on this damned station, the stranger things get. Something's not right, that's for damned sure."

"What do you want to do?" Rosie asked, sitting next to her.

"Whatever it is, I can't... rush into it."

"No."

"But how am I supposed to pretend that everything is normal? That one of my closest friends in the world isn't in the brig being starved and who knows what else? Did you see the bandages on his arms? What are they doing to him down there?"

"Shh, someone might hear you."

"Maybe I don't care if they hear!"

Rosie wrapped an arm around Delia and held tight. "If anything happens to you, then Thomas will stay in that cell. He needs you to keep it together. Play it smart. Keep your cool."

"I know."

"Smuggling him out on a cargo transport is... risky. Even if you manage to break him out of the brig and get him into a crate before someone notices that he's gone, what is he supposed to do on the other end? Those vessels leave here and end up in a central Coalition hub. He'd have to sneak onto another ship without being seen, and in his current state..."

"What about a shuttle?" Delia asked.

"Does he even know how to pilot a shuttle? Besides, they're short range. They can barely reach Nox Beacon, much less anywhere else."

"Josie can pilot a shuttle."

"There's no way she'd leave her crew."

"She might."

"Even so, now you're talking about breaking *two* people out of the brig." Rosie shook her head. "Even considering it is treason."

"If I ran, would you come with me?"

"Where are we running to, Dee? If we vanish off this station along with prisoners, we're done for. They'll have our faces on public broadcasts. Whoever replaces you will be telling the whole of the Near Systems we're wanted for treason."

"What are we even fighting for? The Coalition? The same Coalition that locked Thomas up and starved him? The ones that target rebel settlements, even the children, I—I don't know how much longer I can go on like this, Rosie."

"Take a breath. Relax. Maybe there's a good reason he's down there. You don't know what he might have done."

"Nothing merits that kind of treatment. Torture." Delia buried her face in her hands. "*Torture.*"

"What if he killed someone?"

"It's Thomas. He doesn't even kill spiders."

"I don't... I don't really know what to say, Dee. I don't know how I can help. Breaking a man out of the brig feels impossible, especially on a station this small."

"Will you just... hold me? Just for a while, just until... I don't know. Until I can collect my thoughts."

Rosie hesitated. Her heart was aching to touch her, to comfort her, but at the end of all of this, she'd be going right back to her husband. "Of course," she relented, unable to hold her stoicism. "Stay as long as you need." What she wanted, of course, was for Delia to stay forever.

"I don't even know where to begin," Delia said, nestling into Rosie's embrace. "Leaving him there feels... immoral. I have an obligation to Thomas, it could have been... it could have been me, in there. No doubt those bandages on his arms are because he refused to give up any information."

"Give you up? Delia, what in hells have you gotten yourself into?"

"You're right that I don't know for sure why Thomas is down there. But I can only guess that it's something to do with the rebellion."

"You shouldn't even be saying that out loud. What if someone was on the other side of the door?"

"Then I'd end up where I belonged, in the cell next to his. At least then maybe they'd stop tormenting him."

"You're making a lot of assumptions."

"Why else would they keep him here instead of on a transport? It's because they think he knows something."

"And does he?"

Delia shrugged. "He might. We never discussed it. I should have assumed, maybe—"

"Why?"

"I have, in the past... altered scripts. To give hints to anyone who may have been listening. Not here, though. Only once, with the report about extra patrols on certain flight paths, and look what happened—Josie showed up."

"Is that the real reason you wanted to know why she was here?"

"Yes. I don't know if reports are even reaching settlements anymore. I feel so... cut off, here."

"Delia..."

"I know."

"You've put yourself in so much danger."

"Are you angry at me?"

Rosie turned away. "Not angry. I could never be angry at you, even when you most deserved it."

"Not even when I left?"

"I wasn't angry, Dee, I was heartbroken. Crushed." She released her grip on Delia's shoulders. "I still am."

"I wonder where we'd be if I hadn't."

"Don't," Rosie said again.

"You don't wonder?"

"I spent most of my life wondering. Every day, wondering. And then you showed up here with your husband on your arm, and what was I supposed to do with that?"

"Can you keep a secret?"

"I sure as hell hope so, or everything you've said for the past ten minutes is about to be your death sentence."

"It's not what it seems, with William."

"What is that supposed to mean?"

"It's an arrangement. I needed his good family name—Dodson—to get into broadcasting to begin with. I couldn't even get a job delivering mail to the offices before we got married."

"And what does he get out of this little arrangement? Or do I even want to know?"

"It's nothing like that. William isn't even remotely interested in women. He is, however, extremely interested in gambling. His family, they cut him off financially. He needed money."

"And where exactly were you stashing all those credits, Delia? I know that when you left me, you barely had two credits to rub together."

"They were a gift."

"A gift?"

"From my mother."

Rosie rubbed at her temples. "Your mother died when we were twelve years old, along with your sister."

"Yes, they did. It was in a trust for me. My father didn't tell me until after I left. Don't be angry with me."

"Everything you tell me is just... littered with lies, Delia."

"To keep myself and others safe."

"What kind of life is that to live? What have you gained by... faking a marriage? By handing over the money your mother left you to some... to some degenerate with a gambling problem?"

"It hasn't all been gambling. At least half of his debt was due to poor investments. He's better now. We're a team."

"Are you? Does he know... about us? About me?"

Delia nodded. "Yes."

"Gods below, this is a mess. Like trying to untangle noodles. Pull on one too hard and it's going to snap."

"So you see why I've kept you at arm's length, Rosie? I can't let on that my marriage is a sham, or every one of those opportunities will dry up like dust. They'll cast me back into the shitty little settlement I came from."

"Where *we* came from."

"I've been able to help people. If I can't do that anymore... what's even the point of any of this?"

"So, what, you're running with..." Rosie trailed off. "Rebels?" she finished, in a voice so quiet it was all but inaudible.

"Not as such. I only met one. In Skelm." Delia picked a piece of fluff from her trousers. "He's dead now. Disappeared, officially, but I saw the blood stains in the carpet of the meeting room. Doesn't take a genius to figure that mystery out."

"This is an impossible situation. You're getting yourself—and me, and Carmen—all mixed up in all kinds of treason, but we don't even have the escape route of having someone to rescue us. Who's going to rescue us, Dee? When this all goes south?"

"I... don't know. I just know that I can't sit by and watch all of this happen."

"And I can't sit by and watch you do this all by yourself." She sighed angrily. "Fine. I'll help."

"I always could count on you, Rosie Posy."

"Don't think I don't resent that you do this to me. Anyone else would already have your ass in cuffs. I'm not in the habit of risking life and limb for just *anyone*." Rosie sighed, letting her hands fall back into her lap. "Even if I can't have you."

"There's going to be enough scrutiny on this station, I don't want to be adding to it, especially with Allemande on my tail."

"I know."

"Maybe someday, maybe... when things are different. When William is—well, when we are safe from inquiry."

"That's never going to happen, Dee."

"It might."

"The higher you climb, the more people you'll be helping, and... and that's more important than reviving whatever died between us."

Delia recoiled. "Died?"

"Not to harp on about it, but you did leave. I woke up alone. I didn't see you for months. I thought you had died until your father showed up at my doorstep, shoving a box of my things at me."

"I am sorry about how that happened. I couldn't face you."

"There's something deeply distressing about seeing a sergeant's uniform at your door. I was already sobbing before I realized it was him."

"Rosie..."

"It was a long time ago. I'm over it. You're over it. We both made our choices. I'll help you, Delia, because you're going to get yourself killed otherwise, and to honor the feelings I did have for you. But it can never be what it once was. We've changed too much."

"He didn't give me a choice, Rosie. My father pushed and pushed for me to leave you, and then one day he sent me off-world for an assignment. I needed him, without him, I was nothing, and had nothing."

"It was still a choice, Delia." Rosie sighed. "We could have made it work."

"I was too young to know that."

"I was young, too, but old enough to recognize abandonment when I saw it."

"But—"

Rosie hardened, turning away. "First things first, we need some sort of plan. In order to have a plan that doesn't land us both in a work camp or in front of a firing squad, we're going to need research."

"Rosie—"

"We'll need to know what times the cargo transports arrive and depart. We'll need to know where the crates go and for how long, and how many MPOs are down there. No doubt there will be more after what happened yesterday. And we'll need to figure out how we'd get him from the brig to the cargo bay without anyone noticing or suspecting us."

"Rosie!"

"What?"

"I think we need to consider alternatives. Just in case."

"You mean in case we are found out?"

"Something like that."

"I'll take the fall if anything happens. You have the power and influence to get vital information out. I'm just a cook."

"That's not what I meant."

"Oh, Delia," Rosie said with a sigh. "It is."

"Of course that's not what I meant," Delia protested. "What kind of person do you think I am? I know that things ended poorly between us, but—" She took Rosie's hands. "But I wish I could take it all back."

"You can't."

"I know I can't, I just…"

Rosie pulled her hands free. "Let's stay focused on making a plan."

Chapter 23

Delia was still sitting at the edge of her bed when the station shuddered early in the morning. Well, whatever passed for morning all the way out at the Rim, anyway. The last unscheduled ship had been pirates. What in hell would it be this time?

She didn't bother changing her clothes, just pulled her boots back on and ran to the stairwell that led down to the cargo bay.

"Cargo's off limits," the same MPO from the medical bay said. "Only those with clearance can go down there."

"Since when?"

"Since none of your damned business."

"Surely I have the correct clearances, I—"

"You don't. Now scram."

Delia stood firm. "What are you going to do? Shoot me?"

"If I have to."

"For going to the cargo bay?" she asked with a sarcastic laugh. "I'm expecting a package."

"The ship that just arrived isn't a mail transport."

"Plenty of post gets diverted onto the cargo ships, if I could just—"

"It's not a cargo ship, either. Get out of here before I call for backup and report you."

"What the hell kind of ship is it, then?"

The guard laid his hand atop the revolver holstered at his hip. "Do I need to escalate this interaction?"

"No," Delia said, raising her hands in the air. "You don't." She backed away slowly, not turning her back until she was at the other end of the corridor. What the hell was going on down there?

She'd try the back stairs, instead, the ones behind the atrium. There was a night patrol every twenty paces, it seemed, and unsettling to see so many of them not switching over to the morning shift.

"What's going on?" she asked one of them.

"Nothing. Why are you roaming around outside your quarters so early?"

"I couldn't sleep."

"I recommend returning to your room." The MPO looked up the corridor. "They won't want many civilians around. Too much risk."

"What in hells is that supposed to mean?"

"I dunno. Something about important visitors, how am I to know?"

"Investors. Of course."

"I... don't think it's investors. The general has us all on triple shifts for the next few days."

"Thanks," she said. Why hadn't she been told about special visitors? Did Carmen know? Or the overseer? Abandoning her plans to try the back stairs, she headed for the broadcasting booth instead. There was nothing wrong with being three hours early for work, now was there? With so many guards, there was no way that the back stairs wouldn't also be heavily guarded.

She inserted her key into the padlock, but it wouldn't disengage. "What *now*?" she muttered. She pulled out the key and reinserted it, twisting with no result.

"Ms. Dodson," the overseer said, emerging from her office. "You're here."

"Did someone replace the padlock?"

"I did."

Delia clenched her fist around the brass key, feeling it bite into her palm. "Why?"

"The general and I decided that we need to rethink some security protocols on this station. Don't worry, you will still be allowed into the broadcasting booth, but only with my key." She held up a long, silver key before tucking it back into her pocket.

"I just wanted to get some work done for... later."

"I already approved the morning script, Ms. Dodson."

"I meant for this evening."

"There will be no need for a broadcast this evening. We have a special guest who will be presenting in your stead."

"Special guest?"

"We have a member of the High Council aboard. I recommend you be on your best behavior."

Delia took a step back, stumbling over her own boots. "The *High Council?*" she repeated. "Here? On Turas-Mara?"

"Were you under the impression that we were a useless backwater? You say it yourself nearly every day, this is the *gateway to the universe.* You should hardly be surprised that a station like this, led by myself—and the general, I suppose—would attract the attention of the High Council."

"Of course, ma'am, I just meant that I thought I would have received more notice."

"She's one of the most powerful people in the Near Systems, Ms. Dodson, and soon, the universe. She can hardly be expected to adhere to a regimented schedule, and in these current times, it's best for her to travel incognito, lest some filthy rebel get their hands on her. You can't be too careful these days."

"Yes, ma'am."

"Most of the station will remain locked down for the next several days. I recommend that you use the free time you would have spent on tonight's broadcast convincing my daughter to do that interview. This has gone on far too long."

"Will she not be joining you with the High Council visitor?"

"Not until tomorrow. The High Councilperson will want to settle in first, of course, and then the general and I will be meeting with her to discuss the financial needs of the station's expansion project."

"I'm sure she will see the importance of the work we do here," Delia said.

"If she's as smart as they say she is, I'm sure that will be more than obvious. It's not every day that you find the largest rhodium deposit ever discovered."

"Impressive."

"Quite." Allemande clasped her hands behind her back. "You're dismissed, Ms. Dodson. I'll unlock the broadcasting booth ten minutes before your broadcast."

"Understood."

"Inform Ms. Rojas of this as well. I won't have time to be delivering personalized updates. In fact, I'm almost late as it is. See that you tell her, and remind her that Emeline's marking is past due. If she cannot keep up with the rigorous schooling, we will have to find my daughter a replacement who's up to the task."

* * *

"A member of the High Council? *Here*?" Carmen asked, anxiously pulling on a dark curl.

Delia nodded. "Strange as it seems, yes."

"That explains why every MPO on this damned station is patrolling the corridors. Did you know she was coming?"

"I had no idea. The overseer said it's because the Councilor keeps her schedule safe, to prevent... you know. Rebels." Delia tilted her head. "I would have thought that at the very least, Intelligence would know."

"We should talk somewhere more private," Carmen said, gesturing towards the observatory. "I can't risk an MPO hearing that."

Delia nodded. "I don't think being seen in an out-of-bounds area is the best idea with this many guards, though."

"It will be fine. Just trust me."

"Okay..." Delia mumbled. "Atrium is bound to be crawling, though."

"We're not going through the atrium." She kicked aside a wide plank of wood, revealing a newly constructed corridor. "They won't come down here. It's not finished yet." Carmen replaced the plank of wood once they were inside, and led Delia a little way further.

"So, how come Intelligence doesn't know about this?" Delia pressed again.

"I'm sure they do, but I'm away from the central hub in the Capital. Can't risk sending that information all the way out here, it could have been intercepted."

"Right. Of course."

"It's certainly an opportunity to really let Turas-Mara shine! We should get to the booth to—"

"We won't be able to get in outside of broadcast times. Allemande changed the lock."

Carmen rolled her eyes. "Of course she did."

"She also said that Emeline's marking is late."

"It's not late. I handed back her assignments a week ago."

"Then Emeline is lying to her mother." Delia pushed up her sleeves again. "I wonder why. Is she doing poorly?"

"I wouldn't say poorly, no. She's very bright. A few marks off here and there, but for small things, nothing major."

"Something is going on with that girl."

"I imagine that many of us would behave erratically if we were ripped away from our families and thrown into a vastly different environment. Humans may be adaptable, Delia, but we're not automatons. She's still just a teenager. It's natural for her to push boundaries, find her own way."

"I don't think her mother wants to hear you say that."

"No, I expect not, which is why I haven't let that slip." Carmen tied back her masses of dark, tumbling curls. "So, what now?"

"The overseer wants me to convince Emeline to do this interview."

"Good luck. She's as stubborn as she is smart."

"I don't think she's going to budge unless she gets her way. She wants to shine a spotlight on Skelm."

"Allemande doesn't want that?"

Delia sighed heavily. "No. Definitely not."

"What about the evening broadcast?"

"It's being taken over by the Councilor."

"Any ideas what they want to broadcast?" Carmen asked.

"No. I wish I did, though. Could provide some insight as to why she's here. The overseer mentioned a rhodium deposit, but it feels like there's something more. The High Council is rarely ever seen in public, and it's even more unlikely they'd travel out of the Capital, much less off-world."

"I suppose this really is the gateway to the universe."

"I don't think one would come all the way out here just for a photo-opportunity and a marketing campaign for the Outer Rim, do you?"

Carmen shrugged. "Times are changing."

"I don't think they're changing that much. Something feels fishy."

"You been feeling many fish lately, Dodson?"

Delia snorted. "More than my share, let's put it that way." She chewed on her bottom lip. "Do you think the general knew?"

"I would imagine that she did, yes."

"Strange that she didn't bring in more troops, then. Keeping them all working triple shifts isn't going to last long before they start keeling over from exhaustion on their feet."

Carmen shrugged. "Maybe there wasn't enough time? It would take at least two weeks on the fastest transport in the Coalition. Given the slow old barge we get out here, it's more like a month. I imagine the High Councilperson didn't give that much notice."

"They'd better hope she leaves before—well, I don't know." Delia sighed heavily, rubbing her eyes. "Gods, I have never felt so tired as I have on this damnable station."

"I know what you mean. My bunkmate snores like a congested grizzly."

"Sometimes I wonder if my life would have been simpler outside of broadcasting. A library, maybe. I did always like reading when I was younger." Delia grimaced. Most books had been banned when she was little, replaced with transparent propaganda, instead—and now she'd basically admitted to an Intelligence agent that she'd had access to books that should have been burnt along with the rest. "Er, you know. Approved stories."

Carmen raised an eyebrow. "I liked to read, too. Pity that there's not much worth reading these days."

"I don't know if I would say that—"

"I would," Carmen scoffed. "Who needs more stories about the glory of war? All anyone has to do is tune in to one of your broadcasts to hear about the grisly reality."

"We're not allowed to broadcast that, not here."

"No, but back in Skelm it was the mainstay of every program."

Delia blinked at her. "You were in Skelm when I was presenting?"

"I, er—that's classified."

"Of course."

"Top secret, in fact."

"I can imagine." Delia tucked part of her shirt back into her trousers. "Were you there when all that happened?"

Carmen didn't respond for a moment, choosing instead to stare intently, searching Delia's face for something. "I was," she said finally.

"I don't remember seeing you at the Administration Building."

"That's because I was never *in* the Administration Building. As I said, it's classified."

"I'd make sure the overseer never learns that about you. She was on a major rampage for weeks after that happened, even in a full leg cast."

"I head about that after I left the settlement. I bet she was a real peach to deal with."

Delia nodded. So Carmen had been in Skelm before and during the destruction, not after. Very curious, given that the docks were closed for an entire fortnight after it happened. She cleared her throat lightly. "You were certainly lucky to miss that," she said. "It was hell until the support transports arrived."

"I heard that the rebuild was very successful, though. Much quicker than anyone had anticipated."

"Largely due to Allemande intimidating all of the builders into compliance and rustling up extra credits from the Capital. It would probably still be a pile of rubble without her."

"Do you think she did that for Emeline?"

"Maybe in part, but she wanted to be the overseer of that jurisdiction. She did whatever it took to get there." Delia checked her pocket watch. "Rosie will be delivering the morning bricks soon. You hungry?"

"I'm *management* now," Carmen said with a snicker. "I'll share, don't worry. But we should get to the booth long before Allemande shows up to unlock it. You know, for optics."

Chapter 24

"What in hells?" Rosie muttered, jamming her key into the padlock again.

"Who are you?" a small, slight man demanded.

"I'm the cook," she shot back. "Trying to get into my kitchen."

"For the next three days, it's my kitchen. Are we clear on that?"

Rosie barked out a laugh. "Excuse me? Who the hell do you think you are?"

"I'm Councilor Tarand's personal chef. Didn't they tell you we were coming?"

"No, and I have to prepare breakfast for the management, so if you don't mind—"

He brandished a shiny new key and unlocked the door, blocking her from entering it. "I work alone. You'll have to make do elsewhere."

"There *is* no elsewhere!"

"It is protocol that all food prepared for the High Council be made in a secured kitchen with a member of staff who has been cleared to do so." He managed to look down his nose at her, despite being nearly half a meter shorter. "Which you most certainly are *not*."

"The *High* Council?" she asked in disbelief. "What would a member of the High Council be doing all the way out here?"

"Whatever it is that she is doing, I am sure that it is none of your business, or mine. I'll be taking over the kitchen on this station until we depart in several days." He gave a disdainful glance at the stovetop. "This will have to do, I suppose."

"How am I supposed to get my work done, then?"

"I am sure you will figure that out," he said, closing the door in her face.

Outraged, Rosie stomped down the corridor, heading to the loading bay. Everyone would just have to get by with protein bricks, because she couldn't prepare food in the corridor, now could she?

"Hey, hold up, the loading bay is off-limits for the next few days," Abara said, holding their hand up to stop her.

"I have to get to the brick ration crates to deliver them to quarters and barracks."

"We're under strict orders."

"I just got turfed out of my kitchen. I can't cook anything. Unless people get bricks, they won't be getting a damned morsel of anything to eat until this High Councilor leaves."

"I'm not allowed to let anyone down there who isn't involved with the Councilor's detail."

"Abara, did you hear me? I need the ration crates."

"I can't let you down there."

"Then can you have someone bring them up here?"

"We aren't supposed to be removing anything from the cargo area, either."

Rosie inhaled deeply, trying in vain to settle her nerves. "Abara. No one. Will eat. Unless I get to those crates."

They shook their head. "I'm really sorry, Ms. Gordon, there's nothing I can do. The general is on all of our asses right now, any minor slip up and we'll be looking at an unpaid, immediate discharge."

"Then I'll have to take this to General Fineglass," Rosie asserted, turning on her heel.

"She's in meetings all day, she's not to be disturbed. In fact, right now, she's probably with the welcoming committee in the atrium."

"I don't see any other option, Abara."

They sighed, arms crossed over their chest. "I want to help you, but I can't."

"Why didn't they plan for this? Surely someone must have realized that

I'd need access in order to feed people. What do they expect, everyone to go hungry for days?"

"Knowing the overseer, that wouldn't surprise me," Abara grumbled. "Alright, fine, I'll see what I can do, but one word of this and my head will be on a platter. You got me?"

"Thank you."

"HEY!" Abara shouted down the stairs. "Get someone to bring up a crate of bricks for the cook."

"But—"

"Now!"

Abara gave a weak smile. "Should be just a few minutes."

"I appreciate this."

"Yeah, you'll owe me one, how about that? Save me something nice when you get back into your kitchen."

"You got it." Rosie rested her hands in the pockets of her navy blue dress. "Did any of you know this was happening?"

"No. Most of us got yanked out of our bunks in the middle of the night to prep. Those who weren't were already on duty for a night watch."

"Feels pretty disorganized, if you ask me."

"Trust me, they won't ask you."

Rosie snorted. "Yeah, I won't hold my breath on that account. I just don't get how they could let me get locked out of the kitchen for days! No doubt I'm going to have management pounding at my door wondering where their real food is."

"Given all our background checks, I'm surprised that you didn't qualify to cook for our esteemed visitor."

"That's just how it is, Abara. Doesn't matter how hard you work, or what you do to prove yourself. Those gates are always kept firmly closed." Saying it out loud made her heart sink in her chest. The new lock on the kitchen was proof that she'd never be good enough for the Capital, no matter what her cooking was like, or how well she ran a kitchen. To them, she'd always just be unworthy.

A disgruntled MPO struggled to the top of the stairs, a crate wobbling perilously in his hands. "Where the hell do you want this, Abara?"

"Ask Ms. Gordon."

"The mess hall is probably best," Rosie said, gesturing down the corridor. "At least there are tables in there."

"I can't carry this all the way to the mess hall!" The guard protested, dumping the crate on the floor. "At least you get to use a trolley!"

"I don't get a trolley, actually," Rosie said, deftly balancing the crate on her hip. "I carry these up three flights of stairs every morning and evening. But you're excused for thinking otherwise."

"You mean I'm going to have to do that *again*?"

Rosie arched an eyebrow at Abara. "Only if I don't get access to the cargo bay."

"Aright," Abara said, sighing. "I'll talk to the general the next chance I get, see what I can do. The gods know I can't stand much more of this one's bellyaching," they said, jabbing a thumb at the other MPO. "It's a nonstop stream of complaints."

"Hey!" the annoyed guard interjected. "I didn't see *you* carrying that crate up the stairs!"

"Can you get me tonight's, too? Will make delivery easier until you get me access."

"I said I'd try to get you access."

"I have faith in you. You're a very persuasive person."

"Not as convincing as you, it seems," Abara said, rolling their eyes dramatically. "Go get another crate for Ms. Gordon, please. Feel free to use a handcart if the general's fitness regime kicked your ass yesterday."

"Fuck you, Abara."

"Back atcha."

When the MPO disappeared back down the steps, Rosie shifted the weight of the crate onto her other hip. "Trouble in paradise?"

"I'd hardly say this station is paradise, but let's just say the others aren't exactly thrilled about pulling triple shifts." They sighed again. "It will be a miracle if we don't get at least a dozen requests for transfer by the end of the week. Not that they'll be honored, of course. Recruitment has fallen behind."

"Why is that?"

"Who knows? Maybe some of the letters home, even censored, are painting the Outer Rim as less than hospitable."

"Probably a fair analysis," Rosie said.

"Yeah. Still, it makes for a pissy squad."

"Do you ever think about going back home?"

Abara rubbed their bald head, dark skin shining in the glare of the harsh lights. "Every gods-damned day." They blew out a harsh breath. "But I can't. I was reassigned here by the general herself."

"I bet it will get better once the expansion project is complete. Bigger barracks, more space, a training room, maybe—"

"We'll see. Anyway, you better get to the mess hall, or our disgusting protein bricks might get cold."

"They're already cold."

"That's the joke, Gordon. I'll send my effervescent colleague up with the second crate. You alright with that one?"

"Yeah. Same as every damned morning, to be honest." Rosie nodded and marched back up the hallway, scowling at the locked kitchen door. She had half a mind to kick it in and prove that she was a good enough cook for this High Councilor, whoever the hell she was. She didn't. She walked right past and landed in the mess hall, as planned.

The protein bricks were as gelatinous as they always were, slightly damp and sticking to each other. She pried them apart, wrapping each one in brown paper and stacking them in a tight pyramid on the next table over.

Through the service hatch, she could hear clattering and swearing from the kitchen. No doubt the clod had misunderstood just how bare-bones it was out here. She snorted at the thought of him desperately raking through the drawers, searching for specialized equipment; she frowned when she realized what a mess he'd likely leave behind. Capital chefs weren't accustomed to cleaning up after themselves.

She hummed inanely to herself, something not quite tuneless, but neither was it melodic. She'd never been a very good singer. Her mother had always said she couldn't carry a tune if her life depended on it. Thinking about home was just one more painful ache, so she buried the thought.

"Hey! You!" the chef shouted, peering through the small gap in the service hatch.

"Yes?" she asked, ready to spring into action.

"Shut up with that racket, I'm trying to work in here!" He slammed the hatch shut again, and she resisted the urge to rip the shutters off their hinges. What a nasty, self-important little man. He'd probably attended the Capital Culinary Institute. All of the ones like him had.

When all the bricks had been wrapped, Rosie laid them back into the crate, making sure to tuck the edges of the paper wrapping so the bricks wouldn't get dust on them. They were gross enough without extra dirt making them worse.

Just like every other morning since she'd arrived, she started in the port side barracks, dropping one brick on top of each trunk that laid at the end of every bunk, neat, tidy, and uniform. Next, she hefted the crate to the starboard side barracks, and did the same there.

Carmen's bunk was the only one that diverged from the lifeless grey blankets, with a bright, colorful shawl draped across the end of her bed, the long fringe brushing against the top of the trunk. She wasn't military, and so wasn't expected to follow their living area protocols, but there were plenty of builders on board who went along with the standard-issue bedding, complete with the yellow and purple piping at the edges.

It was eerie in the barracks. Usually Rosie would be shuffling around in the dark, so as not to disturb the ones who were sleeping off a night shift, but now all the lights were on, and the room was completely empty. They'd all be patrolling the ship, an endless cycle of walking, checking, and repeating.

Next, she visited the management quarters. She knocked on the first door. "Breakfast," she said lightly, knowing that some of them wouldn't be happy about the development in the kitchen.

"Since when do we—" someone said, opening the door. "What the hell is that?"

"A protein brick."

"I'm management."

"Unfortunately, the kitchen is closed for the next several days. As such, I am unable to prepare the usual meals." Rosie held out the wrapped brick. "You'll get three a day. I'll deliver the others this afternoon."

"I don't want *that*."

"I appreciate that, sir, but there's nothing I can do."

He harrumphed noisily. "I didn't drag my ass all the way to the Outer Rim to eat the equivalent of livestock feed."

"It's a nutritionally complete meal—"

"It's disgusting, is what it is," he said, throwing it back at her. "I'll be speaking to the overseer about this."

"I encourage you to do that, sir. I don't like this arrangement any more than you do, but with a High Councilor on the station—"

"Balderdash. Why in hells would they be all the way out here?"

"I assure you, I don't know. All I know is that I have no access to my kitchen, and this is the replacement." She held it out to him again. "It's all any of us, except her, will be eating until she leaves in a few days."

"This is an outright lie. The High Council hasn't left Gamma-3 in years, nor would they be all the way out at the Rim."

"Why would I lie?"

"To get out of doing your job. The gods know there are enough lazy louts on this station to sink a naval ship."

"I don't imagine that would work, do you? The general and the overseer would find out immediately, would they not?"

He sniffed the brick. "I've seen stranger ways to get reassigned."

"There's no guarantee that my next assignment would be any better than this one. Check the kitchen for yourself if you must, but I assure you that the chef in there is remarkably unpleasant."

"Is there anything you can do to... spice these up?"

"I'll see what I can do," Rosie offered.

"It's any wonder how the MPOs live on these. It looks like it's already been digested. And why is it... *green*?"

"It's the spinach."

He took a bite. "It doesn't taste like spinach." He grimaced, swallowing in a theatrical manner. "It doesn't taste of much of anything other than slime."

"The pectin in the fruit is to thank for their portable yet slimy texture." She grinned with encouragement. "They're not so bad once you get used to them."

"I very much doubt that," he said, setting the brick on his desk. "I can't say I'll be looking forward to another one later."

"I hope to be back to normal as soon as the High Councilperson leaves." She waved as he closed the door and then sighed. If every member of management was that tetchy about a protein brick, she'd be running behind the rest of the week.

She breathed a sigh of relief at each of the next three doors, as their occupants were elsewhere. She left their bricks in the wire mail basket that hung on the outside, hoping they wouldn't get covered with too much post – but if the cargo bay was off-limits, it was likely there wouldn't *be* any mail.

When Rosie reached Delia's door, she hesitated, even though she knew that she'd be in the broadcasting booth. There was something about the proximity to where Delia slept that made her pulse quicken. Old memories, perhaps. She didn't want it to be any more than that. It had been hard enough to get over Delia Forrest the first time. Doing it again might turn her heart to stone permanently.

Dropping the brick into the basket, she moved on down the corridor. First, Overseer Allemande's office, which was empty, and then the sciences division, where someone named Dr. Arteo tried to steal an extra brick.

The crate empty, Rosie returned to the mess hall. No one ever said this job would be glamorous.

Chapter 25

Delia wrinkled her nose at the protein brick nestled in the mail basket, but took it anyway as she unlocked her door. What a gods-forsaken day. Nothing but more problems to deal with. They'd never get Thomas out of the brig if the security stayed this high.

She sat at the edge of her bed and kicked off her boots, wiggling her toes in her patterned socks, the stripes wobbling back and forth. New boots would be nice. Hers were fine, but getting worn thin at the soles. Off the station, she'd just go purchase some new ones. Here, though, she'd have to have them shipped specially, and William still hadn't written back. One more thing that was keeping her awake at night.

The chime from the radio announced the evening broadcast. Delia laid back on her bed, nibbling at the edge of the protein brick. It was a hell of a thing to be hungry, yet absolutely repulsed by the available food. Fluffing her thin pillow, she loosened the cravat around her neck, tossing it to the side, where it landed on her chair.

"Good evening to each and every listener. I am High Councilor Cecelia Tarand, and tonight, I am broadcasting to you from Turas-Mara Station, all the way at the Outer Rim, the gateway to the universe. No doubt some of you may be surprised to hear my voice, given that the High Council is preoccupied with making wide scale plans for our collective future."

Delia scoffed. "Bullshit."

"The expansion project here at the Rim is of the utmost importance. We are recruiting the best of the best to work on this station, pioneers who will be long remembered by their families and in our history books as the ones who helped expand our reign into the furthest reaches of dark space."

Gods, these protein bricks tasted awful. She swallowed a chunk without chewing, hoping it would bypass her taste buds entirely.

"Furthermore, we are committed to prosperity and opportunity for every Coalition citizen. Expansion and growth are the best way to achieve that, with efficiency, honor, and pride. We must ask something of every one of you out there, and of those here on the station. You must—"

The radio roared with static.

"Gods be damned, that's loud," Delia shouted to herself, turning down the volume dial. "Another interference? What in hells—" Before she could finish her thought, there was angry, threatening pounding on the door.

"Dodson, get out here!" the overseer boomed.

Delia threw open the door, already on the defensive. "I don't know what's causing it!"

"Get in there and fix it!"

"I'm not an operator, I—"

"I don't care *what* you are, you fix it or you're on the first transport off this station and headed straight for the judge!"

She bent to grab her boots, but the overseer grabbed the collar of her shirt and dragged her into the corridor. "What are you doing?" Allemande barked. "Get going!"

"Alright!" Delia snapped, tucking in her shirt. "Gods!"

"Excuse me?"

"*Ma'am*," she added, already halfway down the hall, rolling up the cuffs of her sleeves. Fucking High Councilor. Allemande didn't give one shit about the interference before she got here, and suddenly it was some grand emergency. When she turned the corner, Carmen was already strong-arming her way into the broadcasting booth.

"Hello, yes, excuse me, ma'am, I'm here to see if I can fix the problem we're having. Oh, Delia, good. I'll head into the next room to check connections, if you can stay in the booth here to test."

Delia nodded. "Of course."

"Great!" Carmen chirped. "I'm sure we'll get this sorted out in no time."

A lie, plainly. The two of them had already spent weeks working on a solution to no avail. "I'm glad you're here," Delia said honestly.

"Me too. Here, take this jack. Have a look for fraying wires or something."

Delia took it, pretending to inspect the almost brand-new cord. There was no way it was fraying already, and that wouldn't cause interference, besides. "Hello, ma'am," she said in an absent-minded tone, trying too hard to seem casual around one of the most powerful people in the Near Systems. "It's good to have you aboard."

"I am glad to see such skilled technicians attending to my needs," Councilor Tarand said, the wooden beads at the ends of her braids clacking gently. "If only for a cursory broadcast." She gave Delia a reassuring smile, her dark eyes kind, peering out over high cheekbones.

"We take these things very seriously around here. After all, it's just about the only contact we have with anyone off-station."

"Do you not have the ability to send wires back home?"

"We do. Most of the crew can't afford them."

"Perhaps if the station reached maximum efficiency, there would be more allowance for payment. As it stands, however, there is room for much improvement."

"Delia, anything?" Carmen called from the next room.

"No, nothing. Try something else—the connection, maybe."

"Aye. Give me a minute."

The councilor sat on the stool with irritatingly impeccable posture. "Does this happen often?" she asked.

"No," Delia lied, knowing that the overseer would probably stuff her through an airlock if she told the truth. "But there's a first time for everything!"

"Indeed."

A woman with long, pin-straight, platinum hair poked her head into the booth. "Ma'am, there are reports of a station-wide communications outage. This is a significant security risk—"

"It's alright, Olivia. There is no immediate threat."

"But what if—"

"I think you will agree that despite my reliance on you as my administrative right hand and security detail, I can make my own decisions. We will wait until these fine people repair the equipment."

"Of course, madam."

"Anything now?" Carmen shouted.

Delia tapped on the microphone, and it let loose a metallic shriek. "We have air," she said. "But there's too much feedback."

"Progress! Almost done, then!"

Councilor Tarand tilted her head slightly. "I used to listen to your broadcasts back in the Capital."

"Oh!" Delia exclaimed, taken aback. "I didn't think members of the High Council would have cause or occasion to listen to a public program."

"Some of us like to keep in touch with what our citizens are hearing." Tarand's gaze was fixed on Delia, a calm, cool stare that was somehow unsettling intense. "I feel as though it is important to understand how people think about the Coalition. I preferred your broadcast over the fellow they chose to replace you. He's rather... bland."

"That is quite an honor," Delia said, examining the microphone once again, as though there was anything at all she could do to fix it. "Thank you for telling me."

"Indeed, I was surprised that you left the Capital. For many in your field of work, staying there would have been an easy decision to make. Live in the greatest city in the Near Systems, work your way up until you were the front-woman of the entire station. Yet, you chose to come out here. Why?"

"Turas-Mara is the gateway to the universe."

"Yes, that is the official line. But why did you choose to risk it all to come out here?"

"I felt like it would be making more of a difference than the work I was doing in the Capital."

The councilor nodded. "I admire that, Ms. Dodson. If we had just a few more people like you, this project would already be complete."

"I think we're back on," Carmen said, ducking into the booth. "We apologize for the interruption."

"That's quite alright. Thank you for your hard work and your persistence."

Delia stood. "I think our work is done here, we will leave you to finish your broadcast." She stepped outside the booth with Carmen, closing the door behind them.

"That's not going to happen again, is it?" Olivia asked. "We can't have that happening while the councilor is on the station."

"Hopefully not," Carmen replied, her tone bright and sunny. "You never can tell with these new builds, eh?"

Olivia frowned. "I should hope that isn't the case. Any breach in security would be a danger to her safety. Do you take security lightly here?"

"Respectfully, Ms...?"

"Guisette."

"Ms. Guisette, neither I nor Ms. Dodson here are in charge of security. You would have to speak with General Fineglass about that. Secondly, I can assure you that no one on this station intends her any harm."

"It is part of my job to keep her safe, and as such, I will do whatever it takes to secure her well-being. That is why we made sure the brig was empty before we even docked on the station."

"Empty?" Carmen asked.

"Yes. There are hundreds of considerations I have to keep at the forefront of my mind at all times." The agent smoothed her hands over the folder in her hands. "It wasn't surprising when your overseer said that this station held no prisoners. This place is so small, it makes my skin itch. How can you even stand it?"

"Oh, you know..." Carmen trailed off. "Reading, I suppose."

Delia was still reeling when Carmen elbowed her lightly in the arm. "Oh, err—I tend to focus on my work here, Ms. Guisette. After all that, there isn't much time for recreation, anyway."

"Indeed," the assistant said, distracted.

"We should get going, Delia," Carmen said insistently. "We have that... thing, to plan." She turned to Olivia. "I trust you can handle things from here? Surely the broadcast is almost complete?"

"Yes, I suppose it is. It will have lost all the impact we were hoping for with that lengthy delay, however. We will need to rewrite the script and deliver it again tomorrow morning. Do you think that you can manage to stave off any more malfunctions?"

"We will do our best, I assure you."

"See that you do. We can't spend much longer here, or this station will become a target for every brigand in the Near Systems. No doubt some of them are already on their way here."

"It would be wildly foolish to attack this station, Ms. Guisette," Delia assured her. "We're the most heavily patrolled place by area in the galaxy."

"Quite." She sighed, snapping shut a file in her hands. "Clear off, Councilor Tarand will need the corridor in a moment."

"You don't have to tell us twice," Carmen muttered, pulling Delia around the corner. "Nice to meet you!" she shouted back over her shoulder.

"The brig is *empty*?" Delia hissed as soon as they were out of earshot.

"Maybe they were moved to a secure facility, or put on a prison transport," Carmen offered.

"How can that be? I was just... I was just down there last night."

"They could have been moved in that time."

"In just a few hours?" Delia shook her head. "No, something isn't right. Come on, you're Intelligence, you must know that something about this is strange."

Carmen sighed. "I don't think any ships docked in that time. I was awake all night and I didn't hear anything. Which means they're being hidden somewhere on the station until Tarand leaves." She glanced over at Delia. "Did you speak with that pirate captain?"

Delia hesitated. Carmen was Intelligence, but if she was investigating the station, maybe she could help get Thomas out. "I did. She wouldn't tell me anything. Had two black eyes, though, and they're only getting one brick a day."

"That's in line with prisoner allowances."

"Right," Delia said, because she wasn't about to tell an Intelligence spy that it was barbaric and monstrous to treat people like that, even ones accused of piracy and treason. "Well, she wouldn't answer any of my questions unless I promised to spring her from her cell."

Carmen laughed. "Yeah, that sounds like her."

"You've met her?" Delia asked, her brow furrowed. "You know this captain?"

"I, er—sort of. We've been tracking her for years, and witness accounts all describe her as being rather... tempestuous."

"I'd say that's a very gentle description of her. I think if she had the opportunity, she would have reached through the bars and strangled me with her bare hands."

"Probably."

"What do we do now? Do we try to find her—them?"

"No. There are enough patrols right now that those prisoners aren't going anywhere until the High Councilperson leaves in a few days. Just wait until everything is back to normal, and then you can go back and question her again. Maybe next time she will be more amenable."

"I doubt that."

"Promise me you won't go looking for them, Delia. Now is not the time to be skulking around the station. You will get caught, and then this all starts to unravel in a very dangerous way."

"I promise," Delia lied.

* * *

"Rosie? Rosie, open up!" Delia whispered through the door. "I have to talk to you, it's important!"

There was no answer.

"Rosie!"

"Have you lost what's left of your sense?" Rosie hissed, dragging her away from the door. "The official chef, or whoever the hell he is, is right across the hall!"

"How was I supposed to know that?"

"Didn't you see all the patrols today?"

"Yes, but—"

"Then keep your mouth shut and follow me."

"But—"

"Dee, I swear to all the gods, you have to keep your trap shut, just this once."

"Alright, alright." Delia followed her dutifully, her jaw clenched shut, until Rosie led her into the same hidden corridor that connected to the observatory.

"Out with it. What's going on?" Rosie demanded. "I have plenty to be worried about right now, and—"

"They moved the prisoners. Moved Thomas."

"What? How do you know that? You didn't go down there, did you? Someone will definitely have seen—"

"No, of course I didn't go down there. Councilor Tarand's assistant told me that they refused to dock unless the brig was empty."

"Shit."

"Yeah."

"Any ideas where they've been moved to?"

"No. It's not a big station, they have to be somewhere—but with all the expansion building going on, there's at least a dozen little areas like this one."

Rosie shook her head. "This is barely big enough for the two of us, five people sure as hells wouldn't fit."

"I wouldn't put it past Allemande to cram them in. I'd hoped to get Thomas out, but now..."

"I know. The cargo bay is completely off-limits, I'm having to beg and bribe the MPOs stationed down there just to bring the crates of bricks up for me. There's no way we'd be able to smuggle him out, there are no ships coming or going until Tarand leaves."

Delia leaned against the wall, rubbing at her temples. "My fear is that even after she's gone, they're going to keep up this new security standard.

Bring in more guards, pack them into the barracks until this whole place is crawling with them."

"After what happened with those pirates, I'd say that's a fair assumption to make."

"What are we going to do?"

Rosie brushed against her arm. "I don't know if there's anything we *can* do, Dee. It feels impossible."

"Some days, I regret coming out here at all. If I'd just stayed in the Capital, Thomas would be a free man. He wouldn't have been reassigned to the Rim to be my operator—"

"Maybe. Or he'd be in a different cell somewhere else. You can't know what might have happened."

Delia turned to look at her. "I have too many regrets."

"I suppose we all do."

"I never should have left."

"No, you shouldn't have."

All at once, Delia's eyes flooded with tears. "I missed you every day that I was gone, Rose. That life we never got to live, it *aches* in me. I felt empty the moment I closed the door behind me."

"Dee..." Rosie trailed off. Her eyes were squeezed shut, but her hands found Delia's waist, and then her hips. "I know we shouldn't, but—"

Delia leaned forward into the embrace, feeling her resolve melt away like snowdrifts in the spring, or the hoarfrost on Delta-4 when the morning shone over the distant red mountains. "I never stopped wanting you, Rosie Gordon," she whispered, just before their lips met.

She couldn't help but let little gasps of excitement slip as Rosie deepened the kiss, sending them both tumbling back through time, back to the tiny apartment they shared, when the dust danced in the sunbeams in late afternoon. Back to when they'd lay in each other's arms, daydreaming about the future they'd have together, the curtains drawn to hide them from the world, and to hide the world from them.

Rosie pressed against her, and Delia wept from the proximity to the love of her fractured life. She wrapped her arms around Rosie's ample waist, pulling her closer, as though they would phase into one being, a fusion of self.

It was everything, and then it was nothing, as Rosie pulled away from the first kiss they'd shared in over a decade of loneliness.

"What's the matter?" Delia whispered, her hands still grasping for Rosie.

"I'm sorry," she replied, "I can't."

And then she was gone, and this time it was Delia who was left alone with her tears, and her aching heart, and a pile of broken, irreparable dreams. Nothing was right, and everything hurt. Delia curled in on herself in that hidden corridor, silently weeping bitter tears for a long while, before she picked herself up and returned to her cold, empty quarters.

Chapter 26

She'd spent hours wandering the station after that kiss, the feel of it still lingering on her lips like too much static electricity. It threatened to consume her, the same way Delia's kisses had before. Rosie resisted it, pacing purposefully through the corridors.

One MPO after another asked what she was doing out of her quarters. She told all of them that she was just stretching her legs. There was no rule against that. Not yet, anyway, though Councilor Tarand's presence aboard was already prompting too many changes to keep up with.

Turas-Mara was becoming a jumbled mess of expansion, with corridors that led only to dead-ends, most of them covered with draped tarps to keep nosy civilians like her out. There were too many guards to explore without raising suspicion, so she logged anything out of place in her mind. An abandoned toolbox, a tarp left askew, a slightly crooked 'No Entry' sign. None of it was enough to suggest that's where the prisoners were hidden.

Rosie made one more loop of the station, her eyelids finally growing heavy with exhaustion. Before she traveled out towards the Rim, she'd frequently spend long walks back home, trying to fit life into boxes that she could process and understand. Hell, after Delia left, she had spent every waking moment walking. To work, to the tailor, to nowhere in particular. Up here, though, walking was far less restorative. Panels of steel didn't have the same impact as tall, ancient trees.

She unlocked her door, looking left and right before she nudged it open. The last thing she needed was someone taking note of her late night wanderings. In the solace of her own room, tears leaked from the corners of her eyes. It was too hard to be so close to Delia, knowing they would never be together, not so long as she had to be seen as her husband's wife.

Her foot slid across the floor, a note trapped beneath her boot. Locking the door behind her, she greedily broke the seal on the envelope. What information would there be this time?

Look behind the atrium.

Her heart seized in her chest. Whoever was sending the notes must have known that they were looking for the missing prisoners—did they also know about their little excursion to the brig? How could they? Had they been seen?

Rosie's stomach churned in angry waves, threatening to bring up the protein brick she'd eaten hours earlier, or whatever was left of it. Probably no more than bile, now. She had to tell Delia about the note, but it was the middle of the night, and what were they going to do about it now? Too many patrols, too much surveillance to even get near the atrium.

She sat on her bed, her legs crossed beneath her skirts. Tracing lines from one name to another, she drew a web in her notebook of who could be sending the notes. Who would even have access to that kind of information? One of the ranked MPOs? Carmen? She wrote more names on the page. "Emeline," she whispered.

It had to be her. Who else would have access to Allemande's office, and know that there was a secret file? Who else would have that kind of insider information, and want to share it with a nobody like her? Was it a cry for help, or maybe a plot to incriminate Delia? Emeline hated her, after all, but then why not send the notes directly to her?

Rosie rubbed at her temples in a bid to beat back the encroaching headache. She'd barely slept, and the past few days had blurred into a muddy puddle of confusion in her mind. Coming out to the Rim had been a mistake. She should have listened to her grandfather, but she was stubborn. He'd warned her that the expansion project would be fraught, but she boarded that transport, anyway.

The gods be damned, he was nearly always right, he always had been. It's probably why she was so bull-headed, never listening, and look where it landed her—at the edge of the known galaxy, with only Delia as an ally, a daily reminder of everything she'd lost all those years ago.

She buried her face into the thin pillow and screamed, but instead of the rage and frustration she'd expected, the muffled sound died out halfway through the breath. There wasn't even enough energy within her to shout. Nor was there the will to get out of bed and turn off the single light bulb that hung over the small desk, so she rolled onto her side and expected to sleep.

Still, though, no sleep came, only more questions that swirled in her mind like a deadly poison that threatened to rot her from the inside out. She needed answers if she was going to survive on this station, if she was ever going to get real rest again. Ever since she stepped foot on the station, it had been one problem after the next, mystery after conundrum, and somehow they were all up to her to solve. She was no inspector, no spy for Intelligence, yet there she was, the one being given the trail of crumbs.

Rosie slipped her boots back on, yawning despite her insomnia. She'd just have to go look behind the atrium herself, and damn the consequences.

Chapter 27

"Alright, Ms. Dodson, time to lock up," Overseer Allemande said, waving the long, spindly, silver key from the doorway.

"Of course," Delia answered, gathering up her notes, and the approved script. Getting extricated from the broadcasting booth made her feel like a common criminal, or an unruly child.

"We wouldn't want anything to go wrong again this evening, now would we?"

"No."

"Come now, don't give me such a sour expression. This is for the good of everyone. After all, if the booth remains locked during the hours it isn't used, then no one can be accused of *tampering*."

Despite the overseer's words, it certainly sounded like an accusation. "I can assure you that neither I nor Ms. Rojas tampered with the equipment."

"If I thought you had, you'd already be destined for a prison transport," Allemande said with a smile that barely curved at the edges of her lips. "This is just for peace of mind."

"Will I regain access after Councilor Tarand has departed?"

"Certainly not. This will be the new standard operation procedure from here on out, I'm afraid, but it will disrupt any potential problems. Though the booth was locked yesterday, something still went awry with the transmission. What was it?"

"You'd have to ask Carmen, she was in the operations room. I was in the booth, testing as she worked. It sounded like it was due to a loose wire."

"Strange, as the cables were only just replaced, wouldn't you say so, Ms. Dodson?"

"Yes. Very strange. But it had happened before, and you didn't seem overly concerned."

"What? That never happened before. Why would you say such a thing? I would never allow myself such a dereliction of duty, and I won't have you spreading those lies."

"Of course not, ma'am. Understood. My apologies."

"You will be on hand tonight during the broadcast, in case there are further troubles. Though," she said, holding the key aloft, "I do not anticipate it."

Chapter 28

Rosie waited until past midnight to head back to the atrium. The guards were exhausted and getting sloppy in their rotations. She'd spent most of the day observing them as she walked rings around the station. They were past their prime, half-asleep and angry. That combination was a volatile one that would either let her move around unnoticed, or land her in that strange room with the others.

"Psst. I'm back," she whispered through the heavy metal door.

"Did you bring what we asked?" Josie asked from the other side, her voice hoarse.

"I did."

"Pass it through, then."

Rosie slid the extra protein bricks through the narrow slat in the door, one after another, eight in total. No doubt someone would notice the discrepancy, and she'd have to answer for it—but that was a problem for another day. "That's all I have," she said, easing the slat closed.

"Better than nothing," one of the other pirates muttered. "Can't you get us some real food?"

"Not until I get back into my kitchen. I'm locked out until Tarand leaves."

There was a shuffling from inside the room. "When will that be?" Josie rasped. "I thought the damn brig was bad, but this is categorically worse. We haven't seen light in days."

"She will leave soon, I hope. The station can't go on like this."

"What about getting us out of here?"

Rosie grimaced. "I'm working on it. It's not easy, you know."

"No shit, but if I was on the other side of the door, we'd have been long gone by now."

"Easy for you to say, when you're not the one trying to figure it all out."

Josie coughed. "Just find the key. I'll take care of the rest."

"They'll kill you on sight, just like they did the others. You don't have any weapons!"

"I'll make some."

"Thomas? Are you alright?" Rosie asked, desperate to shift the conversation. There was no way they'd be able to get him out without springing Josie and her crew, too.

"I'm alright. Does Delia know where we are?"

"No, I haven't seen her all day. The High Councilor's presence means she has to be on deck for all the broadcasts."

"Pff," Josie snorted, "as if that High Council asshole has anything important to say. We all know everything that comes out of her mouth is horseshit."

"Will you keep it down? The last thing any of us need is for me to get thrown in there alongside the rest of you. I can't steal protein bricks from inside."

"Barely even worth stealing these things. Once I'm out of here, I swear I'll burn the whole damned crate of them."

"There won't be any time for that. You're going to have to do exactly as we say if you're all going to make it off this station alive."

"I hope I get the opportunity in my life to blow this place to smithereens."

"For now, I just need you to keep your mouths shut, alright?" Rosie whispered. Trying to keep Josie from alerting the whole station with her mouthing off was already proving to be an irritating struggle. "I'm doing the best that I can, but with the increased patrols—"

"Excuses," Josie spat. "I bet you're working for them. I bet this is just some stunt to get us to admit to more crimes than we committed, just so you can justify throwing us into some deeper, darker cell than this and throwing away the key."

"I can promise you, that's not the case."

"If you really wanted to get us out, we'd be out already."

"And what then?" Rosie challenged. "You run through the corridors like a wild woman? Do you think the MPOs won't shoot you on sight, along with what's left of your crew? There are more weapons here than any place outside the gods-damned Armory in the Capital."

"I'd manage."

"You might, but Thomas wouldn't. He's been in a cell for months. Do you think he'd be able to fight his way off this station?"

"I don't give a good goddamn about him," Josie hissed, and then added, "Sorry, Thomas, but my loyalty and responsibility is to my crew, not a random cell mate. For all I know, you could be someone who'd turn us in the second you had a chance. Hell, maybe you already have."

"Why do you think I'm in here?" he wheezed. "Charged with treason. Conspiracy against the Coalition." His hacking cough was muffled by what was left of his sleeve and the thick steel door. "I wouldn't turn you in, Josie."

"I can't know that for sure."

"It doesn't matter," Rosie interjected, watching the corridor with wary eyes. "You're not getting out of there unless Thomas does, too."

"So where's your little girlfriend?" Josie sneered.

"She's not my girlfriend."

"I saw how you two looked at each other. I'm not a fool, you know, it was plain as day. Not that I'm even going to remember what daylight feels like by the time you louts get me out of here."

Rosie blinked. "Delia isn't my girlfriend," she repeated, "not that it's any business of yours, but she's married."

"That doesn't mean she can't be your girlfriend."

"In this case, it does."

"Long lost love, then?"

"I am not discussing *this* with *you*," Rosie seethed. "You're lucky I'm even considering this at all. If you weren't such a... a—"

"Brilliant negotiator? Quick-witted strategist?"

"*Pirate*, I'd leave you in there."

"No, you wouldn't. You've got a conscience. I can smell them a mile off. Rare these days, you know."

"Conscience or no, you still tried to, what, hijack this station?"

Josie let out a restrained breath. "No. You may think I'm an empty-brained sack of horseshit, but I wouldn't do something like that. It's a recipe for disaster. We just wanted to steal some cargo. Bad intel."

"Where was the intel from?"

"You're not doing a great job of convincing me that you're not a Coalition plant."

"I'm merely suggesting that someone may have set you up."

"Maybe. You can bet your ass I plan to find out as soon as I get my hands on that two-timing weasel." There was a soft thud as Josie leaned against the cell door. "So what's the over-under on getting us out of here? How long do we have to wait for you to get your shit together?"

"As long as it takes," Rosie said. "One wrong move, and we're all done for. The overseer will take pleasure in sending us all to camps."

"You don't know the half of what that woman, that—thing, is capable of," Thomas whispered. "Monstrous, to take joy in pain. It is no wonder that she rose through the ranks so quickly. I can only imagine how many bodies have littered her path to success."

"We'll get you out of there as soon as we can," Rosie reassured him. "No matter what it takes."

"You better hurry it up, or that top-hatted beast is going to start carving us up, too. No doubt we've only been spared this long because she's busy kissing ass."

"I'm doing the best I can, I—"

Josie shuffled closer to the door. "Yeah? Then your best isn't good enough. Try harder, unless you want five bodies weighing on that clear conscience of yours."

* * *

"Delia?" Rosie whispered at her door. It was late, though not as late as it usually was when she went skulking around the station. "Dee, I'm sorry about—I'm sorry that I walked out, but I have to talk to you."

"You're out of quarters rather late, aren't you, Ms. Gordon?" Emeline was leaning against the corner at the edge of the corridor, still dressed in her green day dress, though her usually neat braid was messy and unkempt.

Rosie spun around, alarmed. "Eme—I mean, Ms. Allemande. Nice to see you again."

"What do you need with Ms. Dodson that's so important that it can't wait until morning?"

"It's, uh—a private matter."

Emeline smirked. "There isn't much private on a station this size. Everyone's business is everyone's business, if you catch my meaning."

"It's about—" Rosie fumbled for an answer. "It's not that important, actually."

"You know, I can't imagine much that would keep me from the comfort of my quarters, especially this time of night." She arched an eyebrow. "Is everything alright?"

"Fine, fine."

"Then perhaps you should get back to your own quarters, before my mother finds us both out of bed. It's inefficient to spend so much time on personal relationships and recreation, you know."

"I apologize. I've been at a loss since I got kicked out of the kitchen."

"At least it won't be for much longer. Councilor Tarand departs the day after tomorrow."

"Oh, does she? I'm sure the management staff will be happy to return to regular meals. Many of them aren't accustomed to protein bricks." Rosie cleared her throat. "Do you know where Delia—Ms. Dodson, is?"

"Why, are you going to go sneaking off to find her?"

"No, I just—"

"The last I saw of her, she was outside the broadcasting booth, waiting for the end of the nightly program, but that was hours ago now. If she isn't in her quarters, I suppose she could be anywhere. Making the rounds with an MPO for a story maybe, or in a late meeting with the councilor's assistant."

"But—"

"Or," Emeline mused, "she might be in the atrium."

"I just came from there. I mean, around there. The surrounding corridors, that is. I didn't see her."

"Trespassing, Ms. Gordon? And for what reason?"

"As if you don't know," Rosie replied, without thinking. Panic washed over her. Even if Emeline was the one sending notes, she shouldn't even be acknowledging they exist in front of her.

"I can assure you that I don't. What precisely are you talking about? Are you *accusing* me of something, Ms. Gordon?"

"What? No! I just meant that you of all people should know what it's like to be cooped up on this station, being so young and full of life. It can't be easy not having anyone your age to—"

"Those trivial matters are of no concern to me. I am here to further the cause for the Outer Rim expansion and to advocate for the people of Skelm, whether my mother likes that or not. If I wanted to leave, I would. I am not a prisoner here, Ms. Gordon."

Rosie grimaced. "No, of course not."

"Some of us have more important missions in life than petty romantic dalliances," Emeline said, staring coldly. "Or, for that matter, pithy political posturing. There are fools among us who would use their lofty positions to barter for their own advancement, or to line their own pockets. They do not have any of our best interests at heart, and, in fact, I find them utterly contemptible."

"I understand."

"Do you? Because from where I'm standing, it seems as though you aren't doing what's best for those around you, Ms. Gordon."

"Sometimes, it is hard to know what the right path is."

"Maybe for some. I've always found it quite simple. Work for a better future."

Rosie leaned against the wall, her arms crossed, as though she were protecting herself from an incoming blow. "Who gets to decide what's better, though?"

"Very philosophical, Ms. Gordon. I think you'd agree that better means more food to go around, more wealth. Fewer struggling or in pain. Wouldn't you agree?"

"Sure, but—"

"I think you'll find that most of us working for the greater good have similar aims. We just disagree on how to achieve them."

"And how would you achieve that?"

Emeline frowned. "That, I'm afraid, is far more complex a matter. Some, even in the High Council, would disagree on methodology. Some would use force and coercion. Some would use incentives."

"And you? What would you choose?" Rosie asked.

"What I would choose is immaterial, as I am not a policy-maker. I am an advocate, yes. I am also a spokesperson for Turas-Mara. But I do not make the laws, nor do I implement them."

"Seems to me that someone as level-headed as you would make a vast improvement on... well, on some of those in power that I'm aware of."

"That is kind of you to say, Ms. Gordon, but I am not a fool. It is plain to me that you are trying to reel in an answer, or cover something up."

"I am not trying to do either of those things."

"You should consider your words carefully, especially here. You never know who might be lurking around the corner, waiting for the perfect opportunity to misconstrue what you say. I know all too well what damage the press can do."

"Damage?" Rosie asked.

"They craft a narrative, weaving a story that is palatable for an average reader or listener. The facts are inconsequential when they are telling fairy tales that shape public opinion. Take Ms. Dodson, for example. How much of what she says is true? How often does she lie?"

"I don't think that—"

"Spare me your arguing. I've seen first hand how narratives can be twisted to support the indiscriminate goals of certain people." Emeline brushed a stray hair from her face. "I have never been a fan of the press, and less so of Ms. Dodson. She schemes, and I know there is something inconsistent about her story. I just haven't figured it out yet. Still, I've said too much. I suggest you get back to your quarters, and I will return to mine."

Chapter 29

Delia tapped the end of her pencil impatiently against the side of the metal desk. She'd looked everywhere on the damned station, and still no sign of Thomas or the other prisoners. Rosie hadn't said a word to her since the kiss two nights ago either, and that was its own disaster.

She sighed with impatience, crossing out what she'd already written. Writing these fluffy recruitment-drive interviews was the last thing she wanted to be focusing on, yet it was the only thing she was allowed to work on until they were approved. Even then, it would be another cycle of sanitized news, picked over and censored by Overseer Allemande. Did any of this even have a point anymore?

"Dodson!"

Jumping in her seat, she leaned over and opened her door to find General Fineglass, her face red with rage. "General?"

"What does your scrawny, good-for-nothing husband think he's playing at?"

Shit.

"Ma'am? I don't quite know what you're talking about."

"The *parts*, Dodson."

Dread settled into her stomach, insidious and threatening. "I'm afraid that is William's venture. I don't know much about it."

"They're *late*, and that is affecting the expansion schedule. Do you know how specifically humiliating it is to have to explain that to a member of the High Council?"

"I'm sure it's just a problem with the cargo transports, maybe the blockades—"

"I think you and I both know that the transports don't have a damned thing to do with it." The general leaned on the desk, her long auburn braid swinging like an executioner's blade. "Tell me. Where the parts are."

"I don't know!" Delia shouted, the panic rising in her voice, shrill and childlike, her breaths quickening in pace. "He was doing the deal with a middleman."

"Who?"

"I don't know his name."

General Fineglass raked her arm across Delia's desk, sending papers flying, fluttering through the air. "Do you know *anything*, or are you completely useless?"

"We try to keep our business dealings separate! It's the only way to be sure that ethical—"

"Do you think I give one single, rancid, maggot-infested shit about your ethical obligations right now? The future of this station, and thereby, my position, is on the line, and it's entirely the fault of your stinking husband!"

"I'm sorry, I—"

"The shipments are weeks past due. Here I was laboring under the impression that the builders were to blame, but now I discover that isn't the case." The general leaned down until she was all but nose-to-nose with Delia. "I won't be made a fool of on my station."

"I'm not trying to make a fool of you! I haven't even heard from William in weeks."

"And why is that? So that you can keep your nasty little habit of breaking into classified areas a secret?"

"No, it's because our careers are separate, they don't intersect. If I used my influence to secure deals for him—"

"Haven't you, though?" The general said with a sneer. "He sure as hell wouldn't have access to this station if you weren't here, now would he? Yet here he was, staying just long enough to assure me that this would be the best deal for the expansion. How very convenient."

Delia's jaw was clamped shut with anxiety. What could she even say that would calm the general's temper? No doubt William had gotten mixed up in something again, and now she'd have to pay the price for it.

"Well?" General Fineglass prompted. "What do you have to say for yourself?"

"I can only say that I do not control my husband, ma'am. He makes his own choices, and I make mine."

"Doesn't sound like much of a marriage then, does it? Mine thought he could do as he liked when I was stationed out here. He soon discovered that wasn't the case." The general narrowed her eyes. "I know a marriage of convenience when I see one, Dodson."

"You've got it all wrong, General. We have a mutual partnership—"

"Bullshit."

"My relationship is none of your business."

"No, but missing parts I've already spent half our yearly budget on *are* my business, wouldn't you agree?"

Delia swallowed hard. "Yes," she admitted.

"You're going to get him to find what he promised, what he is contractually obliged to send, or I'm going to toss you into the brig until they can drag him in for questioning. How does that sound?"

"I haven't been able to get a hold of him. My letters have gone unanswered, except for one which he sent last month."

"Show it to me."

"It's private, I—"

"*Now.*"

Opening the drawer of her desk, Delia retrieved the letter. Before she could offer it to the general, she snatched it, tearing a piece of the corner, and the tiny piece fluttered easily to the ground. "It's not much," Delia said. "He's been busy, he said."

"There must be more than this. He said the parts would be arriving a month ago, Dodson. Where are they?"

"I don't know!" Delia shouted, her voice strangled and tight. "I don't even know who his contact is, he never told me!"

"When did you last write to him?"

"Shortly after this. I didn't receive a reply to that or the others I wrote."

General Fineglass' mouth twisted into a snarl. "Maybe he's trying to destroy us both. What a coup for a little snake like him."

"He wouldn't do that to me."

"We're about to find out."

"What?"

"Come on," the general spat, grabbing Delia by her arm with such force, she could feel a nasty bruise already forming beneath her skin.

"Don't take me to the brig!" Delia pleaded. "I'll write to him again, or—or I'll get on a transport back to Gamma-3 and find him for you!"

"And let the both of you slip through my fingers? Not a chance in any hell, Ms. Dodson."

"I didn't do anything wrong!"

"Guilt by association," the general said, dragging her down the corridor. "And by my measure, a marriage is a hell of an association to have, no matter how desperately you try to distance yourself from it."

"Ma'am, please! I'll do anything, please—"

"Maybe now you'll learn that you should choose your associates more carefully, and stop cavorting around with any two-bit conman who will have you."

Panicked tears flowed freely from Delia's eyes, her nose running, her throat choked with dread. She'd die out here. The general would starve her in a cell, and shove her cold corpse out an airlock, just like they said they'd done to Thomas. "Please!" she shouted again, desperate now. "I promise, I'll pay back the cost—"

"You wouldn't earn that in three lifetimes."

Delia tried again to wrench her arm away, but the general held it firm in her grip. How many credits had William taken? Why hadn't he told her? The pit in her stomach sank deeper, dragging her further into despair. "Please," she whispered.

"Pick your feet up and walk properly. I'm in no mood to drag you, and if you force me to carry you, I can promise that you won't enjoy that outcome."

"Don't take me to the brig. Please, ma'am, General—I'll do anything, I—"

The general swept her off her feet as though she weighed no more than a child, throwing her over her shoulder, carrying her down the long, twisting corridor before stopping at a steel gate, rusted at the handle. "Get in."

"What?"

General Fineglass shoved her towards the door. "Get. In."

"But this is the wire room."

"Very astute of you, Ms. Dodson. Now open the door and get inside."

Delia did as she was told, her hands shaking. "What now?"

"Sit down."

"Is this because you can't keep prisoners in the brig?"

The general's head jerked back. "Who told you that?"

"An MPO," Delia lied.

"Which one?"

"I don't know his name."

"Useless, gods-damned—enough. We'll discuss my incompetent troops in a moment." She pointed at the brass keys on the desk, each one labeled with a letter, and a few on the end with various punctuations. "You're going to send him an urgent wire."

"Oh."

"Why you haven't done that before now is a mystery to me."

Delia ran her fingers over the buttons. "I—we can't afford it. Sending wires from here back to Gamma-3 is expensive."

"Given the pile of Coalition credits he's currently sitting on, I would venture to say that *he* very much *can*."

"What if he doesn't respond?"

"Oh, I think that he will."

"What should I say?"

The general shrugged, in an almost sarcastic manner. "Tell him the truth, for all I care. That you're being held hostage by big, bad, General Fineglass, and that she's going to throw you into the brig until those parts arrive. Tell him that unless he has a very good reason as to why they've not yet arrived,

I'll let the overseer take the late fee out of your flesh."

"Okay," Delia whispered, typing carefully, her fingers moving in a methodical motion over the keys.

Dear William, she began, the lump in her throat swelling until it almost hurt to breathe. She typed out the message, doing her best to hold back the imminent tears. *Please respond promptly,* she ended the letter, and sent it.

"And now we wait to see if your dashing prince writes back to save you from my clutches."

"How long will it take to reach Gamma-3?"

"A matter of minutes. The real question is, how long will it take him to respond? Assuming he hasn't already skipped town with his pile of stolen gold, that is."

An hour passed in stoic silence, Delia chewing the nail on her thumb back to the quick, until it was shredded and bleeding.

"It's not looking good for you, Ms. Dodson, is it? How frightfully terrible for you." The general sidled up to the side of the desk and leaned against it. "Who else might he care enough about to respond? How about family? His esteemed mother, perhaps."

Delia shook her head. "His family disowned him years ago."

"*What?*"

"They didn't make it public, and they lied to the press when it came up in interviews. They didn't want it to inspire gossip. Or headlines."

"Why would they do that? Just walk out on—on family, like that?"

"I don't know. He never told me," she lied. Telling the truth would only make things worse; the admission that William frequently found himself the victim of poor investment advice wasn't going to help. "I'd always assumed it was a difference of opinion."

"You know something you're not telling me."

"I am telling you everything that I know."

"If that was true, then he would have responded by now. Yet, here we are, sitting in this cramped room, waiting for your beloved to at least try to keep you from the lion's jaws." The general gave a terrifying, wide smile. "It's me. I'm the lion."

"I assumed as such." Delia chewed on her thumbnail again. "How long are you going to keep me here?"

"We'll give your man one more hour. How about that? And then you can join your—that is, and then you can enjoy your time in the brig, Councilor Tarand or no."

"What if he responds later? Maybe he's at a show, or—"

"I guess we'll just have to find out, won't we?"

"This isn't my fault!" Delia protested. "I don't have the first idea of what he's been up to down there!"

"Then we discover that together. I'm in no mood for whining or pitiful displays of pathetic begging. He made a deal, and now he has to answer some hard questions about it. This isn't personal, Ms. Dodson. Anyone else in your position would be treated exactly the same."

"I doubt that," Delia spat, tired of the threats and mistreatment. "If I was the overseer's daughter, maybe, or your family, I wouldn't be sitting in this chair waiting for a death sentence."

"The overseer's daughter wouldn't be running around, married to a conman, now would she? And I have no family, so that supposition is moot."

Delia raised her chin in defiance. "Don't you, though?"

"No. My parents died five years ago in a steamcar accident."

"Oh. I'm... sorry."

"I doubt that very much." The general checked her pocket watch and frowned. "It's not looking very good for you, Ms. Dodson."

"He'll reply, just give him a chance. William wouldn't leave me high and dry like this."

"I doubt *that* very much, too."

Despite her confidence in William's moral compass, doubt began to seep in at the edges, lightly rimmed with despair. If he had forsaken her, thrown her to the wolves... well, she'd probably die on this station. Could she even blame him, after years of keeping up appearances, to aim for the lofty goals of power and influence? Her jaw set firm. Yes. She could.

"The bastard had better, or I'll haunt him into an early grave," she muttered.

Fineglass laughed. "I don't, however, doubt *that*." She cracked her knuckles one by one, each joint making a soft pop. "What you have yet to learn about the Coalition, Delia, is that we don't allow this sort of thing to go on. Can you imagine the unadulterated chaos if we let contractors who ran off with huge sums of credits go unpunished?"

"Does this happen often?"

The general cracked another knuckle. "Not anymore, it doesn't."

The machine whirred softly, the keys tapping out a message inside that they couldn't yet see. Delia didn't allow herself to hope that it was William. Every letter printed within was slower than the last, time dragging out with excruciating length.

Delia snatched the letter from the tray before it floated to the ground, scanning it for only a split second before Fineglass pulled it from her grasp.

"I think you'll find that this is for me," she said coldly. "Ah. He claims that the transport was delayed at Nox Beacon. A likely story, indeed."

"You can verify that, surely, with the port authority there."

"Why would the port authority be holding up goods and cargo destined for a military base?" The general asked in a rhetorical fashion. "They wouldn't. This is nothing more than a clever ploy to buy you some time outside the bars of the brig." The general tore the message into pieces before dropping each one into the waste basket, letting them flutter down before settling atop a mountain of discarded messages.

"I suggest you do verify it," Delia challenged, "I think you will find it is the truth. William wouldn't do something like this." She frowned. "In truth, General, he isn't clever enough."

Fineglass barked a laugh. "Those are the first honest words out of your mouth all day, Dodson."

"Am I free to leave?"

"For now. But I will be watching you, and rest assured, if those parts aren't where he said they will be, then your ass isn't long for freedom. Do we understand one another? Is that clear?"

Delia nodded. "Crystalline."

"Good." The door slammed behind the general, and Delia stood, her legs still shaking, now from hunger, too. Protein bricks never quite filled that hole, and left her perpetually hungry.

Her hand on the doorknob, the wire machine began to whirr again. Delia looked around and glanced down the corridor, but no one was there. General Fineglass must have kicked out the regular operator, the one responsible for censoring any incoming transmissions.

Hell, she was already in trouble, why not stay for a little bit more? The page slid off the receiving tray and lilted towards the floor, listing back and forth in the air. She caught it just before it reached the ground. Another message from William.

Dearest,

I'm sorry about this. It's all a misunderstanding, I assure you. I know this message will be censored, so I can't give you any more details than that right now.

Delia frowned. Gods be damned, of course he'd anticipate a censor. He might be an easy mark, but he wasn't that foolish.

I can say that my new business partner is... well, to be frank with you, my love, he is everything I have ever wanted in a business partner. He is kind, and considerate, and has helped me broker this and other deals throughout the Near Systems that will pull us closer to our goals.

She narrowed her eyes. Business partner?

In fact, I dare say that he and I share a connection not unlike yours with that old school friend of yours. I won't share her name here for propriety's sake.

A rock fell into Delia's stomach. No wonder he hadn't been writing. No wonder he never sent her the parcel that he promised. He was in love.

Please don't be angry with me, Dearest, you know how these things are. We've been spending a great deal of time together working on these deals, and, dare I say, it turns out we are quite compatible in every way. I never thought I would find a business partner so well-suited. We can talk about it all in due course, but for now, keep your chin up, and remember that you are on a small ship, with many eyes. I love you, even still. Yours, William.

Delia read the letter once more, and then a third time, memorizing it.

Then, she shredded it into fine strips, and then tiny squares, and pushed them to the bottom of the waste basket. Something like anger, or perhaps anticipation, burned inside of her. It was obvious he wanted her to stick to their bargain, even as he created a little love nest for himself and this new business partner, whoever in hells he was.

"No," she said aloud, closing the door behind her. "I'm done with that, now."

Chapter 30

Rosie opened her door to find Delia, her face flushed, her eyes glistening with tears. "Dee?" she asked. "What's wrong? What happened?"

"Rose…"

"Come in, don't stand out there in the corridor, someone might see—"

"What if I said that I didn't care anymore?"

"I'd ask how you managed to smuggle whiskey aboard the station." Rosie closed the door and leaned against it, her brow furrowed. "What's gotten into you?"

"You."

Rosie laughed. "What is that supposed to mean?"

"I know that you don't want this—me—anymore, and I know that I deserve that," Delia said, reaching out for Rosie before pulling back, tentative, almost shy. "I know that I ruined whatever life we might have had, once."

"Why are you saying these things?"

"I never stopped thinking about you, Rosie. Every day we've been apart has been like an ache in my chest. I thought about you in every moment, I yearned for you. I built a wall inside myself to block out the pain. But the moment I saw you here on this station, that all started to fall away." Delia reached out again, resting her fingertips on Rosie's hips, her touch so light it was almost like a summer breeze.

"Dee…" Rosie started, but her words faltered. She never had been very good at resisting her, not when they were teenagers at school, and not when they were starting careers a decade ago. The passion, and the insistent hunger, pulled her to the brink every time.

"I won't, if you don't want me to."

"Won't what?" Rosie whispered.

"Kiss you."

"Only if you can promise that you won't leave again."

"I promise that I'll do whatever you want until the end of time," Delia breathed, pressing herself closer, pulling at Rosie's hips. "I want you more than I have ever wanted anything in my entire life."

"You are an impossible woman to resist," Rosie said, tilting Delia's chin upwards, before kissing her soft and slow, their lips lingering. "I can't decide if coming out here was my best idea, or my worst." Her hands found Delia's waist, and then the waistband of her trousers, where she rested her thumbs while pulling her closer.

Delia's hands drifted down, and then snaked up Rosie's skirts, running her hands over the soft, dimpled flesh, pulling a quiet gasp from her lips. What could be more all-encompassing than the feel of the only woman you'd ever really loved, pressing, and pulling, and begging without words to be swallowed whole?

"We should be careful," Rosie said, finally coming up for air between kisses. "What if—"

"Shh," Delia hushed, pressing a finger to Rosie's lips before letting her own rest against Rosie's neck, kissing gently, her hot, eager breath panting against bare skin.

Small moans emitted from Rosie's throat, unintentional yet unrestrained. She'd waited years for Delia to return to her, and now they were together again, after over ten years apart. Her flesh hungered for touch, for the sweet, delicate tracing of fingertips on skin, lips against collarbones, the insistent, needy pulse between her thighs. "The problem with all the others was that they were never you," she whispered, almost involuntarily.

Delia responded with another kiss, each one deeper and more desperate than the last. Her hands pulled at the hem of Rosie's skirts.

"I wish I could just melt into you," Rosie said, gasping from the surprise of the intensity and the temptation of Delia's body, pressed up against her, a sweet yet dangerous crush that threatened to throw her out into the vast, endless space between love and wanting.

Delia's hands on Rosie's thighs now, skin on skin, gently grasping her flesh greedily, a long-buried hunger finally set free, that might yet devour them both, if they weren't careful. Her palms slid across smooth skin with a small growl of wanting.

Her breath quick and shallow, Rosie closed her eyes, letting herself fall into what was about to happen, anticipating the touch, the joining back together, and the plunge over a cliff of desire. No one had ever known exactly what she wanted more than Delia, and nothing had ever changed about that. She'd never believed in fate before, but if this wasn't fate, then what was it?

Delia pushed closer, pulling at fabric, whispering, "Rosie Gordon, you are all I ever needed in this world."

With three sharp raps on the door, they sprang apart.

"Um, who is it?" Rosie managed to utter, pulling the green fabric of her dress back down, smoothing the wrinkles.

"It is Overseer Allemande. Is someone in there with you? Open this door at once!"

"I, er—"

"Now!"

Rosie gestured for Delia to hide under the bed and draped blankets over the top as she opened the door. "What can I do for you, ma'am? Unfortunately, I am still locked out of the kitchen, so I can't—"

"No, no, I don't need *that*. Who's in here? I'm sure I don't need to remind you about workplace dalliances, Ms. Gordon."

"Of course not, ma'am. There's no one in here except me."

"Are you sure about that?"

"Yes."

Allemande's permanent frown grew deeper and more discontented. "Of course."

"Was there something else?"

"Clearly. Do you think I wander around this station nightly, looking to police my employees? Do you think I don't have anything better to do than that?"

"Definitely not, ma'am."

"I am looking for Ms. Dodson. Have you seen her?"

Rosie smiled prettily. "No, I haven't. Why do you ask?"

"I am told you two are... associates. Old friends. I thought maybe, if she was ignoring her duties, it was perhaps to do with an outdated school friendship."

"Is she late for something?"

"I shall discuss these matters with her alone, and no one else," the overseer said in an icy tone that made Rosie's room frosty with threats. "She had a meeting with General Fineglass earlier. An important meeting that I was incorrectly left out of. Scheduling error. I need to discuss some very important things with Ms. Dodson, so if you do see her, tell her I am waiting in my office."

"Of course," Rosie repeated, smiling.

A slow, seething sneer grew on the overseer's face. "Get out of my way."

"Ma'am?"

"Move."

"I can assure you, there is nothing in my quarters worth looking at." Though her face was calm, a swarm of panic nested at the base of her skull. "Just my clothes, and some stationery to write home."

"You don't fool me, Ms. Gordon. You must think that I am some kind of easily led child to not see what is going on here."

"I assure you, I don't know what you are talking about."

Allemande swept past her and into the room. "Insubordination, that's what I see in here. Where is your regulation apron? Your gloves?"

"They're—"

"In here?" the overseer cried, yanking open the door to the tiny closet.

"—in the kitchen," Rosie finished. "Which I am locked out of, on account of Councilor Tarand."

"You should be keeping them in your quarters."

"Coalition policy—"

"You think to speak to *me* about policy?" Allemande asked. "I *write* the policy. Rules and regulations here and in my sector do not come into force without my say so."

Rosie swallowed hard. "It is to help prevent food-borne illness, ma'am. Far easier to clean the hard counters in the kitchen, than all the soft furnishings of a bedroom."

"Aha!" Allemande cried, wrenching open a trunk, and then frowning.

"Those are my underthings," Rosie replied flatly. "Is there something you are looking for?"

"I know she's in here."

"I haven't seen Delia Dodson all day. In fact, I've done nothing other than to work on some methodology to increase both efficiency and supply management by coordinating recipes, if you'd like to—"

"*No.* Definitely not."

"Then I'm afraid I can't help you, because that is all I have done today."

"Far from efficient."

"I would hasten to agree with you, ma'am, but without access to the kitchen, what I can accomplish is frustratingly limited."

"You will be reassigned to a cleaning detail until Councilor Tarand departs."

"But—"

"That is my final word on the matter, Ms. Gordon," Allemande said, aiming a kick under the bed with the toe of her boot. Much to Rosie's surprise, there was no whimper of pain, or any sign of a soft whump where foot met flesh. "Report to the starboard side main corridor at midnight sharp. You will be provided a mop and a bucket with which to shine the floors until I can see my own reflection in them, and you will be sure to be finished long before the rest of the ship awakens for the day."

"Ma'am, I—"

"I never should have taken you on board here," the overseer sneered. "Nothing but a lazy, entitled brat, using her position as the cook to obtain favor and extra rations. Oh, yes, I've seen it all before, with people like you.

From your meager background."

"I am not afraid of work, ma'am."

"Excellent! Then I am sure this will be of absolutely no consequence to you. Good day." She swept out of the room as quickly as she had entered, and Rosie waited until the sharp clicks from the heels of her boots faded down the corridor.

"Are you alright?" she uttered, reaching under the bed to help Delia up.

"Mostly. She landed that kick right between my ribs, feels like."

"I was so surprised you didn't scream."

"Trust me, I'd end up screaming far more if I'd let her know that I was in here."

"Yeah, poor Thomas." Rosie smacked herself on the forehead. "Dee, I forgot! I found them. I got a note a couple nights ago that said to check behind the atrium, and there they were, in a weird, dark little room."

"Why didn't you tell me?"

"I tried! I couldn't find you!"

"How is he? Is he okay?" Delia asked.

Rosie grimaced. "He's alive, at least, but he doesn't look good."

"Did he say anything?"

"No, not much. As you can probably imagine, Josie is doing most of the talking."

Delia shook her head, brushing back a loose curl. "So, the atrium. It's good that we found them, but who do you think is sending the notes?"

"I thought maybe Emeline, but now... now I'm not so sure."

Delia sat on the bed, tucking a few loose curls back into their pins. "It worries me, Rosie. Makes me think all of this is some kind of elaborate setup."

"Set up? For who? Why?"

"Why would someone be telling us this stuff? Who even has that level of access?"

"That's why I thought Emeline." Rosie sat next to Delia on the bed, snaking her arm around her waist. "It's going to be hard to do anything while Tarand is on the station, and I'm afraid it will get even harder once she's gone. They're going to have the cargo bay locked down so tight, a roach won't be able to get in."

"And we'll still have to deal with Josie," Delia said with a grimace. "No doubt she's being a real peach."

"The peachiest. I feel bad for Thomas, being locked up in there with her."

"How's he doing? Is he alright?"

"I've been taking them extra bricks. No doubt Allemande will notice the discrepancy, but that's a problem for another day."

"It's a shame you never learned to pilot," Delia teased. "Would be much easier to steal a ship."

"Oh, it would be a walk in the park to waltz onto a cargo vessel, commandeer it without anyone noticing, and smuggle five people off the station, absolutely." Rosie smirked. "I get too airsick to be a pilot. The trip here from Nox Beacon, I spent the entire time in the washroom revisiting my breakfast."

"We've gotta figure something out, Rose. I'm worried—well, I'm worried that Thomas won't make it much longer."

"I know. At least, for now, he's getting a little more sustenance, even if it's bricks."

"Who *invented* them? They're absolutely vile."

Rosie snorted. "Someone who hates joy."

"And cake."

"And lightly roasted potatoes, seasoned with—"

"No," Delia groaned, falling back onto the bed. "Don't. I'm hungry enough as it is. I'm almost ready to start gnawing on the walls. At least they might have more flavor than bricks."

"Someday," Rosie said, kissing her lightly on the nose, "I will make you a feast."

"Yeah?"

"Promise. I always loved cooking for you, Dee. You were always highly appreciative, as well as honest."

"Just don't make... gods, what was that thing?"

"An aspic. They're beautiful!"

"Put it in a museum then. Just not in my mouth."

Rosie laid next to her and sighed. "Do you think we'll ever get off this station? What happens now?"

"I don't know. We have to help Thomas, but it just seems impossible. We'd have to... I don't know, incapacitate the entire station. All the guards. Fineglass." Delia groaned. "Allemande."

"What if we could?"

"Could what?"

"Incapacitate everyone on the station."

"What, are you hiding several weapons under those skirts?" Delia asked with a laugh.

Rosie arched an eyebrow. "I don't know, you tell me, you were the one having a thorough inspection."

"Yes, uh..." Delia's face grew as red as a beet. "No weapons, then. What did you have in mind?"

"Food poisoning."

"Rosie!"

"Not fatal, just... uncomfortable."

"Uncomfortable how?"

"Let's just say there aren't enough facilities on this station to support that level of... well. You get the picture."

Delia leaned in close, whispering. "How?"

"Undercooked kidney beans."

"Is it really so simple?"

"On a station where everyone is ready to start roasting their own boots in order to eat something other than those damned bricks, it just might be. I'd have to get access to the kitchen, though... and keep the plan away from Allemande."

"I think we could manage that. And then what?"

"The loading bay is going to get locked down after Tarand leaves. Fewer deliveries, almost no ships heading out other than the short-range research shuttles."

"So..." Delia puffed out her cheeks and tilted her head to look at Rosie.

"You're telling me our best plan is going to be to smuggle four people off this station on a High Council transport?"

"Six."

"*Six?*"

Rosie ticked the names off on her fingers. "Thomas, Josie, her two crew, you, me—"

"Whoa, hang on there, Gordon. Why in hells are *we* smuggling *ourselves* off?"

"Well, after the entire station gets food poisoning, it's not going to take a genius to figure that one out, is it? Even if I request a transfer, there's no way it would come in time before it became obvious - and even if it did, they'd know exactly where to find me."

"Oh. Right, of course."

"If we do this, I'm a fugitive, just like Thomas, just like the pirates."

"You'd do that for Thomas? For me?" Delia brushed a hair from Rosie's face.

"I'd do anything for you, you fool. That's always how it's been."

"But my job, everything I've worked at..."

"Is it worth staying? Really? Canned propaganda? You're better than that."

Delia frowned. "If I run, I'm giving up all of that. Every opportunity, all the work will have been.... Been for nothing."

"Drip-feeding information to the rebels for the better part of five years is hardly nothing. Think how many deaths, how many imprisonments may have been avoided—"

"What if you go with the others, and I'll stay here, just for a little while longer, just until the station is complete—"

"Once the station is complete, they'll be wanting a new head of program-ming out here."

"Yes."

"And..." Rosie sighed. "And you want it to be you. Of course you would."

"I could do a lot of good here, Rose. I could have more control over the narrative."

"Do you really think Allemande or Fineglass would allow that? It's still a Coalition station, Dee, hardly hard-hitting investigative journalism. That hasn't existed for years."

"Maybe I could be the one to bring it back into the fold."

"Maybe. Or maybe not."

"You don't think I could do it?" Delia asked, a sharp edge to her tone.

"I don't think anyone can overcome what this has all become. The best we can do is try to bear it the best we can. Why do you think I even ended up all the way out here? After everything that happened back home, I couldn't stand to be there anymore. I wanted to get as far away as—"

"You used to have faith in me."

Rosie blinked and then pulled away. "I've always had faith in you. But some things are bigger than we are. Some things can't be torn down from inside the structure. You have to... I don't know. Blow it up. From outside."

"I'm closer to the information here."

"Information you're not allowed to disseminate."

"Maybe I could be another secret note passer, slipping information out."

"If we do this, I want you to come with me."

Delia shook her head. "I can't, Rosie. I have to see this through. Giving up now would mean the last decade was a waste. That I had accomplished nothing."

"When you came into this room not fifteen minutes ago, you swore to me that you wouldn't leave me again."

"Rosie, some things are more important than... well, I don't know, whatever this is!"

"What made you come here tonight?"

"I missed you."

"Tell me the truth. I deserve that, at the very least."

Delia sat up, tucking her shirt back in, trying in vain to smooth out the wrinkles. "That is the truth."

"Then what is all this business about Allemande looking for you? What happened with Fineglass?"

"It's nothing. Just disagreements about the broadcast scripts. The two of them are nearly always at each other's throats, you know, and—"

"Don't *lie* to me, Delia Forrest. Not now. Not after everything you put me through back then." Anger flushed Rosie's cheeks, and she turned away to hide it and the tears threatening at the corners of her eyes. "I want to know."

"I didn't want to worry you by telling you that the general dragged me to the wire room." Delia sighed. "There was a parts contract. William organized it with Fineglass when he was here, said he had some contact back on Gamma-3 who had a warehouse full of the stuff for cheap. The parts never showed up. Fineglass got angry. She threatened me. But it's all okay, they're just delayed."

"Do you really believe that?"

Delia gave a sad laugh. "No. But I trust him, even still. I don't think he'd do anything to put me in danger."

"He might not, but this contact of his might. Do you even know his name?"

"No. Some *business partner* he's found."

"Right. So you came to my door, begged me to kiss you, because of a parts deal? You were ready to follow me to moons and back, and now you're rethinking?" Rosie rubbed at her temple. "Something isn't adding up."

"He met someone. This contact, apparently, they hit it off. He's in love, they're gallivanting around doing gods know what, and he wanted to make sure, before he left, that I would be... careful."

"Careful?"

"Around you."

Something like a knife twisted in Rosie's gut. "I see."

"I care about you, Rosie Posy. I just—"

"So what you're saying to me right now is that..." she blinked, letting tears cascade down her pink cheeks. "Is that you only decided to choose me when he wasn't an option anymore. Your aesthetic marriage. You didn't... you didn't choose me over him. I was the second-place prize after you decided to be done with him."

"Of course I chose you over him! I'm here now, aren't I?"

"And telling me that after I give up everything to save your friend, you're going to let me board that *fucking* transport alone."

"Thomas will die if we don't get him out of here."

"What about me, Delia? Don't you want—you know what? Forget it. Get out."

Chapter 31

Delia buried her head in her hands. How the hell had everything fallen apart so fast? It was only a couple of short months ago that William was promising her he'd be back soon, that this new business venture of his was going to solve all their problems, take them to the top of the heap. He was so busy trying to prove his parents wrong, that he'd proved that they were right all along, and now she was caught in the middle.

She swore under her breath and pinched at the taut skin on her arm. It was time to snap out of it before they all wound up dead. Her pathetic pity party wasn't going to save Thomas, nor was it going to solve the problem that William had created. Poor, sweet Will. Such an easy mark. So desperate to get rich quick that he never stopped to consider that someone was getting rich off of *him* instead.

Smuggling Thomas, Josie, and her crew onto Tarand's ship was their best option. No matter how many times she tried to work through the problem, making crude sketches in her notepad, she always came back to this. Cargo transports were notorious for getting diverted, spending months taking the slower flight lanes to allow the faster transports to pass them by. There was no way four of them would be able to exist on a ship that long without being found. It was going to be hard enough to do it for only a few days.

Tarand's ship was heading for Delta-4. Delia had overheard Olivia demanding extra patrol ships from General Fineglass, outraged that they only had short-range shuttles out this far. The ship was state-of-the-art, making long journeys in mere fractions of the time. It would take three days to reach Delta-4 from Turas-Mara.

She'd need help - especially now that Rosie wouldn't even speak to her.

The station had a strange current of energy in the air. It wasn't electrical, nor was it excitement. Whatever it was, it felt dangerous and unpredictable. Delia closed the door to her quarters and wandered down the corridor that led to the stairs, looking as nonchalant and unsuspicious as possible. It didn't matter much—almost every one of the guards was barely awake, struggling not to fall asleep standing up. Nearly a week of triple shifts had exhausted them all.

She crept around the final corner and silently celebrated when she saw that Abara was on duty at the top of the stairs. "Abara!" she whispered. "Wake up!"

"What?" they snapped awake, hand on their gun. "What happened?"

"Relax, it's just me. No need for firearms."

"It's almost midnight, Dodson. What do you want?"

"I need your help."

"I'm not letting you down into the loading bay."

"I don't need you to."

Abara lifted one eyebrow in suspicion. "Why don't I believe you?"

"I need you to let someone *else* down there."

"I knew it. No. Absolutely not. I'm barely keeping the overseer off my ass for bringing up the crates of bricks for the cook to hand out. Said we should have prepared for this and stored them elsewhere, as though any of us knew beforehand that someone from the High gods-damned Council was going to show up."

"Come on, Abara, please? I'll do *anything*."

"Whatever you're up to is bound to land my ass in front of the judge." They fumbled with the pocket of their uniform. "Go back to your quarters, Delia."

"It's a matter of life or death."

"For who?"

"I can't tell you."

"You're a real piece of work, you know that? Asking me to put my career on the line for a favor that you can't even give me details about. Does anyone else fall for this bullshit, or just me?"

Delia recoiled. "It's helping a friend. It's not like I'm asking you to help me smuggle pirates aboard."

"No." Abara narrowed their eyes. "But something tells me you want me to help you smuggle pirates *off*."

"Not just pirates." She looked both ways before she continued. "My friend, Thomas. Did you know him?"

"Yeah. Nice guy. Shame what happened."

"He's not dead."

"Piss off."

"It's true!" Delia insisted. "They've been keeping him in the brig for months. He's all torn up, the gods only know what they've done to him down there, and he's wasting away."

Abara searched her face. "Is this the truth?"

"I swear on my own mother's grave, I wouldn't lie. Not about this."

"Why would they keep him aboard?"

"From what I can tell, to stay in line with Coalition regulations on... less methodical means of information extraction."

"Torture."

"Yes."

"Everyone knows the inspectors do as they like, regardless of those laws. Why bother here?"

"Because some former inspectors are trying to keep their noses clean," Delia answered. "In order to keep climbing the ladder of success."

"This could all be a lie to manipulate me into admitting something, or to being an accessory to a crime. I'm barely keeping out of trouble as it is, with all of the things I've seen lately." Abara shook their head. "No. I'm sorry, Delia, I can't help you. What I saw back on that mining asteroid—I can't."

"Are you going to report me?"

"Should I?"

"I guess that depends on where your loyalties lie."

"My loyalties lie with the Coalition," Abara answered. "You know I can't say anything other than that. None of us can. Not without consequences."

"He'll die, Abara."

"His family already thinks he's dead, anyway. Maybe that's just how it needs to be. We don't even know what he did to land him in the brig in the first place."

Delia grimaced.

"Unless we... do?" Abara asked. "What aren't you telling me?"

"I can't say, I really can't—it's mostly supposition, anyway—"

"What in all the gods' names are you mixed up in, Delia?"

"I don't even know anymore. I just know that I... I don't want to see my friend die. Not when I had the chance to do something about it."

"I can't help you."

"But—"

"I can't help you," Abara repeated, their voice barely above a whisper now, "but there is a cleaning cart that comes down this corridor early in the morning. It's large, for bed linens. It heads down to the next deck for cleaning. If someone—or someones, were hidden in there, I doubt I would notice."

"Thank you, *thank you!*"

"I don't know why you're thanking me, Dodson. I already said that I couldn't help you. Now, piss off back to your quarters before I call for backup and have you escorted there."

"Thank you," she whispered again.

"I mean it."

"Alright, alright, I'm going!"

"And Dodson—I don't know what you're planning, or how you're planning to carry this off, but I have to tell you—even if you get him off this deck, I doubt you'll get him off this station." Abara tipped their cap before leaning back against the wall. "And we never had this conversation."

*   *   *

"Psst. Hey," Delia whispered through the small slat in the door. "Are you still in there?"

"Of course we're still in here, you pineapple. Where did you think we'd go? Out for a leisurely stroll?" Josie spat back. "Your little girlfriend hasn't managed to get the key yet."

"She's not my—"

"Sure, sure, whatever you have to tell yourself to sleep at night, darling. Now, get us the hell out of here already!"

"I'm working on it. I have a—"

Josie groaned loud enough to echo down the corridor. "You're so *tedious*, you know that? I'd have found four ways to escape already, if I wasn't trapped in here."

"But you are, so you're going to have to keep your damned voice down unless you want to get caught."

"Why, what are they going to do, throw me in the brig? Oh, look! I'm already there!"

"Just shut up for a moment!" Delia snapped. "There's a laundry cart near the stairs, that—"

"Find me a gun, that's all I need."

"You're not getting a gun. Not now, anyway."

Josie pressed her face to the slat. "I bet you've never even fired a weapon. You're too *soft*."

"I'm a broadcaster, a journalist, not a soldier."

"Just as I thought, then. Another weak excuse for a rescue."

"I'd fire you out the airlock myself, given the opportunity," Delia hissed. "I am doing this for Thomas. Thomas? Are you alright?"

He gave a weak, breathy cough. "I'm alright. As much as I can be, anyway."

"There's a laundry cart," she began again, "near the back stairs that lead down to the loading bay. I'm going to find a way to get all of you on it."

"All of us in one cart?" Josie interjected. "That's a recipe for obvious disaster."

"We'll take two trips, that should be sufficient. The guards... won't see us."

"Who'd you bribe?"

Delia sighed in exasperation. "No one. Shut up. We'll get all of you to the loading bay that way."

"And then what, genius?"

"Then we smuggle you onto Tarand's transport, you keep quiet for a few days, and when it docks on Delta-4, you carefully make your way off the transport and into the crowd."

"That's got to be the most ridiculous, foolhardy, fatal plan I've ever heard." Josie laughed. "I fucking love it. If we survive, it will be the best story I've ever told."

"I'm so glad you approve, given your obvious myriad of choices right now," Delia said in a flat, unimpressed tone. "Thomas, when you get to Delta-4, I'll make sure that there will be some credits there in a fake name. You'll use the old pass code to access them. Should be enough to get you passage on a cargo freighter. *Don't* take a transport, they ask too many questions."

"I know, Delia," he answered. "If you—if you really manage to get me out of here, I'll be sure to disappear into the wind. No one will ever hear my name ever again, except as a sad footnote."

"What about your family?"

"They'll be fine. My parents have got my brother and my sister, they aren't alone. It's a good thing I never married that girl back in Skelm, eh?"

"She never liked you much anyways."

"Shame. I liked her well enough."

"You should be holding out for someone who suits you better."

Josie gave an impatient sigh that escaped her lips as a hiss. "Not to break up this little love fest, here, but when can we expect this plan to snap into place? I have places to go, people to see, you know?"

"Councilor Tarand is leaving tomorrow, before lunch. We'll need to get you into those carts at shift change early in the morning."

"And the key?"

"What?"

"The key, brainless. Where are you going to get the *key* to *unlock* the *door*?"

Delia smirked. "Some pirate you are. You can't pick a lock?"

"Not with my elbow, I can't. Shockingly, they didn't allow me to keep my lock picks when they tossed me in the brig."

"Here," Delia said, removing a long pin from her hair. It matched the dark blond of her hair and glinted in the dim light of the empty corridor. "Take this."

"Yeah, that'll do."

"Don't leave until I come for you with the cart. I mean it, Josie."

"That's *Captain* Josie to you, darling."

"Not much of a captain without a ship, are you? If you try to bust out of here, they'll shoot you on sight, do you hear me? You'll ruin this for yourself and for your crew. And Thomas."

Josie snorted. "Don't get your bloomers in a bunch. I heard you the first time. You'd better hope I can get the door open, or your precious Thomas isn't going anywhere, either."

"Somehow I get the feeling that you've broken more challenging locks with less."

"I'm not much of a lock pick, but I think the motivation of getting the hell out of here, combined with the crushing boredom of this shithole might well do the trick."

"Good. Once you're on board Tarand's ship, you'll have to shut up, so I suggest you get all your mouthing off out of your system before then."

Josie flicked the hair pin over her shoulder. "Here, Dirk. You were always a better lock pick than me, anyhow."

"Aye," he grunted in response.

"Don't think it hasn't dawned on me, Ms. Dodson, that you could have flipped us a pick at any moment, yet you waited until now to grace us with a means of escape."

"You really are a foolish woman, aren't you?" Delia scoffed. "What are you going to do without a weapon, when a dozen MPOs are bearing down on you and what's left of your crew? Ask them politely to let you escape?"

"Wouldn't be the first time that's worked."

"I'll bet."

"What are you suggesting?"

Delia tucked a loose curl behind her ear. "Nothing untoward, just that MPOs in other settlements, well... let's just say they aren't protecting the same kind of stuff we have out here."

"Oh, yeah? What kind of *stuff*?"

"Research. Experiments." She sighed. "Rhodium."

"Rhodium! Here?"

"Not on the station, obviously. A mine they're about to open up on a nearby asteroid. Could be the key to expansion beyond the Rim, if everything they're saying is true."

"We could do with some rhodium, couldn't we, boys?" Josie said with a mischievous laugh.

"Don't get any big ideas, *Captain*. It will be a long while before you get anywhere near your ship again, and by that time, they'll have that place packing more weapons than the Armory on Gamma-3."

"Just get us the hell off this station, Dodson. I'll worry about what comes next."

"Thomas," Delia whispered through the slat. "I'll come back for you later, I promise."

"I know you will," he replied. "You've never let me down before."

"And neither have you."

"Don't make a habit of this, Dee."

Delia's brow furrowed. "A habit of what?"

"Rebellion. It's a slippery slope from helping a friend, to..." he trailed off and rattled the chains at his wrists. "Well, this."

Chapter 32

"Here," an MPO said, tossing a mop at Rosie. "Get going. It might be a small station, but it's a long damn corridor."

"What happened to the rest of the cleaning staff? Shouldn't they be—"

The MPO barked a laugh. "Cleaning staff? Where do you think you are, the Capital? We barely have room for the small teams that are up here, much less a dedicated janitorial staff. It's us who do the cleaning, Chef."

"I'm just the cook."

"And I'm just some poor fool who volunteered to spend two years at the edge of known reality. Doesn't mean that the floors don't need mopping and the toilets don't need scrubbing."

"I'll work faster if you stay out of my way," Rosie grumbled.

"Is this why there are no scraps anymore? No food? You decided your true calling was cleaning up after a bunch of MPOs?"

"The overseer put me on cleaning duty. I don't have access to the kitchen while the High Councilor is on board the station."

"Figures. I only rotated in two weeks ago. I thought maybe it wouldn't be so bad out here, but the only thing I've had is damned protein bricks."

"You get used to it."

"That true?"

Rosie sighed. "No."

"You'd better get to work. I'd hate for you to get written up."

"Thanks. I just—"

The MPO interrupted her by spitting on the floor, the glob of saliva and mucus landing with an unpleasant thwack on the metal floor. "Have fun."

"Disgusting," Rosie muttered, running the mop over the wad of spit, dragging it across the textured ground with limited success. Maybe all MPOs weren't inherently bad, but most of them enjoyed throwing their authority around at the very least.

"You missed a spot," the MPO said with a cackle, now down by the end of the hall. "I'd hate to have to report you to Allemande."

Rosie waved at him, the gesture dripping with sarcasm. "I think she's going to have a lot more to worry about in the next few hours," she mumbled under her breath. She didn't mind cleaning—after all, it was an important part of cooking—but she resented that it was meted out as punishment, and that she was still locked out of the kitchen. Fancy-pants chef was still in there, no doubt making a mess, not putting anything back where she liked it.

Though, if she went through with all this, it might not matter for much longer. Maybe her grandfather had been right about something—there wasn't much point in fighting to get to the top. Not inside the Coalition. It was nothing but inside favors and backroom deals from the top down.

The mop left tiny pools of water on the floor no matter how many times Rosie wrung it out. She had to resort to kneeling down with a cloth to sop it up, and before long, it was soaked through. The water in the bucket was nearly black, just a few feet from where she'd started, proving her theory that mopping was rarely at the top of anyone's priority list aboard this station.

Rosie sighed and wiped her forehead with the back of her hand. She dumped the dirty water down the drain and filled the bucket anew. Without the inbuilt filtration system, there was no way this station could ever run. Mop, dry, dump, refill. It was an endless, grueling cycle, and by the time she reached the end of the main corridor, she wanted to collapse. If the exhaustion didn't kill her, then boredom very well might.

Gods below, but she wished she'd never come out to the Rim in the first place. It seemed like the furthest place she could run to, and yet, she found herself feeling more trapped on Turas-Mara than she ever had back home in Dubhmoor where she grew up.

"Got the early shift, eh?"

"What do you want, Delia?" The question was rhetorical, because it was obvious what Delia wanted.

"I need your help."

"I know."

"It's just, with the patrols, and—"

"Shh. I know. I've already made preparations."

Delia leaned closer. "What kind of... preparations?"

"As we discussed."

"But... how?"

"I'm working on it. Give me time."

"Time, Rosie, we don't *have* time. Tarand leaves today!"

"What is this *we* you're talking about, anyway? You made it very clear that you're not taking part in this... this little *excursion*."

"It's for the greater good."

"It's for *your* greater good. Please stop confusing the two."

Delia reached out and laid a hand on Rosie's arm. "I'm sorry, Posy. I am still trying to work out how to know what's best. Things feel..."

"Complicated?"

"Different."

"Oh yeah?" Rosie asked, dunking the mop back into the bucket. "Different how?"

"I don't know. More dangerous, maybe."

"I imagine that planning a prison break might feel that way, yes."

"You know, I... I didn't think you'd still agree to help me."

"We aren't all heartless monsters, you know." When Delia recoiled from the barbed remark, Rosie sighed again. "I'm sorry. I don't think you're heartless. I just think..." she trailed off for a moment, letting the remains of sentiment hang in the air. "I just think that you have different ideals."

"Ideals?"

"You're more big picture. I'm more about... well, people, I guess. It's why I'm still going to help you. Help Thomas. I couldn't live with myself knowing that I did nothing when I could have."

Delia visibly bristled. "I still care about people."

"I don't want to argue, Dee."

"Do you really think I don't care about people? Why do you think I'm doing *any* of this? Gods, Rose, if I didn't care, I would just—I would just—"

"Just what? Leave me to fend for myself again? Sneak out in the middle of the night?"

"I thought we were past all of that!"

"We were, until you told me that you'd wave goodbye as I folded myself into a cargo crate after doing something for you." Rosie splashed water across the floor. "Again."

"Rose—"

"Stop. I said, I don't want to argue. I don't want that to be my—your—my last memory of us. We're all making our choices, aren't we?"

"So what now?"

"I need to finish my work or they'll know something is up. Move, I need to mop under your boots."

"I talked to Abara."

"So did I."

"You did? When?"

"Earlier, when I got up. They were getting ready to clock out."

"Clock out! But—"

Rosie swished the puddle of dirty water around. "Don't worry, they'll be back on shift when we need to make our move."

"So you know the plan, then?"

"I do. I have to mop the corridors, then I get a break, and that's when I'm going to steal a bag of beans from the kitchen."

"What? How? And... why?"

"The chef in residence usually takes a break after he makes breakfast, and, careless clod that he is, hasn't been closing the padlock all the way. I'll heat them enough to make them palatable and leave the pot in the barracks. Should be enough to buy us time if something goes wrong. Fewer patrols, too."

"Rosie Posy, what would I do without you?"

"The universe will never know, Delia, because I am too much of a silly fool around you." Rosie wiped up the remaining water off the floor, her knees aching from the constant kneeling on the grate floor. "We could never be equals, because I just do whatever I know will make you happy, even if it means... making myself a... fugitive. But this is the last time, I swear it by all the gods, do you hear me? After I'm on that transport—after I leave, I don't ever want to see your face or hear your voice again. I can't handle it."

"But Rosie—"

"No buts. This is how things have to be, now." Rosie pushed a smile across her face, knowing that it was flat and lifeless. "Maybe you'll finally figure out who was writing all those notes. If you do, I'm sure I'll hear all about the big scandal on Turas-Mara Station. Something worth waiting for."

"You know I don't relish staying without you, right? That I'd give anything to join you—"

"We both know that's not true, and it's time we stopped lying about it."

"I'm not lying."

"Go. I'll take care of everything."

Delia chewed on her lip. "What can I do?"

"Creating some kind of diversion would help. Keeping whatever MPOs left on their toes, keeping Allemande and Fineglass away from the loading bay would be the best use of your time."

"So I guess... I guess I won't..."

"Live a good life, Delia," Rosie said, reaching out to squeeze her hand. "I won't ever forget you. If we get caught—if we die—make sure my family knows the truth about what happened. I would want them to be... proud."

"I'm sure they already are."

"I don't know about that."

Delia ran her thumb over the back of Rosie's hand. "And nothing bad is going to happen. It's a foolproof plan."

"Promise me you'll tell them."

"I, uh..." Delia sobered. "I promise."

"Goodbye, Dee."

* * *

Rosie pushed the laundry cart from room to room, collecting linens and depositing fresh ones on the thin, bare mattresses. The management quarters were all the same, small, yet serviceable. She left a tub of under-stewed kidney beans on every desk with a note.

It's not much, but it's better than bricks.

She didn't bother pretending that the food was from anyone else. They'd all know that it was her who had fed everyone toxic food. In a couple of hours, maybe less, depending when they ate it, most people on the station would be grievously indisposed.

Guilt weighed on her even as her cart grew lighter. She never wanted to make anyone sick, but... well, without an extra dose of chaos as they tried to get Thomas off the station, he'd almost certainly be caught. They all would. A shiver skated over her skin, and she shook it off as she pushed the cart into the main barracks.

Here, she left a large pot of the beans in the center of the room, with a stack of plates next to it. The MPOs were the ones they most needed to be occupied as they escaped. She repeated this in the nearby secondary barracks, arranging the pot in the most attractive and tempting manner, not that she need to have bothered. One guard wandered in as she was completing the linens switch and helped herself to a heaping plate.

"The hell is this?" she asked, shoveling a bite into her mouth.

"Not much, but it's better than bricks," Rosie answered in a casual tone, her hands shaking.

"When are you going to get us some real food in here, eh, Cooky? It's better than a brick, but I'd sell my elbows for some nice roasted tofu."

"I'm doing my best. The restrictions and monitoring of ingredients have increased significantly in recent weeks."

267

"Just remember, if you want to survive, you keep us on your side, yeah?" The MPO licked the plate clean. "Don't piss us off."

Rosie smiled. "I'll do my best," she said. No doubt there would be an entire station of enraged MPOs in just a few hours, as soon as they figured out what she'd done. No one would die, but some egos might get decimated in the process.

"Don't forget to get some of this to the corporal. They just left for another double shift. You piss them off, you piss all of us off."

"Uh huh, I got it."

"Abara doesn't take kindly to being left out of the food."

"Don't worry, I have a special portion for Abara."

"I hope that's true. I don't want to hear them bitching all night."

"Mhmm," Rosie murmured, dragging the cart out of the room. She wouldn't miss being around so many MPOs. It was an exhausting experience, having to smile and nod along to veiled threats and demands. They were bored out here, and no one to take it out on other than her and the other civilian builders.

Three more rooms came and went as she drew closer to the atrium. Rosie's heart was already pounding in her chest, and she hadn't even gotten the prisoners in the cart yet. Sweat prickled on her brow.

"Ms. Gordon," General Fineglass boomed, coming around the corner. "What are you doing on cleaning detail?"

"Overseer Allemande assigned me."

"Of course she did."

"She thought that as I don't have kitchen duties right now—"

"Yes, yes, I understand. She thought that undermining my authority by taking away the punishments I'm able to mete out for my troops was the best solution."

"Ma'am?"

Fineglass sighed, towering over her. "It's fine, Gordon, just carry on as you were. I don't have time nor the energy to argue with her on this right now, not while Councilor Tarand is still aboard. Gods be damned."

"Understood, General."

The general paused, her brow furrowed. "What can I smell?"

Rosie froze. "It's, uh… it's nothing." Poisoning a general was bound to land her in the hottest water if she was caught.

"Do you have food? Illicit food?"

"No?"

"Are you feeding my troops, Gordon?"

"Uh—"

"Good. They can't exist on bricks alone. I know, I know what I told you—but they've all been pulling triples for nearly a week. I'll have a damned mutiny on my hands if they don't get something soon. What is it?"

"Stewed beans. Nothing special, but—"

"That's perfect. Good job, Gordon." The general peeked under the cart. "Can I have some?"

"Ma'am?"

"I love stewed beans. The crap that chef has been putting out, the portions are so small! How is a woman like me supposed to subsist on rations like that?"

"Of course you can have some. There are a few tubs on the bottom, still."

"Thank you," the general said, taking the lid off the aluminum tub. "Smells great."

"I don't think some of your troops agree."

"Oh, don't mind them. They're just tired and cranky."

"Thank you, ma'am."

"Don't take any notice of the overseer. I'll deal with her."

"Are you going to push back on the brick-only policy?"

"Gods, no, she'd want to argue the semantics for weeks. I only just got out of that meeting with my sanity intact last time. No, I'll just be sure to fudge the numbers. What she doesn't know won't hurt her. Or me, for that matter. I can't endure another round of nutritional diagrams with that woman. Did you know that she eats her protein bricks with a knife and fork? Who even does that, I can't—" Fineglass hissed out a sigh, cutting herself off. "We'll fudge the numbers," she repeated.

"Understood."

"Off you go, then. Finish your rounds. No doubt you'll be pleased to get back into your kitchen, eh?"

Rosie nodded and pushed the cart past the general. Her stomach churned, bile spitting up into the back of her throat, and she almost convinced herself that *she'd* eaten the beans, too.

Dumping the majority of the laundry in her own room, Rosie dragged the cart behind the atrium. No guards around, not yet, anyway. No doubt once they figured out that the prisoners were missing, all hell would break loose. She just hoped that wouldn't be until after Tarand's ship had left the station.

"Finally. I was beginning to think you'd forgotten about us."

"The timing is important. If we—"

"Yeah, yeah, whatever. Come on, get us out of here."

"I can only take two of you at once."

Josie pressed her eye to the slat in the door. "Then you start with my crew."

"No, we start with Thomas."

"Do you think I'm a fool? You'd get him on that ship and leave them here to rot. They go first."

Rosie clenched the handle of the cart. "Fine. We don't have time to argue."

"Right, you two, get into that cart and keep your wide traps shut. Don't do anything stupid, do you hear me? I mean it. You fuck up down there, and it's curtains for me and our new pal Thomas here."

"Aye," one of them grumbled.

The door swung open, and the two men climbed into the cart. Rosie covered them with laundry and closed the cell door again. "I'll be back as soon as I can," she whispered.

"I'm not going to wait forever for this little plan. If that ship leaves without us, we're screwed."

"I said, I'll be back."

The cart was surprisingly easy to push, given the size of the men inside it. She didn't waste any time in bustling down the corridors, keeping her eyes on the floor in front of her. When she reached the stairwell, she pulled the cart onto the lift, powered by a complicated set of pulleys operated by the rider.

"You ready?" Abara asked.

Rosie nodded. "As I'll ever be.

"You do realize that you're unlikely to make it off the station, right? There's still time to—"

"I have to do this."

"Whatever you say."

She yanked on the lever, and the lift began to sink, first one deck, and then another, until she was at the loading bay. There was no guard posted here; Abara must have made sure of that. There were also several crates near the stairs marked IMPORTANT - FOR DELTA-4 DISPATCH.

Josie's crew climbed into one of the crates, pulling the lid over their heads. Good. One batch down, one to go.

As planned, she took the cart to the opposite stairs, so as not to look like she was retracing her steps on the barracks deck for anyone who might be paying attention. She'd learned from her grandmother's mistakes.

"That took so long, I'm pretty sure I've aged a decade," Josie snapped.

Rosie pulled the door open. "I'm not going to miss you."

"The feeling is entirely mutual, I assure you."

"Thomas? Are you alright?"

He gave her a thin smile as he exited the room. His face was gaunt, his cheeks sunken in from months of being malnourished. "Smells like food," he said, climbing into the cart.

"Don't eat it."

"Why?"

"Undercooked. It will make you sick."

He pulled a pile of sheets over his head. "And here I'd always heard you were an amazing cook."

"Oh yeah? And where exactly did you hear that?"

"Delia never stopped talking about you all those years. It was obvious to anyone who heard it that she loved you so much."

A pang shot through Rosie's heart. "Did she tell you to say that?"

"No. She told me not to, in fact."

"Why?"

"She said it was going to be hard enough to say goodbye without adding insult to injury."

"It's her choice. What's done is done."

Thomas reached a hand out and squeezed Rosie's. "For whatever it's worth, thank you. I know that I can never repay you for what you've done for me."

"Don't thank me yet, we're still on the damned station. Put your heads down and let's get the hell out of here."

"About time," Josie grumbled.

The cart moved smoothly throughout the halls, aside from one wheel that had begun to wobble under the unexpected weight of two stowaways.

"This better be the last trip," Abara said as they approached. "I can't keep the bay clear for much longer."

"Don't worry, it is. We'll be gone before you know it."

"I hope so. Rosie—good luck. Don't tell anyone I said that if you get caught."

"Don't eat the beans in the barracks."

"What?"

"Just trust me. And don't tell anyone that if there are questions after we go. In fact, you might want to... you might want to pretend that you did eat them."

Abara cocked an eyebrow. "You're not making much sense."

"I know. But believe me, okay?"

"Hurry up now, patrols are going to swap for the takeoff in ten minutes."

Rosie nodded, wheeling the cart into the lift and pulling the lever once again. If everything had gone to plan, at least a third of those guards wouldn't be showing up for their shifts. They descended to the loading bay.

When Josie climbed into her crate, the temptation to find a hammer and nails to lock her in there was definitely tempting. Rosie helped Thomas into his own crate, being sure that the lid was on securely. They were almost free.

With a sigh, she approached the final open crate, ready to seal herself in.

"Ms. Gordon? What are you doing?"

Emeline emerged from behind one of the thick metal pillars, a revolver in her hands.

Chapter 33

"Ms. Dodson, good that you are here on time, for once," Overseer Allemande said, unlocking the broadcasting booth. "Councilor Tarand will be here momentarily for her final address from the station."

"Yes, ma'am."

"Where is Ms. Rojas?"

"She should be here any moment."

"I should hope so. It's not as though her time is so valuable that she should feel entitled to keep a member of the High Council waiting."

Olivia appeared from around the corner at the end of the hall. "Overseer, we're almost ready. The last of the councilor's cargo is being loaded onto the ship."

"Very good. May your journey be swift and clear."

"We plan on it. Not much can impede the Peregrine Gloriosa." Olivia shuffled through some papers on her clipboard. "Ms. Dodson, Councilor Tarand wanted me to extend her deepest gratitude for your assistance aboard Turas-Mara Station. The broadcasts from the past several days are polling beautifully, and we have already seen an improvement in recruitment across all sectors."

"It has been my pleasure."

"Where is Ms. Rojas?" Allemande barked. "This is unacceptable behavior."

"I can run the broadcast without her," Delia offered. "She has taught me enough to manage on my own. Maybe she got sick, or—"

"Unacceptable, simply unacceptable. Ms. Guisette, please accept my sincerest apologies for the unreliable nature of some of our staff. You can see why a recruitment drive for the Outer Rim is of such importance."

Olivia blinked. "So long as Ms. Dodson can run the booth, I don't see a problem."

"Good morning, everyone," Councilor Tarand announced, dressed in her signature long, flowing cloak of iridescent yellow and purple. "I trust we are all set for my final address?"

"We are," Delia said, before Allemande could start shouting again. "I will be your operator for today."

"Fabulous. Today, we will tell everyone what a delight it has been living on Turas-Mara Station. Beautifully catered food, suitable accommodations, and most of all, some of the bravest, most ingenious Coalition citizens I have ever had the privilege to meet."

"And some of the most efficient management," Allemande added.

"Yes, that too, how callous of me to forget to mention it in the first place."

"I just find that it is important to highlight that. People prefer to work under competent leadership, much like your own, madam councilor. None of us could even begin to compare to someone such as yourself."

"You embarrass me, Overseer Allemande. I am but another member of our glorious empire." Tarand stepped into the booth and sat on the stool near the microphone. "Ms. Dodson, if you would be so kind as to patch me in?"

"Of course, if you'll just give me a moment at your microphone, I will make sure that it is hooked in. We don't want any more mishaps, now do we?" Delia asked lightly, as she wiggled at the connection. It was better that Carmen hadn't showed up. It would be much easier to create a diversion this way—yet, her absence sat heavy in Delia's gut. What if she was dragging Rosie and Thomas off the loading bay right now, having them thrown back into the brig?

Delia nodded. "All set in here. Live in thirty seconds, Councilor."

"Much obliged."

Her breaths shallow and quick now, Delia sat in the control room, flipping the switches to prepare for the broadcast. She hovered over the final one, her mind on Rosie. Instead, she reached under the counter and yanked on the wire that connected the local broadcasting stream to the antenna atop the satellite, just enough to jar the locked screw at the end.

"We're live in five, four, three..." she trailed off.

"It is a glorious morning here on Turas-Mara Station," Councilor Tarand began, her voice soothing and clear. "I am desperately sad to be departing, for my time here has been some of the most enriching of my life. Life out here at the rim is invigorating, tempting out the sense of adventure that lies within us all."

Delia clenched her fists and released, over and over again, digging her nails into her palm to keep her mind focused. Now or never. No going back, if she changed the plan this late in its execution.

"The food out here is to die for, with catered options for every diet. I have to say, some of the dishes I have been served here far surpass even the best and most beloved dining establishments on Gamma-3. The quarters are spacious, and you'll want for nothing once you come out here to the Rim. It may even be the adventure you've been dreaming of—"

Delia bent the microphone's wire, introducing a hideous static into the line, then wiggling the connections to create a piercing shriek of feedback.

"Ms. Dodson!" Allemande roared, throwing the control room door open. "Fix it!"

"I—I can't!" Delia lied, her eyes wide and convincing. "Our signal is being interrupted again!"

"The military knows very well what's going on here, they wouldn't dare—"

"Ma'am, it's pirates!"

"*What?*"

"They're the ones who have been upsetting the broadcasts, that's why we were never able to halt it!"

Allemande yanked her up and dragged her into the hall by her elbow. "Get in that booth and tell them to release our frequency, or we'll rain the powers of every hell down on them."

"Aye," Delia said, picking up the microphone.

Tarand was still seated on the stool, bewildered. "What's going on?" she asked.

"Just some ruffians we mean to dispatch," Delia said. She cleared her throat and spoke into the microphone with authority, knowing full well the only people who would hear it were the ones on the station. "Release this frequency," she demanded to the dead air, the shriek still echoing through the corridor. "If you do not desist immediately, we will be forced to dispatch every gunship in the Coalition's armada to remove your ship from space. Give up now, and you may be shown mercy."

"They don't want my message of hope to be delivered," Tarand whispered. "You see? It is our resilience as an empire that threatens the brigands the most."

"You have twenty seconds to release this frequency!"

Olivia shoved Delia aside. "Ma'am, we need to move. If there are pirates or rebels about—"

"I will not be frightened into submission like a mouse," Tarand declared. "I have no interest in allowing myself to be cowed by filthy pirates who don't even have the courage or tenacity to try to board this station themselves, choosing instead to make shots at messages of hope and peace from afar."

"But ma'am—"

"Olivia, do not argue with me about this. We wait until the line is clear. I'm sure Ms. Dodson will have it free in no time."

Allemande towered in the doorway. "Ms. Dodson, get down to the wire room and send an immediate message to Nox Beacon. Tell them to send every reinforcement they can. Have you been able to isolate the location of this disruption?"

Delia nodded. "Yes," she lied.

"Where?"

"Approaching from the starboard side of the station."

"It's *them*, I know it is," Allemande hissed, her fists clenched white with rage. "Evie Anderson and her gang of unlawful tyrants."

"Ma'am?" Delia asked, pretending she had no idea about the crew.

"The Cricket. That... that ship. It must be them, it must—" She whirled around. "They must be coming for Councilor Tarand. They mean to take her hostage, and—" Overseer Allemande's eyes flashed with a dangerous thirst for vengeance. "What are you still doing here, Ms. Dodson? Get to that wire room!"

"Yes, ma'am!" The sound of Delia's boots on the metal floor echoed throughout the corridors, a pounding rhythm that drove her faster towards the back stairs. There might still be time to fix what she'd nearly broken forever.

"Delia! Delia *no*!" Abara shouted as she approached. "They're down already, they'll be loading, you could—"

"Get out of my way!"

"You'll draw too much attention! Have you lost your sense?"

"Just let me pass!"

Abara put a hand on her shoulder. "I... I can't let you do that. I could be in enough trouble as it is, I—"

"Corporal!" General Fineglass shouted, one arm clasped around her stomach. "I need you to—" She interrupted herself with a retch, covering her mouth with her hand. "I need you to get to the atrium right away."

"Ma'am? But that's not my assignment."

"Some kind of—" She retched again. "Stomach bug. We're thin on the ground, Abara. I need you protecting Councilor Tarand, not guarding the laundry stairs."

"Aye." They turned to Delia, their eyes pleading. "Don't."

"Get going, Corporal." Fineglass wiped her clammy brow with the back of her hand. "What in hells are you doing here, Dodson?"

"Heading to the wire room."

"Via the back stairs?"

Delia took a step backwards. "I have to... see something first. Overseer's orders."

"You finally figured it out, did you? Took you long—" Another retch. "Enough."

"Figured what out, ma'am?"

"Go."

"Ma'am?"

The general bent in half, cradling her stomach. "Go!" she shouted.

Delia sprinted down the stairs two at a time, using the handrails for stability as she swung from one step to the next. Gods, don't let them have left already.

Finally, at the loading bay, she swung around a support beam and stopped dead in her tracks.

"I—I have a gun!" Emeline shouted, waving a revolver in the air. Her eyes were wild, unhinged.

"We can see that," Josie replied in a bored voice. "Why don't you put that nasty thing down, Sweetpea? You're scaring my big, strong, manly crew members."

"It wasn't you?" Rosie asked. "Em—Ms. Allemande, it wasn't you who sent me all those notes?"

Emeline's hands were shaking, but the gun was still pointed at Josie. "Notes? What notes?"

"Who else would have access like that? It must have been you who wanted us to know where the prisoners were being held."

"I would never do that! I would never—" Emeline cocked the gun to punctuate her point, yanking back on the silver hammer. "*Ever* give away classified information!"

"But your family—"

"They're dead to me!" Emeline shouted, her eyes filling with tears.

Delia crept closer, keeping to the shadows. They'd all get caught and publicly executed if they didn't get on the ship soon.

"You could come with us," Rosie offered, her voice kind and welcoming. "We can get you out of here."

"No!" Emeline shouted. "No, no!"

Josie, quick as lightning, ducked under Emeline's aim, ripped the revolver from her hands, and cracked her on the skull. "That was enough of that, I think."

"She's just a girl!" Rosie shouted, bending over Emeline.

"Yeah, a girl who was about to make sure we all said our goodbyes on a public broadcast before lining us up for the firing squad. Not quite how I wanted to end my day."

"You could have just taken the gun from her!"

"What, and let her run straight to her mother? Are you *trying* to get us all killed?"

"Take her with," Delia said, emerging from her hiding place. "If you leave her on this station, she'll never see her family again. She deserves better than being a pawn."

"Dee, what are you doing down here?" Rosie demanded. "You were supposed to—"

"I did cause a diversion. They think pirates are off the starboard side of the station. We need to get you loaded up, and fast. Get in the crates, seal yourselves in. I'll deal with Emeline."

Delia hoisted the girl up under the armpits and set her down inside a crate. "Please, don't scream when you wake up," she whispered, using the fabric belt at Emeline's waist as a gag. "We're trying to help." She set the lid on top, tapping it into place with the heel of her palm.

Muffled voices across the bay came from the front stairs.

"Councilor, we need to get you off this station immediately," Olivia shouted. "It's too dangerous, and we can better defend you onboard The Peregrine Gloriosa. We can outrun any pirate or rebel ship that tries to pursue."

"Where are all the guards?" Tarand asked.

"The general redirected them to be sure we can make a hasty exit from the station. Come, ma'am, please, I'm sure we don't have much time—"

Delia climbed into a half-empty crate, nestling herself in a pile of small droids. What were droids doing on a High Council ship, anyway?

"Yes, Ms. Guisette, I understand completely. Thank you for doing all that you can in order to keep me safe."

"It's my job."

The voices were closer now, and Delia focused to slow her breath to a quieter, more manageable rate. If Emeline woke up and started screaming, they were all done for. Gods, the journey would take at least two days to Delta-4. There was no way they'd be able to keep her quiet that long. She should have suggested they lock her in a utility closet, or—no, there had been no time.

"Horace!" Olivia shouted. "Why aren't these crates loaded in already?"

"I didn't realize we'd be leaving so soon!" he said, his tone apologetic and harried. "Won't take but a minute."

"Hurry up, we need to leave right now!"

"Yes, yes, as soon as, yes." He used a cart to drag the crates up the ramp, one at a time, and slammed the cargo door shut. The ship's engines roared to life, deafening all other sounds. The hiss of the pressure pumps slithered through the bay, and the ship lifted off the station and into space. The ultra-fast speed made Delia's stomach turn, and she tilted her head back to swallow down the bile in her throat.

The raw, rough wood of the crate bit into her palms, sliding a sliver beneath her skin with a sharp stab of pain. Her knees pulled to her chest, Delia struggled to regulate her breathing, her lungs insistent on pulling shallow, short gasps of air, threatening her with hyperventilation. Gods, what had she done? There was no going back after this, not after kidnapping, and escape, and—no. She shook her head, desperate to clear her thoughts.

The others shifted in their crates, with someone stifling a dry cough in their throat. The insistent hum of the ship thrummed beneath her boots, forcing her to stay connected to the reality of what had just happened.

"Alright, boys, we need to deal with the girl," Josie said, climbing out of her crate.

"What are you doing? Get back in!" Rosie hissed. "What if someone comes?"

"Then it's a good thing this kid brought me a gun, isn't it? Did you seriously expect me to spend two days in a crate?"

"But the plan is—"

"Oh, shut up. You're boring."

"So boring that I just saved you and your crew from torture and probably death. Real boring, me! Poisoning an entire station to make sure we got out! Boring!"

"If we don't do something about her, she's going to wake up and scream the place down. Sound might be muffled from back here, but it sure as hells wouldn't take them long to hear that once she gets going."

"You're not going to—kill her, are you? I can't allow you to kill her. I won't—I won't stand for it."

"Oh, look who just grew a spine!" Josie mocked. "Of course I'm not going to kill her. What do you think I am, a monster?"

"Good."

"We're going to use her as a hostage."

Delia coughed, clearing her throat from the burning acid. "Josie, you can't! She's just a girl!"

"Looks mostly grown to me, and besides, if she's the daughter of that monster back there, I'm sure she can handle some light peril. We won't hurt her. So long as she cooperates."

"Delia?" Rosie cried, throwing off the lid of her crate.

"Yep, it's me," she replied, unsealing her own.

"But you said—"

"I couldn't leave you. Not again. Not after... everything."

Rosie's eyes filled with tears. "You silly, foolish woman. What about all those big plans?"

"Turns out, I'm less interested in them without you."

Josie rolled her eyes. "Well, isn't this just a dreadful, maudlin display?"

"What, Cap, you've never been in love?" Dirk asked.

"Sure. But I got over it."

He grinned. "I think it's sweet."

"Keep that to yourself, or I'll toss you out of an airlock myself." Josie yawned. "We use her as a hostage to get this ship landed somewhere. A big transport beacon is best. They're going to figure out she's missing in a few hours, a day at the most."

"They won't care about a girl, they'll let you kill her and then string all of us up," Dirk said.

"She's the overseer's daughter and the key to their marketing success for the Outer Rim. They'll care."

"So what, we just... give her back?" Delia asked. "I thought we'd get her back to her family."

"After that little display in the loading bay, I'm not so sure she wants to get back to them." Josie shrugged. "People change. Sometimes for the worse."

"She was taken! Abducted! She was brainwashed!"

"That may be the case, but I'm not about to risk the rest of our lives on keeping her when she doesn't want to be kept. We use her as a hostage and get as far away from Turas-Mara and this ship as we can. Once we get to Delta-4, my crew can pick us up from there."

"What the hell is a pirate crew doing on Delta-4? That's almost as overrun with Coalition as Gamma-3!" Rosie interjected. "They're going to have all our faces in the papers as soon as they figure it out. You really think we won't be seen there?"

"Listen, Cupcake, I've been at this a long damned time, alright? In case you've forgotten, my ship looks just like the Coalition cargo vessels. I would say thank you for getting us out, but I'm not so foolish as to think you'd have done it if you didn't need to in order to save our buddy Thomas over there. Maybe you can close that trap of yours and let me do what I'm best at. If I need a cream puff, I'll ask you."

"I'm not a damned patissier!" Rosie shot back. "I can't stand making choux dough!"

"Gods below," Josie said. "You're *not* a *patissier*? Whatever will we do?"

"Rose, I hate to say it, but she's right," Delia relented. "If we stay on this ship very long, they'll get notified we escaped, and then we're as good as dead. We need to be the ones holding the cards."

"But—"

"Saying that, though, I don't think we should hand her over."

Josie gave an exasperated sigh. "Are you aware that's not how this hostage thing works?"

"Are *you* aware that she's the one who organized the labor rally back on Skelm?"

"That was *her*?"

"Yes. And then Allemande had her picked up and deposited into her home, where she legally adopted her and kept her under tight control. She was brainwashed."

"I wasn't brainwashed," Emeline said, climbing out of her crate. "And you didn't tie my hands, Ms. Dodson, so I'm not sure what good you thought a gag would do. You're not very good at this, are you?"

Josie whipped the gun from her waistband and trained it on Emeline. "One wrong move, kid, and it's curtains for you."

"You won't kill me. I'm your only ticket out of here. I have to tell you, I have no interest in being a hostage, and I don't intend on cooperating."

"You will, unless you want a hole in that pretty little skull of yours."

"Without me, you lose all your leverage."

Josie pointed the gun at Emeline's feet. "Don't need both feet to live. Just ask Dirk. He's doing just fine, aren't you, Dirk?"

"Aye," he grunted. "Just fine and dandy."

"Hear that, Emeline? He's fine and dandy. So I recommend that you pipe down and let the adults talk."

"Do you really think that my mother won't have every shuttle out looking for me? That she won't inform this ship's captain immediately upon realizing that I'm gone?"

"Considering the chaos back on the station right now, I would guess that we have at least a few hours before that happens. They're going to spend some time hunting for a pirate ship off the starboard side that isn't there, and is probably hundreds of thousands of kilometers away."

"But the guards—"

"Are mostly indisposed," Rosie said. "It will be a few hours before they recover. Maybe longer, if they had second helpings."

"You *poisoned* the guards?" Emeline asked, horrified. "You poisoned them!"

"They'll be fine. It's not lethal."

"Thomas? Thomas!" Delia cried, prying lids off crates. "He's not here, he—"

"I'm right here, Dodson," he said, pushing his fingers through a gap in the slats. "I'm too weak to get the lid off."

Delia ripped the lid off and pulled him up, hugging him. "Thomas, I'm so glad that you're alright."

"Thanks to you."

"I thought you'd died."

He laughed. "I know." Thomas gave her a weak squeeze. "Any food around?"

"Here, have this," Josie said, tossing him an apple. "Stole it from the loading bay, along with some other food supplies. Might be a bumpy ride before we get to my ship."

Thomas took a bite. "Thanks." He groaned quietly. "I never thought an apple could taste so good."

"After months of those disgusting bricks, I'm not surprised that a mealy apple tastes like the finest food in the Capital. Careful, there might be a worm."

"Protein," he said, taking another bite. "At least a worm would be a welcome change from what I've been having lately."

"Once we get my ship, we'll get you fed proper."

"Full of altruism, all of a sudden?" Delia asked. "Doesn't seem like you to go out of your way for someone."

"Once you've shit in the same bucket as someone, it tends to bring you closer. Thomas is a good man. I can see why you wanted to free him. Besides, all that knowledge knocking around in his brain about broadcasting might prove useful." Josie eyed Emeline with suspicion. "But we won't talk any more about that, in case the little brat here decides to share every bit of conversation once they get her back."

"Please, as if pirate radio is anything new. The Coalition has spent decades shoring up technology to defend against those pitiful takeovers."

"Yet your mother fell for it hook, line, and sinker," Delia said. "Seems it might be more of a threat than you think. Information is a dangerous thing."

Emeline scoffed. "My mother is one of the foremost politicians in the

Near Systems. She is smarter than most of the brainless animals she has as superiors. She has the best interests of everyone at heart, and—"

Josie kept the gun trained on Emeline's feet. "She carved chunks out of Thomas' skin. Is that what a kind and empathetic leader does?"

"She wouldn't do that."

"Oh, she did it, alright."

"You're all a pack of liars. Why else would you be on this ship, if you weren't? I have no reason to believe any of you. Pirates, rebels—all you do is destroy, and take, and act according to your own selfish desires."

"You're right, Dodson. She *is* brainwashed."

"I'm not brainwashed!" Emeline shouted. "For the first time, I see things clearly! You can't help people by burning down buildings like they did in Skelm. You have to be part of the system to change it!"

"The system is broken," Rosie whispered. "It has been for a very long time. You can't fix the Coalition. It was designed to be what it is, from the ground up. Brick by brick, they built up an empire that pushes people down, that shields the rich and powerful, that rewards cruelty. You can't... you can't *change* that, Emeline."

"Failures always say that," Emeline shot back.

Josie laughed. "Enough of this. I don't need to hear lectures from a child."

"I'm eighteen."

"Good for you."

"If my calculations are right, Cap, we need to get a move on. We could land at Faaion Beacon in an hour," Dirk said.

"Beats two days in these crates," Delia grumbled.

"Right then," Josie said, grabbing Emeline by the arm. "Time to call the bridge."

Chapter 34

"No one is calling the bridge," a crate in the back of the loading bay said, muffled.

"Gods below, how many fucking stowaways are on this ship?" Josie huffed. "Show yourself, or I start shooting the crate."

"No need for that." Carmen emerged from the crate, her hands in the air. "Don't waste shots on me. You only have six."

"I will waste my ammunition on whoever I see fit."

"Carmen!" Emeline cried. "Carmen, you have to help me!"

"I am helping you. Just relax, there's no need to go upsetting the captain, here."

Josie pulled back the hammer on the gun. "Who are you?"

"She's Intelligence," Delia whispered. Things were going downhill, and fast.

"Wait!" Carmen shouted, her hands still up. "Do *not* shoot me. There are more deserving targets, I promise."

"I don't let spies live. Tell us how you found out about the plan."

Carmen stepped out of the crate, only lowering her hands once to pull her skirts free of an exposed nail. "She's right, I am Intelligence. But I am not Intelligence for the Coalition."

Josie hesitated. "What in hell is that supposed to mean?"

"I work for the rebellion based out of Brad—well, you know the place. I used to fly with Captain Violet, for a time."

"That just makes me want to shoot you more."

"Yes, I've heard about your... disagreements."

"Hardly a disagreement. She killed my captain."

"From what I understand, he was trying to board and ransack her ship." Carmen lowered her arms to her sides. "Emeline, are you alright?"

"I'm fine."

"I trust you aren't interested in being a hostage today."

Emeline shook her head. "No. In fact, I'd rather not be a hostage *any* day."

"A fair point. Captain Josie, would you be so kind as to lower your weapon? No one needs to get shot here today."

"Are you sure?" Josie asked. "I can think of at least two people in this room right now that I'd love to have an excuse to shoot."

Carmen blinked. "I have no doubt about that in the slightest. However, once you alert the bridge that you're in here, with the overseer's daughter as collateral, what makes you think there won't be at least three dozen squads waiting for you?"

"The threat that I'll put a round into her skull if they don't comply."

"Captain Josie, I know that you are smarter than this. You've led your crew across the Near Systems, you've ransacked all manner of ships and reunited countless families."

"I don't know if you've noticed, but we're running low on options, here. We can't keep her. She'll alert the whole damned ship the second we drop our guard. Or our gun, for that matter." Josie kept the revolver trained at Emeline's feet. "If Intelligence managed to figure all of this out, then there's not much hope that they won't already be onto us. Staying on this ship is a death sentence."

"No one is suggesting to stay on the ship." Carmen produced a pair of wire cutters from the pocket of her bright yellow dress. "I am suggesting, though, that we force a landing with some creative mechanical engineer-ing."

"Are you a mechanic?"

"No."

Josie snorted. "Oh, great, we have an untrained pineapple armed with scissors, this definitely won't end with our frozen corpses floating through space."

"I said I wasn't a mechanic. I never said I was untrained," Carmen replied, prying open a gear box on the far wall. "I've worked with one of the best mechanics in the Near Systems. She spent months studying the blueprints for this vessel."

"And how did you get your paws on that?"

"We have several contacts within the Coalition."

"Who?"

Carmen examined a wire. "I can't tell you that. Not unless you're ready to join us."

"I don't need a band of blithering fools to get the job done," Josie snapped. "I've done perfectly fine on my own."

"Not to split hairs, but you did need me to break you out of the brig," Rosie said. "Seems like an important distinction."

"I'd have gotten out days ago if I wasn't having to wait on you two."

"And been shot on sight."

"And gotten away without having to drag the rest of you along with me!"

Emeline cleared her throat. "Take me to Skelm."

"Skelm?" Delia asked. "But that's—"

"It's where I need to be right now. If you agree, I will cooperate."

"What does cooperation look like?" Josie asked. "Does it look like you selling us out the first chance you get?"

"I am a reasonable person," Emeline mused. "Get me to Skelm, and I won't say a word about what happened. They'll know, of course—people don't just evaporate off the most remote station in the Near Systems—but I'll be sure to not... cause a scene. At the transport beacon."

"It will take a week to get to Skelm from all the way out here, even in this high-powered ship."

"Yes."

"Why Skelm?" Josie asked. "Why have such an affinity for a place that's no more than an outdated backwater?"

"You may be able to dismiss an entire city based on outdated assumptions,

Captain Josie, but I care about the people there, and they deserve better."

"What do you think you're going to do there, build homes? Start passing out pamphlets to the contract holders there that encourage them to pay their workers more? Get real, kid."

Emeline smiled. "No. I have a few ideas of my own."

"What?" Delia burst out. "But what about your family? What about—"

"My family became dead to me the moment they put Skelm to the torch. My sister made choices that were not to benefit the citizens. She did what she did to save her own ass and escape. I thought that we were in it together, but—but we weren't. She never even tried to come for me when I was taken, you know. I spent two weeks in a cell off-world before my mother came for me. *She* fought for me. *She* had me released. My sister ran away."

"I'm sorry that happened to you," Carmen said gently. "That must have been so difficult."

"Don't insult me by trying to ply me with pretty words, Ms. Rojas. You lied to me, too. You said that you would always look out for me."

"That wasn't a lie. I *am* looking out for you. You'll notice that your person is still intact and not riddled with bullet holes."

"If you really want to help me, then you'll take me to Skelm. Take me to Skelm, or I start screaming right now, and I'll happily watch the whole pack of you get marched off to the firing squad."

"We will—*I* will get you to Skelm. But we have a few stops to make first, in order to make sure that everyone can remain safe. Is that acceptable?" Carmen held out her hand to shake on the deal.

Emeline considered this for a moment, before nodding. "Agreed."

"Why not just make a run for the first transport back to the Rim?" Rosie asked. "After all, as you told me, you weren't a prisoner on Turas-Mara. If you can leave whenever you want, why would you even need us to get there?"

"My mother and I have differing ideas on how to achieve similar goals. She is lonely sometimes. She wants me to stay with her at the Outer Rim, work on my studies, and do interviews to promote the expansion project. I was not a prisoner, but as you know, transport to and from the station was hardly comfortable or regular. Even this loading bay is far superior to the kinds of vessels we had coming and going."

"What are you doing over there?" Josie asked, nodding her head towards Carmen. "Are we going to get to land, or what?"

Carmen brandished a large socket wrench now. "I need to wait to trigger the boiler alarm, or they might land at a fuel station instead. We don't want that. We're only going to get one shot at this, so we have to be patient and wait for the right moment."

"Where are you keeping all of those tools?"

"What, you don't keep yours in the same place?" Carmen asked, pulling a hammer from a tool belt around her thigh. "Being prepared is always important. I never leave home without it, now. Best gift I was ever given." She grinned. "Roger gave it to me."

Josie made a face. "Gross."

"Don't be jealous. I can ask him where he got it. Maybe for your birthday, Josie?"

"Shut up."

"Almost there, besides." Carmen peered out the small porthole. "Three, two, one, here we go." She wrenched a nut off the side of the panel, sending it rolling across the floor. Then, prying open the access panel in the floor, she unscrewed a hinge and smacked the hammer inside. "That should do it."

"What the hell was that, some kind of choreographed show?"

"Should cause the boiler to trip a safety valve."

"But what if—"

The ship shuddered gently and slowed. "There you have it," Carmen said proudly. "It worked."

"What now then, genius?" Josie scoffed. "They'll open the doors and see all of us standing here like useless produce."

"Oh," Rosie said. "They won't come into the loading bay. They'll check the boiler room. Protocol is to not open the bay unless absolutely necessary. In case stowaways were to try to board."

"How do we get *off* the ship, then?"

Delia pointed to the far wall. "Through that emergency door, I imagine. Just have to hope no one sees us."

"The private loading bays at Faaion Beacon are sequestered off from the main area. We should be able to exit, lie low, and wait for the ship to depart," Carmen said, replacing the tools in her thigh belt.

"Did you have all of this planned out?"

"I had a hundred different scenarios planned, though, to be honest, I always assumed that I'd be leaving when I rotated back off the station. I never quite anticipated... this."

"I don't like spies," Josie announced. "Once we're free, I don't want to see you hanging around, you hear me?"

"I wasn't spying on *you*."

"So you say."

"If I was going to spy on you, I'd already have known you were going to try to ransack the station before you did it. If I'd been spying on you, I would have told you not to bother, because what you're looking for wasn't ever even on board."

Josie narrowed her eyes. "You don't know that."

"I *do* know that."

"My crew took it. I saw them load it onto my ship."

Carmen shook her head. "You saw them load a decoy."

"No!"

"What in hells are you talking about?" Delia interjected. "What decoy? What were they—you—looking for on Turas-Mara?"

"Don't you worry about that," Josie said. "Though no doubt this spy here is going to spill her guts to Captain Violet the second they meet."

"I don't work for Captain Violet," Carmen said. "We're friends, yes, but she gave up looking for it over a year ago."

"Then she's a bigger fool than I even thought. It could turn the tide of the war."

"War?" Emeline said with a scoff. "What war?"

"The one you've been lucky enough not to notice, kid. Battles are being won and lost every day. Unfortunately for most of us, the Coalition is doing most of the winning and we're all doing the bulk of the losing."

"A few rebels is hardly a war."

Josie grimaced. "I think you are sorely misinformed about what's going on out there. What's been going on out there for years, now. People being starved outright by people like your mother. People dying, all because they dared to dream of something better than being born to work until their bodies give out."

"What is society without rules and regulations, though? Nothing more than chaos."

"Your mother teach you that little tidbit, too?" Josie asked, snorting back a laugh. "There's plenty of chaos to go around, even in the most tightly controlled sectors. That's just how it is."

"Enough with the philosophizing," Carmen scolded, though her tone was gentle. "They'll be landing soon, and we need to make sure we're the hell out of the loading area and onto another ship before they figure it out. Assuming, of course, that they haven't already."

"We should split up," Delia said. "Far too recognizable as a group, and staying together means we're easily tracked."

"She's right. So who's going with who?

"I want to go with Carmen," Emeline announced. "I don't trust any of the rest of you to not sell me to the highest bidder."

"Whatever," Josie grumbled. "I'll go on my own. Dirk, Owen, pair off. Head for Delta-4, but don't make it obvious. No direct flights, and I mean it this time. I don't care how good the in-flight snacks are."

"We'll stick together," Rosie announced, weaving her arm around Delia's waist. "And we'll take Thomas, too. Where are we going?"

Carmen leaned against the access panel. "The sooner we get off main transit ships, the better. I say we all try for Captain Josie's ship, and then go from there."

"I'm not a gods-forsaken transport service," Josie grumbled. "I have other things that need attending to."

"Oh yeah?" Carmen asked. "Like what, exactly?"

"Just—*things*!"

Delia rolled her eyes. "So much for working towards getting your hands on that—that thing. What things do you have plans for? Sitting around all day, face-first in a puddle of moonshine?"

"Sounds like a plan to me," Josie said. "Boys, add that to the list."

"Aye, Cap," came the gruff reply.

Rosie rankled at the flippant remark. "This isn't a joke, you know. It's all well and fine for your crew to make wisecracks, but we're in real danger here."

"I'm not a nanny for grown adults on their first foray into rebellion," Josie snapped. "You want that, you can hang around and wait for Captain Violet to show her face." Dirk elbowed Owen, and Josie's face cracked into a wide grin. "Come to think of it, you know, you're right, Rosie."

"I am?"

"Of course! We should stick together, help each other out. After all, it won't be long before they're looking for us, and I don't trust you lot to not rat me out the second you get the opportunity. We'll split up and meet at the Brushstroke Inn in two days. It's in Chalidon, the main port on Delta-4."

Delia shook her head. "Two days? How are we all going to make it there in that time?"

"Guess you better hurry. We can't hang around in case they come looking for my ship."

"Fine."

Josie held her arms out in triumph. "Excellent, we're all agreed."

"The ship is descending," Carmen announced, peering out the porthole. "Won't be long before we're docked. We should keep quiet, now, we don't know when the engine will cut out and leave us vulnerable to detection."

"Yeah, let's all listen to the spy. I'm sure she has our best interests at heart."

"If you want to make it off this beacon alive, you'll listen to me. I can promise you that I don't intend any of you any harm."

"The feeling isn't mutual."

"Shut up, Josie," Delia hissed. "You're going to get us all caught."

"You've done an excellent job of causing problems already, bringing that kid along, so I'd suggest you climb down out of the royal tower you're inhabiting and join the rest of us in reality."

Rosie grabbed Delia's hand and squeezed gently, a non-verbal cue to ignore Josie's taunts. Whatever the reason she was being so petulant, it didn't matter—one wrong move and they'd all end up dead.

"Almost there," Carmen whispered, and the ship gave a gentle shudder as the engines ground to a halt, letting the ship silently coast into the loading bay. The porthole went black for a moment, and then the starry view of deep space was replaced with the rusted rivets of Faaion Beacon, cast in an unpleasant orange light.

"What now?" Delia asked in a hushed tone."

"Shh. We wait for them to pass the bay, and then we sneak out."

Josie holstered the gun, finally, wedging it into the back of her waistband. Emeline's shoulders dropped, no longer under immediate threat. "There's the pilot. Let's go."

One by one, they ducked under the emergency hatch at the side, squeezing between the ship and the wall of the loading bay. Thomas leaned against Delia as he shuffled through, holding his side, his brow furrowed. The blunt metal hinge of the hatch pressed into Rosie's hips, and she grimaced from the pain, biting her tongue to keep from crying out. She wedged herself into the gap, shuffling along behind Delia and Carmen.

They moved from behind the ship to a pile of crates, and then a pallet of fuel canisters, until they slipped undetected into the main area of the beacon. It was run down and dirty, being so far from the usual trading routes, the overhead lamps flickering with damaged bulbs. The entire place smelled vaguely of vomit.

"Gross," Rosie said, stepping around a pile of errant trash. "No wonder people never come out this way."

"Oh, they will soon enough," Delia replied. "With the Turas-Mara expansion project, no doubt more paths will become commonplace. I bet in a year this place looks completely different."

"Yeah, and all the vendors you see in the wings will get pushed out to make room for something shinier," Josie interjected. "A year ago, Nox

Beacon looked a lot like this. Now, it's all... sanitized. I think dirt has a certain charm to it."

"Which flight are you taking?"

Josie stared up at the departures board as one line after another appeared, each letter flipped with an overhead pulley system. "I'll take the one to the hub outside Epsilon-5 and grab a transfer from there."

"I want to go to Skelm," Emeline announced again.

"We can't yet, Precious," Josie replied in a mocking tone. "There are no flights that will get us there. We need my ship first. Do you have any idea what security in Skelm looks like, now that it's been chosen as the main producer of raw materials for the expansion?"

"No."

"It may as well be Gamma-fucking-3 over there. Inspections, paperwork, chip scans—" Josie's face drained of color. "Chip scans! You three—four—five? You still have Coalition chips, they'll be tracking you any minute!"

Rosie pressed hard on her arm, wincing from the inevitable bruise. "Four. Mine is... well, mine isn't a problem."

"Well, aren't you the intriguing mystery? Doesn't help us for the rest of them, though—"

Carmen sidled up beside them, lifting the hem of her skirt to pull out a small, snub-nosed gun, pressing it against Delia's arm. It chirped angrily, and she moved then to Thomas, Emeline, and finally, herself. "I was saying, it's always important to come prepared."

"How'd you manage to smuggle *that* aboard Turas-Mara?" Josie asked.

"Creatively." Carmen looked at her sideways. "Not like that." She replaced the gun into the belt at her thigh and smiled. "A spy never reveals her secrets."

"I have a feeling that gun has seen more than one of your secrets."

"Josie!" Delia scolded. "She just saved our asses. Again, I don't think we need to make rude comments."

"We didn't all grow up in the aristocracy, Dodson. Some of us call it how we see it."

Carmen steered them all towards the departures deck. "The way I see it, they're going to notice that the last location tracked was here, so we need to move. Now."

"Thomas, we can take the freighter to Epsilon-6. I know for a fact there are shuttles that connect over to Chalidon," Delia said.

"Oh no," Josie said. "I don't think so, Muffin. You two will scamper the first chance you get, sell the rest of us out."

"I wouldn't do that."

"Easy to say, harder to deny once you've gone and done it. No, Ms. Dodson, you'll travel with me."

Delia turned her chin up in defiance. "And what if I tell you to go to hell?"

"Then you're on your own. It's my damned ship you need to get to—well, places selling grey market chips and new identities. But, hey, if you want to take chances on your own, then go right ahead. I look forward to seeing your face alongside the public broadcast, with a nice, big, *wanted* stamp."

"I can't think of much I'd rather do less than spend two days traveling with *you*," Delia spat. "But I guess you get to call the shots if I want passage to a safe area for Thomas and the rest of us."

"I'll go with Thomas," Rosie offered. "We'll be fine. There's a flight in twenty minutes from bay seven over to another beacon, we can get a few connections from there. It's a major transport hub in those parts."

"Good," Delia nodded. "Hopefully, it may throw them off that we're all headed to the same place as Tarand. Maybe Delta-4 won't be the first place they look."

"We'd all better hope so, or that port is going to be locked down tighter than a—"

"We get the picture, Josie."

"Get on board, all of you," Carmen said. "Don't speak to anyone you don't need to. Don't even speak to each other if you can manage it. Try not to be seen. And don't try to use your chips to pay for anything, you risk a reboot."

"How are we supposed to pay for anything, then?"

"I will hopefully have that sorted out by the time we all reach the

Brushstroke Inn. Here," she said, handing out lumps of metal. "This should be enough to barter passage and a little food."

"What else do you have hiding in those pockets, a whole ship?" Josie asked.

Carmen gave a half smile. "Unfortunately not. Now, Emeline and I are going to take a quick shuttle across to another transport beacon half a day from here, and get a flight from there. We'll see you at the inn in two days."

Chapter 35

Delia's bones ached with exhaustion. Two solid days of travel, with no sleep, and nothing but protein bricks for food. They were lucky to get even that, huddled in the drafty loading bay of the freighter. The crew hadn't asked many questions, at least.

Her hair was tangled and matted, the curls flattened against her head and frizzy. It was a damned good thing the freighter was light on mirrors, or she'd end up with a crisis of confidence. Josie had barely spoken two words to her, as agreed when they boarded.

Did William already know that she was missing—that she was a fugitive now? How many MPOs were out looking for them? Would they even make it past the port on Delta-4, or would they get snatched off the ship's ramp and thrown into a cell?

"Relax, Ms. Dodson," Josie said, half asleep. "We're almost there, now."

"If you're the one telling me to relax, then I know I should be at least thirty percent more panicked."

"I've been in worse scrapes than this, don't you worry."

Delia snorted. "Oh yeah? When? When was the last time someone broke you out of a cell and you had half the gods-damned Coalition fleet after you?"

"Three months ago."

"What did you do, rob a fuel beacon?"

Josie pulled her sleeves down and buttoned them, the cuffs dirty and grey from weeks in the brig. "No, I loaded fifty refugees onto my ship. They got away. I stayed to distract the chuckleheads in the settlement. Worked. They got free, and eventually, so did I."

"I'm surprised they haven't decided to execute you on the spot."

"They would, if they knew who I was. But every mission, it's a different name, a different chip, a different vessel—or at least, one that looks different. For all they know, I'm twelve different pirates." Josie laughed, smoothing back a stray blond hair. "By the time they figure any of it out, I hope that the tide has turned in our favor."

Delia turned away. "We should wait to talk until... until later."

"Don't mind me," the crew member said, pulling a hat over her eyes. "I can barely hear anything over the engines."

"You heard enough to hear that, though."

"Whatever secrets you have, I'm not interested. Secrets complicate things, and I'm looking for a simple life. Load the crates, unload the crates, get paid, spend all my credits at the Banríon tables. It's all anyone needs."

"I'm not so sure about that," Delia grumbled. "Besides, I'm terrible at cards."

"You won't have much time to think about it. We'll be landing soon."

"Finally," Josie said with an exaggerated sigh.

The crew member swung out of the hammock. "What do you mean, finally? We're bang on time, unlike most of the freighters that make this journey."

"I could have done it with plenty of time to spare. You took the long way around the belt."

"Yeah, because most of us actually enjoy living. You can't get through that thing at speed, not without a few holes in the hull. Trust me, lady, the belt isn't something you want to mess around with."

Josie scoffed. "I do it all the time. Minimal damage, if any. You just need a navigator who isn't a chicken."

"Buckle up, we're about to hit atmosphere. I don't know if you've ever been to a terraformed city, but the landings can be pretty rough."

"Maybe for amateurs."

The crew member rolled her eyes before clipping herself to the restraint at the far wall. "Don't say I didn't warn you."

"Please, I've landed here—"

The ship lurched hard to the left, throwing Delia and Josie into a crate piled high with produce. A cabbage toppled off and rolled across the floor, wedging itself into a corner barricaded with mops and a stack of nested buckets.

Delia grappled her way across the cargo, a splinter wedging its way deep into her palm. When she reached the wall, she slid the belt over her shoulders and clasped the lock shut. "Gods," she said, gasping for air.

"I told you so," the crew member said, laughing. "Can't say I didn't warn you."

"Is your pilot *drunk*?" Josie demanded, her knuckles white as she pulled herself upright after the ship lurched again.

"Probably. Man likes his rum. What can I say?"

"What kind of captain—" Josie was interrupted by another sharp turn, and this time, the ship's engines shuddered. "After everything, I'm going to wind up dead because some pissant pilot can't manage to stay off the booze for a couple of days."

"We haven't crashed yet, don't get your underwear in a knot. Look out the porthole, we've almost descended all the way to the dock."

"If my pilot drove a ship like this, then I'd—"

The crew member snorted loudly, "If you had a pilot like him, my guess is that you wouldn't be booking passage on freighters in the middle of dark space and paying extra for the privilege. We're not fools, you know. It's no mystery that you're running from something."

Josie's jaw set firm. "You said you wouldn't say anything." Her hand strayed, reaching for the revolver she'd hidden in her waistband.

"And we won't, so you can stop reaching for that pea-shooter you've got in your pants."

"How did you—"

"I've been at this a long time. I can spot a concealed weapon from a hundred meters. Trust me, you don't want to travel down that route. Are we understood?"

Josie's arms fell to her sides. "Yeah."

The ship's landing gear engaged, and they set down in the middle of the busy port.

"Now get the hell out of my bay before we get flagged for an inspection," the crew member said. "And don't let me catch you on this ship again. You're too mouthy for your own good. Gonna get someone killed someday."

"Joke's on you, I already did!" Josie barked, tucking in her shirt. "Let's go, Dodson, we have a meeting to get to, and I don't want to spend even one more second on this piece of shit ship."

"Yeah, good riddance!" the crew member yelled, unbuckling herself. "Fucking arrogant little shit."

"Which way to the Brushstroke Inn?" Delia asked, ushering Josie out of the loading bay before she started a fist fight. "I've never been to Chalidon before. I don't know my way around."

"I'm not surprised a delicate princess like you has never been left to fend for yourself. Take a right out of the dock's gate, and the inn is half a kilometer up the hill, set back into an alley."

"Sounds very above-board."

"Listen, you're welcome to find your own way off this rock if you're going to criticize everything."

Delia put her hands up in surrender. "I'm not criticizing. Just an observation, that's all. Trust me, I've been in my share of speakeasies."

"Yeah." Josie barked a laugh, sharp and percussive. "I'll bet. Get a move on, Dodson, we don't want to be late for our own party."

* * *

The Brushstroke Inn looked normal, at first glance, if slightly dingy. Delia rested her palms against the reception desk, frowned, and then wiped the dust off on her trousers. "Place looks like no one has stayed here in a decade," she said.

"That's probably true, at least top-side. Maybe an errant traveler here or there, but it's hardly on the main drag of the city. Come on, the basement is this way." Josie waved her over to a narrow, steep staircase. "We'll take the stairs. My navigator will need the lift, if he's not here already."

The thick, greasy cobwebs in the corner made Delia wary. "This looks like heaven for spiders."

"You afraid of a little bug?"

"Ones that can bite you? Yes. I am suitably hesitant to bunk in with them." The old stone walls had long lost their mortar, and parts had crumbled away. The steps were carefully kept, though, with bright yellow paint at the edge of each stair.

"Don't be such a baby. It's only a few more to go."

"We'll see who's a baby when you get bitten."

"Gods below, just walk."

Delia descended the rest of the steps into a basement piled high with old, empty crates with jagged edges and an empty utility shelf. "Some speakeasy."

"Shut up," Josie said, pulling the shelf away from the wall. "Get in."

Delia slid through the opening before it was fully wide, into a small room lined with maps tacked to the walls from floor to ceiling. The bar itself was brightly lit, though the patron tables were dim and secretive.

"Look, everyone's here," Josie said, gesturing to where three circular tables had been pushed together. "Right on time."

Delia squinted. "It's not everyone. Rosie and Thomas—"

"Just sit down so we can hammer this out. We'll fill them in later. We've at least got Dirk, Owen, the kid, and the spy here, so let's get started." Josie turned to the barkeep. "A round of ales for my friends, if you please."

"Anything for you, Cap," he said, his bushy mustache obscuring the broad grin. "New shipment in from off-world. Good stuff. Barely even tastes like piss."

"That's what I love to hear!"

"Where are the others?" Delia asked, pulling up a chair. "Have you heard anything? Were they here already?"

Carmen shook her head. "We haven't seen them, but it's only just now time. Maybe their ship was delayed getting through the atmosphere."

"Rough landing?" Josie asked. "Seems no one around here knows how to pilot a ship."

"I wouldn't call it rough, so much as death-defying," Emeline quipped, a thick, silk scarf draped around her shoulders. "I can't say I would be thrilled to come here again."

"With any luck, you won't have to," Carmen said. "The terraformers here have to work harder to keep the air pure, and it makes for a little bit of a tumbled ride. We got here okay in the end."

"Cap, the broadcasts picked up the story," Owen said. "In a sense. Says rebels captured the girl here, and they've got patrols heading in every direction. I don't think they know where we ended up, though."

"What about Tarand?" Delia asked.

"Nah, nothing about her. I reckon they want to keep that quiet. It doesn't look good for them to admit a bunch of convicts escaped on a High Council ship."

Carmen sipped from her pint of ale. "None of you were even supposed to be on the station, remember? Tarand herself may not even know."

"Do you really think they'd let us escape with Allemande's daughter without coming after us?" Delia asked. "No, we should still be careful. They won't let us get away that easily."

Emeline nodded. "My mother will be coming to rescue me. I can promise you that."

"And what are your thoughts on the matter? You gonna sell us out at the first opportunity, start screaming in the streets?" Josie leaned across the table, nose-to-nose with Emeline. "Boys, I hope you blindfolded this little angel on the way in here."

"Of course, Cap. Only let her take it off once we were at the table."

"Good. I'd hate for her to ruin good establishments by running her big mouth."

"So long as you get me to Skelm, I'll never say a word about how I got there. I will begin my work there, publicly, and then my mother will know that I do not intend to go back to Turas-Mara unless it's on official business."

"Let's not get ahead of ourselves," Josie said, after draining her pint.

"We still need to make it off this rock with my ship and my crew, and get to... well, you'll see when we get there."

Carmen nodded. "It's for the best that we realign there before carrying on to Skelm. However, you..." she trailed off, and looked at Emeline apologetically. "You may want to have her in the brig. We can't risk it."

"In the brig!" Emeline shouted, outraged. "I'm not your damned prisoner! That wasn't the deal we made!"

"It's for the best," Carmen explained. "For your benefit and everyone else's. If you saw where that ship was heading, if anything happened after, they'd all think it was you. There would be... repercussions."

"Please, everyone knows there are secret rebel bases all over the Near Systems. It's hardly a secret."

"Carmen is right," Josie announced. "We can't risk it. They'd have my head on a spike before sundown if I waltzed in there with one of the most high-profile figures." The captain frowned, drumming her fingers against the worn wood tabletop. "You're presenting more problems than I care to solve, kid. If I'd had it my way, we would have left you on that station, dead. You've put more than one target on our backs, now that I think of it."

"Let's focus on regrouping and getting her to Skelm, and then hoping that she keeps her word," Carmen said. "You *will* keep your word, won't you, Emeline?"

"I told you, I won't utter a word about any of this, so long as you get me where I need to go. We can part ways after that."

"Nah, I don't trust her," Dirk said. "She'll sell us out first chance she gets."

"I won't!"

"That's what they all say, until they're strapped to a chair with an inspector firing questions at them. Then, they all sing like canaries."

"My mother wouldn't allow that."

"You should ask your mother how she questions prisoners," Josie said. "Just ask Thomas—"

"They still aren't here," Delia interrupted. Every movement of the clock on the wall dragged on her heart.

"Hmm. So they aren't."

"We need to wait for them."

Josie shook her head. "No, what we need to do is get the hell out of here before someone recognizes the little princess here."

"We can't just leave them! Thomas is the only reason any of you are free!"

"Thomas isn't my problem. My crew is my problem. My ship is my problem. Your friend, your girl… they aren't my problem. They aren't my responsibility."

Delia stood up so fast, the chair she'd been sitting on toppled over behind her. "No. No! I'm not leaving here without Thomas and Rosie. I choose to stay here and wait for them."

"Oh, dear, what a conundrum," Josie mused. "Boys?"

Delia barely had time to scream before the blinding pain made the room spin around her.

Chapter 36

"What do you mean, they aren't here?" Rosie demanded, leaning over the bar. "They're supposed to be here. We're only an hour late, our ship—"

"Listen, lady, how many times do I have to tell you? I didn't see anything. This place has been empty all day."

"This *is* the Brushstroke Inn, isn't it?" Thomas asked, his voice still weak and raspy.

"Yep."

"And there isn't another one somewhere in the city? Or—or somewhere else on Delta-4?"

The barkeep tossed a soggy rag into a bucket. "I don't keep a tally of every place on the planet, buddy, but as far as I know, we're the only one." He shrugged and disappeared into the back room.

"Something doesn't feel right," Rosie whispered. "They can't all have been later than we were."

"No, he's lying," Thomas agreed. "He knows something. Maybe he was paid off. Or threatened."

"Why would they have paid him off to lie to us?"

"I think we both know it could only have been Josie."

Rosie shoved her hands into her pockets. "What do we do now, then? We don't have much to barter with, we don't know where they could have gone..."

"I have an idea where they may have gone."

"Where?"

"I've only ever heard about it in whispers. Fragments of information, really—but there's a secret pirate settlement called—"

The barkeep poked his head out from the door. "I'd be careful what you're saying, and where," he cautioned. "If you're trying to get there, saying the name aloud is a big clue that you shouldn't even know that it exists." He narrowed his eyes. "How *do* you know that it exists?"

"I've spent many years passing information to pirates and rebels," Thomas croaked. Sometimes, they pass tidbits back to me."

"I know where it is," Rosie said, resigned.

"What?" both men asked.

"It's a long story. I've never been there, myself, but my grandfather always talked about it when I was young. Said it was like heaven. My grandmother helped to establish it."

"Does Delia know that?" Thomas asked.

"No. I never told her."

"Why?"

"Because my grandmother was killed for knowing where it was. She never gave up the location, so they... they killed her."

Thomas laid a sympathetic hand over her arm. "I'm sorry."

"I tried to forget for years. I ran as far as I could after she died. It's how I ended up at the Rim."

"But you know its location?"

"I do. She taught it to me in a song."

"I don't understand."

Rosie sighed. "It's like a puzzle. If you have all the pieces, it makes sense."

"If you're looking to get there, you'll have a hell of a time from the docks here. Too regimented. Too many checks. Not as bad as Gamma-3, but it's gotten worse over the years," the bartender offered. "You'd do better to get a shuttle up to the second moon. There's a small transport hub there that some of the rum-runners use."

"Do you think they'd give us a ride?" Thomas asked.

The bartender shrugged. "I doubt it, but as you got here by hitching rides, I'll go ahead and assume that stowing away isn't outside your skill set. Don't get caught. They'll kill you."

"Isn't there a better way?" Rosie asked.

"No. Not unless you've got a big pile of credits, and judging by your appearances, no offense intended, you two don't."

"We've been traveling for days, and he—" Rosie started to say.

The bartender held his hands up to stop her. "Don't say anything else. I prefer not to know what's going on. Harder for an MPO to beat it out of me if push came to shove."

"I understand." Rosie snapped off a chunk of the ore in her pocket and laid it on the bar. "Are you sure you didn't see anything earlier?"

"I'm sure. I'd be less sure if that was a bigger piece."

"You're a damned thief," Thomas spat. "A common brigand, a—"

"Listen, pal, we've all got to find a way to live nowadays, yeah? Josie's a good customer, and—"

"So they *were* here," Rosie interrupted. "I bet we can assume the rest."

The bartender nodded. "I'll bet you can, too. But you didn't hear that from me, alright? Not a damned word of it. I have enough problems without losing loyal patrons. This place is barely staying afloat as it is, with all the new laws in place." He ran his hands over his bald head. "Hold on. Wait here," he said, disappearing into the back once again.

"What do you think happened?" Thomas asked.

"Hard to know for sure, but Delia wouldn't have left us here without a fight."

"No, she wouldn't have."

"Which tells me that Josie... well, I don't know for sure, but I worry they may be in trouble."

"Do you think she'd sell them back to the Coalition?"

"Maybe. I wouldn't put it past her."

Thomas pulled at a frayed thread on his bandage. "No, me neither."

"We need to get to—well, we need to get to where we need to go. Maybe they'll go there, if we're lucky. If nothing else, we might be able to barter our way onto a ship that knows Josie, knows where she goes."

"It's going to be hard to find someone willing to sell out one of their own."

"Given her attitude problems, I'm hoping it might be easier than we anticipate. Maybe she's pissed off one too many pirates."

"Here," the bartender said, setting a fabric-wrapped bundle atop the bar. "Some provisions. Water, rum, food. Better grub than you've been getting, from what I can tell."

"Thank you, I—" Thomas started to say, when the bartender took the lump of metal and pocketed it. "Hey!"

"I'm not a charity," the bartender said. "Trust me, that's a bargain. You got information and supplies. Most would pay double for that, but I... well, I'm hoping you tell people about this place. We'll go under if we don't start seeing more patrons in here soon."

"We will," Rosie assured him, taking the parcel. "And thank you for this. You're right that it's the best we've seen lately."

"Now, get out of my sight before I change my mind. Speakeasies have been raided for less, you know."

* * *

They had to use the rest of their bartering metal to buy passage on a shuttle to the transport hub. If they couldn't find passage to the pirate settlement, they'd end up stranded in a small transport hub—or have to sneak onto a ship. Neither was an attractive option.

"Can I have some more of that bread?" Thomas asked after they settled into their seats.

Rosie handed him the parcel. "Have the rest."

"No, no, I couldn't. That wouldn't be fair."

"You've been in a cell for months. Have the bread. I'll be fine with some of the dried fruit."

Thomas groaned with happiness as he took a bite. "You don't know how important real food is until you've been denied it. When I was in that cell, I thought I'd never taste bread again."

"When we're out of this mess, Thomas, I'll make you ten loaves."

"You bake?"

"Bread, cakes... not pastries. To hell with making pastries."

"I like pastries."

"Everyone likes them. I, however, hate laminating dough with the substitutes available these days. Back on the farm..." she trailed off. "Never mind."

"Alright, no pastries," he agreed, and took another bite. "Maybe a cake, though."

"Real vanilla, with buttercream frosting. A nice cup of coffee alongside."

"Now you're talking."

"Freshly ground beans, a thick, complex aroma. Gods below, I miss good coffee."

"I've always been more of a tea man, myself," Thomas said. "A nice, floral black tea. Double steeped. Squeeze of lemon."

"You don't find that out at the Rim."

"No."

"What happened to you, then?"

He looked around, craning his neck to see where the other passengers were seated. "They'd suspected us for a long time."

"Us? You mean they knew Delia was in on it?"

"I managed to convince Overseer Allemande otherwise." He patted the bandage on his arm and winced. "She'd gone through months of our scripts from broadcasts long before we even joined Turas-Mara. *Keep your enemies close*,' she said. The broadcasts in Skelm were too much. Too obvious, maybe, but it felt like there was no other option. Not after our Scattered contact there went missing. I bet the bitch killed him herself."

"They told everyone you'd died, even Delia."

He nodded. "Allemande wanted to question me first. To make Delia think I'd talked, maybe, or that I'd lost my senses. To entice her to let her guard down. She didn't, though, and that's the only reason I'm sitting here with you now."

"She was so distraught, you know."

"I never thought she'd find me. I guess, in a way, I have Josie to thank for that."

"Let's not go overboard," Rosie said. "Josie left us here. And I don't think Delia would have gone willingly. Maybe Josie threatened her, or... I don't know."

"If I learned one thing in that cell, it's that you shouldn't ever assume you know what's going on when you don't have the full story." He shoved the last of the bread into his mouth and chewed thoughtfully. "Allemande told me that Delia ratted me out. I knew that was a lie. She also said that my family had written to the general with their suspicions. I didn't know if that was truth or fiction. Maybe I still don't."

The shuttle's engine roared into life, sending them hurtling into the atmosphere. They'd paid dearly for the voyage, but the smooth ride into space was almost worth it. Delta-4 faded from view as they ascended, finally disappearing behind thick cloud cover.

"Should be a short flight, at least," Rosie offered. "Hopefully, someone will help us."

Thomas grimaced. "It's going to be a hard sell, without anything to trade. We might have to—" he looked around again, suspicious. "Stowaway."

"I'll do anything if it means I can make sure that Delia is safe. And Carmen, too."

"What about Emeline?"

"She's too valuable. Josie would be a fool to hurt her. And Josie, despite her past actions, is no fool."

"What do you think she was looking for on the station?"

"I've only heard whispers about it. A weapon."

"It's always a weapon," Rosie said with a sigh.

"They've been testing it out past the Rim, on some abandoned mining camps out there. Last I heard from my contact in the science division, up at the CSA, they want to use it to wipe out rebel settlements for good."

"You have a contact in the CSA?"

"I do. Jhaveri. Never seen her in person, and everything I get comes through three layers of code. Minimal information, but it's better than nothing."

"But Carmen said it was a decoy on Turas-Mara."

Thomas nodded. "By the time Josie showed up, it was. I'll bet my right arm that they were feeding false information somewhere, to see where the leak was. No doubt whoever that was, is sitting in a cell somewhere now. If they haven't been killed already."

"Jhaveri?"

"No. She knew it was a decoy. I wanted to get information out, but... Allemande grabbed me before I could. Had MPOs snatch me right out of bed that night. I didn't even know what was happening until it was too late."

"We'll land soon. We should keep quiet. People might wander back here looking for their suitcases."

Thomas nodded. "Aye."

The shuttle landed gently, coasting into a wide bay at the far end of the transport hub. It was much smaller than Faaion Beacon had been, but almost as busy. Crowds of people bustled to and fro, and as Rosie and Thomas disembarked, they found themselves lost in a sea of bodies.

"Move it!" one man yelled.

"Sorry," Rosie apologized, jumping out of the way. "We need to find where these ships are headed. The one we need won't be listed on the departures board, it will only be cargo." She squinted up at the ceiling, trying to read. "I can't see what that says, can you?"

"I can, but all the bays are listed. Maybe we'll have to wait."

"Bay six is departing right now for Epsilon-6. There should be another ship coming in there, but nothing is listed. Might be cargo. Might be just the ship we need."

"Let's go."

Fighting their way through the crowds, they didn't even reach bay six until the previous ship was long gone, and the new one landed, the ramp rolling down to the floor.

"It's unregistered," Thomas said. "That's a good sign."

"Should we... ask?"

"I don't know. I don't make a habit of this."

Rosie snorted. "Fair point."

The loading bay door rose up, clanking noisily, deafening even over the din of the throngs of people in the hub. At first, there was no one there. And then, there was General Fineglass, her braid unkempt and out of uniform.

"You stay away from us!" Rosie shouted, backing away. "We don't know anything. We didn't do anything!"

General Fineglass stared at them, bewildered.

Thomas turned to run.

"Wait!" the general yelled. "Wait. Who do you think I am?"

"I—we—you mean to tell me that you *aren't* General Fineglass?"

"Get inside. Quick."

"It's a trap," Thomas said, his voice strangled with panic. "It's clearly her, just look!"

Rosie hesitated. "Who are you, then?"

"I can't say out in the open. My—General Fineglass threatened me on pain of death if I was ever seen and confused for her, if that gives you any idea."

Thomas pulled away from Rosie. "I'm not going back to that cell. You'll have to kill me first." He retreated, trying to grasp at Rosie's sleeve drag her along. "We need to get to Josie."

"Hold on, Josie? Captain Josie?"

"How do you know her?"

"You could say we are... acquainted."

Rosie reached back for Thomas. "We're thin on allies right now, Thomas."

"Yes, which is why I'm not keen to trust just anyone," he replied. "I didn't get off that station just to meet my demise because I didn't think things through."

Not-the-general held her hands up. "I'm not going to kill anyone. Please trust me. Look," she said, rolling up the sleeve of her jumpsuit, revealing an intricate tattoo of vines curling around her forearm, disappearing into a thicket of leaves and ferns that peeked out from beneath the fabric. "I can't be Fineglass, see?"

"It could be a fake."

She licked her hand and rubbed vigorously at the tattoo. "It's not a fake."

"Thomas?" Rosie prompted, reaching out for his arm. "Come on, let's just see. If it is the general, we're dead either way."

"I'd rather be dead than back in that cell," he said, hesitant, still leaning on the balls of his feet, like he was preparing to run at any moment.

"No one is going to put you into a cell," the woman said, extending her hand. "I'm Bailey Stockton."

Rosie shook her hand. "Rosie Gordon."

"If you come with me, we can take you someplace safe."

"We're trying to get to... well, you know."

Bailey nodded. "That's our next stop. We have a big delivery to one of the taverns there."

"How do I know you won't throw us out an airlock the moment we leave the hub?" Thomas asked, hugging himself. "I know how they like to toy with their prisoners. This might just be another one of her games."

"I've never been good at playing games, as Bertie here can attest."

"She's awful. Rubbish at cards. So terrible, it's not even fun to beat her," a woman with an unruly mop of greying hair said, poking her head out of the ship. "I don't know who you two are, but I do know that sticking around here for any length of time is a recipe for disaster. Speaking of which, we need to get a move on or we're gonna be late, and you know how much Larkin needs this shipment for the event tomorrow."

"Aye," Bailey said, waving her away. "Please, I promise no one here is going to hurt you. We should talk. I feel like you might have some information that I need, and vice versa."

"Come on, Thomas," Rosie said again, holding her hand out for him. "It's the best offer we've got going. She's right—if we stick around here too long, we'll become too obvious, and that's the last thing we need right now."

His glance shifted between the three women before he relented. "Okay."

"We won't let anything happen to you," Bailey reassured him.

They boarded the ship, a small cargo vessel with low ceilings and one narrow hallway. A loose nail head caught on Rosie's dress, tearing a hole in the wool fabric. Rosie frowned at the fraying fibers. "Damn."

"I know someone who can fix that for you when we get there," Bailey said, leading them into the cramped kitchen area. "She's quick as a flash, too." She sat on the long bench, stretching her legs out along the plank of unvarnished wood, the soles of her boots almost like new. "Marshall!" she shouted. "Let's go!"

"Don't mind our state-of-the-art radio system," Bertie said, an eyebrow arched at Bailey. "I should get up to the cockpit before he throws a tantrum again."

"You know he can't navigate worth a damn," Bailey said with a snort.

"After fifteen years, you'd think I'd have learned my lesson."

After Bertie disappeared up the ladder, Rosie cleared her throat. "Is it... safe? To talk here?"

"Yes."

"Of course they'd say that," Thomas said bitterly. "Why would anyone ever admit that it wasn't?"

Bailey pushed a bowl of fresh fruit towards him. "What can I do to convince you that I'm not her? Here, you should eat something. You look half-starved."

"He is," Rosie said. "They had him locked—"

"Don't tell her anything, not until we know she's not lying," Thomas said, reaching for an apple and eyeing it suspiciously. "Could be poisoned."

"It's not." Bailey grabbed another piece of fruit and took a bite. "See? Would I eat poisoned fruit?"

"I guess not."

"Seems to me you both have met my sister."

Thomas recoiled. "Your... sister? But General Fineglass doesn't have a sister."

"It's *true*?" Rosie said with a gasp.

Bailey's brow furrowed. "Where did you hear this? A rumor? She said that she'd quashed all the press about when I was in the Capital."

"No, it was a note—wait, so Delia's hunch was right?"

"Delia? Delia Dodson, the radio presenter?"

"Yes, that's her!"

"I met her once. She seemed nice."

Rosie took a plum from the bowl. "She is."

"Can we go back to this business about the note? Who was writing notes? And why?"

"I don't know, I just kept finding them in my room." Pulling one of the crumpled slips from her pocket, she smoothed it out onto the small wooden table. "See?"

"Huh." Bailey took the note, examining it. "She wrote this."

"She? She who?"

"My sister. General Fineglass."

"Are you sure?"

Bailey nodded. "I'd recognize her writing anywhere. I should, really, after spending a week signing her signature. See that weird little loop on the letter L? That's her, alright. But why would she be leaking information like this?"

"To ensnare us again, probably," Thomas said, nibbling at the apple core. "You're probably part of this whole charade. How else does someone have a sister like her who continues to be a rum-runner?"

"Oh, don't worry, my friend, she threatened me on pain of death if I was ever seen anywhere someone could think it was her. Which makes it all the stranger that she'd be writing notes to someone about it."

"She caught us in the overseer's office," Rosie offered. "But she let us go, instead of throwing us into the brig."

"Shh!" Thomas cautioned. "Don't tell her anything else!"

"Why were you in the overseer's office?"

"One of the notes mentioned a secret file." Rosie rummaged in her pockets once again and produced the note. "See here, a file."

"Did you find this file?"

"Yes. It was about some ship called the Cricket."

The color drained from Bailey's face. "Shit. Gods. Marshall!" she shouted. "Juice it. We need to talk to Captain Violet. They might be in trouble."

"We're as juiced as we're gonna get," the captain shouted back. "I'll send a message ahead to Bradach. Make sure she doesn't leave."

"What did the file say?" Bailey demanded. "Who was in it? Was I in it? Was... someone named Mae, in it?"

"The suspected crew members, mostly. Outdated or missing photos, but there was someone named Georgina, another called... Henrietta?"

"Yes, that tracks. They both worked for the Coalition before Skelm burned down."

"And Violet, like you mentioned. I don't remember the rest. I'm so sorry. Your name was crossed out. No photo."

Thomas reached for another piece of fruit. "Delia didn't tell me you broke into Allemande's office."

"It's not like we had much time for catching up, what with breaking you out with the rest of them."

"Rest of them?" Bailey asked. "What do you mean, rest of them?"

"Someone named Josie tried to steal something from Turas-Mara Station. Some of her crew died. A couple ended up with her in the brig. The others escaped."

"I shouldn't be surprised that Josie is mixed up in this. What a mess this is. Well, where are the others? Where is Delia Dodson? Where is Captain Josie?"

"We... don't know," Rosie admitted. "We were supposed to meet up with them at an inn in Chalidon. Thomas and I were late, our flight delayed, and they were long gone by the time we got there. The bartender wouldn't tell us much."

"No, I imagine Josie will have paid him well to keep his mouth shut."

"I'm worried that something happened."

"We'll do all we can. It will be a day or so to Bradach, and we'll round up whoever we can to try to track them down."

Chapter 37

Delia groaned. Her head was pounding, and even as she opened her eyes, the cell around her spun. Cell. She was in a cell. "Hey!" she shouted. "Let me out of here!"

"Don't bother," Carmen said from the cell across. "All you'll get for your efforts is another head injury."

"What happened?"

"That little skunk took us prisoner, is what happened," Emeline spat. She was in the last cell against the wall. "I'll string her up myself the moment I get out of here."

"Did they knock you both out, too?"

Carmen sighed. "No. She let us see them give you a few good hits, and asked if we'd play along. There was no point in fighting back. Once her navigator arrived, a few seconds after you got knocked out, we were far too outnumbered."

"Rosie? Thomas?"

"They never showed."

"I don't feel well," Delia managed to mumble, before rolling over and vomiting into a bucket.

"That's common with a concussion. Just take it easy. We can't do anything right now, anyway." Carmen leaned closer to the iron bars of her cell. "We should get you looked at. Head injuries can be serious."

Delia wiped her mouth with the back of her hand. "Somehow, I doubt that Josie is all that concerned with providing adequate medical care."

"She doesn't know who she's toying with," Emeline said, her tone strident and tight. "My mother will—"

"Your mother lied to protect herself and her reputation. They didn't even come after us, because it would inform Tarand that we escaped on her ship."

"She's biding her time. She wouldn't leave me to rot."

"I guess we'll see about that."

"I guess we *will*."

The footsteps descending into the brig made the pain in Delia's head pulse with every rhythmic tap of a boot heel on the iron ladder. "Well, look who's finally awake," Josie said, sneering at them all. "Maybe you should have thought twice before running your mouths."

"What is your game here, Josie?" Carmen asked. "As far as I can tell, you—"

"*Captain* Josie, if you please. We are on my ship, after all."

"Fine. As far as I can tell, *Captain* Josie, you're in a position of limited gain."

"Oh really? And how is that?"

"You're in possession of a high-value hostage that you won't be able to use without risking bringing down the might of the entire Coalition fleet on yourself. And what are you going to do with the rest of us? Delia is a fugitive now, and I'm nobody. A whisper on the wind. A spy."

Josie barked a performative laugh, bending to slap her knee. "What an excellent joke, Carmen! Hell, if being a spy doesn't work out, which, let's be honest here, it clearly hasn't, you may yet have a future as a clown."

"When my mother gets hold of you—" Emeline said, her face contorted with rage.

"Pipe down, pipsqueak. Your mother hasn't even put out an alert. Guess you're not that important, after all."

"She'll be looking. Odds are, she already has a fleet of cloaked ships on their way here already."

"I doubt that. Besides, we have technology that can detect Coalition signatures long before they get close enough to question ours. You're in here for the long haul, kiddo."

"I will get out of here, and when I do, you'll be the first pirate I hunt down."

"Excellent. I look forward to it, in fact. But I won't hold my breath, if that's okay by you, because I'd die of asphyxiation before you got anywhere near me. All of you thought that you were more clever than me. Delia was going to throw me out an airlock the first opportunity she got, and we all know it. Carmen here would have reported me to the first informant she could, telling them all about how I got caught. And you, my dear darling Emeline, haven't stopped making empty threats since the moment I laid eyes on you."

"Believe me, my threats are anything but empty."

"I guess we'll see about that, won't we? For now, you're in a cell on my ship. It doesn't look very good for you."

"You can't keep us here forever," Delia muttered. "If nothing else, you wouldn't have space to imprison anyone else that crosses you."

"Of course I'm not keeping you here forever, you pomegranate. Delia Dodson, the up-jumped jackass of a reporter. You'll fetch a mighty fine price on the black market. No doubt there's someone who will pay for your hide. No one gets as high as you have in the ranks without pissing a few people off."

"So you are ransoming us," Carmen said. "If that's the case, then I have a few names who will pay for my release."

"I'm not going to sell you off to the highest bidder. What do you think I am, a monster? No, I want to be sure that everyone has the option to have their say. Wouldn't you agree that's fair?"

"Just let us go, Captain Josie. We're of no use to you. Release us, and I'll make sure you are beautifully rewarded."

"This isn't about the money, it's about revenge. No one crosses me and gets away with it, do you hear me?"

"Cross you? Rosie is the one who freed you!" Delia protested. "Without us, you'd still be on Turas-Mara at the ass-end of nowhere!"

"Rosie isn't here, now is she? So as far as I'm concerned, you're prisoners, fair and square. Now, if you don't mind, I have a pressing dinner engagement with an enormous bowl of fried tofu. Enjoy your stay." As she began the climb out of the brig, Josie looked over her shoulder with a laugh. "Oh, don't look at me like that. I'll feed you, of course. We have plenty of protein bricks on the ship for you."

"I really dislike that woman," Carmen grumbled when Josie had disappeared up the ladder. "My grandmother always said to look for the best in someone, but Josie really tries my patience."

Delia rubbed her head. "Looks like we're stuck here."

"My mother will—"

"If your mother does track this ship down, she'll kill everyone except you."

"Maybe you deserve it," Emeline spat. "You are pirates, after all."

"I'm a reporter, not a pirate."

"Yet you were passing information to the rebels."

"Hmm," Delia said, distracted by the throbbing in her skull. "There's no proof of that. Besides, weren't you the one who was so desperate to speak about the truth of Skelm?"

"Those are laborers, not pirates. They work for their bread, they don't just steal it."

Carmen shifted on the bed in her cell. "You might be surprised at how many displaced Skelmians turned to piracy, Emeline."

"Then they had no choice."

"What makes you think anyone else did?"

Emeline fell into a silent sulk, and Delia laid down, turning towards the wall.

"You shouldn't go back to sleep. You might have a concussion," Carmen said gently. "She hit you pretty hard."

"Who hit me?"

"The navigator. She came up behind you."

"What did she hit me with?"

"A glass bottle. I'm surprised it didn't break. More so that you didn't get a wound."

Delia rubbed the back of her head and winced. "Oh, I think I did. It's not bleeding anymore, but I'd guess I could use a few stitches."

"We're going to get out of here, you know."

"Oh yeah? And how are you so sure of that?"

"I have a good feeling about it."

"A good feeling?" Delia asked with a snort. "We're locked in cells on a hostile ship."

"Sure, but we're not dead yet."

"We will be as soon as she sells us off."

Carmen laughed. "She'll have a hard time selling us to anyone. Not even the black market allows that sort of thing nowadays. Her best bet is to ransom us."

"I don't know anyone with money who would pay to spring me. No one Josie would be able to find, anyway." Delia sighed. No doubt William would be in hiding by now. Even he couldn't escape the jaws of the general's expectations. "I'm just a reporter."

"Have faith, Delia. Someone will come for us."

"How do you do that?"

"Do what?"

"Act so... positive."

"Oh." Carmen leaned against the wall, pulling a tangle of curls out from behind her. "I guess I've been through worse than this, so I know that this can't be the end. If I survived all those other things, it's impossible that I wouldn't survive this, too."

"I'm not sure that's how it works."

Carmen shrugged. "Maybe not. But it's served me well enough so far. Besides, I was in Skelm when it burned. You were a voice in the darkness. Now I can be that for you, too."

"You weren't there on a tutoring assignment, were you?"

"No."

"Were you one of the escapees?"

"Yes. Soldiers had rounded us up and packed us off to be indentured workers in Skelm. There was a riot when we landed, and I just about got away."

"That's not true," Emeline said, her face close to the iron bars. "There was no riot."

"Okay, maybe riot is somewhat of an overestimation, but—"

"No. There was a labor demonstration. We wanted to form a union. But then, they—we—"

"You were thrown onto the nearest shuttle off-world," Delia finished. "They wanted you executed for it. It's all anyone could talk about at the Administration Building, how some kid tried to overthrow the government during a gala."

"I wasn't trying to overthrow the government."

"I know that. Tell that to the people in charge."

"My mother made sure that I was safe."

"Sure. She was the one who made the calls, being the governor and all. Oh, I heard plenty of rumors. They were going to execute you, but they were afraid you'd be a martyr for the cause. Then they discussed work camps, boarding school. In the end, she adopted you to neutralize the threat."

"She adopted me because she loves me."

Delia turned to face her. "She loves that she convinced you to do her bidding. You're just a pawn, Emeline."

"How would you know? I bet there's not a single person in the world who loves you."

"You're probably right about that. At least I don't lie to myself about it. My mother did, before she died. My father, well... he had strange ideas of what was best for me."

"My father died when I was little. You know, my... my real father."

"I'm sorry."

"He died organizing a rebellion. That's what they said, anyway. The guards. The governor at the time, he announced that twelve people went missing at the docks. That was the official line. We never saw him again."

"Your sister fought hard to get you back, you know," Carmen said.

Emeline's face hardened. "I don't have any sisters."

"What happened to you when you were taken?" Delia asked.

"I was transferred from transport to transport for a while. Spent some time in a cell, a nicer one than this. And then my mother showed up, unlocked the door, and took me home."

"Grubs up!" Dirk said, climbing halfway down the ladder. He threw a protein brick into each cell, laughed, and ascended back into the main part of the ship.

"Great," Delia said, the thought of biting into it turning her stomach. "And here I was, afraid I'd never have the pleasure of eating this crap again."

Carmen bit off a corner. "It's not my favorite, I'll give you that. I can't wait to get my hands on some real food again."

"They can't be that bad," Emeline scoffed, taking a hearty bite, before spitting it out into the bucket. "These are expired!"

Delia snorted. "No, that's just what they taste like."

"It's disgusting. Gods, I'd take the moldy tins of beans back in Skelm over whatever this is supposed to be."

"According to your mother, it's a nutritionally complete meal."

"She eats them all the time."

"Maybe she burned off all her taste buds in the name of efficiency. You're lucky you never had these forced on you."

Emeline scowled at the remainder of the brick. "I'm not going to start now, either. I think I'd rather starve than eat this."

"Judging by Josie's attitude, you might have to."

"I'll be rescued long before that."

"I wouldn't count on that," Delia said, nibbling at her own brick. "This ship is fitted with all kinds of tech."

"Tech they stole from the Coalition."

"Some freely given by researchers who defected, actually."

"It's still proprietary information. It's still theft."

Delia snorted. "What happened to you? In Skelm, you had them all completely terrified that you were about to upend how everything there worked. Just a kid, yet you were ready to march on the Administration Building. Now you... you're just another droid for the Coalition."

"I'm not a droid. I just learned I couldn't change anything from the outside."

"I don't think that's true."

"All *due* respect, Ms. Dodson, I didn't ask for your opinion."

"What exactly is your problem with me?"

"It would be easier to list the problems I *don't* have with you," Emeline said. "But, for starters, you've spent your career playing both sides of the fence. It's cowardly."

"It's not cowardly. It's using access for the greater good. Maybe you could learn something from that."

"You doomed dozens of people back in Skelm. You do realize that, don't you? Thirty-eight people died that night in the blaze and the storm."

"I had nothing to do with that."

"You helped the people who burned down my city, Ms Dodson. You made sure that it happened. You fed them clues to help them evade capture, and you assisted in their escape, and I have no time for snakes like you."

"Those people were never found. They may have escaped, too."

"A fairy tale you tell yourself so that you can sleep at night."

"What would you have done in my position, then? As far as I can remember, you weren't giving up any information once you were captured."

"I didn't have any information by then. The place I had been living had already been raided by the time someone came to question me."

Delia swallowed the last bite of the protein brick with a grimace. "You're trying to tell me that you would have willingly sold out your own sister?"

"I told you, I have no sister. For all I know, she's dead."

"She isn't," Carmen said quietly. "Georgie isn't dead, Emeline."

"Don't even say her name in my presence."

"She's spent all this time looking for you. Your birth mother, too, and your little sister Lucy. They miss you very much. So much, in fact, they convinced some of the coordinators for The Scattered to send me to Turas-Mara to make sure that you were okay."

"Clearly, I'm fine. They needn't have bothered."

"They miss you."

"I don't care."

"Em—"

"Leave me alone," Emeline said, her voice wavering. She turned to face the wall, but not before a tear dripped down her cheek onto the rusted metal floor of the brig.

Chapter 38

"Up and at 'em," Bailey said gently, pouring herself a mug of coffee. "We're landing in less than an hour. "Coffee?"

"Yes, please," Rosie said, stretching her arms over her head. Sleeping in the kitchen area had left her feeling stiff and brittle.

"Sorry that we didn't have quarters for you two. Small ship."

"It's okay. We appreciate the hospitality."

"This is nothing, just wait until we get to Bradach. There are some... ground rules, though. Marsh says you have to sign the agreement before we can enter the airspace. It's the law."

"What, we sign our rights away, or something?" Thomas asked. "No, thank you."

"Er—no, you have to promise not to tell anyone where it is."

"I don't even know where we are right now."

"I can tell you, if you—"

"What happens if I did tell?"

Bailey blinked at him. "Are you planning on it?"

"No."

"Okay?"

"Would they have me killed?"

"Uh... they might, yes."

"Fantastic," Thomas said, reaching for the pen in the middle of the table. "From one fascist authority to another. You know, I used to think I'd be so excited to finally set foot in the legendary hidden settlement. Now that it's mere moments away, it feels... lackluster."

"I can understand that. It's just a formality, really. This place protects a lot of people. A lot of refugees, now, too."

"Refugees?"

"Yes, there's a new building development. It's almost finished now. They'll have to start building another straight away, the refugees just keep coming."

"I thought this was a pirate settlement, not a rebel post."

Bailey shrugged. "In some ways, that's a blurry line, these days."

"I'll sign," Rosie said. She was eager to get to Bradach, to find someone who could help her find where Delia had been taken. With every passing hour, she could be further away. She pushed the page to Thomas. "Come on. This is how we get Dee back."

"Yeah." He took the pen and signed, his signature wobbly and uneven. "There."

"Thanks," Bailey said, before shouting up the ladder, "Marsh! We're good!"

"Approaching settlement," he called from the cockpit. "Shouldn't be too long if the bays aren't full up!"

"How long will it take to find someone who might know where Delia is?" Rosie asked.

"Not long," Bailey said, draining her mug. "It's a short walk to the Purple Pig, and they're pretty tapped into what's going on. If Captain Violet is around, we can see if they have time to chase up Josie. Given their history, though, I bet she'll make sure she has the time."

"Bad blood between pirates?" Thomas mused. "You'd think that there would be some kind of... code."

"Not outside Bradach. Anything is fair game. It does lead to some... grudges. But there's no fighting, no brawling or duels in Bradach." Bailey pointed to the papers. "It's in the contract. Part of the rules."

"How oddly civilized."

"We're pirates, sir, not animals. We're perfectly capable of managing our own society. Though, truth be told, I'm more of a rum-runner. Even more of a builder, nowadays."

"Could I have another?" Rosie asked, nudging her mug across the table. "It's been months since I've had a decent cup."

"Gods, if you think this is what counts as a decent cup, you must really have been drinking garbage juice out there. Marshall barely makes drinkable coffee."

"If you want better coffee, you'll make it yourself," Marshall growled from above. "And it's not like Bertie makes any better!"

"Zip your pie hole, you old fool," Bertie said, climbing up from the loading bay. "I swear he gets more ornery with every passing day. Man should have retired months ago, when we had the chance. I think he's hells-bent on working himself into an early grave."

"We all knew he wouldn't give it up after that job," Bailey said with a smirk. "He's addicted to the chase of it."

"The chase, and the credits. Besides, the rum-running makes good cover for transporting folks like these." Bertie grabbed a mug from the hook behind the pot. "Budge up. I need to sit down before I head up to deal with Marshall's inability to land this thing."

"I can land just fine! Maybe if your nav maps weren't so—"

"We all know my nav maps are fine, you old fool. Just fly the damned ship, I'll be up as soon as I knock back some caffeine."

Bailey poured coffee into Bertie's extra large mug, emptying the pot. "I hope no one else wanted any. The coffee at the Pig is much better, though." She examined the bottom of the pot. "We don't want a decaffeinated Bertie."

"Damn right," Bertie said, taking a deep gulp of the steaming liquid. "We all have our vices. At least mine is cheap and probably won't land me in prison."

"No, I imagine it would be the rum-running that would do that."

"Don't tempt fate, Stockton. We've got enough heat on our tail as it is after that little rescue effort grabbing everyone off that asteroid." Bertie took another sip, closing her eyes to savor the taste. "These two haven't met Captain Tansy yet, have they?"

"Who?" Rosie asked.

"She's head of the refugee movement. Got a whole fleet of ships, resources, the whole package. Might be able to help you with whatever you're after. I would imagine that your accounts will have been locked down by now."

"I don't know for sure."

"If they aren't, they're as good as. They'll be tracking your every move if you use it. Captain Tansy will have some emergency funds, but they're limited by how much they can bring in. You'd be best served finding some work as soon as you can."

"We need to find Delia and the others first."

Bertie grimaced. "It's a fool's errand, I'm afraid. Josie's ship rivals the Cricket in stealth. If you're able to find her, rest assured that girl's mother will, too."

"We're not just going to leave them there!" Thomas protested. "Delia's the only reason I'm not still rotting in a cell, she—"

"Listen. I'm not telling you what to do, hotshot, so relax. We've all been known to take risks. I'm just saying, you might need a hell of a lot of help."

"Bertie!" Marshall shouted. "I need that nav map! I don't know where I'm going!"

"You've been here hundreds of times. You can't set down without a map?"

"Gods be damned, Bertie!"

"Alright, alright, keep your trousers on, man." Bertie set her half-empty mug down and hauled herself up the ladder.

Bailey pushed up the sleeves of her jumpsuit. "Won't be long now. We'll get to the Pig and make a plan, alright?"

"Why are you helping us?" Thomas demanded. "For all we know, you could have flown us right back out to the Rim."

"In this old ship, we'd be lucky to reach the Rim in six months," Bailey said with a laugh. "Just wait. You'll see."

* * *

Bradach was the most beautiful place Rosie had ever seen—at least, since she left home so long ago. The cobblestone streets were lined with vegetable gardens, huge, leafy plants with vines that climbed the red brick walls of the buildings. She wished Delia was there to see it for the first time, too.

"This way," Bailey said, waving her up the pavement. "Pig's not far." She shifted the large crate in her arms, the bottles within clinking in a delicate chorus. "They'll be expecting me, at least."

Thomas stared up the hill at the small, bustling city. "How long has this place been here?"

"Oh, at least sixty years. It was already established during the last rebellion."

"It's beautiful. I honestly—I never... never thought I'd really make it here."

"It's one of my favorite places in the whole Near Systems, second only to Hjarta." Bailey's face fell. "Not that Hjarta exists anywhere outside my memories, now."

"What happened?" Rosie asked, though she already knew the answer. Her heart ached not only for Bailey, but for herself, too.

"Coalition."

It was only one word, but it was enough. The brutal history hung in the air.

"I'm sorry."

Bailey sighed. "Me too."

"You have a library here?" Thomas asked, peering down a side street. "What's in it?"

"Books."

"Old books, or new books?"

"Both. I'm not a big reader on my own, so I couldn't say. Mae might know. We can ask her later."

"Mae?"

"My—Mae. She's my person. She's also the best damned seamstress in the Near Systems. *Don't* go to the tailor across town."

"What? Why?"

"Just don't."

Rosie inhaled deep the air that was far fresher than any she'd breathed for years, maybe. A nearby park was home to a cluster of trees, motionless without wind. "It almost feels like Gamma-3."

"That's mostly thanks to Carmen. Come on, the Pig is just around the corner."

"Gods," Rosie breathed at the sight of the towering tavern. "What a beautiful building." The gilded sign hung over the door, the purple boar smiling broadly over the name. "I've never seen anything like it."

"Let's head to the back door, I have to drop this in the kitchen. Hey! Larkin!"

"You're late," a petite woman with a long, thick braid said, a smile playing on her lips. "Where have you been, Stockton?"

"Oh, you know Marshall. He hates parking in the bays here. Says the spaces are too small."

"Who's this?"

"I need to talk to you both, actually. This here is Thomas, he's a fugitive from Turas-Mara. And this is Rosie Gordon. They got separated from the rest of their group in the escape."

"Oh yeah? And who's in that group?"

"Carmen, for one."

Larkin took the crate from Bailey and set it on a table inside. "Oh, shit."

"And Georgie's little sister, for another."

"No."

"Yes. That's right, isn't it?"

Rosie nodded. "Yes. They have Delia, too. Delia Dodson?"

"The reporter?"

"Yeah."

"Gods on steambikes. We need to get Eves in here. Maybe she's picked up some chatter. Who has them?"

Bailey rolled her eyes. "Josie."

"Oh good, an old friend," Larkin said, sarcasm dripping from her words. "Captain Violet will be thrilled, I'm sure."

"They haven't left yet, have they?"

"No, but they're not here. Not yet, anyway. Henry is probably down at the science lab, along with Georgie and her mother. We should... we should break that news gently, Stockton."

Bailey nodded. "I know."

"It's amazing that they got her. I didn't think she'd change her mind, not after... well. Not after what she did to Mae."

"What did Emeline do?" Rosie asked.

"Drugged Mae when she tried to stage a rescue. We couldn't get her out, then. But maybe all that propaganda has worn off."

Rosie shook her head. "Emeline didn't want to come with us. She held a gun on us."

"Maybe don't mention that to Georgie right off the bat. It's going to be hard enough hearing she's off Turas-Mara Station, but still not here." Larkin poked at a pot on the stove. "Eves!" she yelled up into the rafters. "Eves, we have company!"

"Don't you dare touch that soup, Larkin Flores," a woman with short blue hair scolded from the landing. "You almost ruined it last time."

"I didn't do anything, Evie!"

"You were going to, I can tell."

"I wasn't!"

"Mhmm."

Larkin put her hands on her hips. "Don't you want to welcome our new friends?"

"Yes, but not in the kitchen, you grapefruit. Where are your manners? Show them into the tavern!"

"Evie, they came to the back door! Look! Bailey brought our order!"

"And yet you're still standing there, long after you took that box and set it on the table!" Evie laughed, her shoulders shaking. "Come on, into the tavern. You three look hungry."

"Starved," Thomas said. "Literally."

Larkin waved them through the swinging door that led into an opulent, stylish tavern, with plush, velvet seats and gilded, framed art on the walls.

The beauty of it nearly took Rosie's breath away. "I've never seen anything like it," she breathed.

"All of the interiors were decided by Captain Tansy. We did a few things ourselves, Evie and I, but this place would be a pile of rubble if not for Tansy. She's expected back in the docks later this evening. They had a layover that took longer than anticipated."

"Welcome," Evie said, extending her hand. "I'm Evie, as you heard, and you've already met my other half, here."

"This is Rosie and Thomas," Bailey said. "We need to get everyone in here. It's big."

"Big how?"

"They got Emeline."

"Oh, my gods! Where is she?"

Bailey shook her head. "We're going to need Captain Violet. Maybe Captain Tansy, too."

"Alright," Evie said, a worried look settling into her face. "Let me fix up some food."

"I can help," Rosie offered.

"Don't be silly, you're our guests!"

"Please, I would feel much better if I had something to do. I was a cook out at the Rim. And before that, too."

"I hope you don't judge us on the content of our menu. Larkin is a wonderful bartender, but a terrible cook. I get by. Not too many complaints."

"Anything will be better than the protein bricks they had us eating."

Larkin made a retching sound. "I don't think I could ever go back to eating those things. Eves has me spoiled, now."

"Alright, then, we have some soup, and there's fresh bread from this morning."

"Sounds perfect," Rosie said, her stomach already rumbling. She followed Evie back into the kitchen, and, as though automatic, began to slice through the loaf of crusty sourdough bread. "It smells divine."

"I imagine anything would after a protein brick."

"No—I mean, yes, but this loaf is perfect. It's not under proved, the crust is fantastic, and just look at this crumb! So lovely and dense!"

Evie beamed with pride. "I have been practicing. Early loaves were... well, they weren't great, let's just say that."

"Bread is hard to perfect. Even I can't assume I'll get it right every time." Rosie cut another slice, letting it fall over onto the wooden board. "What's the soup, if you don't mind me asking?"

"Potato and leek, fresh from the community garden—"

A woman burst in through the kitchen door. "Where is she?"

"Georgie! We were just going to send someone down—"

"Where's my sister?"

"She's not here," Rosie said. "We took her off the station, but we got separated on Delta-4."

Georgie's face fell. "Oh. I thought..."

"How did you even hear so soon? They only just got here!" Evie said.

"Lucy was playing hide and seek with one of the kids that arrived last week. She heard someone say they'd found Emeline, and she ran down to the labs to tell us. I ran all the way back." Georgie covered her face with her hands. "She already told my mother, too. She'll be on her way up, thinking Em is here."

Rosie stopped slicing. "I'm so sorry," she said softly. "We're going to do everything we can to get her back."

"Who are you?"

"I was the cook on Turas-Mara Station. We had a bit of a jailbreak."

"Gods, does it ever stop?" Georgie asked in a sad voice. "Seems like we're having to break someone out every other week now."

Evie laid a hand on Georgie's shoulder. "It's only going to get worse before it gets better. Come on, let's go sit down. Everyone else will be here soon."

"I've got this," Rosie said, waving Evie away. "I know my way around a kitchen." She finished slicing the loaf, halving the pieces and arranging them on a plate before ladling the soup into equal portions. It smelled divine and tasted even better. A perfect amount of leek. Evie was selling herself short as a cook.

She delivered the food to the table, deftly carrying the bowls four at a time, stacked against her forearms. "Grub's up," she said, sitting down to eat. "Thank you, Evie and Larkin."

"Yes, thank you," Thomas echoed.

Georgie gave her soup a forlorn look. "I really thought she'd be here."

"I know," Evie said. "She will be, soon. This is a big step forward."

"I should tell Lucy and my mother before they get up here. Before they run into the others and tell them, too." Georgie stood from the table, leaving the food untouched. "I'll be back. Someone can have my dinner. I've lost my appetite."

Thomas swapped his empty bowl for Georgie's without a word, and the doors of the tavern swung wide, allowing the warm afternoon glow to pool on the floor for just a second as several silhouettes entered.

"You rang?" a petite woman with a scar across her face announced. "We have a ship to raid. We don't want to miss it. Not if we want their cargo."

"Captain Violet, I found these two out at the transport hub off Delta-4," Bailey said. "They know something about Emeline, and the reporter, Delia Dodson. It sounds like that's where Carmen ended up, too."

"Emeline?" the captain asked, an eyebrow raised. "I thought we'd lost communication with Turas-Mara Station." She turned to a woman behind her of similar height, but dressed in a long black tailcoat. "Kady?"

"We did lose comms, yes. Our attempts to patch in were too obvious."

"So that's what that was?" Rosie asked. "We thought it was the military."

"Yes, by design. Still, the Rim was just too far for our antennae to reach. We thought that maybe Carmen had been captured, or worse."

"Well, she was, but not until we escaped the station."

Captain Violet pulled up a chair. "What does that mean?"

"Another captain, she—"

"It was Josie, wasn't it?"

Rosie nodded. "Yes."

"I told you she was up to something, didn't I, Alice? I told you that she was going to cause more trouble for us."

A tall woman with an eyepatch behind her tugged at one of her long, silvery braids. "I thought that maybe, since we saved her daughter—"

"I told you she wouldn't see it that way. I should have listened to my gut." The captain turned back to the table. "Where did they go?"

"I don't know," Rosie said, shaking her head. "Thomas and I arrived at the Brushstroke Inn on Delta-4 hours after they departed. The bartender wouldn't tell me much, but he did confirm they'd been there."

"Damn. They could be almost anywhere by now. Bailey, did you pick up on any chatter when you were out rum-running?"

Bailey shook her head. "No, we didn't hear anything. But given what we know of Josie, that doesn't surprise me."

"Someone needs to take her out," Larkin muttered. They all turned to look at her, and she shrugged. "Relax, I didn't mean me. Those days are behind me, I promised Evie. I just meant that Josie is going to piss off the wrong pirate one of these days, and running back here to Bradach isn't going to save her."

The tall bearded man standing next to the captain sighed and leaned on his cane. "I can start charting a course to some known locations, Boss, if you want."

"Yes," the captain agreed. "That seems like the best course of action, for now. But we'll need to be careful. No doubt that monster of an overseer will have her hounds out looking for Emeline. She's not going to give that up easily. Alice, make sure we load the bay with all the extra fuel we can fit. We'll have to be flying stealthed the whole way through."

Alice nodded. "Sure thing, Vi."

"Wait," Rosie said, standing up. "What about Thomas and I? What can we do?"

"You can stay out of the way," Kady said icily. "You're civilians. You'll just get us killed. We'll come back here when we have them in hand."

"I can help. I could cook for the crew!"

"Ned does our cooking."

"I'll help however I can. I'll even scrub the walls if you need me to."

Georgie came back into the room through the kitchen entrance, her sister and mother in tow. "If anyone is going, it's me, and I think we all know that."

"Absolutely not," Kady said. "Too much risk of emotion clouding your judgment. Thomas should stay here in Bradach, he looks like what he needs is plenty of rest. Rosie, you should stay, too."

"Emotional?" Georgie shouted. "This is my sister we're talking about! I've spent almost two years looking for her, trying to get her back, I—"

"Georgina," her mother said gently. "This is for the best. I think that Henry would agree."

"I do agree, in fact," a woman said, coming through the front doors. "I was calling after you, George. Didn't you hear me?"

"No," Georgie said, reaching out for her.

"You know our faces are all over the bounty feeds. We can't risk getting too close to a Coalition ship. Even if we were careful, someone might recognize us. Especially if we end up anywhere near Skelm."

"Henry, I know." Georgie buried her face in her hands. "I know. I just want to be there when they get her. I want to make sure it all goes okay."

"I'll go," Bailey offered. "I know how important it is to get your sister back."

"I don't need you fighting my battles for me, Stockton."

"It's not about that. It's about doing what's best for all of us here."

"You have a much more recognizable face than me. What makes you think you going is any better as a solution?"

Bailey rolled up the sleeves of her worn green jumpsuit. "I can use mine to our advantage, just like I did—"

"No," Georgie's mother said. "I cannot accept you risking yourself like that. If that general finds you again, she'll kill you for sure. They won't even have the opportunity to break you out of a cell, and even that is getting harder by the day."

"We need a plan," Henry said. "Arguing about who is or isn't going doesn't help, and doesn't get any of us closer to getting them back from Josie. Ned, where are Josie's usual haunts?"

"From what I can tell, that ship doesn't have a home dock anywhere.

They frequent Delta-4, but they won't be going back there so soon after leaving, not when holding prisoners. They sometimes visit Bradach when they have goods to offload. What were they looking for on Turas-Mara in the first place?"

"We don't know for sure," Thomas said, taking a third piece of bread from the plate. "Even in the brig, she wouldn't say. Thought I was a planted spy."

Captain Violet turned to look at Ned. "You don't think she's working for—no, it couldn't be. Could it?"

Ned shrugged. "I haven't spoken to Barnaby in months. He stopped writing me letters when I told him about Davey."

"Do you think he'd be trading in weapons, now?"

"Anything is possible." Ned's face had descended into a frown. "Anything that would line his pockets."

"Then we have to assume that's a possibility. Where was the last letter from?"

"Kilper Station. It's possible that he was just passing through, though."

Alice leaned over Rosie and snatched a piece of bread. "We have to assume Josie might be headed there. Who else would agree to deal with her? Hasn't she burned most of those bridges?"

"She earns credibility from the refugee sweeps, just like she helped with ours last year. Though I can't imagine who else would be equipped to try to ransom an overseer's daughter. It's the height of foolishness."

"Josie will be expecting us to retrace her steps," Kady said, perching atop the bar. "I vote we head for Kilper Station and nab her in the act."

Captain Violet nodded. "I am inclined to agree. Ned?"

"On it," he said, already turning for the door. "I'll have nav maps in an hour. We can leave directly after."

"I still think that I should go with," Georgie said again, but quieter this time. "She's my sister. She's my responsibility, and I—I can't fail her. Not again."

Henry laid a hand on her arm. "What happened wasn't your fault."

"It doesn't matter. She's my sister. Ma, come on, back me up here."

Georgie's mother shook her head and pulled Lucy close to her. "You aren't going to listen to me, anyway. You never have. I don't want to lose another daughter, Georgina."

"You won't. I promise."

"Fine, then I'm coming too," Henry announced. "I told you, I'm not spending any more time away from you. We had enough of that in the beginning."

"What about the lab?"

"The lab will be fine without me for a few days, wouldn't you agree, Mrs. Payne?"

Georgie's mother nodded. "We're in fine shape down there," she admitted. "Georgina, if you insist upon going after your sister, please be careful. Don't take any unnecessary risks."

"When have I ever done that?" Georgie asked with a smirk.

"Every moment since the day you were born."

"Alright, crew, get together whatever you need," Captain Violet said. "We leave as soon as the nav maps are ready." She looked over at Georgie, an eyebrow raised, and then sighed. "Come on then, Payne. I know there's no hope in even trying to keep you off my ship for this."

As the rest began to filter out of the tavern, Rosie caught Bailey by the sleeve. "I need to get on that ship."

"They'll bring everyone back safe and sound, don't you worry."

"*Please.*"

Bailey sighed. "Come with me. I have an idea. Mae isn't going to like it, though."

Chapter 39

"I wonder where we are," Delia mused, staring up at the cracked ceiling of her cell. "I suppose we could be almost anywhere by now."

"Hard to know without at least a porthole," Carmen said. "Hey, Emeline, you don't have a porthole, do you?"

Emeline sighed heavily. "No."

"Too bad they took your tool belt, Carmen."

"We'd already be out of here if they hadn't. I had five lock picks in there, and a retractable knife. Though, what we'd do after we got out of the cells, I don't know. Knives don't tend to fare well against revolvers."

"Where could Josie be taking us?"

"Only the gods know. I just want to get out of this damned brig. My legs are starting to cramp."

"Will you two shut up?" Emeline snapped. "I swear, it's just constant blathering, it never ends! We don't know where we are, we don't know where we're going, and I will be gods-damned if I have to listen to another round of what-ifs."

"What do you suggest we do, then, Emeline? It's not as if Josie left us with reading material. Hell, not even a slapdash Banríon deck."

"We can just sit here in silence. That's my preference."

Carmen swung her legs down off her bed. "Come on, Em, we're just trying to keep spirits up. Being in a cell is bad for the brain. Does a number on your coping skills. People aren't meant to be caged."

"I'm not so sure I'd classify either of you as people."

"You sound hungry. Why don't you have a few bites of your breakfast?"

Emeline kicked the bucket by her bed. "I'd rather starve."

"To be honest, I'd rather not listen to your constant negativity," Delia said. "And yet, here we are. Listen, let's make a deal, shall we? You eat your protein brick, and Carmen and I will promise not to break into song for at least another hour."

"I never thought I'd be so lucky."

"Maybe take a bite, and keep your strength up, because we don't know if or when we'll have to make a run for it."

Emeline swore under her breath and took a bite. "This tastes like vomit."

"That will pass," Carmen said. "You get used to it."

"Someone should make these taste better. I'll bet the MPOs wouldn't hate them so much if they tasted of... of *something*."

Delia snorted. "According to your beloved mother, that would undermine the efficient nature of a protein brick. How can we know if it is peak efficiency if it isn't also borderline impossible to eat?"

"She does her best, you know. Running a prison, or a city, or a sector isn't an easy task, especially with vigilantes like you wandering around. You think it's so easy, balancing the needs of the people with the lack of resources brought on by—" Emeline took another bite, and then spat it out. "—By fucking piracy! Do you not see that the constant raiding of cargo vessels is what causes shortages in the first place? If the rebels would stop hiring the pirates to do their dirty work, this war would be over in two days, and we'd all get to eat some real damned food!"

"Do you really believe that?" Carmen asked quietly. "Truly, and deep down, in your heart of hearts?"

"Yes."

"Then you're not the girl I thought you were."

"I don't give a shit who you thought I was, what fairy tale you cooked up in your head. Right now, I'd give my left arm to be back on that backwater station. Even watered-down vegetable soup was better than this."

"Your left arm, eh?" Josie asked, descending the ladder. "Good to know, in case negotiations go south. I know which limb to show them, to let them know that we are serious."

"Most people start with fingers," Delia said. "More of them to go around."

"I think an arm sends more of a message, don't you? Really tells people that you mean business, with the added bonus of making sure people don't mess with you."

"Back home, people talked about you like you're some kind of hero," Carmen said. "Turns out, you're just another mercenary."

"I'm a hero to those who deserve it. As it turns out, I don't care much for pampered princesses or Coalition reporters. Or spies, for that matter."

Delia grasped the iron bars. "We sprung you from that cell. You repay that debt by putting us into one?"

"You wouldn't have sprung me if you could have gotten away with it. You'd have left all three of us in there to rot."

"But we didn't. We could have killed all three of you and taken Thomas instead."

"You don't have the guts for that." Josie laughed. "I know it, and you know it. That's why you're worthless to me as anything other than a hostage. You don't have what it takes to do what needs to be done. All three of you are nothing more than a liability I can't wait to be rid of."

"Then drop us at the nearest beacon and we'll be out of your hair," Carmen said. "Job done, and you get to fly off with your prize in peace, heading to bother some other innocents, no doubt."

"And lose out on a nice, fat credit reward? You are dreaming, my friend."

Emeline snorted a laugh. "You're no better than the people you claim to fight against. You do know that, don't you, Captain Josie? You'll do anything for a pile of credits, with no regard to what's right or moral. I bet you'd sell your own child for a chance at riches."

"What in hells do you know about morality?" Josie roared, kicking the door of Emeline's cell. "You sold out the people you claimed to care about in half a second. You took one look at the inside of a cell and happily signed away their rights to save your own skin. Don't you dare talk to me about morality, little girl. And don't you ever talk about my child ever again."

"I didn't sell anyone out! What choice did you think I had?"

"The choice to keep your fucking trap shut for a few more days before someone could get to you and break you out. They all thought you were this beacon of hope in the darkness and *you threw it all away!*"

"I didn't have a choice," Emeline repeated, but now her voice was strangled by a silent sob. "They never told me what I was signing."

"You should have let them cut off that arm before you signed anything, you stupid, *selfish* little girl. Those people you're so desperate to advocate for from within the confines of your precious Coalition are suffering, Emeline."

"It would have been fine for them if my fucking sister hadn't *burned the city down!*"

"Oh, that's bullshit and we both know it, kid. You ran scared the second the heat came for you."

"We were living in a basement for... for months. Running from the guards, organizing rallies. We were going to have a union! They were going to listen! Until... until..."

"Until the governor—now overseer—made sure none of that happened. She's the one who organized that, Emeline," Delia said. "I was there. I heard the orders being handed down."

"She only did what she had to. My sister was threatening the safety of the city, the storms—the gala—it wasn't the right time for a union. It is now. I can go back and make everything right, now."

Josie laughed. "Wow, they really did a number on you, didn't they? And I'll bet they didn't even have to lay a hand on you in order for you to fold like a cheap pack of cards. I've met some real rebels in my time. People who withstood torture and never sold anyone out. But you did it without a second glance."

"Lay off, Josie, she was just a kid," Carmen said. "I'd bet my ass you'd have done the same at her age."

"Bullshit."

"Not from what I've heard."

"You haven't heard shit."

Carmen smirked. "I've heard plenty. She's right, you are a mercenary. Not a shred of morals in your entire body."

"You don't know anything about my morals."

"I know that you're harassing an eighteen-year-old that you already have in a cell over something that happened almost two years ago. Where the hell were you, Captain Josie, when Hjarta got overrun? When they were loading hundreds of people onto transports to send them off to only the gods know where?"

"I was otherwise engaged."

"Yeah, I'll bet you were. Engaged with keeping your own ass safe."

"Need I remind you that I raided Turas-Mara?"

"How much did The Scattered offer to pay you?"

Josie's palm rested against the revolver on her hip. "Not many would have done that without offer of payment, and you know it."

"So much for selfless altruism," Emeline said.

"Altruism doesn't pay the bills, or put food in my daughter's stomach. We do what we have to do, within the confines of what we *can* do."

"Yet you're suggesting that a teenager somehow had the power to topple centuries-old power structures in Skelm?" Carmen scoffed. "Please. Listen to yourself. You sound ridiculous."

"That girl had power in the palm of her hand, and she damn well squandered it," Josie spat. "She could have achieved so much more if she had just waited it out a little longer."

"Don't talk about me like I'm not here!" Emeline shouted. "I'm not just some pawn willing to let everyone else make all the decisions for me. I can do as I damned well please!"

Josie smirked. "That's the kind of attitude I want to see from you. Don't let people choose your life for you, Emeline. One day you'll wake up and realize that you're ten years older and still spinning your wheels in the same mud."

"I don't need bullshit platitudes from you."

"I'm just passing on a little bit of sage advice. Take it or leave it, kid."

"I'll leave it, thank you very much."

Delia stretched her arms out, reaching above her head to grasp the bars of her cell. The metal was cool, but rusted, and left orange residue on her palms. "Don't you have somewhere to be, *Captain* Josie?"

"As a matter of fact, I do. I have a wire to send about the price on your heads. From what I understand, the bounty for you will feed my crew for a year."

"I hope they aren't hungry, because there's no way you'll get those credits."

"We'll see about that."

"I guess we will."

Chapter 40

"Bay Leaf, you said you'd come straight home when you got back. Here I've been waiting and waiting, thinking something happened—"

"I'm sorry, Mae, I'm sorry," Bailey said, wrapping the woman in a tight embrace. "We got hung up."

"I told you those blockades would cause trouble."

"No, nothing like that. We ran into a couple of strays at the hub off Delta-4, I took them up to the Pig." Bailey swept Mae off her feet, pulling her in for a deep kiss.

Rosie stepped into the shop, closing the door behind her with a gentle jingle of the bell hung under the open sign. She cleared her throat noisily to announce her presence. "Hi, I'm Rosie."

Mae pulled away, straightening her collar. "Nice to meet you, Rosie," she said, shaking Rosie's hand delicately. "I'm Mae, just like it says on the door." She turned back to Bailey with a stern expression. "Whatever this is, I don't like it. I can sense trouble."

Bailey pulled Mae closer. "Don't be mad—"

"Damn it to hell, what now?" Mae demanded, pulling away. "Don't tell me that you're going back out—"

"Rosie needs a favor."

Mae raised an eyebrow. "And what would that favor be?"

"She wants to go with the Cricket crew. They're heading out to look for Josie. She has Carmen and Emeline, and—do you remember that reporter back in the Capital?"

"Delia Dodson?"

"Yeah, she has her, too."

"Gods. Alright, Rosie, what do you need?"

"She needs—"

"Let her speak, Bai."

Rosie pulled at her skirts. "If you could repair this tear for me, I have a little ore left to pay you."

"Are you planning on coming back to Bradach?"

"I hope so. It's not like I can go anywhere else now."

"Good. You can pay me when you get back. You look resourceful. I'm sure it won't be a problem."

"That's too kind of you, but I just need the hole patched—"

Mae marched over to a rack of clothes along the wall, the taffeta of her sapphire blue skirts swishing gently. "Nonsense. If you're going with the Cricket, you'll need the right attire. You never know what they'll get up to, and we wouldn't want to risk you not having what you need. Alice is much too tall for you to borrow anything from her, and besides, I can assume your styles don't match up."

"Er—"

"Dresses, skirts, or jumpsuits?" Mae asked, sliding hangers along the rail. "We have several styles, all in your size. If you'd like a different fabric, I can have it made for you while you are gone."

"Oh. I don't much mind. Whatever is easiest."

"A dress and a jumpsuit, then, to cover the bases. And we should send you with—"

"Mae, they don't want her to go," Bailey said, lingering by the door. "They don't even want Georgie to be on the ship."

"They'll have a hell of a time keeping her off. I don't think she's thought of anything else since her sister was taken."

"Can you smuggle her onto the ship? Aren't you sending some crates for trade?"

"Absolutely not."

"But Mae—"

"I'm smart enough not to cross Captain Violet. She's one of my best customers, and if you haven't noticed, my love, she's rather good with a gun."

"She wouldn't shoot you. She likes what you make her too much."

Mae sighed and chewed her bottom lip. "Why are you so desperate to get on that ship, Rosie?"

"Delia is out there. I have to find her. We were friends—more than friends—at school, and then—"

"I see. And I understand."

Bailey grinned. "So you'll help?"

"I can't promise Captain Violet won't turn that ship right around the moment you're discovered. She may well do that, and that will only make the rescue take longer, and it will be more dangerous for them."

"I understand. I think she will let me stay."

"And why is that?"

"I'm a cook. Crews love me."

"Crews might, but I doubt Ned will." Mae folded several dresses over her arm and gestured toward a fitting room at the back of the store. "Try these on to start. I can't have you gallivanting across the Near Systems without appropriate clothing."

"I—thank you," Rosie said, pulling the dressing room curtain closed. "I would have been happy with the tear being patched.

"That's all you'd have gotten from that hack tailor across town," Mae muttered darkly. "Man couldn't even sew on a button properly if his mortal life depended on it."

"I'm just not sure this is all necessary. It's very kind of you, but I've never been one for a large trunk of clothes."

"How many dresses do you own, Rosie?"

"Just this one."

"Then I think it's time we expanded your wardrobe. Here, try this one first. The green will pick up the flecks in your eyes." Mae passed the dress through. "If you don't like the fit around the hips, then this blue one might work for you."

Rosie dropped her torn dress to the ground and pulled on the new one. The fabric was crisp yet soft, cinched lightly at the waist, the corset over the top a complementary damask in a deep forest green. "This is far too nice for smuggling aboard a ship. It's so beautiful."

"Everyone deserves beautiful clothing, Rosie. Let's see."

Rosie drew back the curtain. "It's the nicest thing I've ever worn."

"Mm," Mae mumbled, nodding in approval. "How are you with small spaces? The crates I am sending aboard aren't very big."

"I don't mind, so long as I fit."

"You won't be able to stand."

"I'll manage."

Mae turned to Bailey, a hand on her hip. "You aren't going, are you? Because you promised me after last time—"

"No, Mae, I'm not. I wish I could find some way to help them get Emeline back, but I'm not sure I'd be anything more than a hindrance."

"Not to mention that if she... well, if she decides to rejoin Turas-Mara, there're no guarantees she won't tell the general exactly where you are and who you are running with."

"I'm pretty sure that Overseer Allemande thinks I'm dead."

"What? Why?"

Bailey gave Rosie an apologetic look. "They found a file."

"A file?"

"About the Cricket. My name was crossed out."

Mae gasped. "Did you tell Captain Violet?"

"Not yet. They should get Emeline back first before we worry about that."

"Bay Leaf, I'm not so sure that's your decision to make."

Rosie rested her hands in her pockets. "I'll tell them once we are underway. They should know that Allemande is after them. It's like some kind of... obsession."

"That in no way surprises me." Mae sighed again, pulling a jumpsuit from a hanger. "This may be a better choice, if you're about to be running for your life. Less fabric to trail behind you."

"I hope not."

The jumpsuit fit perfectly, a deep v-neck at the front, closed with brass toggles at the center and a wide belt at the hips. The pockets were deep and the sleeves cropped just below the elbow, the fabric an olive twill that looked surprisingly good. Rosie never would have picked it out on her own.

She threw back the curtain. "I think this is better for now."

"We'll get you in that dress when you get back, what do you think? A night out at the Pig?"

Rosie nodded. "I'd like that."

The door jingled as it opened and shut.

"You got those crates ready yet, Mae?"

"Yes, Abigail, they're in back. Four this time."

"That's twice as many as last time!" Abigail pouted. "I thought you said they were scaling back on trade!"

"That was before they made a nice, fat cut of a four-hundred percent profit. Don't worry, you'll have help. Bailey can take the largest one, and our new friend Rosie here can take one."

"That still leaves me with two, which is twice as many as anyone else."

Bailey lifted two crates under one arm. "I've got it."

"You'd have to start paying me more if you didn't have your enormously strong girlfriend to carry all this to the docks, you know."

Mae laughed. "I know. But think of it this way, now we have room for new fabrics, and the merchant comes next week."

"I'm choosing at least half, you promised."

"Not if you miss that ship, you're not. Get going, all of you. And Rosie—make sure no one sees you climbing into a crate. They don't like stowaways on the docks."

"Understood."

"Let's go, my arms are already aching," Abigail announced, backing through the front door. "And I have a date tonight that I almost don't want to bail out on."

"I'd hate for you to miss that," Bailey said with a snort. "Maybe he's a dream come true."

"Depends. He might be more of a nightmare. Found him on the docks two days ago, loading up a freighter."

"What's it like?" Rosie asked, shifting the weight of the crate in her arms. "Living here?"

"Beats the alternative," Abigail said. "I'd rather live free here than be a prisoner anywhere else, which is likely if I were to leave."

"You're a fugitive?"

"Worse. I'm a refugee."

"Oh."

Abigail scowled at the crate in her arms. "I can barely see over this thing, and it's heavy as hell. What did Mae pack it with, bricks?"

"I think just fabric," Bailey said. "Though who knows, maybe she did throw in a few bricks, for good measure."

"No one asked for your searing wit, *Bailey*. Gods be damned, we really need a cart if we're going to keep this up. Even you can't carry more than that."

"They aren't that heavy."

"No, but they're huge and unwieldy. How far are we from the docks? This crate is blocking my view."

"Not far."

"That's what you always say, and then I end up walking for kilometers with these things."

Bailey snorted a laugh. "It's not even half a kilometer to the docks. A quarter, maybe."

"Feels further."

"So, Rosie, you ready to smuggle yourself aboard?"

Rosie hugged the crate to her chest. "I guess so."

"When was your first smuggle?"

"Um... a long time ago. And I was smaller then. Shorter. I was six years old."

"Oh, yeah? Where were you headed?"

"Gamma-3. It was before the checks got bad. Lots of people did it in those days."

"Where from?"

Rosie shook her head as much as she could with the crate in her way. "I don't remember." It was a lie, but an easy one to tell. She'd been telling it nearly her whole life.

"Lots more movement in those days. The Coalition was still afraid of its people, then. That's not the case, anymore."

"No," Rosie agreed. "It's not."

"Listen, if Captain Violet wants to know how you got aboard, maybe don't mention Mae. She doesn't like confrontation with people she admires."

"Sure thing."

"Where you headed?" Abigail asked. "Somewhere with good trade, I hope."

"I'm not actually sure. They're trying to track down a ship."

"Refugees?"

"Sort of. More like hostages. We'll see, I guess."

Bailey looked both ways before climbing up the ship's ramp. "We're here."

"Where are we supposed to put these?" Abigail asked. "It's wall-to-wall fuel crates in here."

"Pile them in the corner. I'll make sure Alice knows they're there."

"How long until takeoff?" Rosie asked.

"Not long. You better get yourself hidden before someone sees you. Climb in, I'll put the lid on. I'd wait at least a few hours after they take off to make yourself known. You're not carrying any guns, are you?"

"What? No!"

"Good. Kady will be less likely to shoot you on sight if you look unarmed. Good luck!"

* * *

There were worse crates to be smuggled in. At least this one was filled with soft, silken fabrics, even if she was folded up on herself, trying not to breathe too loudly. It had been at least an hour, hadn't it? She couldn't quite read her pocket watch in the darkness.

Her bladder was full, and her stomach was about to rumble any moment. She wasn't built for being smuggled. It wasn't the small space she minded so much, but the boredom, the time ticking by a hundred times slower than it should, that was filling her nerves with anxiety.

With nothing to distract her, all she had were thoughts, worries about Delia and the others. Wondering if she'd made a crucial error in smuggling herself aboard. Maybe Kady was right—she had no place on a pirate vessel. What could she do, besides cook?

The crew airlock door opened with a pneumatic hiss, and Rosie held her breath.

"I told you, Al, I already cleaned the fuel connections."

"Ivy, I know. I'm saying that the fuel pump isn't powerful enough to inject more, faster. The boilers are maxed out as it is."

"But that doesn't make any sense. We upgraded all the components barely three months back."

"And then we ran that mission where we took a few hits on that side, remember?"

"Oh yeah."

"The increase in particulates is what's causing problems. If I can't fix it, Vi is going to make me sleep in the engine room."

"No, she wouldn't."

"You're right. But I'd deserve it. Best damned mechanic around for old boats like this, and I can't even get us at max fuel consumption. The solar panels aren't doing enough of the heavy lifting."

"Alice... don't be so hard on yourself. This ship would have fallen out of the sky two years ago without you."

"Maybe so. Doesn't fix our problems right now."

"Is there any way we can ease off, even for a few hours? We could swap the injectors—"

"Captain Violet is hell-bent on getting out there as fast as possible. She doesn't want to risk missing a handoff." There was a rustling, and then the clank of a crate being pried open. "We can at least get all this down to the boiler room, as much as we can fit. Maybe we can save some time there, if we're not having to run back and forth every few hours."

"Alrighty. Hand me that crowbar."

"Aye."

Rosie's heart pounded in her chest. They were going to find her any minute. Did they carry revolvers, too? She'd hoped to climb out and present herself in a neutral, non-threatening way. Springing out of a crate like a child's toy was the opposite of that.

The cacophony of crates being opened, examined, and emptied was amplified inside her own. Her hands over her ears to dull the noise, she braced as it got closer and closer, until one of them was right next to her.

"What the hell!" Alice shouted, holding an enormous wrench over her head.

"I'm sorry! Don't hit me!" Rosie yelled, covering her face with her hands.

"The cook? What are you doing in there?"

"I needed to come with you. It's important."

Alice sighed, slipping the wrench back into her tool belt. "I nearly split your skull open."

"I didn't mean to scare you. I had planned to make myself known in a less terrifying way."

"Hiya," a young woman with bright green hair said, extending her hand. "I'm Ivy."

"Hello," Rosie replied, shaking her hand. "I'm sorry for intruding."

"You've exposed a weakness in our security. See, Alice? I told you we needed bio-scanners."

"Bio-scanners are far too expensive," Alice refuted. "We've been over this. Vi isn't going to approve the expense."

"She might once we break the news that we found a stowaway."

"A stowaway from Bradach is hardly the same as a battle-worn MPO."

Ivy shrugged. "Only takes once."

"You just want the bio-scanners because it's new tech."

"What, and you don't?"

"I didn't say that. I just said Vi isn't gonna go for it."

Rosie cleared her throat gently. "Not to... intrude, though I suppose I already have—"

"Yes, you have."

"Please don't turn the ship around. I just want the chance to help. Delia is... she's important to me. So is Carmen. And Emeline."

"They're important to us, too. That's why we're going after them."

"I know, I just—I felt like I could help, maybe, and... well, it's not like I have anywhere else to go now. Not after what happened on Turas-Mara."

"No family?"

"It's complicated."

Alice laughed. "Sounds like you'll fit right in. We're a band of strays and orphans, we are. Ivy here got tossed out because she got caught hustling card tables and dice games one too many times. Her parents got sick of bailing her out of lockup. I don't know what happened to mine, though they're likely long dead by now. I've got a brother I haven't spoken to in twenty years. A Coalition trader."

"I'm sorry."

"He was a jackass, anyway."

"Do you think Captain Violet will make us turn around?"

"Not if you let me break the news."

"They're married," Ivy announced. "Cap says there are no special privileges, but Alice can always convince her of something. Unless it's about installing bio-scanners."

"Gods, Ivy, enough with the bio-scanners. We'll get them when we can pick up some older models. You and I both know this old ship can't interface with new tech easily."

"It would be a fun challenge."

"Can't you challenge yourself to unpack these fuel cells a little faster?"

Ivy pried open a crate. "Yeah, yeah."

"And the tertiary boiler needs maintenance. The safety valve keeps sticking."

"I fixed it already."

"Great. Er, good. Yes. Rosie, you come with me. Be quiet. Don't let Kady see you or she'll blow a gasket. She's already pissed that Georgie insisted on boarding."

"But Emeline is her sister."

Alice pulled the lever, and they stepped through into the ship. "Yes, but sometimes emotions make things... difficult. Dangerous. Georgie's been looking for her for years. She's spoken to half the pirates in the Near Systems trying to track her down. When we heard the broadcasts from the Rim, we knew she was there. Georgie talked Davey into sending Carmen out there to try to get her."

"Davey?"

"Works for The Scattered. He's our contact there. Bit of a loose cannon, but Bailey vouched for him."

"I'm not so sure Emeline wants to be... rescued. She held a gun on us when we were leaving the station."

"Yes, that's the other reason Kady didn't want Georgie to come along. It may be painful to see her sister this way. We may have to put her in the brig if we want her to cooperate. We all want Emeline back, but she's a liability now." Alice glanced sideways at Rosie. "Do you think she can be saved? I don't mean getting her on the ship. I mean, do you think she'll ever be... one of us, again?"

"She's been through a lot."

"Yeah. That's what I thought."

"She cares deeply for everyone back in Skelm. I think she has confusing feelings about her family. I think she does miss them."

"I guess we'll find out when we get there."

"Where are we going?"

"Kilper Station. Vi—Captain Violet has a hunch that's where Josie is going to be."

"Why?"

"She has something she's going to want to sell to the highest bidder, and I know who that might be. He's an ignorant fool, and lucky Vi didn't shoot him when she caught him stealing from the cargo bay. The bridge is to the right. Stay in the corridor."

"Should I be worried?"

"Probably not."

"Probably?"

"Shh." Alice climbed the steps up to the bridge. "Hello, Violet."

"You want something, I can tell."

"I'm just saying hello! Is it a crime for a wife to want to visit the woman she loves most in the world?"

"Out with it, Al. What is it?"

"We, er... Ivy and I, that is—"

"I told you three times already, we can't afford bio-scanners. Maybe in a few months, when we run a few more jobs, but it depends."

"It's not the bio-scanners—although, now that you mention it, there is the possibility that we could lift one if we pillaged the right vessel—"

"Alice."

"We found a stowaway."

"Who? Where?"

Rosie saw the captain reach for her revolver, and she flattened herself against the wall in a desperate attempt to be as invisible as possible.

"Put the gun down, Vi. It's the cook from the Pig. The one who landed with Bailey."

"Oh. I thought we told her no."

"We did."

"Then why in hells is she on my ship?"

Alice sighed. "I think she wants to help."

"We have enough mouths to feed, and hardly enough room on this ship as it is, especially with Georgie insisting that she come, too. Has she even ever pulled a job? Seen combat? Gods, she's probably just like you when we first met. Inexperienced. A liability."

"Probably."

"Am I to assume you're on my bridge in order to vouch for her?"

"Something like that."

"I should turn this damned ship right around. We'll lose time, but we can't be filling up with extra bodies, not when we're hoping to pick up three more. Four, if I get my hands on Josie long enough to throw her into a cell."

"Going after Josie is a bad idea, and you know it."

"I'm tired of these games with her, Al. Leo was nothing more than another two-bit pirate with a gun and an attitude. Josie's much smarter than he ever was, except she lets this vendetta steer her actions."

"Oh, and you don't?"

"That's different. She shot Ned."

"You killed her captain."

Captain Violet scoffed. "He deserved it." She holstered the gun and turned back to the controls. "We can't risk it, especially not when we're facing off with Josie. This cook probably doesn't even know the ass-end of a heat gun."

"I do," Rosie said, leaning her weight onto the first step, though tentative. "I can use a heat gun."

"So you're an eavesdropper *and* a stowaway, are you? Well, heat guns are irrelevant. We don't have any spare."

"I'll do whatever you need me to. I just want to be able to help in some way. Help get them back."

"What would you do if Josie got hold of you?"

"I'd bite her."

The captain laughed, her eyes crinkling at the edges. "That's not the answer I expected, I will grant you that."

"With respect, Captain, I've known Delia almost all my life, and Carmen is the first friend I've made in years. Emeline is a sweet girl, deep down, and—"

"So sweet, she drugged Mae."

"Who?" Rosie asked, feigning ignorance.

"Please, I recognize her work anywhere. It's no mystery how you ended up stowed in the only shipment we took on board. Don't worry, I'm not angry at her. My point is, Emeline gave her truth serum. It nearly exposed all of us, and the whole of Bradach, too. Emeline is dangerous now, whether her sister wants to admit it or not."

Chapter 41

Delia was already grasping the bars of her cell when the ship's engines cut off. "We've landed somewhere."

"Might just be a fuel beacon," Carmen said, still reclining on her slab of metal that was meant to be a bed. "Hard to know without a porthole."

"We could try to escape," Emeline said, her arms reaching through the bars, her fingers fumbling for the keyhole. "I might be able to pick this lock."

"And what, prance past the crew on this ship? How do you figure that?" Delia asked. "It's not like they're going to let you leave."

"There's no need for talk of breaking out," Josie said, descending the ladder, a large ring of keys in her hand. "We're here."

"Where?"

"It's not necessary for you to know the specifics. I'm sure your new captor will tell you everything you need to know."

"You sold us?"

"It's what I promised, wasn't it?"

"That's illegal!" Emeline shouted.

"I'm a pirate. I'm not very concerned with legality. Delia, you first. Put your hands through the bars so I can cuff you."

Delia did as she was told. "Why cuff me? Are you afraid?"

"No, but I don't want you causing problems until we've gotten the handoff. Carmen, you next."

"The Scattered will find out about this," Carmen said, presenting her wrists. "I won't be able to save you once they do."

"The Scattered can kiss my ass. What have they done for me lately? Nothing. Fuck all. They're impotent and ineffective. I doubt they could catch a mouse in a trap. Besides, once I sell this thing to them, they'll be eating out of the palm of my hand. Emeline, your wrists, please."

"My mother will come for you."

"I'm sure she will, but so long as she's hiding the news about the escape of prisoners, it will hardly be the might of the Coalition coming down on me. Face it, sweetpea, you're not as important as her success. As climbing the ranks, inflating her career. You're space junk."

"Enough, Josie," Delia said. "Just get us the hell out of here. Your ship stinks of piss and vomit."

"It does not!"

"Open the cell, get on with it. No matter who you've sold us to, it's got to be better than this rickety old thing. It's a miracle it stays in the sky at all."

"I'll have you know, this is one of the foremost vessels in use. We have more technology than—"

Delia interrupted her with a laugh. "Yet it still smells like a basic training barracks."

The cells sprang open when Josie pulled a lever, her revolver in her other hand. "Get up the ladder. Move. There's another gun at the top, so don't think about trying anything."

"I wouldn't dream of it," Delia muttered, pulling herself up the ladder. The metal was slick under her boots, and her legs ached from being cramped in the cell for so long. "You alright back there, Carmen? Emeline?"

"Just get a move on. We don't have all day."

"No, you've probably got more people to sell."

"Keep your mouth shut. You don't even know what's going on. Delia Dodson, voice at the Outer Rim. You think you know everything, don't you? Well, you don't."

"I know more than you."

"I could fill several libraries with what you don't know."

"Sure," Delia said with a laugh, pulling herself up out of the brig.

"Move it," Dirk growled. "We have a meeting to keep."

"Alright, alright. Don't get your underwear in a twist."

"Hurry up!" Josie shouted from below. "I want to have time to get some pastries from that place I like before we leave."

Dirk poked the barrel of his revolver into Delia's side. "Walk."

"Where?"

"Forward until the corridor forks, then left out of the loading bay."

"I have to say, the service on this ship isn't exactly up to my expectations."

"You're awfully mouthy for someone in irons."

"I try not to let circumstance dictate my attitude."

Emeline huffed loudly. "Will you shut up, Delia? You're going to get us all killed."

"If I did, it would be a damned improvement from having to be on this urine-soaked pile of flying scrap metal."

Josie laughed. "We'll see how mouthy you are in a few minutes."

They walked down off the ship's ramp into a large trading station. Delia squinted up at the sky, but couldn't see anything beyond the huge mirrors that hung to reflect sunlight down into the city. "Where the hell are we?"

"That's for me to know, and you to find out."

"It's not home," Carmen muttered. "It's not Skelm or Delta-4, either."

"Correct on all accounts."

"This isn't—you haven't brought us to Kilper Station, have you?"

"You'll know soon enough."

Delia sidled up alongside Carmen, despite the revolver pointed at her rib cage. "What's wrong with Kilper Station?"

"Black market dealings. Some say human trafficking."

"I'll scream," Emeline threatened. "Then everyone will know exactly who I am."

"Go on, I dare you," Josie said, throwing her head back to laugh again. "Odds are that half the miscreants on this rock would be even happier to kill you than I would."

"Cap?" Dirk said. "Which stall?"

"There, on your right. See? Our buyer is already waiting for us." She shoved Carmen from behind. "Move it."

"I don't know who you think you are," Emeline shouted over the din of hundreds of traders, all making illicit deals, "but I'll have you know that my mother will be here any moment."

The man, short and impeccably well-dressed, shook his head. "Not judging by what I've heard."

"Good of you to be on time," Josie said, holstering her gun. "I can't stand tardiness."

"So I've heard."

"Oh yeah? From who?"

"Here and there. My contacts aren't important. Do you have what we discussed?"

"I do."

"Where... where is it?"

Josie gave him a smug smile. "Safe on my ship, where it will stay until I get the payment that was promised."

"I can assure you, The Scattered is good for the payment, but I cannot release funds until I see it intact. There have been... rumors. Of a counterfeit."

"It's not counterfeit."

"I'm sure. Nevertheless, protocol is protocol. I don't make the rules, Captain Josie, I merely abide by them. If you accompany me to your loading bay, I will verify the veracity and transfer funds. I've already hired several strapping dock workers to help me transport it onto a waiting vessel."

"No. You transfer the funds now. How do I know you won't steal it once you see it?"

The man frowned. "On the contrary, how do I know that you won't take the transferred funds and run? After all, no one has ever even seen what you stole. For all we know, this is some elaborate ruse."

"It isn't."

"My business partner and I, we have worked very hard to secure this contract, and we aren't willing to take any chances."

"I'm the one who stormed the gods-damned station," Josie spat. "I lost three of my crew. Good, strong people that didn't deserve the end they got. Now transfer the credits, or we walk."

"That is wholly inadvisable. I am merely asking for verification, Captain. Your reluctance to provide that is a rather red flag, if you forgive the expression."

"And your reluctance to transfer what I'm owed tells me that you don't even have what you promised, so I guess we are at an impasse, Barnaby."

Delia studied the man. He was certainly William's type, and given what he was dealing with, it made her wonder. "Is your business partner... William?"

"No."

"Shut up, Dodson," Josie said, elbowing her in the ribs, "or I'm going to make sure you get the worst deal of all of you."

Barnaby's eyes widened. "Dodson? Delia Dodson?"

"You do know William, don't you?" Delia asked, sidestepping another jab from Josie. "He's my—well. It's complicated, I guess, and—"

"What the hell are you doing with her, Josie?" Barnaby demanded. "You said you had the item we asked for. You never said you'd be using blackmail."

"Blackmail?" Josie barked. "How was I supposed to know you'd know who she is?"

"She's a broadcaster, Josie. Almost everyone knows who she is." He sighed, jamming his hands into his pockets. "I'll ask you again—why do you have her? And who are the other two?"

"None of your business. Now, transfer the credits so we can be on our way."

"What are you doing with them?"

"Getting rid of them, the easiest way I know how. I have an appointment with Dennis in twenty minutes."

"No."

Josie laughed. "Yes. Who do you think you are?"

"I'm not letting you give them over to a damned bounty hunter."

Delia's blood ran cold. Bounty hunters weren't known for their kindness or their reason. She yanked at her cuffs, trying in vain to break the links that joined them.

"Relax, Dodson," Josie said. "He's just going to turn you over to the Coalition. I'm sure you'll be living the high life on two bricks a day, and even that's better than you deserve."

"I'll pay a million more than Dennis is paying," Barnaby said.

"A million is nothing."

"Ten million, then."

Josie feigned a snore. "You're putting me to sleep with this. Let me be crystal clear with you, here. Make it worth my while or piss off. The enjoyment I'll get from handing them over is worth a lot, financially speaking."

"Twenty million?"

"Barnaby Meier!" a tall woman roared, striding down the center aisle. "You have sunk to a new low. Here I thought that you were making amends, and I find you here, trying to... to buy them for their bounties?"

"Alice! Wait, Alice, no—it's not what you think—"

"I vouched for you, Barnaby. I begged Violet to let you stay, and then you stole from us. I told them all it was just a mistake, the sad, malformed tinge of your past life, that you would work to undo all of that, and yet—yet I find you here!"

"He's not lying," Carmen said. "He's trying to save us from Dennis."

Alice spun, turning on Josie. "So it's you. I should have known. From the moment we met, I knew you'd be a thorn in my side until the day I died."

"Hopefully I won't be a thorn too much longer, then," Josie said sweetly.

"We knew we'd find you here."

"I'll have to cover my tracks more thoroughly next time, then, so I don't have to risk looking at your ugly mug."

"How much do you want for them?"

"Barnaby here just offered twenty million. You gonna outbid him?"

"Twenty—Barns, how do you have that many credits?"

He looked up at the sky. "I have a new business partner."

"You're conning someone new, you mean."

"Al, if you'd just let me explain—"

"Enough. Josie, just tell us what you want for them. We don't have time to waste."

Josie performatively twirled a lock of blond hair between her fingers. "A hundred million."

"Piss off. Dennis can't be giving you more than five."

"Maybe so. Why don't you go and ask him? I'm sure he'd be willing to up his bid if he knew that we were having an auction."

Alice squeezed her eyes shut, her fists in tight balls. "Fine. A hundred million."

"That was far too easy," Josie said, an eyebrow raised in suspicion. "Make a big score recently, did you? Well now, if that's the case, I think the price just doubled."

"We already agreed on a hundred million."

"It's a seller's market, Alice."

"Josie, I am appealing to your humanity. We just want our people back, the same way you'd want yours back."

"Three of my people are dead, going after the thing this one wanted," Josie replied, jabbing her thumb in Barnaby's direction. "I think the rest of my crew deserves some restitution."

"We had nothing to do with whatever deal you made with him. We kicked him off our ship years ago because he's a lying, thieving, two-faced little imp."

"Anyone who has ever had favorable dealings with Violet is permanently on my shit list. Do we need to revisit that? Do you need me to remind you why that is?"

"For all the gods' sakes, Josie, have a little mercy, will you? Delia here has never even met Violet."

"And yet it's Violet who has come rushing to her rescue. Why is that?"

"Because—" Alice faltered. "Because Emeline's sister has spent two years looking for her, and she happens to be standing behind you."

"Then her sister can pay for her, if she wants her so bad. The price for Emeline just went up to three hundred million."

"This is sick extortion, Josie, and you know it. What if it was your little girl—"

"Don't you *dare* bring her into this, you enormous ogre. She has nothing to do with this, and I'm not going to allow you to manipulate my emotions in the name of morality. Piss off, before you make me really angry."

"I'm not leaving without these three. I don't care what you do with Barnaby. You can throw him in your brig, for all I care."

"Hey!" he protested. "I was trying to help!"

"And making a mess of it, as usual. No doubt this whole thing was cooked up to give you a nice slice of the ransom money, eh? You've broken enough trust, Barnaby."

"As brilliant a plan as that may have been, that's not what's going on. You have to believe me, Al."

"I wouldn't believe you if I were standing in a burning building, and you told me that I was on fire."

Josie pulled out her revolver. "I've had enough of this. Pay me for my prisoners, or leave. I have plenty of other business to attend to."

"What are you going to do, shoot me in the middle of the trades tent?" Alice scoffed.

"If I have to, yes."

"I'd like to see you try."

"Don't tempt me," Josie said, her thumb on the hammer. "We both know they'd just throw your body into a shallow grave rather than risk the tent being shut down. I'm home free."

"Not when I get done with you, you cretinous little rat—"

"Emeline?" someone shouted through the crowd. "Emmy, is that you?"

"Georgie, I told you to stay on the ship," Alice yelled, not moving her glare from Josie. "It's too dangerous to—"

"Emeline!" Georgie cried, pushing her way through a group of well-dressed, dangerous looking people. "Em, we finally found you! I never stopped looking, I—"

"Get *away* from me," Emeline hissed, holding her arms out. "I want nothing to do with you."

"What are you talking about? You're free! You don't have to do that... that monster's bidding anymore. We're going to take you home, and you can see Ma, and Lucy, and—"

"Home? We don't have a home anymore, thanks to you. Skelm was in ruins. You certainly can't ever go back there, not after what you did."

"Skelm? Skelm is fine! It was rebuilt in record time—"

"People died that night, Georgina! Or did you think that you could set an entire city on fire and walk away from what you'd done? Get out of my sight."

Alice shoved past Josie. "Let's all just calm down for a minute, here."

"You can get out of my sight as well," Emeline said. "I'll bet you were there that night, too."

"Yes, but—"

"Murderers."

"No, we—"

"*Murderers!*"

"We evacuated refugees!"

Emeline leaned in close until she was nose-to-nose with Alice, standing on the toes of her boots to reach. "Horseshit."

"It's not. We can take you to meet some of them."

"There were no refugees in Skelm. You abducted workers."

"Emmy," Georgie began, reaching out a gentle hand for her sister, "please, just listen. I promise I will explain everything that happened after they took you. I would never lie to you, I promise. You have to know that, right?"

"I don't trust a word that comes out of your mouth." Emeline turned to Josie. "Are you going to sell me to this bounty hunter or what? I'd like to get back to my life now, and away from these liars and thieves."

"I've got news for you, cupcake. There are more liars and thieves where you came from than in this entire trading tent." Josie sighed and holstered her weapon. "Are you going to pay for these three or not? I'm tired of... of whatever this is."

"How much?" Georgie asked, a sharp edge to her voice.

"Three hundred million for Emeline."

"And the others?"

"One hundred million each. Five stacks, in total."

Alice held her hands up in surrender. "Fine. Done. Barnaby, pay the woman."

"Me?" he spluttered. "I don't have that kind of—"

"Cut the crap. We all know that you have it."

"Al, I am responsible for—"

"If you ever want to set foot on that ship again, you'll pay her what she's asking. Right now."

Barnaby rolled up his sleeve and held out his arm. "It's extortion."

"Of course it's extortion," Josie said, grinning, pulling a chip scanner from her back pocket. "Pirates have to adapt. Adjust. Innovate. That's all I'm doing. It's not personal."

"Of course it's personal," Alice snapped.

"Only a little." The scanner's gears turned silently and chirped when the funds had been transferred. "An absolute pleasure doing business with you."

"Come on, Emmy, let's get you on the ship," Georgie said, taking the cuff key from Josie and unlocking them. "Lucy is going to be so happy to see you."

"I'm not going with you."

"I get that you're angry at me, Em, but—"

"You can't make me go. I'll send word, and my mother will send for me. Don't touch me."

"Your mother?" Georgie asked, disgust washing over her face. "Your real mother has been waiting two years to see you again. Be mad at me all you want, but you're getting on that ship."

Emeline shoved Georgie back. "You're dead to me."

"What about Ma? What about Lucy?"

"They chose their side, just like I chose mine. You just want to burn everything down! You let our people down, Georgina! You were letting them starve!"

"What was I supposed to do with that tyrant bearing down on us? There wasn't enough food! Because of *her!*"

"No, because of—of pirates like you! Stealing everything, disrupting the transports! I don't give a damn if you live or die, Georgina. I'm leaving." As she turned to march off through the trading tent, a woman streaked out from behind a stall with a small stun gun and thrust it into Emeline's neck. She fell hard to the floor.

"Kady, what the fuck do you think you're doing?" Georgie bellowed, rushing to Emeline's side.

"This is why I told you not to come, Georgie," Kady replied softly. "The rest of us knew that this might be difficult."

"You could have killed her!"

"It's only small. She'll be fine in a few minutes. Come on, we need to get her on the ship now. Before she wakes up."

"This feels wrong." Georgie brushed tears from her cheeks. "This isn't how it was supposed to be."

"She's been gone for two years. A lot can happen in that time." Kady hooked her hands under Emeline's arms. "Alice, will you grab her legs?"

"Of course." She cast an angry glance at Barnaby. "Whatever you're doing, I don't want to know about it."

"It's for the Scattered, Al," he replied. "I'm just trying to help."

Alice lifted Emeline's legs, wrapping the fabric of the girl's skirts around her legs so it wouldn't drag on the dusty dirt floor. "Your definition of help is rarely accurate."

"Will you tell Ned that I say I'm happy for him? That I hope he's well?"

"No."

"But—"

"*No,*" Alice replied, turning to walk back to the ship. "Write a letter, if you're so inclined."

Barnaby turned to follow her when Josie caught him by the wrist. "Oh, no. We have business to attend to," she said. "Though I suppose you've proved that you have the funds."

"Please, just five minutes—"

"I'm not here to give time to your petty squabbles with the self-righteous crew of the Cricket. I have my own errands to run." Josie unlocked Delia and Carmen's cuffs. "Go on, piss off. It hasn't been a pleasure, and I hope we don't meet again."

Delia rubbed at her wrists, the skin raw. "The feeling is mutual."

"Come on, Dee," Carmen whispered. "Let's get you the hell out of here."

"I feel like someone is about to jump us again."

"Me, too. We'd better stay close to the others, just in case. I hate this place."

"You've been here before?"

"Unfortunately. It's a nasty place, a breeding ground of greed and excess. These are the places that most think represent all rebels, when it's just as much Coalition managers and higher ups in here as there are pirates." Carmen glanced over her shoulder. "I need to go see to that deal. Something doesn't feel right."

"Where are you going?"

"I'll meet up with you all soon." She flashed a wide grin. "Don't worry about me."

"Hurry up," Kady barked over her shoulder. "We don't have time to take a leisurely stroll. We need to get out of here."

When they exited the tent, a small droid descended, hovering over Alice's left shoulder. "Good job, BEEP," she said affectionately.

"Are you sure it worked?" Kady asked,

"I'm sure. Your programming is sound. It should have intercepted that credit transfer," Alice said, adjusting her grip on Emeline's legs. "We need to figure out what to do with her."

"You're not putting her in the brig," Georgie interjected. "She's my sister, not a criminal."

"If she takes note of where we're headed, we risk her giving the location away if she... if she escapes," Kady said. "We can't take that risk."

"Then I'll paint the porthole while she's unconscious."

Alice gave Kady a sideways glance. "That might work."

"Alice, we agreed!" Kady protested. "We made a plan for a reason!"

"I know, but it's her sister. We wouldn't want one of us in the brig."

"*You* were in the brig not so long ago."

"A misunderstanding, and that was over two years ago. I wasn't a kid who'd been kidnapped, either."

"Fine. But I'm not telling the captain."

Alice sighed. "No, I expect I'll have to."

"Open the door!" Kady shouted at the ship. "We got her, and the others, too."

The old, rusted metal of the ship creaked as the gears ground against each other, lifting the loading bay door until they could all fit underneath without crouching. "Better lock it again, Ivy," Alice said. "We don't want any more stowaways, do we?"

"Aye."

"Not to... draw attention from Emeline, but I was hoping your crew could help me track some people down," Delia said. "I'm looking for two others that were meant to be on Josie's ship, a man who was probably malnourished, and a woman, she's beautiful, a cook—"

"Delia!" Rosie shouted, bounding through the open airlock. "Delia, it really is you! Gods below, I thought I'd never see you again. I didn't believe them when they said Josie would be here—"

"Rosie!" Delia yelled, burying her face in Rosie's neck. "Rosie, my posy, you're alright. After they took us, I feared the worst for you and—where's Thomas?"

"Don't worry, he's fine. Needs feeding up and to rest, but he'll be just fine."

"How did you end up on the Cricket?"

"It's a very odd story. Turns out, General Fineglass really *does* have a sister. They look almost identical."

"Gods be damned. I knew it."

"Ivy, can you ask the captain to meet me on the bridge when she's back from the market?" Alice asked over her shoulder. "We're going to get Emeline settled in. Hopefully, she doesn't tear the room apart when she wakes up."

"She's not an animal," Georgie said, following close behind. "She just needs time to adjust."

"We'll see about that," Kady muttered, guiding Emeline's unconscious body through the doorway, protecting her head from lolling against the sides of the glass.

"One of yous will have to bunk in with me, unless you want to share a room," Ivy said, tugging on a latching bar. "With Emeline staying, and others, we don't have any room, and that's after Kady gave up a section of her lab for temporary accommodations."

"I think we can share a room, Rosie, what do you think?" Delia asked.

"Sounds good. Ivy, what's the plan? Where are we going?"

Ivy shrugged. "You'd have to ask Ned. I heard something about going back to Bradach right away."

"Bradach?" Delia asked.

"You'll love it there, Dee. It's like Gamma-3 used to be."

"That's a tall order."

"We can start over. Together."

Delia hesitated. "I'm worried about William. That trade back there, I think... I think he's gotten himself mixed up in something terrible."

"Why is he your problem? It's not like he sent a pirate crew after you. *I* did. *Me*."

"I think that man back there knows William. I think that was his business partner, and he's the one who paid to have us released."

"Where is he?"

"I... don't know. Back on Gamma-3, maybe? But then, why would he be doing this kind of business from there? It's foolish. He's going to get himself caught."

"What do we do, then?" Rosie asked. "We don't have a ship of our own. We can't just go chasing off after him all over the Near Systems if we don't even know where he is."

"That trader might. Barnaby, they called him." Delia turned back to the door. "Ivy, can you open the door, let me out? I'll be right back, I just need to talk to him."

Ivy shook her head. "I don't think that's a good idea. He'll be loading that thing off of Josie's ship now, and she could just snatch you up again."

"I'm willing to take that risk."

Rosie caught her by the wrist. "Dee, I just got you back. I don't want to see you running back into the jaws of danger."

"What do you expect me to do?"

"Take a breath. Make a plan. We'll find him, I promise. If he's sitting on that pile of credits, he'll be able to buy himself some time."

"If he's sitting on those credits, they'll know exactly where he is." Delia tugged at the buttons on her dirty, stained shirt cuffs. "For all I know, he could be dead already. I can't just give up on him, Rosie. I can't abandon him."

A fierce pounding on the door interrupted the conversation. "Ivy! Open up, it's Captain Violet! We need to leave, right now. Tell Ned to fire up the engines."

Ivy yanked hard on the pulley. "Ned!" she shouted into the radio on her hip. "We need to go!"

"Aye!" came the gruff, staticky reply.

The huge door raised upward with a cacophony of metallic screeches, protesting their use, until it was just high enough for a petite woman with a shining scar across her face to clamber underneath. "I knew that rat-faced bastard was up to no good. Ned!" she shouted into her own radio. "Plot a course to Terringgough Gulch, full speed. I'll be on the bridge as soon as I can."

"Boss? What's up?"

"Barnaby, the gods be damned, is screwing us over again!" The captain hooked the radio back onto her hip. "Is everyone else aboard, Ivy?"

"Yes. We got everyone. You were the last to return."

"Hyun? Jasper?"

"Never left. She said she never gets medical supplies from this market. Too likely to be cut with adulterants. Jasper is with her in the medical bay."

"Good. And Emeline is...?"

"In one of the quarters."

"Not the brig?"

Ivy locked the loading bay door, latching it closed with a heavy clank. "Georgie protested."

"Yes," Captain Violet said with a sigh. "I was afraid of that. Alright, up to the bridge. Gods, and here I thought we had enough problems, now we have to deal with yet another gods-damned faction. Obsidian Enclave, *please*. As if the Near Systems doesn't have enough in the way of fractured leadership."

Rosie released Delia's hand and stepped back towards the door. "Obsidian Enclave?" she repeated.

"Why? I don't suppose you know anything about them?"

"I'm afraid I do, Captain. More than I wish."

Chapter 42

Rosie's mouth was dry with anxiety as she followed the captain through the ship. Delia was following, but tentative, cautious. Was what she was about to admit going to split them apart again?

"Ned," the captain said, taking the steps onto the bridge two at a time. "What's our journey looking like?"

"If we take it full speed, we'll have to refuel before we head back if you want enough juice for stealth. Last time, you complained that the fuel prices were too high."

Captain Violet waved him away. "I don't care about that right now. Just get us there as soon as possible."

"What... happened?" Ned asked, preparing the ship for takeoff. "With Barnaby?"

"Alice got him to pay for the release of the hostages—prisoners—and then he bought that thing from Josie. We thought he was buying it for The Scattered. For Cass."

"But he wasn't?"

"No. It's for Obsidian Enclave. Carmen radioed and told us. She'll meet with us later."

Ned scratched his thick ginger beard. "Boss, are you sure? They've been defunct since... well, since the last rebellion. Decades. You'd have been just a kid." The ship's boilers, and then engines, roared into life, bringing a gentle shake to the threadbare floor as it lifted into the sky.

"No one has heard from them in years. Even the old loyalists to that cause finally stopped talking about it in taverns. It's nothing I would have expected, and yet here we are." The captain rubbed the bridge of her nose. "This is the last thing we needed, especially with Emeline on board."

"It didn't go well, I heard."

"We expected that, unfortunately."

"Atmosphere pressure is normal," Ned announced, pulling a lever in front of him. "Kady had to zap her."

"Damn. See, this is why I didn't want Georgie along. We knew it might get difficult. I don't think she realized how different her sister might be, now. Might always be."

"Mm," Ned murmured in agreement. "So what's the plan, Boss?"

"We need to tell Cass what's going on. I don't trust the communication lines, not knowing Obsidian Enclave is out there. That was their specialty last time, you know. Intercepting, decoding. If any of the old ones are left, that's exactly what they'll be doing." She sat in her captain's chair, looking out the wide glass as the ship burst from the atmosphere into dark space. "Rosie," she said. "You don't have to lurk in the corridor. You're allowed on the bridge. This isn't a Coalition ship."

Rosie took several tentative steps, teetering in the doorway. "Old habits," she said.

"What can you tell us about Obsidian Enclave, then? You said you might know something, so, out with it."

"My family was very involved, for a time."

"What family?"

"My grandparents, on my mother's side."

The captain raised her eyebrows in surprise. "I thought you were raised on Gamma-3."

"I was, mostly. Brought there when I was very young. Obsidian Enclave tends to avoid Coalition-controlled areas, for... obvious reasons. I didn't know much. My mother didn't want me getting all wrapped up in that. Her mother was killed by the military when she was very young, so she was raised by my grandfather. He's still... sympathetic, I guess. To the cause."

"Where is their base?"

"I can't know for sure. But last year I heard rumors about the expansion project, that they found something beyond the edge of the known galaxy. I volunteered to go out there, to the Outer Rim. I thought maybe… I don't know. I don't know what I thought. It was more instinct than information."

"That would make sense why they've cropped up again after so long. If they have a base out there, they'll be wanting to protect it from whatever the researchers are doing."

"Mining rhodium," Delia said from behind. "I spoke to a researcher aboard Turas-Mara Station. A Dr. Arteo."

"Arteo?" Ned asked. "Didn't we know an Arteo, once?"

"Probably no relation," the captain said. "But we'll look into it. Rhodium is a hell of a thing to be sitting on. The Coalition isn't going to give up on that easily." She swiveled in her chair to face Rosie. "Can you get into contact with your family? See what they might be able to tell us?"

Rosie shook her head. "I haven't heard from them since I left. My mother is probably furious with me for leaving without a word."

"What about your grandfather?"

"We were always very close—but we haven't been in contact since I left. I suppose it's also possible that…" Rosie swallowed hard. "He's an old man."

"Maybe so, but old Obsidian Enclaves don't die easy. Where do they live now?"

"Dubhmoor, on Gamma-3. It's where I grew up, and Delia here, too. It's small. There's not much there, never has been. We both went to boarding school, and would go home for summer holidays. I… I don't know if they would have left. Without knowing the whole story, I can't say for sure."

"Ned, do we still have contacts down on Gamma-3?"

"Aye, but only a few now. The rest have gone dark in recent months."

"Could be they were rounded up."

"Maybe. Or the heat got too close. Some of them have families to protect, Boss."

The captain drummed her fingertips against the warped metal dashboard in front of her. "Yes, that's understandable. Rosie, we'll have someone reach out to them, if that's okay with you."

"I don't know if you'll get a response. My mother was always insistent that we walk a straight and narrow path. She didn't want to draw any attention. If people knew that we were related to my grandmother, they might execute us, too."

"Who was your grandmother?"

"Norah Gordon."

The captain stared. "No."

"I didn't know her, Captain. She died long before I was born. But that was her."

"*You* are the granddaughter of Norah Gordon?"

Ned studied Rosie's face. "You don't look much like her. Not much resemblance to the old photos you see in the taverns in ghost settlements."

"Everyone always said I took after my grandfather's side. She was tall, willowy, with golden hair. My grandfather is a short, stocky man. He always said it made us better cooks. Closer to the fire, you know."

"Are you playing us for fools?" Captain Violet demanded. "We have no time for such games. Lives are on the line, Rosie, and—"

"I'll swear on anything that I am not lying. Swear on my own life, even."

"Don't think I won't follow that through if it turns out you are."

"The only other place I can think they might be, if they ran, is an old settlement out past Epsilon-6. There's a big asteroid out there, devoid of rhodium for at least one hundred years. If they aren't on Gamma-3, they might be there. We stayed there for a time, when I was young."

"Have someone check on that for us, Ned."

"Aye, Boss," he replied. "I have heard that was an old stopover, back in the day, for people wanting to stay under the radar. There used to be a man who lived there, specialized in grey-market chips."

Rosie nodded. "I was very young, but I sort of remember a big tent there. The chip I have in my arm is untrackable, but the Coalition doesn't know that."

"Those are very expensive," the captain said. "You're lucky to have one."

"My grandfather spent what little money he had left on them after my father was killed. He was an Obsidian Enclave, too. It was then they decided to hide. That it... wasn't worth fighting, anymore."

"Clearly, the rest of them didn't agree."

"I wish I could be more help," Rosie said, her hands in her pockets. "I was just so young, I don't remember much."

Ned clapped a hand on her shoulder. "You've helped immensely. We're glad to have you aboard."

The captain turned back to the window, still drumming a rhythm into the metal. "You'll still have to pull your weight, though. Maybe you can make dinner tonight. There's not much in the kitchen, we didn't pick anything up at the market. Hyun swears it's full of pesticides."

"After months on that station, I feel like I am uniquely qualified. We barely had anything when I first got there. Not even flour."

"Not even flour?" Ned asked. "Impossible."

"Most of the crew only ever got protein bricks."

"A sorry excuse for food. Still, I usually cook on board, so there's no need for that, Rosie. We'll find another job for you."

"Ned, I'm going to need you and Kady to be tracing these contacts," Captain Violet said. "You won't have time to make us all dinner."

"I can handle it, Boss."

"Let the woman make us dinner, Nedrick."

He scowled. "Fine. But don't rearrange the spices. I just re-alphabetized them last week."

"I wouldn't dream of reorganizing another cook's kitchen. It's tantamount to treason, as far as I'm concerned," Rosie said, cracking a smile. "I hope I will be able to prepare something that meets with your approval."

The captain snorted a laugh. "Don't mind him, Rosie. He's just a little territorial about the kitchen."

* * *

"Let's see what we have here," Rosie mumbled, standing on her tiptoes to see into the high cabinets. "Some cans, several bags of pulses, flours..."

"Are we going to address the elephant in the room?" Delia asked, standing in the doorway to the kitchen, leaned gracefully against the frame.

"What would that be?"

"Rose, please."

Stacking several cans on the counter, Rosie sighed. "I was telling the truth on the bridge. I don't remember much."

"Clearly you remembered that much, though. How come you never told me?"

"My mother always made it very clear that it was life or death, that kind of information."

"You could have trusted me. We've known each other almost our entire lives."

"When would I have told you, Dee? When we were digging for carrots in my grandfather's garden as kids? Or when we were away at school, as teenagers? You were already on a path, even then. I was nothing more than the daughter of rebels, trying to survive. You would have—you might have dropped me, had I told you."

"Of course I wouldn't have."

"And how would I know? You don't remember this, but you said an awful lot of things about rebels then. Parroted from your father, I'm sure, but still, I couldn't have known."

"You didn't tell me on the station, either."

"I never expected to see you there. Never in a million years, Delia. I was out there to try to... I don't know, learn about my grandmother. About my father. About why I'd spent my entire life hiding in plain sight, drifting under the radar. Then there you were, all important and successful, the way I always knew you'd be, and closely tied with the likes of Fineglass and Allemande."

"We broke into her office together."

"Yeah, by that time we had other priorities, didn't we?"

"I guess we ended up here, anyway. In spite of all that."

Rosie walked into the pantry, partly to look for produce, and partly to hide the tears gathering in her eyes. "I guess we did." She wiped her face on her borrowed apron. "There are onions and potatoes in here. Some mushrooms, too."

"Posy, what's wrong?" Delia had followed her into the pantry, her brow furrowed with concern.

"I'm just so glad I found you again. On the station, and now here. I just keep thinking—what if I hadn't found Bailey at that transport hub? Thomas and I would still be flitting around, looking for any sign of you."

"You would have found me. I know you would."

"I see now why my mother was always so adamant we stay out of trouble. Once you're in it, that shadow just keeps following you with one thing, and then the next."

Delia rested her hands on Rosie's hips. "Maybe we should look at it more like liberation, like freedom... rather than a kind of prison."

"Isn't it, though? We'll never be able to show our faces in the Capital again."

"Would you really want to? You always said it smelled of rotting petals and fumes."

"It *does* smell like rotting petals and fumes. That doesn't mean I don't already miss the freedom to go there." Rosie picked a few more potatoes from the near-empty bin, nestling them in her gathered apron. "Don't you worry about what comes next?"

"Surely finding William is next on the agenda... I wonder if this Cass person is Cassius Calvetti."

"Who?"

"Leader of The Scattered. She hasn't been at the helm for long."

"You'd better be careful, Delia, or someone will think you're gathering information for some kind of scoop."

Delia shrugged. "Old habits."

"Make yourself useful. Peel these." Rosie dumped the potatoes out onto the counter and handed Delia a paring knife. "I notice they didn't tell *you* that you had to pitch in."

"I'm a poor, rescued reporter, torn from the jaws of death. You're a stowaway."

"How did you know that?"

"I overheard Ivy talking about it." Delia ran her hands over the fabric gathered at Rosie's thick waist. "You're wearing something new. I... I like it."

Rosie blushed, but cleared her throat and turned towards the sink. "The seamstress thought it would be best for this. I did try on a dress, but it felt so opulent and fancy. I've never worn anything like that before."

"Maybe someday I'll see you in it."

"Yeah, maybe. Assuming we survive this."

"Don't worry, if there's anything we do well, here, it's survive," a woman said from the doorway, the plush, purple crushed velvet of her jacket glinting in the dim light. "It's nice to finally meet you, Delia Dodson."

"I'm very sorry that I don't know who you are," Delia replied.

"Hyun. I'm the medical technician aboard. Well, Jasper too, but I know more than him. But he's learning fast." She sauntered in and leaned on the back of a chair. "Did either of you see Emeline brought in?"

"Yes. She was... incapacitated."

"I was afraid that might happen. I'm on my way to go and check on her. I promised Georgie that I would. I've never seen her so angry. I thought Alice might have to pull her and Kady off each other."

"I can't even imagine what it would be like to find family again after so long," Delia said. "And after those experiences."

"It's a hard road ahead, no matter what happens," Hyun agreed. "I worry there may not be a path back for Emeline. We can't keep her prisoner forever, and neither can her sister, despite what she says."

"What happens if she doesn't come around?" Rosie asked.

Hyun shrugged. "I wish I could say. It's not a scenario we wanted to plan for, even if it seems likely, now. I imagine the crew will have a vote, if it comes to that. An anonymous vote. Emotions will run high, whatever the outcome."

"What if someone could give her at least part of what she wanted?" Delia asked. "I don't know if maybe that would help?"

"Worth a try, I guess. I didn't know her before. She was on the ship all of five minutes before she sneaked out of the loading bay to try to return to her brewing revolution in Skelm. It's hard to know how to help, when I barely know the girl beyond what Georgie has told us, and what we heard on the broadcasts."

"You listened to my broadcasts?"

"Sure."

"Did you... like them?"

"Liked them more when you were dropping us information."

Delia grimaced. "My scripts were heavily edited, in the end."

"Last we heard that was useful, you mentioned patrols on flight paths out towards the Rim. Didn't do us any good, we were on the other end of the Near Systems—but obviously Josie heard you."

"I've never really known what's right. I tried to do what I could, but it's such a challenge when one wrong word means that people can die."

"I didn't envy you," Hyun said, brushing a stray hair back into the elaborate braid coiled atop her head. "At least as a med tech, I have one job, and that's trying to fix the person in front of me. Stop the bleed, set the bone, remove the foreign object, heal burned lungs. Once you've seen the inside of a ribcage, it hits you that really, we're all just sacks of meat and bone."

"It's not a job I could do. Blood makes me squeamish," Rosie said.

"Let's try to keep you out of my med bay then, shall we?" Hyun eyed the counter. "What's on the menu? Where's Ned?"

"Potatoes au gratin, and I'm preparing dinner tonight. Ned is working on something else for the captain."

"I'm surprised he even let you in here."

"I don't think it was by choice."

Hyun laughed. "No, I imagine not. He's very protective about the kitchen. Gods, but he complained when we first started taking turns cooking. Now he barely lets anyone in here, for fear that they'll misplace a spoon."

"I promised him I'll behave."

"I'd better go check on Emeline. Hopefully, she doesn't throw anything at my head."

"If in doubt, duck," Delia said, grinning. "You can't go wrong."

"Thanks for that sage advice. Hopefully, that works out for me."

After Hyun left, the odd silence in the kitchen nagged at Rosie's nerves. Delia wasn't saying anything, and the only sounds were those of the knife pulsing against the worn, wooden cutting board, scraping the sliced, peeled potatoes into a large dish.

"Dee, are you upset with me?" Rosie asked. "You've barely said a word in ten minutes."

"Just lost in thought."

"Don't get too lost, or I'll have to climb in there to guide you back out."

"Very funny. No, I'm just wondering how we can... *defuse* Emeline. No one wants this to end badly, least of all her sister. But despite all that time on the station, I'm not sure I can say I know the girl any better than Hyun, who apparently only saw her for a few minutes two years ago."

"Are you going to make *every* problem your problem?"

"I can't help it. I just... I want to help, Rose. I feel pretty useless right now, and I hate it."

"It's too bad I don't have more potatoes for you to peel."

Delia laughed and laced her arms around Rosie's waist. "I have to admit, that wasn't my favorite job. I would like to help in other ways that don't involve knives—"

"You could do the dishes."

"—or soap."

"Yeah, by the looks of you, it really looks like you have an aversion to soap."

"You'd look like a rat dragged in by the cat if you'd spent that long in Josie's brig, too. I'm very grateful to be out of there."

"And I'm glad to have you back."

"What do you think is going to happen now?"

Rosie leaned her head back, allowing Delia to rest against her neck. "I don't know. I wish I did. I wish I had more information, but everything is so hazy in my memory. My grandfather only told me shreds of story in whispers. He didn't want my mother to overhear."

"What kind of stories?"

"Tall tales, mostly. Stories about brave rebels who nearly took down the Coalition. It felt almost like magic, dreaming about a different kind of world. Hells, a different kind of universe, even. But I got older, I grew up, and I learned that no one was ever close to taking it down. Anyone who posed a threat was wiped out." Rosie wiped her hands on the apron, her skin raw from handling the wet potatoes. "It felt achievable, when I was small. Now, it feels impossible. How can you even begin to undermine something so huge, so powerful?"

"Posy, you're a damned genius."

"I am? What did I say this time?"

"I have an idea. Do you have cornflower?"

Chapter 43

Delia rapped quietly on the heavy iron door. "Emeline?"

"Go away."

"I thought you might want some company."

"The only thing I want right now is to be left the hell alone."

"Sure, I understand that. It's been a tough week."

"With respect, Ms. Dodson, piss off."

"Alright," Delia said, but hesitated, still balancing the steaming plate in her hand. "I have something for you, though."

"Whatever it is, I don't want it."

"It's cornbread."

"I don't want anything you made. It's probably poisoned, anyway."

"Rosie made it. Here, I'll take a bite myself, I'll show you." She unlatched the door's exterior lock. "Can I open this?"

"...Fine."

The door pushed open, casting a thin strip of yellow light from the corridor lights into the dark room. "See?" Delia prompted, taking a big bite of bread. It was still warm from the oven, the butter melting into every crumb. "It's good."

"I'll wait. It might still be poisoned. Or laced with truth serum."

"That's what you did to Mae, wasn't it?"

"She was a fool to trust me. She underestimated me, and I... and I..."

Delia sat on the edge of the bed. "Do you regret it?"

"No. Yes. I don't know anymore."

"This must be very difficult for you."

"I'm very tired of being snatched up by people and waking up in a cell. This time makes four. The first was Skelm, and then Tarand's ship, Josie's brig, and now here. Wherever *here* is." Emeline picked at her nails. "You people are no better than all the rest."

"That might be true. Probably is, in fact."

"Where are they taking me?"

Delia shrugged. "I'm not sure, really. It sounds like there is some important business to attend to before we can go... home."

"Have you ever been there? This new home?"

"No, I haven't."

"How do you know you'll like it there?"

"I don't."

"Won't you miss people?"

"The people I care most about are already on this ship." Guilt breathed into Delia's lungs. "Well, most of them, anyway."

"What about the Capital?"

"I never much liked it there. Crowded. Lots of back-stabbing."

Emeline eyed the cornbread, half-wrapped up in the clean kitchen towel. "I didn't like the Capital, either. Everything was so... censored."

"Including the radio broadcasts."

"I guess you won't be going back to your job now."

An ache settled deep in Delia's chest. "No, I guess I won't. Your mother will know I had something to do with all of this."

"Yes, she will."

"I'll have to go into hiding for a while. Until people forget my name. Until... well. That's enough of that, I think. There's no sense in wallowing in self-pity."

"It's inefficient," Emeline agreed.

"I haven't keeled over or started spilling my life's secrets yet. Do you think you might have a bite of this cornbread?"

"You might have only dosed one of them."

"What secrets are you hiding that you'd be worried about? We saw the secret file in your mother's office. We know that she's after this ship already, and has been for years."

Emeline's fingers brushed against the cornbread. "I saw it, too."

"Oh, *really?*"

"She trusted me. More than my sister does right now." Emeline laid the cornbread in the palm of her hand, tasting a small crumb. "I had full access to Turas-Mara, even though I wasn't supposed to. She gave me access, because she trusted me. I went through all of her files. I found the secret one in her desk. Saw my sister's name in it."

"That must have been hard."

Emeline took a bite. "It was... expected. Of course they would be tracking Georgie and Henry. They were Coalition employees who committed treason."

"I guess they did."

"This bread is very good. Not as good as my—as my..."

"Other mother?" Delia offered.

"Why are you being so nice to me? What do you want?"

"Just to figure out how we can all move forward. Your sister loves you. She cares about you. Everyone on the ship is talking about how she spent every waking moment over the past two years trying to get you back."

"She has a strange way of showing it, kidnapping me and throwing me into a locked room."

Delia shifted, the conversation uncomfortable. "I wish I could change that for you, but I don't have any authority on this ship. I'm a stranger to them."

"A stranger, yet you're not locked in a room."

"They are afraid you will try to contact your mother."

"They'd deserve it," Emeline said, stuffing the rest of the cornbread in her mouth.

"Maybe so."

"You'd deserve it, too." Emeline brushed the remaining crumbs into her hand, and then funneled them into her mouth. "Actions have consequences."

"I'm not arguing that point. We all make choices. Some of those choices affect other people, and we all have to decide how that impacts any future decisions. Hells, I've made all kinds of mistakes in life, and they follow me, even now."

"Oh yeah? Like what?"

"Like leaving Rosie all those years ago, for one thing. Chasing fame and fortune, for another. Leaking information that got people killed back on Turas-Mara. It all keeps me up at night."

"It should."

"I can get you more of that, if you want," Delia said, gesturing at the empty towel. "I asked Rosie to make a whole pan of it."

"You'll just drug the next one you bring me."

"Not everyone is trying to drug food, alright? No one is doing that. I wouldn't even know where to start, for one thing. I don't exactly have access to things like truth serum, nor would I have the first idea on how to make it myself."

"You know I can't trust you, right?"

"I know. I get that."

"But I appreciate the food. Anything is better than those bricks. I should tell my mo—" Emeline cleared her throat. "Someone should adjust the formula, make it taste better than the underside of an old shoe."

"Come on, we both know that's an insult to old shoes."

"You can go now."

"Alright, and I will. I had an idea, though. And I'd need your help to do it."

Emeline turned and faced the wall. "I'm not interested in helping you."

"I realize that, but it occurs to me that you might be interested in helping the people of Skelm."

"And how do you propose we do that? Ask my sister to burn the city down again? Make sure it stays thick with MPOs until the end of time?"

"I thought a broadcast about how things really are there might work."

"Are you that delusional to think they'd ever let you anywhere near a broadcast room again? You'd be lucky to get out of this with your head still attached to your neck."

"There are ways."

"You'd hijack the official signal, wouldn't you?"

"Yes," Delia admitted. "I would."

"I want no part of that." Emeline looked over her shoulder. "Once I make it back to civilization, if you people ever decide to release me, I'll make sure that signal security is the first thing I suggest."

"I understand your objections. It's risky, and not a Coalition signal. But telling people about the plight of workers is worthwhile, no matter how that happens." Delia stood and hesitated by the door. "I'll do it with or without your help, Emeline."

"That's Ms. Allemande to you."

The door latched closed, and Delia let out a long sigh.

"How did it go?" Kady asked, leaning against a stack of crates.

"I'd be lying if I said I hadn't hoped for better."

"Walk with me. Almost time for dinner, anyway. I'll have Ivy bring the girl a plate."

"Sure."

"What do you think? Will she come around?"

Delia picked at the frayed edging of her suspenders. "It's hard to say. Sometimes it feels like there is progress. Other times, she pulls back, and it's like she puts up a wall."

"Hyun said that might be normal. Emeline didn't say much to her, either."

"She doesn't like being locked in that room. She thinks no one trusts her."

"We don't. Kid is the daughter of a powerful overseer who would give anything to have us in her sights. One wrong move and we're all yesterday's news," Kady said.

"Might go a long way in showing her that she's welcome."

"It's risky. We'll wait until we're all back on Bradach to try that approach. We just can't right now." Kady's steps were graceful and nearly silent. "I can't agree to risk everyone else's life to make a teenager feel better."

Delia nodded. "I understand that. I'm just relaying what she said."

"I've already got Georgie shooting daggers at me from her eyes whenever I see her on the ship. She doesn't understand that it's not about any kind of grudge or personal slight. I want to make sure we all stay alive and out of Coalition prisons." Kady pressed a hand to her temple. "I didn't want her to come because I knew that it likely wouldn't be the loving reunion that Georgie was imagining."

"I think we need to give Emeline some more time. It's too soon to make a judgment on it all."

"Time is the one thing we don't have. With Obsidian Enclave cropping up out of nowhere, this new weapon that Josie supposedly stole and sold to Barnaby, and knowing what Cass needs for the next phase—well, it's all converging at once."

"I think Barnaby is working with my—uh—with William," Delia said carefully.

Kady arched a perfect eyebrow. "Does the captain know that?"

"It didn't come up."

"Any way we can get closer to Barnaby, to figure out if the weapon was the real deal, we should take it. Where were they working out of? What's their ship?"

"I don't know. It's been months since I saw William last. He was supposed to have some deal with the Coalition for rare parts. The shipments were late, if there were shipments to begin with."

"Is this Will a con artist?" Kady asked.

Delia shook her head. "More like an easy mark. He's had some... troubles, in the past."

"No wonder he's working with Barnaby, then. No doubt that ratfink sniffed him out from half a million kilometers away."

"What's that supposed to mean?"

"Nothing. Listen, don't say anything to the captain about this just yet. Or Alice. She has a soft spot for Barnaby, even after all this time, and all the shit he's pulled. Let me throw out some lines, see what I pull in. We may yet find your William. Is he your...?"

"We have an arrangement," Delia replied.

"And what arrangement is that?"

"I married him for his name. He married me because he needed someone to pay his gambling debts."

"Right. And how upset would you be if we used him to get to Barnaby?"

"I don't want him to get hurt," Delia said. "I realize he might have gotten mixed up in something—again—but he's a good man, really. He doesn't deserve to get hurt."

"If it all goes to plan, no one will get hurt."

"And if it doesn't?"

"Listen, Delia, just let me worry about that, alright?" Kady steered her back into the kitchen area. "Smells good in here. What did Rosie make?"

"Some sort of potato thing, I don't know." Delia shrugged off Kady's hand. She didn't want to talk about the food, she wanted to find out what she knew about William and this Barnaby person. What in hells had he done, now? She should have known that he would find trouble the moment she went off-world and left him in the Capital. He was easily led by charm and a friendly demeanor.

"Food's up," Rosie announced, setting steaming trays on the table. "It's not much, but—"

"Oh, my good gods alive," Ivy said, already filling her plate, "this smells like heaven."

"It's potatoes au gratin. There are also some trays of roasted beans that I found canned in the pantry. For dessert, we have—"

"There's dessert?" Alice asked, pulling up a chair. "You never make us dessert anymore, Ned."

"Oh, I'm sorry," Ned said with a scowl. "I'm usually too busy plotting flight paths around new blockades that crop up every other gods-damned day."

"Relax, Ned, we still love you. Rosie is just helping out, isn't that right?"

Rosie nodded. "Of course. I'd never want to take over another cook's kitchen, in fact, I—"

"Whatever."

"She's just trying to pitch in," Delia said pointedly. "There's no need for your attitude."

Ned stared at her as he flicked one potato slice onto his plate. "I don't have an attitude."

"Dee, it's fine," Rosie said, laying the final tray in the center of the table. "For dessert, we have a butterscotch pudding."

"Where in hells did you find butterscotch?"

"I made it."

"With what?"

Rosie sat down and served herself. "Ingredients," she told him with a smirk.

"Oh good, dinner," Captain Violet said, swanning into the room. She kissed the top of Alice's head on her way to get a plate. "We're on track to meet Cass at Terringgough Gulch. Should land tomorrow morning, eh Ned?"

He nodded. "Aye."

"I want you all to be extremely careful in the messages you are sending and receiving, not just on the ship, but at all times. Obsidian Enclave may already be intercepting communications, and we need to remain vigilant. Do not contact any of our Coalition contacts until further notice." She sat down next to Alice, fork in hand. "That includes Jhanvi Jhaveri."

"But Jhaveri is our best source!" Kady protested. "How do you expect me to get a jump on Coalition tech without her?"

"We'll just have to do what we can for now."

"When can we schedule a meetup with her, then?"

"Not until we can know for sure if our comms are being intercepted or monitored."

Alice swore under her breath. "Nothing can ever be easy, can it?"

"Not for us, darling. You knew that when you signed on with this crew."

"Let's not get into that argument again, shall we?"

"In any case, when we get there, keep your eyes out for anything that looks suspicious. We don't know what Obsidian Enclave is planning."

"Surely having more people on our side can only be a good thing, right?"

Delia asked. "More forces for the rebellion? More opportunities to knock the Coalition off guard?"

"You won't remember what it was like, back then," the captain said, a dark tone to her voice. "Obsidian Enclave, at times, made The Scattered look like harmless amateurs. Both sides were ruthless, but the Coalition had bigger guns and better armor. Too many lives were lost. Almost everyone my age lost family, friends. The war raged for almost twenty years."

"Maybe ruthless is what we need now. Seems like so far, all the rebellion has managed to do is irritate the Coalition."

"We've done plenty more than that, but it never gets reported on. As you well know."

Delia sat back in her seat and stared at her plate. "There's only so much I can do."

"No one is asking to lay the weight of the Near Systems at your feet. But in a similar fashion, we can't sit by and let innocents get slaughtered by the thousands in another war that will have the same damned outcome unless we get a handle on things first. That's why we are going to meet with Cass, and that is why we're going to track down Barnaby if it's the last thing I do."

Heavy silence hung in the air for a moment. "How come no one ever tells us when dinner is ready?" Hyun asked, striding in with a tall, handsome man. In a way, he looked a little like William.

"I told you half an hour ago," Ivy protested. "You said you'd be right down."

"Oh yeah."

"I'm half-starved," Jasper said, piling his plate high. "You wouldn't believe how you can work up an appetite reorganizing the medicinal vials."

"Yeah, I'm sure that's all you two were doing," Ivy said with a snort.

"Anyway," Alice said, shooting Ivy a look, "we have to schedule a pickup soon for some parts. We really need to rewire some of the panels before we wind up in another firefight."

"*Another*?" Delia asked.

"That copper isn't strong enough to handle the current running through it, Vi. If you want to keep running at max capacity, we have to prioritize maintenance."

"Okay, Alice, I hear you," the captain said, before shoving in another forkful of potatoes. "But we need to see Cass first."

"I know we need to see Cass first!"

"And she's probably going to ask us to track down Barnaby. You know as well as I do that we have a better chance of flushing him out than any of her people do."

"Yes, alright, but then we need to have at least four days for repairs."

"Fine, fine."

"I mean it, Captain. This ship doesn't stay in the sky with hopes and wishes."

"And we won't stay in the sky at all if we don't figure out what the hell is going on with that weapon."

"Not to... interrupt, but these potatoes are absolutely divine," Hyun said, piling more onto her plate. "It might be one of my new favorites."

"I'm glad you're enjoying it," Rosie replied, looking a little bit smug. It was fine for her to be proud of her work. She'd earned it.

Delia finally took a bite of her own meal, savoring the rich, creamy sauce and the lightly browned cheese. It had been the best thing she'd eaten in... months, probably. "It really is amazing, Rosie."

"I guess it's alright," Ned admitted, helping himself to a second portion. "How did you keep the sauce so consistent?"

"You have to be careful with the temperatures when making the roux," Rosie explained. "Otherwise, you risk breaking the emulsion."

"I suppose you used *all* the cheese, did you?"

"No. There's still half of that small wheel back there."

"How did you roast those beans?"

"Rinsed, and tossed in oil and seasonings."

Ned took a bite, trying his best to suppress a smile. "It's good."

"I'm glad it meets with your approval, sir."

"I suppose I can allow you to cook for us a while longer. I still have more charts to complete, and it was kind of nice, having someone else cook for once. Gods know Kady hates it."

"There aren't enough words to describe how much I detest cooking," Kady agreed. "I love eating. Hate preparing the food."

"Plenty of science in cooking, too," Rosie offered.

"Sure. Not enough coding, though. You get too lost in thought with a dish and suddenly you have a burnt pile of nothing."

"Yeah, and we had enough burnt piles of nothing to last us a lifetime," Ned said with a snort. "She can code us all under the table and come up with all kinds of amazing solutions, but the woman is not a chef. It's alright, Kady. We love you anyway."

"You love me because I keep our asses out of trouble."

"That, and your sparkling personality."

"Piss off, Ned."

"Eat your dinner, Kady."

"Rosie, in light of your... familial connections, I think we should have you reach out to your mother and grandfather via a wire," the captain said. "If someone is monitoring us, then it may be helpful if they know that Norah Gordon's granddaughter is aboard."

"Norah Gordon? *The* Norah Gordon?" Georgie asked.

"I guess," Rosie admitted. "I never met her."

Georgie set her fork down. "My father idolized her. Said she was the true leader Obsidian Enclave really needed. He said the rebellion died when she did."

"I'm not so sure that's the entire truth, but I have heard that said."

"This could be the ticket to everything, Captain. We could fly wherever we wanted without a problem. They had the most amazing network of flight paths and signal reflectors."

Captain Violet shook her head. "That was a long time ago. Technologies have changed now, and much of the stories that remain about Norah Gordon have all but passed into legend on both sides. Young rebels want to be her, young military recruits and inspectors all want to capture her, or whoever the next face of the rebellion is. We have to be careful."

"That's the most important thing on this ship now, isn't it?" Georgie spat. "Being careful. So careful that you've locked my little sister in a cage."

"We are careful so as not to see more of us behind bars," the captain replied calmly. "And I hardly think that a soft bed with fresh linens is akin to a cage—or maybe you should ask Evie or Larkin what it's like in a Coalition prison. Hell, ask Ned!"

Without a word, Ned stood, cleaned his plate, and left the room.

"Ned, I'm sorry, but she needs to know that what we're doing is not the same," Captain Violet called after him. "We don't know what Emeline would do, given the opportunity!"

"She might have learned all manner of things while she was gone," Kady said. "For all we know, she'd rewire the communications column on the bridge and send a beacon a kilometer wide. Then where would that leave the rest of us, Georgie? In cells, and you can bet your ass they wouldn't be as nice as the room she's currently in."

"What if we just monitored her closely?" Henry suggested. "I could keep an eye on her, or—"

"I don't think you realize what that girl is like," Delia interjected. "She's so conflicted that if I was in her shoes, I wouldn't even know where to begin. She needs time and space, and frankly, someone to talk to who isn't one of us."

"I'll talk to her," Georgie said.

"She doesn't want to talk to you. Not yet. You have to give her time. She's not the same sister you lost two years ago. She probably won't ever be again."

"I know her better than any of you," Georgie said, standing up, her fists balled at her sides in quiet rage. "I swear on my own mother's life, I will do whatever it takes to—"

"Pipe down," Ned replied from the doorway. He was steering Emeline by her shoulders, and gently pressed her into a chair.

"Nedrick, this is tantamount to mutiny," Kady hissed. "We didn't agree on this, and you had no right to endanger the entire crew by letting her out."

"What is she going to do at the dinner table, Kady? Eh? Steal a potato?

Throw a fork at you? I'm not going to be on a ship where we lock up people who did nothing against us. It was wrong when we did it to Alice, and it's wrong now."

"Captain?" Kady asked, glaring across the table. "Are you going to let this stand?"

"Who the hell do you think you are?" Georgie snapped.

"The second in command on this fucking ship, thank you *very* much."

"She's my sister, not some MPO we picked up off the streets!"

"For all we know, she's a full-blown Coalition operative by now. She's said nothing to imply that she wants to do anything other than sell us out the first chance she gets. Including you."

"Especially her," Emeline chimed in. "But, in the interest of... diplomacy, I will desist from any scheming, so long as you don't lock me in that room. I am beyond done with being confined."

"There, you see?" Ned said. "Problem solved. For now, at least." He filled a plate and set it in front of Emeline. "Kady, I am sorry. Boss, the same to you. I just... I can't be party to some sort of moral backslide. We're better than that." He gave Kady a half smile. "All of us."

"Ned..." the captain said with a deep sigh. "You could have at least asked first."

"It just would have been arguments. See? Now we have progress. She promises not to sell us out. We can all build on that."

"A Coalition promise isn't worth shit on someone's boot," Kady muttered. "How many times has a promise turned out to be nothing more than a ploy?"

Georgie stood again. "If my sister sells us out, you can put both of us in the brig. I will take full responsibility for anything she does."

"Sit down, Payne," Captain Violet said. "That is wholly unnecessary." She chewed another bite of her dinner before continuing. "Ms—Emeline, why should we trust you? Clearly, my navigator does, but my second in command is somewhat less than convinced. So, convince her."

"First of all, I don't have the skills to rewire a console. Engineering was never my strong suit, and it wasn't what I trained for. I realize you may not take me at my word, but it is the truth. I can barely tell a hammer from a wrench."

"So what were you trained for on the station, then?" Kady demanded, scraping her fork noisily against the plate. "To be a spy?"

"To be a diplomat."

Kady snorted. "Liar."

"It isn't a lie."

Delia cleared her throat. "She spent most of her days with Carmen, who you all know and trust. Emeline had a heavy workload of academic studies, and unless she was getting lessons from one of the two engineers on the station, she wouldn't have learned anything like that. Not there, anyway."

"In any case, while I understand why you don't trust me, especially after the unfortunate circumstances with Maevestra Machenet, I will extend trust to you all that you won't shove me out an airlock at the first opportunity. I'm well aware that aside from my sister's rather irritating insistence, you have no real reason to even keep me alive."

Kady shoved her plate away. "You're right on that count."

"Let's all just take a breath, shall we?" Captain Violet said. "First of all: Emeline, I appreciate your candor. I can't help wondering how things would be if you hadn't left this ship that day in Skelm, but it's of no consequence now, anyway. No sense in dwelling on the past. We will take the lock off of your quarters, but I will firmly request that you stay away from restricted areas. For our purposes, that will be the bridge, boiler room, crew quarters, and the loading bay."

Emeline nodded. "This is acceptable."

"Kady, your objections are noted. As such, if we discover that our verbal contract has been breached, then the lock goes back on for the duration of our journey. Georgie... I will gently suggest that you give your sister the space that she needs right now. I know—we all know—that you've spent years waiting for this moment, but I can tell you from experience that if you push too hard, it will not go as you like."

Georgie shook her head. "But—"

"She's right, George," Henry said, laying a hand on Georgie's. "You can't force her to talk to you."

"Damned right," Emeline said, holding a forkful of potatoes aloft. "I'll be happy when I never have to look at you again, Georgina."

Georgie stormed out, knocking the chair over as she went, already burying her face in her hands. Henry followed, casting an apologetic look back at the rest of the crew.

"Enough, now," the captain said. "We all know our roles on this ship, and I know that you can perform them admirably. This is not an ideal situation, but we have all dealt with far worse. Rosie, thank you for the meal. It was delicious."

Other crew members murmured their agreement, and Delia nodded along with them.

"Ned and Kady, meet me on the bridge in twenty minutes to discuss landing procedures for meeting with Cass. Hyun, let's keep the med bay prepped... just in case."

Hyun nodded. "Of course, Captain."

"Alice, I'll make sure we schedule in days for repair after all this."

"Thanks, Vi."

"Now, is everyone satisfied with that?"

Kady sighed angrily, but said nothing.

"Good. I'll see the rest of you in the morning. Be ready for a landing, and to load up."

* * *

"So," Rosie said, her hand on the doorknob. "I guess this is it."

"I guess it is."

"Should we go in?"

"That seems like a better option than sleeping out here in the hall, don't you think?"

"You did good, going to talk to Emeline earlier. I feel like what happened at dinner would have been much worse, otherwise."

Delia closed the door behind them and flipped the latch closed, a force of habit brought forth from years of surprise inspections at the school they'd attended. "Wouldn't have done any good without a bribe of cornbread, so thanks for that."

"Of course. I'd do anything for you, Dee."

"I can sleep on the floor. I don't mind it."

"You'd rather sleep on the ground than share a bed with me?" Rosie asked.

"No! No, that's not it, I just—" Delia stopped and shook her head. "You'd think with me being a broadcaster that I wouldn't struggle so much with words, and yet I always seem to say the wrong things to you. I'm going to... I'm going to take a bath, and clean up. I feel like today has lasted approximately nine hundred years."

"I bet you're exhausted."

"I haven't even begun to process the half of it. I can say one thing for sure, though, and that's that I really don't want to end up in a brig again."

"We'll have to do our best to keep you out of trouble, then."

Delia laughed. "I feel like that might be harder than it sounds."

"Knowing you, it's going to be damned near impossible. Go on, go clean up. I'll wash your clothes and lay them out on the radiator for you."

"You don't have to do that."

"Of course I don't, but I'm offering it, because you just spent time in a cell. Plus, it's not as though I haven't done it before. Remember that time you fell into that mud creek?"

"I think you mean when you pushed me into the mud creek."

"You slipped!"

"Yes, because you shoved me!" Delia said, unbuttoning her shirt. She turned and faced the wall to untuck it, letting her suspenders fall over her shoulders to hang at her hips. "I made you clean my clothes because you were the reason they got muddy in the first place."

"That's not how I remember it."

"I bet."

"I'll tell you what happened," Rosie said, stifling a snort of laughter. "I told you to look at the bank of the creek because there was a snake. You called me a liar, then you saw it, reached out to grab me for balance, and fell in."

"I still maintain that you pushed me in. It wasn't even a real snake."

"No, but it definitely looked convincing enough for you to scream and thrash around in the water. You thought you were about to die."

"I still have a scar from that day, where a rock on the creek bed scraped across my shoulder."

"I can see it," Rosie said, suddenly right behind her, tracing her fingers over the long-faded scar, nothing more than a thin white line running across Delia's skin.

The electricity of her touch was already sending Delia into a spiral. "I should take that bath." She stepped out of her trousers, laying them across the bed alongside her shirt. She didn't know what to say, and nothing came to mind that wasn't trite.

"You still look the same, you know." Rosie leaned against the door frame, her gaze pulling across Delia's body.

"You've only improved with age," Delia replied, a blush creeping up her cheeks. "Like a fine, illegal wine."

"Maybe my illegality is why things never worked out."

"Maybe it's just fate that everything happened the way that it did." Delia let her hair down, matted curls tangled at the nape of her neck.

"Perhaps. Or maybe it's just the way life works."

Delia stepped inside the bathroom, leaving the door ajar. She shed her undergarments as the tub filled, curled loops of steam dissipating as they reached the ceiling. The water was the perfect temperature of searingly hot. She stepped in, stifling a satisfied groan.

"Are you alright in there?"

"Yes. Just glad that I'm out of those clothes."

Rosie laughed. "That makes two of us."

This was a new Rosie, confident, and it pulled at something inside Delia. She scrubbed at the grit in the creases of her elbows with the fresh bar of soap, embedded with pink peppercorns. "That's very bold of you to say, Rosie Gordon."

"Maybe all that illegal aging has given me some fresh perspectives."

Closing her eyes, Delia sank her head beneath the water and scrubbed at her scalp before resurfacing, suds clumped below her left ear. "Sometimes, it feels like no time has passed at all."

"I felt every second you were away, after you left.'"

"That's not what I meant."

Rosie leaned against the door frame, facing the bedroom. "I know."

Passing the soap over her skin once more, Delia didn't say anything. She chewed her lip, surveying Rosie's ample curves through the door. Gods, she was so beautiful, the way she carried herself, the smudge of flour on her elbow, the wisp of hair that hung down over her shoulder. "Rosie, I—"

"Do you need a towel?"

Delia blinked, spreading suds behind the backs of her knees. "Yes."

"I won't look," Rosie said, turning her face away as she hung a towel on the rail.

"You can look. It's nothing you haven't seen." Delia rinsed the foam from her hair, squeezing the water from the wet, heavy curls.

Rosie turned, her eyes skimming across the suds that hid Delia's body. "It's been a while."

"Yes." Delia pulled up the drain and stood, wrapping herself in the towel. "I feel much better, now." She scowled at the pile of underthings. "I wish I had something fresh to wear to bed. I'll wash these for the morning, but..."

Rosie stepped inside the room and slipped her hand beneath the towel, resting her palm against the warm dampness of Delia's hips. "Gods below, but how I missed you," she whispered.

The feeling of her skin and the huskiness of those breathy words melted every drop of caution and reserve that Delia had ever possessed. She sighed into Rosie's hair, drawing closer, and then dropping the towel entirely, feeling the cool air of the room brush against her. "Oh, Rosie," she breathed.

When their lips met, an unstoppable heat began to build between Delia's thighs. She ran her hands over the roundness of Rosie's hips and belly, an enticing, sweet softness that was both familiar and yet unexplored. Delia pressed further into the kiss, desperate to be as close as she could, pulling at Rosie's clothes.

Rosie stepped back. "Not yet."

"*Not yet?*"

"I don't know if I believe you, Forrest. I don't know if I believe how much you want it."

Delia fumbled for words, grasping for the towel. "Of course I do. Of course I want it—you."

"Hm." Rosie arched an eyebrow, locking eyes with Delia as she flipped open the top clasp of her jumpsuit, exposing a hint of round breast peeking at the edges of the fabric.

"Rosie," Delia breathed, her breath catching in her throat. "What are you doing to me?"

"Tormenting you." She flipped open a second clasp, her eyes still locked on Delia. "Is it working?"

"Yes."

"Good."

Delia stepped forward, her hands reaching out. Rosie held up a hand to stop her, a coy smile playing at the edges of her lips. "But—" Delia protested.

"We aren't even, yet."

"Even?"

Rosie nodded, opening the third clasp, the jumpsuit falling open to her waist. Her emerald green, lace bra letting pale skin peek through with just enough mystery to make Delia groan. Rosie continued, "You made me watch you on that station for months from afar."

"I didn't—"

"Shh." Rosie shrugged her shoulders out of the jumpsuit, and it clung to her hips, where she rested a hand, biting her bottom lip. "You *left* me, Delia Forrest."

"I told you, I—"

Rosie lifted Delia's chin, silencing her with a look. "No." She unbuttoned more of the jumpsuit, allowing Delia to sneak a peek at the matching underthings. "I don't think you've convinced me, yet."

"How do I convince you, without touching you?"

"Beg."

Delia had to steady herself, holding onto the empty towel rail. She could barely even breathe for wanting Rosie, and it threatened to push the air from her lungs, consuming her, leaving nothing but smoldering ash. "Please," she whispered.

"I can't hear you."

"Please," Delia repeated, her fingernails digging into her palm from want.

"And?"

"I want to feel your skin against mine, Rosie."

"Why?"

Delia swallowed hard. "Because—because you are the only woman I've ever really wanted. You're beautiful. You make me feel things no one else ever has."

"Better." Rosie released another button, stepping out of the jumpsuit. "What else?"

"You are quite possibly the best thing I have ever seen in my entire life."

Rosie gave a short, throaty laugh. "You're gods-damned right I am." She took a step towards Delia, releasing the clasp on her bra, letting it fall to the ground.

Delia's heart thudded in her chest, blood pounding in her ears from the anticipation. "If you don't let me touch you, I might actually die."

"You might."

"Is that a risk you're willing to take?"

Rosie considered this, and then slid the emerald lace over her hips, and it landed with a soft swish of lace on wood. "I suppose I don't want you to die." She took another step towards Delia, pulling her closer until they were pressed against one another with soft sighs of hungry desperation.

They tumbled together onto the bed, kicking off the covers, their mouths entrenched in each other's with hungry, desperate kisses. Delia knelt over Rosie, kissing down her neck, lingering at the collar bone just long enough to draw a small gasp. Her hands across Rosie's ample breasts, Delia felt a tightness in her that yearned for release, and to have that intimacy she had so long craved, dreaming of their younger years together when they were guiltless and in love.

Delia drew her hands down, running them up Rosie's thighs, kissing across her belly, and hesitating, teasing at the thatch of dark hair just like she remembered Rosie had always liked. They'd always just fit naturally together, without effort. It was like they'd grown together, in a way, until they hadn't, and now here they were, splicing back together as easily as they had in the beginning.

She kissed there deeply, and slowly, feeling her own self pulse greedily with the desire of it. Rosie moaned softly, her breath already shallow and rhythmic, her hands entwined in Delia's damp hair, pulling her closer, her back arching off the bed. Delia was lost in her, enfolded in her core essence, a connection that sprung up from the depths of themselves and seamlessly melded back together.

Rosie gasped for breath and cried out, her hands grasping at the bed, the remaining linens clasped between her fingers. She laughed and then reached for Delia, finding her ready with the anticipation.

Delia had almost forgotten what it felt like to be touched like that, by someone who loved her, and knew every inch of her, and wanted nothing more than to make her happy. She laid back on the bed, Rosie kissing her again with every insistent press, until she was left breathless, too, and weeping, holding Rosie tight in her arms. "That was new," she said after a moment.

"Some things do change, Delia."

"I like change. I liked *that*."

"It's what I deserve."

"It is." Delia kissed Rosie's neck again. "And I am sorry. Truly."

"I forgive you."

Chapter 44

Rosie hadn't slept, not really. She just kept staring at Delia's sleeping form, her hair tumbling over the pillow in loose curls, half of the covers bunched up under her chin. Would she leave again? Walk out on her, again? They were so good together, but then, that had been true all those years ago, too.

She sighed, rolling out of the bed easily. Delia slept like a bear in hibernation, there was no need to creep around or try to be silent. Hells, she could probably make a whole soufflé without waking her, if she wanted. Pulling on her clothes, Rosie tied her hair back in a loose bun, dark tendrils framing her face.

The door clicked closed behind her, and she leaned against it, her eyes closed for just a moment.

"Everything okay?" Ned asked, his voice husky and ragged from sleep.

"Morning."

"Can't sleep?"

"Something like that."

He combed his fingers through his bushy beard. "Breakfast?"

"Yours or mine?"

"Both."

"Okay." She followed him down the corridor, the echoes of their boots bouncing delicately off the metal walls of the ship. "You couldn't sleep either?"

"I did, for a while. I was up late finishing a chart, there's a new blockade on the other side of Delta-4. It's going to take longer to get back to Bradach than the boss wanted, but it can't be helped."

"It's too bad the ship's stealth doesn't help with that."

"Oh, it does, but these blockades run on different tech. It's making things a nightmare for Captain Tansy. She's got a whole transport full of folks trying to get to safety. I worry that one of these days they'll get boxed in. That's why I keep making these charts. Maybe they might help, I don't know."

"Seems to me you're doing a good job."

"I have a lot on my mind lately. Cooking used to help with that."

"I'm sorry, I didn't mean to—"

Ned held his hands up apologetically. "No, no. I didn't mean it like that. I barely have time to keep my head screwed on straight right now. Boss was right to ask you to step in. I'm sorry if I got... defensive."

"I'd never want to hamper the efforts of another cook."

"Let's have a little fun, Rosie, what do you say? It's at least six hours before we reach Terringgough Gulch, and I'm in desperate need of some pancakes."

Rosie raised an eyebrow. "What kind?"

"The fluffy kind. None of that flat bullshit. If I wanted a crepe, I'd make a crepe."

"My thoughts exactly."

He grinned and turned on the lights in the kitchen. "Pick your poison, Rosie. What do you love to make?"

"I've been laying in bed, dreaming of a soufflé."

"And what do you hate to make?"

"Pastry."

Ned sucked in a breath, barely containing his excitement. "I adore making pastry. It's so... perfectly scientific and methodical. Don't you get such a rush cutting in the fat?"

"No!" Rosie said with a laugh. "I absolutely despise it. It takes forever to get all those layers of lamination. It's a nightmare in a kitchen with a deadline."

"No deadlines here, if you want to have a crack at it."

"I'll leave that fun to you. Just save me a pastry."

"I wouldn't dream of depriving you." He tilted his chin, looking at her from the corner of his eye. "Are you really going to make a soufflé?"

"Yes."

"How do you... you know. Keep it from collapsing?" He whispered this as though it was a classified secret.

"It's in the egg whites. You really need to whip them and fold them into the rest of it. And be careful of heavier ingredients."

Ned nodded in appreciation. "Let's get started, then. I think there's room enough in the kitchen for both of us, don't you think?"

"I've worked in smaller."

"So, how are you finding your newfound freedom?"

"I don't know," Rosie said, piling ingredients on the narrow counter top. "I haven't even had time to process it all, really. We planned it all, but it still felt like a dream, even as it was happening. And then Josie, and the market, now here... it's a lot to take in."

"I know what you mean."

"What was it like for you?"

"Oh, it was decades ago now. I was young, foolish. Ran off from my regiment during induction, joined The Scattered."

"Oh, I didn't realize that you were—"

"I left them after about five years. Linked up with the boss, here. She needed a good navigator. I needed a ship to run away from all the shit I'd done." He measured out flour and dumped it into a glass mixing bowl. "I've been here ever since."

"It's a hard thing to detach from your past. I barely remember mine, and it still follows me like a shadow, always cropping up where I don't expect it."

"Lots of people would love to be able to call themselves Norah Gordon's granddaughter."

"I know." Rosie cracked one egg, and then another. "Before I went off to school, a strange man came to the place we lived. He said he wanted me to go with him, restart the resistance. My mother damn near killed him on the spot with a kitchen knife.”

“She sounds fierce.”

“She is. And… unforgiving. I doubt she’ll ever reply to my letters now. She told me not to leave, not to go out to the Rim, but I had to go. I had to know if there was something out there waiting for me, you know?”

“Life comes and grabs us by the hair, sometimes, and you have to just follow it, no matter what people say. Even if, deep down, you know they might be right.” He pulled a wooden spoon from its hook and started to mix the batter, tiny flecks splattering against the wall. “Can I ask you something?”

“Shoot.”

“You’re… you know. With Delia?”

“I don’t really know what to call it, but I guess so. We were apart for a long time. Over ten years.”

“How did you decide to give her another chance?”

Rosie separated another egg, holding the yolk in her fingers. “I don’t know, I guess… I felt like I had to. That maybe one mistake wasn’t enough to throw it away forever.”

“Hmm.”

“Something on your mind?”

“Someone, really. But he’s made more than one mistake. More like… hundreds, probably.”

“This Barnaby guy?”

“Don’t tell the boss. Or Kady. Or Alice. Actually, maybe don’t mention this to anyone on the ship. Or in the Pig.”

“My lips are sealed.”

“He made a bundle stealing from us. Selling stuff off the ship without us even knowing, promising it to shady dealers at trade beacons. The boss had to give up a full shipment just so they wouldn’t kill him. I begged her to save him. She did, of course, but then she kicked him off the ship. I can’t blame her.”

“That sounds pretty complicated.”

“Yeah. I’m supposed to be over it.”

"But you're not?"

Ned poured batter into a sizzling pan until it made a perfect circle. "No." He sighed heavily. "And this stuff with Josie, and the weapon, and Obsidian Enclave, it's only gotten worse. Everyone on this ship hates him, and rightfully so."

"Everyone but you?"

"Yeah. Everyone but me."

"No judgment from me," Rosie said, whipping the egg whites into soft peaks. "I was hung up on the same woman a decade after she walked away from me. And now, I guess, she came back. Life is funny like that. I'm trying not to question it."

"I just wonder how long I'd have to wait for Barnaby to stop... messing around, and decide that I'm more important. I feel like a fool. There's someone who's worked hard to build a relationship with me. He gets along with the crew here, he adores me, really, but..."

"No spark?"

"No gods-damned spark."

"That's tough."

"I keep hoping it will take me by surprise one day, and that will be that." Ned flipped the pancake. "I feel like it's getting to the point I really should end it. It's been months. We don't spend much time together, but Davey... well, he's a good man. He deserves better."

"You're a good man, too. You're letting me make a soufflé in your kitchen." She folded the egg whites into the yolks, mixed with honey and cream, the last of the stores from the icebox. "See, you have to be sure that the cream mixture is good and cooled before you add in. Otherwise you end up with a mess."

"I've never been brave enough to attempt that."

"Yet you gleefully laminate pastry?" Rosie shook her head. "If you can do that without fear, I bet you'll be making soufflés in no time."

Ned cracked a smile. "Try and stop me."

"I refuse."

"I'm going to have to explain to the boss why my next market order has four times as many eggs."

"You could always smuggle them on."

"What a maverick I would be, smuggling eggs," he said, his eyes crinkling with laughter.

"Oh, you joke, friend, but I had to account for every *crumb* on Turas-Mara. The second anything went missing, Emeline's dear old mother was right on my tail." She finished folding in the whites, and poured the mixture into small, makeshift ramekins. "I think you were right to bring her to dinner, if it's not too bold to say."

"Don't let Kady hear you say that. I was almost afraid she'd smother me to death in the night."

"Emeline is going to need a lot of time to heal. And that might have to be away from Georgie, whether she likes it or not."

He nodded. "It's not easy, deprogramming yourself. Many of us have done it to some extent, but never to that degree. That poor girl was indoctrinated by one of the most masterful inspectors we've ever heard of. I'm glad we got her back, and I know her mother—her birth mother, that is—will be, too, but I'm not sure that she'll be the old Emeline they all hoped would return."

"These won't take long," Rosie said, putting the tiny soufflés into the brick oven at the edge of the kitchen, pausing to warm her hands. The heat from the boilers kept their rooms warm in the middle of dark space, and it also cooked their food. "Only about five minutes, judging by the temperature."

"Something smells good," Ivy said, wandering into the kitchen, her green hair sticking up on one side. "Is there coffee?"

"Aye," Ned replied, and poured her a cup. "Early shift?"

"I told Alice I would do an inventory of spare parts before we got to the next beacon. I told her that yesterday, but I... haven't done it yet."

"Don't worry, we won't tell on you."

"What's cooking?"

"A banquet. Pancakes, eggs, and Rosie's got soufflés in the oven."

Ivy sipped her coffee and gave a gratified sigh. "Fancy for a regular old morning."

"Sometimes, cooking helps clear the mind," Rosie said, though her own thoughts were still as cluttered as they had been before. "There's plenty, if you want some."

"Load me up, I'm starved. I know what you mean, though. Sometimes I like to just really get into a project, take something apart and put it all back together again."

"Is counting nuts and bolts not quite the same rush?"

"I swear Alice has me counting every other week. Makes sense, though, with all the blockades, half the usual grey markets are out of reach. Probably shut down entirely, now." Ivy took another sip. "Ned, did you say there was a new one up?"

"Yep. Damned things."

"Hyun is worried that it's going to affect being able to get medical supplies. You know she's been taking crates back to Bradach for the refugees."

Rosie peered into the oven at the jiggly soufflés. "Do many of the refugees need much medical care?"

"Almost all of them."

"Wow."

"For some, it's as easy as some clean bandages and antibiotics. For others, they require extensive, ongoing treatments for their lungs, Georgie's mother included. I think that is Hyun's main concern."

"I'm sure that the medical supervisors in Bradach will have similar concerns. If we can't get at the meds, no one else can, either," Ned said, sliding a plate stacked high with pancakes in front of Ivy. "Eat up, you'll need the energy for all that counting."

"What would help get through the blockades?" Rosie asked. "More stealth? Spies, undercover?"

"Credits."

"That's it?"

"Lots of them, and a flowing stream to grease all the palms needed. Even then, there's no guarantee. Someone could decide they want to have their soufflé and eat it too. Those ready yet?"

Rosie poked at a ramekin with a long stick. "Looks like. Hand me that glove." She took them out, one at a time, setting them gingerly on the counter. "See? No deflation. It's the egg whites."

"Trade you a pancake for one of those."

"Two pancakes."

"Done."

They made their plates, leaving the rest of the food in the kitchen. Rosie plunged a fork into the delightfully fluffy soufflé, blowing on the steam that rose in gentle tendrils up to the ceiling. "Good pancakes."

"This soufflé, Rosie. I might be in love."

"Sorry, Ned, you're not my type."

He burst out laughing, covering his mouth. "The feeling is mutual. I meant with your lovely dish. I'm going to have to perfect them myself, or no breakfast will ever measure up."

Captain Violet appeared in the doorway, her face drawn with worry. "We have a problem."

"What's up, Boss?" Ned was already out of his chair and halfway to the door.

"There's a new blockade between us and Terringgough Gulch."

"Can't be. I just checked the updated maps a few hours ago."

"It's not Coalition, it's... something else."

"Who?"

"I don't know, but it's not good. We need to move around it. Do you think we can, without being seen?"

Ned stroked his beard. "Possibly. It's not going to be easy, we don't have a lot of leeway on this trajectory before we run into patrols from the nearby base."

"I never thought I'd get sick of the skies, but I'll be damned to hell if I'm not dreaming of some shitty little broken down farmhouse right about now."

"Sit down, Boss. Eat something. You look like you need it."

"No, no, I'll come with you to the bridge."

"Don't be ridiculous, I'm fine. You know I'm better with nav than you."

The captain gave him a wry smile. "Fine. But don't plan the fun without me." She sat in Ned's now vacant chair, her weight sinking down and stress weighing at her shoulders.

"Breakfast?" Rosie asked, already filling a plate.

"What's this?"

"Ned made pancakes and fried eggs. I made soufflés."

"Someone might even be fooled that this is a luxury liner, with grub like this." The captain took a bite of a soufflé. "This is fantastic."

"Here, Cap," Ivy said, sliding a mug of coffee across the table. "Fresh up."

"Where's Alice?"

"Boiler room. She had to patch the tertiary, it threw a gasket."

"When?"

Ivy shrugged. "Sometime last night. Why?"

"I'm worried about these repair schedules. With all these damned blockades, it's getting harder and harder to budget days for it. Did she seem worried?"

"No more than usual. She's just cautious, Cap, you know her."

"I know." Captain Violet sipped at the coffee and set the mug back on the table. "Just feel like we could really use a break. All of us. Away from all… this. But that's impossible right now, with Emeline on board, and Georgie at Kady's throat, and Cass wanting to know where Barnaby is, and Obsidian Enclave climbing out of the woodwork."

"We'll get there," Ivy reassured her, refilling the mug. "We always do."

Rosie cleared up the dishes, wiping the utensils clean. "I'll help however I can, even if it's just making meals."

"It's wonderful, really," the captain said, shoving another bite into her mouth. "Food can make all the difference with morale. Gotta feed people to keep them happy and working. I'm sure this will be fine, I just worry we will miss our meeting with Cass; she's an incredibly difficult woman to get hold of. You'd think we were trying to schedule a dinner with a member of the High Council."

"The leader of The Scattered is basically half the rebellion's High Council," Ivy mused. "It's no wonder she's never around. Except for when she needs us, anyway."

"Boss?" the radio crackled. "Boss, you'd better get up here."

Captain Violet pulled her radio from her belt. "What's wrong, Ned?"

"It's not a blockade. Well, it is, but it's not what we thought. They want Rosie."

"What?"

All at once, the room swam in front of Rosie. A blockade? What did they want with her? Air left her lungs, and she gasped for breath as panic nestled into her spine. "Who?" she asked.

"It's Obsidian Enclave."

"Tell them they can't have her," the captain said. "She's ours."

The radio crackled with static. "I did that. They said they'll trade the weapon for her."

"I'll be right there."

Rosie started to follow the captain. "Should I—"

"Stay here. We don't know if this is even legitimate."

"But—"

"Ivy, go tell Alice that she better finish that patch right now. I have a bad feeling about this. Rosie... with me. I've decided you're better off within eyeshot." Captain Violet stood and marched out of the kitchen area, with Rosie scrambling to keep up with her knees like jelly. She never had dealt well with anxiety or fear.

"Uh, Captain?"

"We should get to the bridge." Captain Violet's tone was different now, harsh, on a knife edge. "I knew something didn't feel right."

Was Delia even awake yet? Would she even know what was going on, that Rosie might end up traded to Obsidian Enclave in the middle of a makeshift blockade? Even as she stumbled after the captain, she wanted to turn tail and run in the other direction, back to the safety of Delia's arms.

"Talk to me, Ned," the captain said, stepping onto the bridge. "How did these assholes contact us?"

"A radio transmission, the usual way."

"What did they say?"

Ned sighed. "That they know the granddaughter of Norah Gordon is aboard, and they want her back. They said it's part of their legacy, and they are willing to trade us the weapon for her."

"For hells' sakes."

"I... I don't know who they think I am. I'm not a leader of a revolution. I'm a cook," Rosie said, her voice squeaky with apprehension. "They want my grandmother, not me. I'm not her. I didn't even *know* her."

"To some, there is an awful lot of meaning within a symbol, or someone with the right lineage. If they're trying to revive the resistance, then having Norah's granddaughter at the forefront would pull hundreds out of hiding. Maybe even thousands."

Rosie laughed at the absurdity of it all. These people thought she could change the arc of history, with what? A fork? "What happens if I tell them I'm not interested?"

"They may fire on us," Ned admitted. "Or, they may not. Either way, they have that damned weapon Cass has spent the past year looking for. Seems Barnaby didn't hesitate to turn around and sell it straight to Obsidian Enclave, probably for a tidy little profit, if I had to guess." His jaw was set firm, clenched tight.

"What happens if I... give myself up?"

"They may hand over the weapon—decoy—whatever the thing is. They may not. It's hard to say, given they just reappeared out of decades of dormancy. Do you think someone in your family let it slip that Norah had a direct descendant?"

"No. Yes. Maybe."

"Which is it?" Captain Violet demanded.

"My mother wanted me to take it to my grave. She certainly wouldn't have said anything. My grandfather, though... well, the resistance still lived on in his heart, even all those years later. If he did mention it to the wrong person, I doubt it was on purpose. He's old now. He doesn't get out much, except for a few nights a week at the local tavern."

"A tavern is enough for word to spread. Might be that someone overheard, or a friend of a friend sent a wire..." The captain shook her head. "It doesn't matter how they found out. They know now."

"What's the plan, Boss?"

"Give me the odds on blasting past them without getting shot to hell."

"Low."

"How low?"

"Extremely," Ned said with a grimace.

Captain Violet rubbed at the bridge of her nose, her eyes squeezed shut. "And what about feigning ignorance?"

"Depends on our performance, I would guess."

"We haven't sent any comms about Rosie. How the hell would they know?"

Ned shrugged. "Maybe they tracked that she was out at the Rim, and heard, or suspected, that she escaped. Rosie, did you talk to anyone other than Bailey before you boarded that ship?"

"A bartender down on Delta-4, in Chalidon. He knew Josie pretty well. Sounded like maybe she pays him for his discretion."

"It's always damned Josie," the captain grumbled. "Should have killed her when I had the chance."

"She did help us get out of Skelm," Ned offered.

"Besides that."

Rosie cracked her knuckles at her sides, one at a time, savoring each little pop as a microsecond of space to think. "What if I spoke to them directly?"

"And say what, exactly?"

"That they should give us the weapon and let us pass?"

"I don't think they'll go for that. We should come up with something else."

Ned leaned back in his chair, tying his long hair into a bun. "That might be our best option, Boss. They already know she's here. They're waiting for us to respond."

"Rosie?" the captain asked. "Do you feel equipped to take this on?"

"No," she answered honestly. "But I'll do it. I'm the reason they are doing this. I should be the way we get out of this mess."

"Don't agree to anything right away. You can always back out. It's your decision, but I would rather you didn't leave the ship. We don't know these people, and despite their affection for your grandmother, we don't know their motives or their plans for you."

"Be careful," Ned agreed. "We're here if you need us."

The captain nodded. "Get them on transmission."

"Vessel twelve-three-two, come in, this is the Cricket."

The radio crackled. "Do you agree to our bargain?" a deep baritone voice asked. "We are tired of waiting. We have spent years waiting."

"You'll have to talk to Ms. Gordon herself." Ned stood and motioned for Rosie to sit.

"Hello," she said. It was strange to try to emulate a woman she'd never met. "This is Rosie Gordon. Norah was my grandmother."

"We'd love to have you aboard, Ms. Gordon. You could be the key to the next phase."

"And what does that next phase entail, exactly?"

"We're afraid that is classified information until you are with us. And if you aren't with us, you will be considered to be against us."

"Hold fire, sir, I am not against anyone. I am just a cook."

"The granddaughter of Norah Gordon is far more than just a cook."

"I can assure you, I wouldn't know the first thing about leading a resistance, or a rebellion, or being a spy. But if you want to know how to make perfect poached eggs, then I can help."

"We can teach you."

Rosie took a breath to calm her frayed nerves and her shaking hands. "I'm afraid I don't have any interest in that. Would you take me, against my will?"

"We would rather not. But perhaps if you would come over to our ship—"

"Absolutely not," Captain Violet interjected. "The answer is no. If you want to meet Ms. Gordon, you will do so on neutral ground."

"We are not your enemies."

"Oh, no? Then why in hells have you created a blockade?"

"To get your attention. Clearly, it worked."

"I'm not impressed by this, and neither is Ms. Gordon. Let us pass."

"Let her speak for herself."

"Alright," Rosie said. "What is it you really want from me, then? We know you have the weapon. We know where you got it from. We even know how it was procured. If you have that, why would you need me, also?"

"How did you know all that?"

"I was there when it happened."

"Despite your claims, Ms. Gordon, it seems clear to us that you have your grandmother's fighting spirit. Daring escapes, theft, now you're aboard a rickety pirate vessel."

"It's a good thing Alice didn't hear that," Ned mumbled.

"We have been monitoring your progress since you became visible again. You were lost, for a time."

Rosie fought to keep her breaths even and steady. "I wasn't lost. I knew exactly where I was."

"Tell us, why did you go out to the Rim? It surely wasn't coincidence."

"No. I felt like there was... something out there, that I had to see for myself."

"Then let us take you there. We'll show you everything you ever wanted to see."

"You know, I think the urge has passed, now. My questions about Obsidian Enclave have been adequately answered. I know you have a settlement out there, beyond the Rim. That's why she died. To keep all of the secrets."

"A horrible debt that can never be repaid," the man on the other side of the radio said in a somber tone. "But we can start by doing right by her granddaughter. You could be the new mother of the resistance, Ms. Gordon."

"I am fundamentally uninterested in being the face of your movement."

"Just give us a chance to show you what we can do—what we're capable of."

"The captain here is right. I will not be meeting you on your ship. You've done nothing to prove your identities to me, other than knowing far more than I am comfortable with. If you really want to look into my face, to try and convince me to join your ranks, then we will meet on neutral ground. That means you will have to remove the blockade, and let us pass."

"Where do you suggest we meet? Our people have been banned from Bradach for decades now."

Captain Violet gave a sardonic laugh. "That's your own fault."

"Nevertheless, we need a location."

"Boss?" Ned whispered, gesturing at a map.

"No. That's a terrible idea."

"I'm not sure we have many other options."

Rosie clenched her fists at her sides. "What should I say?"

"Vessel twelve-three-two, we can rendezvous at the old Terringgough Gulch camp," the captain announced. "Do not come armed. In good faith, we won't, either. But if you try to take Ms. Gordon, we will make damned sure you don't leave in one piece."

"These are not favorable terms."

"Take them, or leave them. We aren't going to sit here all day and argue with you. We have a timetable to keep to."

"If we say no?"

"Then I will turn my ship around and find another way."

"We would just blockade you again. We have the time to spend on this matter."

"I'm in no mood for negotiating or games. Either meet us at Terring-gough Gulch, or don't. That's your choice. But those are our terms, and we don't have any intention of budging."

"You know," the radio crackled, "they warned me you would be difficult. I wish I had listened."

"Who the hell is *they*?"

"It's unimportant. Fine, Captain, we will meet you in Terringgough Gulch. We trust you are headed straight there?"

"We'd probably be there already if you clowns hadn't gotten in our way."

"Ms. Gordon, everyone aboard here is very excited to meet you. Your grandmother meant a lot to all of us."

"Great," Rosie mumbled. First she'd spent most of her life running away from her grandmother's sullied legacy, and now she was expected to fill her shoes, as though leadership was genetic. Perhaps it was—but then, she'd always taken after her grandfather, anyway—better as a kitchen grunt than the prize in a dangerous game of tug of war.

Chapter 45

Delia stood at the sink, splashing water onto her face. Gods, she'd slept like the dead. No wonder, after so long in that disgusting brig. What time was it, even? She popped open her pocket watch and stared until the dial came into focus. Mid-morning. Where was Rosie? She must have been up for hours already.

Pulling her loose curls back into a twist, she shoved pins into her hair to hold the style, and slipped the suspenders up over her shoulders. Her clothes were still damp from the night before, and the fabric clung to her underarms. She frowned at her reflection. At least she was clean, but wearing wet fabric felt completely disgusting.

Her stomach growled impatiently, and she jerked the door open in her haste. The ship was oddly quiet without the hum of the engines. Had they landed, already? Why hadn't Rosie woken her up? Delia quickened her pace, striding purposefully to the kitchen area. "Rosie?" she called.

The room was empty, except for a plate of cold pancakes and one small soufflé which had long since collapsed. "Rosie?"

She poked her head back out into the corridor. What in hells was going on? "Captain? Ned?" Had everyone left the ship already?

The sound of her boots pounding against the metal grate gave a menacing, percussive rhythm that bounced down the halls of the ship. She had to find them. What if something had gone wrong? By the gods, she'd always hated being such a heavy sleeper, being able to dream right through loud alarm bells and wake-up calls.

Movement in the loading area caught the corner of her eye through the glass. Slipping into the crew airlock, the pressure gauge was already set to a normal rate. They must have landed, but where? Was it where they'd been intending to go? The door released, and she pushed into the cargo bay, squinting out towards the open door. Beyond, it was dark and desolate. Greying cliffs casting long, impervious shadows over the ravines in the distance. There were no mirrors here, the only light was from the ships in the dock, and a distant moon that faintly glowed on the horizon.

A soft click drew her attention. "Who's there?" she asked, reaching for some kind of improvised weapon. There was nothing, not even a crowbar. "Show yourself!"

The shuttle door swung open, and Emeline climbed inside.

"Emeline! Wait! Where are you going? Where are the others?"

"Get out of my way, Dodson."

"Where are you going?"

"I'm going where I'm needed."

"Captain said—"

Emeline snorted. "I don't give one good goddamn what the captain said. If you consider pirates to even *be* captains. It's nothing more than organized crime."

"What about your sister?"

"What about her? She burned our city to the ground. I won't ever forgive her for that."

"She did it for *you!*"

"She did it for herself." Emeline pulled herself into the pilot seat of the shuttle and smoothed her skirts. "If she really wants to talk to me, then she's going to have a lot of work to do."

"You haven't even seen your mother yet. Or Lucy. You said that you were always close."

"And that's... regrettable. Lucy is just a little girl, she didn't choose any of this. Maybe someday I will see her again."

"Where did the others go, Emeline? Where are we?"

"They left the ship to trade weapons." She buckled herself in. "Some paragons of morality, they are. Probably planning to burn down more cities just to prove a point to the Coalition. What they can't seem to understand is that they are just as bad, if they are hurting innocents, too."

Delia planted her feet behind the shuttle. "I can't let you leave."

"Do you really think I won't just back over you?"

"No, actually, I don't think you would. All that waxing lyrical about the sanctity of human life, and you'd crush my body under that shuttle's landing gear?"

"Ms. Dodson, please. I know that you have no reason to trust me, no reason to believe what I am about to say, but I need for you to hear it."

"Go on."

"My—mother—Overseer Allemande will already have squads out looking for me. She'll be worried sick. I know none of them here care about that, and I know that she's done horrid things, but my point is that she's not going to just stop looking. They will find this ship eventually."

"You won't be on the ship forever, they're taking us to—"

"I know all that, but do you really think they will trust me there? People don't even trust me on this ship. A city of pirates and refugees from the war isn't going to look at me with anything other than outright contempt, unless it's pity. I don't want either of those things."

"Then what do you want?"

"I want to advocate for my people. That's all I ever wanted—the opportunity to lessen their burdens, to fight for... for better living conditions, for an end to the stranglehold that the merchants have over their factories."

"And you're going to achieve that by running away?"

"I will achieve that by running for political office."

Delia laughed. "You can't be serious."

"Think about it—this is the best possible outcome for all of us."

"And how is that?"

"If I show up back in Skelm and announce my candidacy publicly, she won't be able to refute it. She'll have to call back the search squads. I'll be left to campaign for my position, I will have the freedom I have been so denied over the past two years. Do you know what I'd give to even walk in a park alone? To make my own choices about how I spend my time?"

"We could help you do that."

"You think being in league with a bunch of pirates who are apparently chasing after elite weaponry is a good way to win votes?" Emeline shook her head. "No. I have to do this my way. I know that Georgina isn't going to understand. She thinks that democracy is dead. But what she's never been able to answer is, what do we do when we've purged the corruption and rot? What will we be left with if we tear down the framework, too?"

"I... don't know. I can't answer that, either."

"Let me leave, Delia."

"On two conditions."

"And what are those?"

"Number one, you agree to a neutral meeting space for your family. They want to see you."

"Agreed," Emeline said with a scowl.

"Number two, you make your announcement with me."

Emeline shook her head. "Absolutely not. You're a fugitive, now."

"If you want to be the people's advocate, then you have to listen to the people's radio, and I guarantee you that almost none of them are listening to the official channels."

"Skelm eliminated the pirated frequencies."

"I eliminated them, on direction from your—from Allemande. I can uneliminate them just as easily."

"If you try to get into Skelm, they'll have you arrested at the docks," Emeline said. "You won't be able to get within five hundred kilometers of that city."

"I guess it's good that I learned a few things aboard that station then, isn't it? We'll bounce the frequency. People have been doing it for years. Even the Coalition."

"If I were to agree, you'd... let me go?"

Delia considered this, and then nodded. "Yes."

"And you wouldn't send this ship straight after me?"

"I can't stop what they do, but I will do my best to convince them otherwise. What you say makes sense. Your sister won't see it, though, at least not at first."

"No, she won't, and she's who I am most worried about. She's reckless. Did you know that she and her little scientist were the ones who pushed my mother down an elevator shaft?"

"No, I didn't."

"She's not as innocent as she looks. She's as much a monster as any of them." Emeline pulled the fabric of her dress inside the shuttle. "Tell them we will meet in one week at the transport beacon near Delta-4. I'll be there. Tell Georgina not to come."

"She's not going to like that."

"Then tell her that if she shows up, I'll leave immediately. I am allowing this for... for Lucy. She's already lost too much in her short life. She shouldn't have to lose me, too."

"I'll tell her."

"This is for the best, Ms. Dodson. Hopefully, someday you and all the rest of them will see that."

"I trust you," Delia said, and meant it. She stepped out of the way and watched the shuttle pull out of the loading bay and lift up into the atmosphere until it was no longer visible.

* * *

"Ivy! Where are we?" Delia asked. "Have you seen Rosie?"

"She's on the bridge with Ned and Cap. We've landed at Terringgough Gulch, but there are some complications. Captain said to stay on the ship, at least for now."

"Everything okay?"

Ivy shook her head. "It sounded serious."

"Shit. I should get up there, see if I can—"

"It's probably for the best that you stay here. Have a pancake. Rosie made soufflés, too."

"How can I be expected to eat when I know something might be wrong? Do you know what's going on? Should I be worried?"

"You should eat." Ivy slid a plate across the table. "I just heated it up."

"Is it the Coalition? Did they find us?"

"Sounds more like Obsidian Enclave. They want to talk to Rosie."

Delia sank a fork into the soft cake. "Why can't they just leave her alone? She didn't even know her grandmother. What if she needs me?"

"Relax, Dodson," Hyun said, sauntering in, bedecked in a lime green medic coat and matching boots, polished to a mirror shine. "I just heard. They're going to meet us here."

"With Cass?" Ivy asked. "Isn't that kind of... oil and water? Obsidian Enclave and The Scattered haven't exactly been on the best of terms, historically."

"We didn't have a lot of options. Seems like half of dark space is one big blockade these days. Nice to know that we have to worry about it from other factions now, too." Hyun draped herself over a chair and piled a plate high with food. "This looks great. Been ages since we had a hot breakfast. Ned has insomnia again?"

"Probably."

"Jas, hurry up, or I'm going to eat the rest of these pancakes."

"Alright, gods," Jasper mumbled, ambling into the room. "You know I'm not a morning person."

"Here. Coffee." Hyun poured with one hand, while cutting another chunk of pancakes with the other. "It's not even *that* early. I'll even save the rest for you, how's that?"

"Great."

"You two don't seem worried," Delia said, irritated at their lack of concern for Rosie.

"I'm more of a planner, myself. I don't see much point in worrying when you could have a plan instead. But we do have a plan, so fretting will only make me tense up. Better to go into things with a clear mind. Jas here, he's a worrywart, but he's too tired to know what's going on yet."

"I know what's going on, I just can't function without caffeine. I'll be plenty worried the moment it hits my bloodstream."

"How long will it take them to get here?" Delia asked.

Ivy shrugged. "Not long. Oh, gods be damned, I still have to finish my inventory count! Alice is going to—"

"Alice is going to what?" Alice asked from the doorway.

"Uh…"

"Don't worry, I finished your count. We're low on gaskets and the long bolts for the boilers."

"Sorry."

"Did you at least save me some food?"

Ivy gestured towards the kitchen. "Last of it is in there."

"Vi says they're landing in an hour. No guns."

"What if something goes wrong?" Delia demanded. "This is Rosie we're talking about! What if they take her?"

"Then we abandon diplomacy and put as many holes in their ship as we can."

"How are you going to do that without guns?"

Alice tapped her tool belt. "Never underestimate what a motivated mechanic can achieve."

"I don't know how you can all be so… calm."

"Captain Violet has enough anxiety for all of us, trust me. She's probably pacing the bridge, making fourteen different contingency plans already."

"I guess all we can do is wait."

Ivy nodded. "And finish these pancakes." She offered another to Delia, who shook her head.

"Vi says most everyone should stay on the ship. Small crew to deal with these people, then we'll have the meeting with Cass and be on our way," Alice said. "Just her, Rosie, me, Ned, and Kady for this."

"But—"

"We can't risk any complications."

Delia nodded. "I understand." She cleared her plate, washed the dish, and re-pinned her hair. She gave them a smile and a wave, having already decided to defy the captain's orders.

Chapter 46

"Ms. Rosie Gordon, it is a deep honor to make your acquaintance." The man was flanked by four others, two on either side, all of them dressed head to toe in white flight suits, the tint of their visors so dark that their faces were obscured. "I was a great admirer of your grandmother."

"As many were, I am told."

"We imagine you grew up listening to stories about her bravery and dedication to the resistance. The things you could tell us would be mind-boggling."

Rosie wiped her palms, sweaty with nerves, against the fabric that rested over her hips. "That's not entirely accurate," she said. "In fact, the opposite is true. I know very little about her."

The man stepped back. "What?"

"My mother was deeply concerned for our safety after my father was killed. We moved around a lot, until we settled on Gamma-3 with my grandfather."

"He lives?"

"Yes."

"With brutal honesty, I'm surprised no one has had him killed yet. Many blame him for your grandmother's death. If he hadn't doubted the plan, she might still be alive."

"You are grossly misinformed, sir. He knew that hundreds of lives were at risk, including my mother's. Had he stayed on that damned base, everyone there would have died in the blast, and you know it. Now, I understand why

Obsidian Enclave would long for the old days, when my grandmother led them to victory after victory, but I am not her. I am nothing like her."

"We found you on a pirate vessel. You have the same drive for justice. That much is obvious."

"I am still uninterested in joining you or leading you. The death or harm of others isn't a burden my conscience can bear. My grandmother left a trail of blood wherever she went. That is not my path."

"She left a trail of hope, Ms. Gordon. Hope has all but died out in the Near Systems and beyond the Rim."

"What exactly do you want from me? A face for your resistance?"

"In part, yes. Obsidian Enclave has been content to live beyond the Rim for decades now. We've terraformed. It looks like most other cities, except there are no MPOs. But now that the Coalition is exploring past Turas-Mara Station, they have gotten much too close. If they find us, they will kill us."

"I am not the savior you are looking for, sir."

"We need hope, Ms. Gordon. Many have all but given up. We can't match the artillery of the Coalition. If—*when* they discover us, they will wipe us out."

Rosie sighed. "And what, you want me to... go with you? Be a poster woman for your cause? Live in your settlement?"

"We would wish for you to travel the Near Systems with us, to recruit new members. If we can swell our ranks, if we can claw back the numbers we once had, we may yet have a fighting chance."

"This is such bullshit," Kady said, rolling her eyes. "We know you have the weapon. You're anything but helpless."

"That weapon isn't enough to save us. It is merely... a deterrent."

"You don't even know that it's not a fake. It could be filled with sawdust and rusted gears, for all you know."

The man tilted his head. "I can assure you, it is not a fake. It is the genuine weapon, bought and paid for, fair and square."

"What exactly are we all doing here?" Kady demanded, her long black cloak swirling gently in the breeze from the Obsidian Enclave ship's exhaust nearby. "Seems to me you just want Rosie for her name, and you're threatening us to get her."

"We didn't threaten anyone, we merely created a gentle blockade."

"Oh, please. You and I both know that forcing ships into Coalition flight paths is as good as a death sentence."

He shrugged. "No one was forced. You made your own decision. Now we are here, explaining our position."

"Not much of a choice, though, is it?"

"A choice nonetheless."

"Enough of this," Rosie said, her hands shoved deep into her pockets. "I am not going to go with you."

"We will continue to create blockades until you see reason. We want the same things, Ms. Gordon. If you would just give us the chance to show you—"

"Where is it?" a voice shouted from behind a cliff. "I know you have it, you dirty fucking rat."

"Ah, Cassius Calvetti. How I'd hoped we would never meet again." He turned back to Rosie. "You didn't mention that it was going to be a party, Ms. Gordon."

"You didn't leave us much choice," Rosie answered. "We were all but backed into a corner."

"Indeed."

"Give it to me, you shit," the woman, now on the ridge, yelled out across the barren landscape. "You know full well I'm the one who paid Josie in the first place."

"And yet, she chose to sell it to me, instead. I wonder why that might be? Perhaps she felt that it would be better off in *our* hands."

"Alice, you told her they have it?" Captain Violet hissed.

"No! Carmen must have when she stayed behind on Kilper Station," Alice replied. "Cass is... very persuasive."

Cass smirked. "Damn right I am. You don't get to be where I am by skulking around behind makeshift blockades and strong-arming strangers into being your propaganda."

"No, from what I hear, you get to where you are with petty politicking and backstabbing your elders," the man said.

"Didn't you *literally* stab someone in the back, Gregor? Or was that just a rumor? Either way, no one has seen that council elder in years."

"Change doesn't happen incrementally. It happens all at once, or not at all. The Scattered have been dancing around it for years now, and what's changed, eh? Tighter restrictions. More patrols. Bigger prisons and work camps. Looks like you've done a hell of a job, Cassius."

"Piss off. At least I'm down here trying, and not fucking about beyond the Rim playing house with a bunch of resistance rejects."

"We've created a sustainable future. That's more than you can say."

"If you're so happy out there, then explain why you're suddenly back here stealing my shit? What do you need it for, then?"

"A defense protocol. You know as well as I do that the voyages from Turas-Mara are a threat to us all."

"Speak for yourself, pisshead. I've got my own plans for it. Hand it over."

"Not on your life. You'd have to kill us all first, and we all know that your aim has never been very accurate."

"I've been practicing, Gregor." Cass' hands hovered above the revolvers at her hips.

"Don't even try it, kitten. You're outnumbered."

"I've got plenty of backup."

Captain Violet cleared her throat. "Can we all just take a breath, please? Our medical bay doesn't have enough room for all of us, and I think Hyun might let us all die if we end up pumped full of lead because we had short tempers."

"It's not us, Captain. Clearly your friend Cassius is the one with the hot head."

"Don't play innocent with me. You all but forced us into a Coalition flight path to get your way. Rosie isn't going to be going with you. While I won't get involved in your... financial dispute, I do think it's bad form to have taken that weapon."

"Taken? My good captain, we purchased it." Gregor waved at another suited Obsidian Enclave soldier near their ship. "I can prove it, in fact."

"Somehow, I don't think that Josie would have written you a receipt."

"We don't need a receipt. We have witnesses."

Two men were shoved out of the ship's loading bay and down the ramp, one of the faction's bodyguards close behind them with a heat gun.

"Al!" the smaller one shouted. "Alice, you have to help us!"

"What have you gotten mixed up in now, Barnaby? Still pissing around with fellow con artists, I see?"

"They promised us payment!"

Gregor turned. "Payment which you duly received, sir."

"We didn't agree to be taken prisoner!"

"You aren't prisoners. You are our guests! You just aren't allowed to leave of your own accord until the unit has been verified."

"So you're the two pissants who bought my weapon off of Josie, are you?" Cass said, stepping forward, her hands still resting in the belt loops nearest to the holster on her hip. "Where I come from, that isn't very well regarded." She stepped forward again. "I've seen men killed for less."

"We aren't killing anyone today, so let's all just relax, shall we?" Captain Violet ordered. "We came to tell Cass that we might know where the weapon was. Turns out, the answer is on the Obsidian Enclave ship. We've done what we said we would, and our agreement has been fulfilled, wouldn't you agree, Cassius?"

"The agreement was—"

"The agreement was to locate it for you, which we have. As such, I anticipate payment will now be made. Promptly, and without argument."

Cass arched an eyebrow. "I suppose you may be right, Captain. However, let me offer an extension of our previous agreement. Help me take it from these fools, and I'll pay double."

"Give us Ms. Gordon, and we'll give you the weapon," Gregor said. "No jokes or angles. She is worth more than the weapon."

"Come on, Gregor, even *you* must know how ridiculous this is."

"The likes of you would never understand the importance of a real movement. All The Scattered does is hide in the shadows and make small, pitiable strikes against trade shipments and roving patrols. It's pathetic, really, that you can't think any bigger than that."

"She's not going to save your dying faction, you know. She's just one person."

"This is all moot, because Rosie Gordon isn't setting foot on any ship that isn't ours," Captain Violet said. "We are not in the business of trading people for weapons. We're not barbarians."

"Captain, Ms. Gordon wouldn't be our prisoner—she'd be our esteemed guest!"

"Oh, like those two sacks of bullshit over there are? No. Absolutely not. We're no fools. We're pirates."

Cass snorted. "I bet this old fool doesn't even have the weapon. I bet it's all a ruse, it's already packed away somewhere in one of their bunkers, I'll bet."

Gregor folded his gloved hands, interlacing his fingers and holding them at his waist. "I'll tell you what, Cassius. We will roll the weapon out for you to look at. You may cast your eyes upon it and see that I tell no lies. Not today, anyway."

"Cassius isn't the one making decisions about whether Rosie goes with you or not," Captain Violet said, squaring her shoulders.

"Isn't she? You took her orders so far. Why not now?"

"We were being paid for a job. As I said, that job has now been completed."

"Double pay, though. That's quite the incentive."

"I have enough problems without adding Obsidian Enclave to that list. If we help her take it from you, we'll be running forever. We all know that you monitor comms. I'm in no rush to be looking over my shoulder for the rest of my days."

"What if I record some messages for you?" Rosie suggested. "I can do that."

"I'm afraid that's not good enough," Gregor replied. "Though your willingness to negotiate proves that you do have a slice of your grandmother's wisdom within you."

Rosie bristled. "No, I'm just tired of listening to the three of you bicker. The longer we stay here, the larger the risk of being discovered, wouldn't you agree?"

"I'm not the one trying to run away."

"Alright, try this on for size. Show them this weapon. If it's genuine, I will go with you."

"Rosie, no!" Delia shouted from the mound of dirt behind them.

"I have to, Dee. It's what's best for everyone."

"It's not what's best for *you*!"

"Sometimes that doesn't matter."

Delia was skidding down the slope now, the dry dust from the dirt floating into the air and hanging like a fog. "It does matter. You matter! I only just found you again, don't leave me now. I know that I have no right to say that, not after what I did all those years ago, but—"

"Delia!" William shouted. "Dearest! You're alright?"

"William! You're alive!"

"Only just," he replied. "I was so worried about you after that wire. I thought for sure they'd throw you in a cell."

"They almost did, they—"

"You're here with Rosie?"

"I am, but—"

"Gods below, but this is dull," Gregor grumbled. "I have no interest in a lover's spat. Either we do this deal, or we don't. And if we don't, you can be sure, Ms. Gordon, that we will always know where you are. We will never stop trying to show you how important you are to the cause."

"Shut up," Delia snapped. "You're nothing more than a two-bit resistance fighter who can't manage to do a single thing you set out to do."

"We're just getting started. In six months, in one year, the whole of the Near Systems will know that Obsidian Enclave has returned to power. Then we'll see what little traitorous ghouls we round up to set examples for the rest of them, shall we?"

"Leave her alone," Rosie said, stepping close to Gregor. She blinked at her reflection in his visor. "I named the terms. Agree, or don't. You can follow me to the edges of the Near Systems, if you want, but I am not so easily bought, and neither was my grandmother."

"You went to the Rim to find us, Ms. Gordon. You know that you belong with us."

"That was before I knew what shits you were. The terms, Gregor."

He sighed heavily and waved his hand in the air. "Wheel it out then, comrades," he said in a flat tone. "We shall do an equal exchange, but we will have Ms. Gordon in hand first, lest young Cassius here decide that she's going to have her cake and eat it, too." He grabbed Rosie by the arm and pulled her off to the side.

"You're being a real weasel to the woman you want to run your resistance, Gregor," Cass said. "Better be careful with that one. She looks dangerous."

"The difference between you and me, Cassius, is that I'm willing to do what it takes to get the job done while you play in piles of your own excrement, I imagine." He gave a lazy wave. "Roll it out. No further than halfway between our ship and theirs."

"Alice, you've got to do something!" Barnaby shouted.

"I can't keep bailing you out like this," Alice replied. "When are you going to learn to keep your nose out of trouble? Fuck's sake, Barns, I can't stick up for you when you're always pulling this shit!"

Two other Obsidian Enclave soldiers descended from their ship, rolling a small cart down the ramp. On top of it was a silvery box with an antenna shooting out from the side. "Here it is, Cassius," Gregor said with a smirk. "As promised."

"How do I know it's not a fake?"

"It's not."

"You could be lying."

Gregor leaned against the cart, a hand resting atop the box. "Even if I was, it's not as though you lose anything. Ms. Gordon was never yours to begin with, according to the good captain here. It's a win-win scenario for you."

"Prove it. Show me that it works."

"I can't, not without causing major destruction to all of us, my people included." He pulled Rosie by the elbow, closer to his ship. "Though you're welcome to use one of your own for purposes of demonstration. Hell, you could even use this crew's ship. We all know you've been known to do worse, but that's The Scattered's style, isn't it?"

"You're one to talk, you conniving snake."

"Stop pulling me," Rosie said, pulling at her elbow. "I already said, I—"

"It's a fake!" William yelled, falling to his knees. "I'm sorry, I'm so sorry—it's a replica, and I've known all along!"

Gregor tightened his grip on Rosie, his gloved fingers biting into her skin, now shoving her towards the ship. "Bad luck then, Cassius," he shouted as the others of his team sprinted aboard.

Rosie twisted in his grasp, trying to push him away even as he dragged her up the ramp. "Let me go!" she shouted again.

"I promise you, once you've joined us, you'll never regret leaving this life," Gregor said. "We will show you the life of opulence and leadership that you'd never see if you stay with them."

"You can't take her!" Delia screamed, running at the ship.

Gregor pulled a gun from his hip and pointed it at her. "Stop!" he shouted, before the noise of an explosion rang in Rosie's ears, sending her to her knees.

Chapter 47

Delia flinched from instinct, at first expecting to see a red bloom through her damp clothes. When there was nothing—no pain, no blood—she craned her neck to the sky, strewn with showers of yellow and purple sparks. Coalition flares. Someone had been tracked.

Scrambling to her feet, she ran at the ship again, her ears still ringing from the explosion. More MPOs would be landing any minute, now that their scouts had sent up the flares. Rosie was crumpled on the ground, and Delia grabbed at her in a panicked haze.

"Rosie! We have to go. Come on!"

Gregor stumbled back onto the ramp, spotting the sparkling flares floating in the sky. "She's coming with me!"

Delia wound her arm back and launched it into his visor, sending him sprawling backwards. Her knuckles were bloody from the crack in his helmet. It didn't matter. "Rosie!" she shouted again.

"I thought he'd shot you," Rosie said, a sob welling in her throat.

"He didn't! I'm alright, but we have to go!"

"Let's go!" Captain Violet shouted above the sound of the explosions, already sprinting back to the Cricket. "We need to leave now!"

Kady and Alice took off running for the Cricket's loading bay ramp. "Go! They're almost here!" Kady yelled over her shoulder.

Ships were already descending through the settlement's thin atmosphere, large military transports plastered with the florid logo of the Coalition. Delia pulled Rosie towards the Cricket, their hands clasped together as they ran.

"William!" Delia shouted. "Come with us!"

"Right behind you!" he replied, his wrists clasped in iron cuffs.

"Come on, people," Captain Violet shouted from the ramp. Her chest heaved with short, panicked breaths, her tone much more frantic than before. The sound of it sent rocks of anxiety hurtling down into Delia's stomach.

A shot rang out over the gorge, and William crumpled to the ground.

"No!" Delia screamed, flinging herself down at the ground to cover him. "Will, come on, we have to get on the ship!"

A rich tapestry of blood wove its way across his crisp white shirt in neat rivulets, a droplet pooling on the iridescent button at his waist.

"They're here!" Captain Violet shouted, unholstering her own revolver. "Get ready! Find cover!"

"Help me," Delia said, and Rosie lifted William under the arms and dragged him behind the ship, his boots dragging tracks in the orange clay soil. More shots echoed dully beneath the sharp explosions from the flares, the light dancing across the ground, the spectrum of color shifted by the cool light of the mirrors overhead. "How many are there?" Delia asked, pressing against his wound.

Rosie ducked her head around the side before darting back. "At least three squads. Too many. And they keep sending up flares."

"We need to get on the ship."

"They're shooting at the loading bay, there's no way we'll be able to get inside."

Ned emerged from behind a crate, a heat gun in one hand, and his cane in the other. "There's a secret entrance underneath. Follow me. Be as quiet as you can. Once you're on the ship, find Hyun and Jasper. Tell them to get ready for injuries. Find Ivy. Tell her we need full speed and power. Tell her to re-route whatever she needs to. We'll need it if we're going to get out of here alive."

Delia followed him under the ship, swallowing back the hacking coughs in her throat from the dust kicked up by their boots as they shuffled along, hunched under the metal body. "How do you think they tracked us?"

"Could have been anything," Ned replied in a whisper. "There are three groups of outlaws here—The Scattered, Obsidian Enclave, and us. It's probably not us, but you never know. The Coalition has been known to put trackers in almost anything."

"What about the weapon?" William asked, his voice a soft wheeze.

"You said it was a fake."

"I lied."

Ned, impressed, cocked an eyebrow. "That gives us leverage. Come on now, up you go." He popped open a small latch. "It's a secret room, meant for captains during a raid or a mutiny. There's a ladder at the far end." He boosted Rosie through first, and she reached down for William.

"You next, William," Rosie said.

"Wait," Delia said, hesitating. "What about you, Ned? Come with us, we'll pull you up."

"I have to get to the boss, tell her it's not a fake." He looked back. "I have to find Barnaby. He was right behind you and then..." Ned shook his head. "And then he wasn't."

"But what if—"

"Do what I said and then get a gun from the kitchen. It's hidden under the fourth floorboard from the entrance. There's another one hidden in the loading bay. Go!"

Delia scrambled up into the hatch, closing it behind her. William's shirt was already drenched with blood, and he was sweating. "We have to get him to the med bay."

"I'll pull him up the ladder," Rosie said, jumping up the rungs. She pulled William up onto the ship's deck and cupped her hands around her mouth. "Help!" she shouted. "Hyun!"

Hyun was there almost right away, already bent over William, with Jasper close behind with a rolling cot. "He's lost a lot of blood. Jas, load him up, we've got our work cut out for us." Without looking away from William, she asked, "Who else?"

"We don't know," Delia answered. "There are shots all over the place,

I saw three bodies, none of them ours, not sure if they're alive or… or not. The Coalition showed up and threw up flares."

"Gods," Hyun said with a small gasp.

"Ned said to be ready."

"And we will be. Jas, let's get him to the med bay. The sooner we stabilize him, the better. You two…" she trailed off.

"He said to find Ivy."

"She's in the kitchen."

Delia and Rosie peeled off down the corridor, running on the balls of their feet, just in case an MPO had already found themselves aboard.

"Whoa, where's the fire?" Ivy asked with a laugh. Her face sobered immediately. "What happened?"

"Gunfire. The trade went bad. The Coalition is here."

"Holy gods on fire in a chariot."

"Ned said to tell you—"

Ivy nodded. "Full power at the ready. I'll rewire. It's going to be close."

"He said there's a gun?"

"Fourth floorboard." Ivy took off out the doorway, tightening the tool belt at her hips as she ran.

Delia snatched a dull knife from the drawer and pried at the floorboard. It came away easily, revealing a well-kept silver revolver, fully loaded, with an extra long barrel engraved with a merfolk's tail. "Got it."

"Should we go to the loading bay?"

"They might need help."

"Let's go," Rosie said, tucking a large kitchen knife into her waistband.

"What in hells are you going to do with that?"

"It's insurance. I don't want those assholes dragging me onto their ship."

"Rosie, my posy… you are everything I ever wanted."

"Good. Come on."

The lights in the corridor flickered and went out. Ivy was already rerouting power. The boilers kicked on, one by one, until the ship had a low, growling hum.

The gun in Delia's hand was heavy and cold, yet fit into her palm easily.

Sneaking through the open airlock, they crept behind crates, straining to hear where the gunfire was coming from.

"Enough!" someone yelled, and the shots ceased.

Delia crept closer, hiding behind a small crate near the ramp down to the ground outside the ship. Dust hung in the air, a sickly yellowish brown that stuck to every surface. Captain Violet was crouched behind a boulder, reloading her revolver with ammunition from her breast pocket.

"This isn't over, Allemande," the captain shouted back. "You don't even know the half of it." Her stern, confident tone echoed across the flat ground, halted by the nearby cliff faces that reached high into the sky, their intimidating size making even the ships look miniature.

Allemande tilted her chin upwards, an unconscious attempt at intimidation. "I know enough. I know that you have my daughter on your disgusting little ship. I should have known when she went missing that it would be *you* that took her, squirreled her away from me, kidnapped her and forced her off the station. I know that she didn't go willingly."

"You're not getting her back."

"I strongly anticipate that statement to be false. Return her to me before I riddle the rest of your crew with bullet holes."

The Captain stood her ground, the smoke from the flares swirling around her. She smirked, lifting an eyebrow. "Seems like we're in a standoff, doesn't it? You're outnumbered, Overseer."

Allemande laughed. "Outnumbered? I have three squads, with more on the way. Your tiny, insignificant crew is powerless to resist."

"Let's make a deal, then. You piss off, and we carry on as we always have."

"A very droll joke, Captain. Or should I call you Cadet? That's what you were when you failed out of flight school all those years ago."

"I didn't fail, I ran."

"It's the same thing, I think you'll find—after all, you ended up here, defeated, regardless. Where is Evie Anderson? I know that she's here."

Captain Violet snorted a laugh. "Still pissed off about that broken jaw she gave you, eh? I can't say you didn't deserve it, after what you did to her."

"Bring her to me."

"She's a hundred thousand kilometers from here, more, even. Navigation was never my strong suit. But I can guarantee you that she's not with us."

"Nonsense. I know full well that she's the leader of your little brigade."

"Overseer, I could fill the Capital library with what you don't know."

"Bring her to me! Both of them! My daughter first!" Allemande's voice now was cold, steady, forceful in a way that made Delia's skin crawl as she crouched behind the crate. She stole another peek, snapping her head back when an MPO turned in her direction.

Kady crouched nearby. "Maybe we should just hand her over," she hissed to the captain. "Would solve some problems. She doesn't want to be here with us anyway, no matter what Georgie and Henry think."

"You can't have her!" Georgie shouted from the other side of the plateau. "You've taken enough from my family!"

Delia shifted her weight, sitting back on her haunches as she stole another look. Whatever happened, it wasn't going to be easy to get out of it, if any of them got out of it at all.

The overseer raised an eyebrow and then gave Georgie a condescending smirk. "Ms. Payne, how wonderful to meet you again. I presume your little scientist is around here somewhere as well? Indeed, I never expected to find so many targets here at the same time. It's like my birthday, except better. I never got to thank you for pushing me down that elevator shaft. Turns out, all that metal in my leg saved me from a different early demise."

"You brainwashed my sister. You carved up Evie, and Thomas, and—and—"

"Don't get hysterical. I never brainwashed Emeline. I care for her deeply, and as such, she has been educated to the highest standard, something you and your mother never bothered to do. She's far better off with me, where she can unfold her potential, instead of lying in squalor with *you*."

"You're a monster." Georgie started to raise the heat gun at her side, but Henry rose up from behind the same crate and pushed her arm back down.

"Don't," Henry said. "They'll kill you without a second glance, and then what will happen to your sister?"

"Ms. Weaver is correct," Allemande said coolly. "She always has been a brilliant scientific mind. An admirable dedication to her research, until your toxic desperation for power polluted her plans. Henrietta, your parents were so distressed when I told them what you had done. It's such a shame to see you wash your potential down the drain. Don't let the same thing happen to Emeline."

"If Emeline truly wants to go with you, we'll let her," Captain Violet announced. "But only if she agrees, without threats or force."

"I think we're past that now, don't you, Cadet?" Allemande asked. "I have three squads and ships filled to the brim with ammunition. I've already beaten you. Bring out my daughter."

Delia stood, shoving the barrel of the gun into the back of her trousers. "She's gone."

"Oh look, Ms. Dodson is here as well. Given your penchant for lies, you'll forgive me if I don't believe a word of it. Bring her to me, or I will start firing on all of you."

"It's the truth. You could search this ship from top to bottom, you won't find her. She left an hour before you arrived. Tell your navigators to check the radar logs—a shuttle flew out past the atmosphere."

"You let her go?" Kady and Georgie screamed in unison.

Kady shot Georgie a look, continuing, "She could be headed straight back to the Capital!"

The overseer's face darkened with rage. "What do you mean, she flew a shuttle? Emeline doesn't know how to pilot a ship!"

"She does, actually. Carmen taught her as a part of her diplomatic training," Delia explained.

"You let her take *my* shuttle?" Alice grumbled. "I just got it a few months ago!" She glared at the captain. "I told you we needed bio-scanners in the loading bay."

Captain Violet rubbed at the bridge of her nose. "There will be plenty of time for I-told-you-so later."

"Nonsense!" Allemande roared. "Bring her to me at once!"

"She isn't here, Overseer," Delia said again. "She's gone."

"Then where did she go?"

"I don't know. She didn't find it necessary to tell me," Delia lied. "Judging by the technology on this craft, I imagine that once she was out of radar range, that shuttle will be a challenge to track."

"But we're within shuttle distance of half a dozen different transport hubs! She could be anywhere, about to get snatched up by brigands like you!"

"Emeline is all but grown. She has learned how to handle herself."

"I'll make sure that you regret the day that you crossed me, Ms. Dodson. Officers! Arrest them! Capture them all, and I don't care if they die in the struggle."

The MPOs began to advance, their weapons drawn, closing the distance between their ships and the Cricket one heavy boot thud at a time. An Obsidian Enclave soldier rushed forward and fell dead with the crack of a gunshot.

"We have nothing to do with this," Gregor shouted, his voice strangled with emotion. "We don't know your daughter!"

"I know who you are, Gregor Zink," Allemande said. "If you think that I'm unaware that your sniveling comrades are camped out beyond the Rim, you are desperately mistaken. Embarrassingly so."

"Just let us get back on our ship, and we will leave with no further bloodshed. Your quarrel isn't with us."

"The hell it isn't." The overseer raised her own revolver and fired it. Gregor fell to the ground, clutching his stomach. "Obsidian Enclave are like cockroaches. Though they may seem at times to be innumerable, all you need is a good exterminator. Guards! Round up the rest!"

"Don't shoot," Captain Violet said, defeated. "We are outgunned."

An MPO slapped a pair of cuffs around Kady's wrists, and she spat in his eye. "Fuck you," she growled. "I'll never talk."

"You always talk, in the end," Allemande said.

Kady smirked. "Evie Anderson didn't."

The overseer's eyes flashed with anger. "She will, once I've gotten my hands on her. I was too merciful with her last time. I won't make that mistake again." She waved her hand in a graceful twirl. "Kill the rest."

"Wait!" Cass shouted, emerging from a scrape in the cliff side. "Wait."

"Cassius Calvetti. I did not expect to see *you* here," Allemande said. There was a tiny waver in her voice, though not enough to show fear to the guards. "What were you doing here, I wonder?" The plateau grew quiet, the only sounds those of shuffling feet against dusty clay and Gregor Zink's quiet groans of pain.

"Trying to recruit your daughter into my ranks. After what she pulled in Skelm, I thought we might have a surefire chance."

"You disgust me."

Cass shrugged. "I don't really care. We could get into a tit for tat of who has committed more atrocities, but that doesn't seem like an efficient use of anyone's time, now does it, Overseer?"

"You're a fool, Ms. Calvetti. Now you'll end up in a cell, just like the last person who stood in your shoes, in that position. It wasn't even that long ago, was it? He begged for his life at the end, you know. A coward to the last. He told us everything we wanted to know."

Cass laughed. "Not so fast. You don't know where you are, do you?"

"A derelict asteroid mining camp."

"Yes, but it's *my* derelict asteroid mining camp, and as such, the tunnels all across this rock are filled with The Scattered. I think you'll find that it's *you* who is outnumbered, Overseer."

"Run a scan," Allemande barked to an MPO.

"At least three hundred," the guard responded.

The overseer smirked. "Three hundred isn't going to be much against the might of the Coalition. You can bet there are at least a dozen more squads headed here right now, armed to the gills with enough explosives to wipe your little encampment off of the map."

"You and I both know those squads are at least twenty minutes away. I wonder what could happen in twenty minutes?"

"Whatever you do to me, it won't stop the reinforcements from mowing you down."

"No, and you're right about that," Cass said, approaching, her close-cropped hair covered in the dust kicked up from the ships' engines. She folded her arms over her chest, the brass buttons of her jacket glinting in the cold light. "I am going to suggest that we make a deal, what do you say?"

"I don't make deals with outlaws."

"No, but you might, if you knew that it was the best option. Think about it, Overseer. You can try to overpower us before your troops arrive. You will lose." Cass laughed. "We'll kill every last one of you Coalition rats! Sure, we'll have a hard go of it once those squads land, but it won't matter, because you'll be dead."

"Many have tried to kill me, and all have failed."

Cass whipped her revolver out before any of the guards even flinched. "I have impeccable aim, Overseer. I can promise that you won't survive our encounter."

"Then what is your alternative proposition? We let you all free, I suppose? Allow you to continue to undermine and extort the Coalition for your own selfish gains?"

"I will humbly turn myself over to you, relinquish my weapons, but you have to turn the rest of them loose." She glanced back towards the Obsidian Enclave ship. "Except them. I don't care about them."

"What a moving display of solidarity," Allemande said. "How selfless of you to throw yourself upon my mercy and beg for your life."

"If anyone winds up begging today, I can promise you that it's not going to be me."

"Why do you think I would allow such a flagrant display of weakness? None of you will leave this asteroid alive if you so much as lay a hand on me."

"Think about it, Amaranth. There are two paths that diverge from this moment. In one path, you're dead, cold in the ground, and no one, not even that girl you kidnapped, will remember you. Not even a footnote in history. *Pathetic. Or*, you can be the overseer who successfully tracked and captured Cassius Calvetti, leader of The Scattered. You'd be celebrated across the Near Systems for your tireless dedication to eradicating the rot of piracy and rebellion."

"And what do you get out of it, besides a short, imprisoned life and a public execution?"

Cass flinched. "To save bloodshed. No one else has to die here today. You take me, you're free to go chase your daughter down. You start shooting, no one leaves this rock breathing, I guarantee it."

"Uh, Overseer, we're picking up an explosive signature somewhere below us," the guard said.

"You wired the entire asteroid with explosives," Allemande said coolly. "You would murder your own people? To what end?"

"We are all called to make unpalatable decisions in war," Cass replied.

"This isn't a war. It's a tantrum, dragged out by lazy little cretins like you, who are afraid to work towards the greater good of something. You and your ilk would rather destroy than build."

"There's no greater good until there aren't children starving in your streets. How can you call it progress when the rich build space stations while refugees of your abandoned mines die alone from preventable illnesses?"

"You have no understanding of leadership. You play games, that's all—and the time for childish pretenses is at an end. It doesn't matter what happens today, Ms. Calvetti, because either way, The Scattered are at an end."

"Make your choice, Overseer."

Allemande considered her options, taking the scanner from the guard and running it herself. "I will need to search this ship. For all I know, my daughter is being held prisoner, and the shuttle was a diversion."

Captain Violet nodded, and three guards boarded the Cricket. "Ned, go with them," she said. "Make sure they don't steal anything."

"It's not us that engage in thievery, Cadet," the overseer said with a sniff. "I believe you'd need a mirror to see the culprits there."

Delia jerked back from the door as the guards entered the ship, leaning back into Rosie. "There are three in the medical bay, and one in the boiler room," she said.

"Don't worry," Ned replied, holding his heat gun at his hip. "They won't get into any mischief, now will you, boys?"

"Fuck off," one of them said. "Lay one finger on me and I'll put a hole in your gut wide enough to reach through."

"Hurry up, you have ninety seconds."

"We have as many seconds as we want. We're the ones with squads inbound."

"Yeah, and we're the ones with the trigger for enough explosives to make sure that even your mother couldn't identify the remains, so keep it moving."

Allemande cleared her throat. "You do realize, Ms. Calvetti, that even if you do give yourself up, those squads will land here, regardless? Your people aren't going to have a chance."

"You'd let squads land on a rock, knowing they'll die in the explosion?" Cass asked.

"As you said, we all make difficult choices."

"You should know, Overseer, and if you look up right now, you will see that I have my own reinforcements arriving. If you want to get me off this rock, you're going to need your own squads to escort me to whatever disgusting cell you have in mind. I might go willingly, but they certainly will not allow it."

"Well, haven't you just thought of *everything?*"

"You don't get to where I am without a little forward-planning."

"Yet, it's still going to land you in prison."

Cass tilted her chin up, a smirk playing on her lips. "You may win the battle today, Overseer, but you'll never win the war."

"Take her," Allemande said, her tone icy.

The guard with a gun to Alice's head holstered the weapon and turned to cuff Cass, who was kicking her own guns away, her hands held aloft in surrender.

The overseer smiled. "You know what I find most amusing? That this all came to pass because another one of you miscreants thought to steal a weapon from Turas-Mara. Oh, yes, we knew as soon as the ship scurried away, fleeing back into dark space, that it was taken. But it didn't matter, because it was a counterfeit. How many have died, now, in pursuit of it? Three? Four?"

Delia reached back and rested her palm on the gun from the kitchen. The tension in the air was thick and uneasy, like an unset gelatin, or that rice pudding Rosie's grandfather used to make them when they were kids.

"And it was all for nothing," Allemande continued, striding along the length of the Obsidian Enclave ship. "Lives lost for a piece of useless garbage. You fools think that you can overcome the might of the Coalition, but you are wrong. We will always be two steps ahead of you. We will always know where you are, and how to find you."

The two guards that had boarded the ship reappeared, dragging Ivy behind them. "Ma'am, we found a teenage girl aboard—"

"That's not my daughter, you incompetent fools!"

"No, but... maybe we should take her, anyway. There's no record of her in the archives."

"No record? Who are you?" she barked at Ivy. "Where do you come from?"

"I'm Ivy, and I come from none of your damned business! Take your hands off me!"

"Bring her. If she has no record, she was likely born off-world in a rebel settlement."

Alice launched forward, tackling one of the guards outside around the knees and taking his heat gun. "You're not taking her! That wasn't the deal!"

"You'll soon learn that I always win," Allemande said, a grin spreading across her face. "Always."

The guards began to drag Ivy off the ship. She was kicking her legs out and sobbing, trying to wrest away from their grip. "No!" she screamed. "Leave me alone!"

"Fuck this," Rosie muttered, and before Delia could reach out to stop her, she sprang out from behind the crate and sank the kitchen knife deep into the calf of one of the guards.

He fell, screaming, clutching at his leg. The other released Ivy, reaching for his gun, but Delia got hers first, firing wildly but hitting him in the thigh. Ivy took the gun he dropped and backed away, inching back up the ship's ramp, her hands shaking.

"Kill them!" Allemande shouted, her eyes cold and empty.

All at once, the plateau erupted into gunfire and heat bolts, singing through the air before they smashed into metal, rock, flesh. Ivy shot at another guard trying to make it up the ramp, and Ned fired his heat gun at the other ship, where a red-hot hole appeared in the leg of the landing gear.

Delia was pulling at Rosie, trying to get her back into cover. Ammunition was everywhere, zinging past their ears, putting wide dents into the metal of the ship. Someone was screaming—was it one of their own, or an MPO?

They were leading Cass away, dragging her up the ramp of one of the Coalition ships. "Take it!" she was screaming, but Delia couldn't hear her, only read the words on her lips.

"Where's the weapon?" Delia asked.

"It's out there still!" Ivy responded, diving behind another crate.

"Stay here. I'm going to go and get it."

Rosie grabbed her arm. "Dee, no! It's too dangerous!"

"I'll be back before you know it." Their lips met for a brief moment before Delia pulled away, moving for the loading bay door. Whatever that thing was, whether it was genuine or counterfeit, William had nearly died trying to deal with it. That couldn't just be for nothing.

Ducking down behind a boulder, she spotted it, toppled over onto the ground next to the cart it had been wheeled out on. Obsidian Enclave ships began to pull off the surface of the asteroid, kicking up so much of the yellowy-brown dust that visibility bottomed out, leaving Delia grasping along the ground towards the weapon.

The dust caught at the back of her throat and made her eyes stream, but she knew better than to rub them. She pulled her thin, damp shirt over her face, suddenly grateful that her clothes hadn't dried that morning. Hacking back a cough, she grappled with the dirt, fumbling for the weapon. Some of the gunfire had been replaced with the sound of wheezing, but shots continued to ring out, the sound echoing off the metallic exterior of the ships.

"Go!" Cass was yelling, until her voice was strangled into silence.

"Get on the ship!" Captain Violet shouted between coughs. "Everyone, now!"

Delia squinted, but she couldn't see, even with her eyes shielded from the grit in the air. She scraped her fingers through the dirt, clawing furiously until she found the smooth finish of the weapon. It was lighter than she thought it would be, with a rounded edge.

Holding it in her hands, she sprinted back in the direction she came from, though the swirling clouds of dust and dirt confused her sense of direction.

"Where do you think you're going?" Kady shouted, grabbing at her suspenders and pushing her off to the side. "You'll go over the cliff if you keep going that way."

They stumbled back onto the Cricket, and Kady snatched the weapon from Delia's hands.

"Captain! She got it!"

"Ned, pull us out! Now, right now!" the captain shouted.

"Do we have everyone?" Ivy asked, her hands on the lever for the door.

"Yes, yes! Close the door!"

Rosie wrapped Delia in a tight embrace. "Please don't ever do that again."

"No promises," Delia replied with a wry smile. "Nice work with the knife."

"I told you we might need it."

The ship lifted off the surface of Terringgough Gulch, thrashing and rocking as it ascended. No one said a word, as though they were all anticipating being shot down, and sent spiraling back to the asteroid.

"Boss!" Ned's voice crackled over the radio. "I need you up here, pronto! Visibility is shit and all this damned dust is blocking the autopilot sensors!"

"On my way!" the captain responded, already running for the bridge.

"Ivy, with me," Alice announced, moving her eye patch from her good eye back to her missing one, the scar a long, jagged line over her eyelid. "We need to make sure none of the conduits come apart."

Kady cradled the weapon in the excess fabric of her cloak, wrapping it up to cushion against any unexpected blows. "We need to get this back to the science division in Bradach. If it's what we thought... if it's what Bailey said it might be... this could change everything."

"What if it's a fake?" Rosie asked.

"That's why we need to get it somewhere safe, where we can study it."

"Someone get on the goddamn cannon!" the captain's voice boomed through the speaker. "If we don't shake these assholes, we're not going to make it!"

"You two," Kady ordered, "over there. Shoot at anything coming after us. I need to hide this in case we get boarded."

"You think we'll get boarded?"

"We definitely will if you don't get your asses in gear!"

Delia ran to the cannon, running her hands over the smooth metal. "Heavier than I thought," she said. "Rosie, I'll guide, you light."

"Have you lost your senses? We both know I'm a better anchor than you. I'll guide, *you* light."

"Whatever happens, we'll do it together," Delia said, grabbing Rosie's hand. "Together, we're unstoppable."

The cannon fired, one blast after another, explosions lighting up dark space, the orange flames glistening through the Cricket's portholes, until every other ship had pulled away from their pursuit, leaving them alone on their path.

"Captain, we're clear," Kady said, nodding at them with approval.

"Good," the radio echoed with the captain's voice. "Get out of the bay, we can't risk depressurization."

Delia and Rosie pressed themselves into the crew airlock and pressurized, before tumbling out onto the ship, both of them sprawled on the floor. "I love you, Rosie," she said, holding onto her as the ship lurched into maximum speed. The lights were out, the corridors dark but buzzing with the hum of the ship's engines.

"I love you, too."

Epilogue

"Thank you for tuning in to tonight's broadcast with our special guest, Ms. Emeline Allemande. Join us tomorrow for an in-depth look into work camp living conditions. I am your host, Delia Forrest, signing off."

"We're out," Carmen said with a smile. "Emeline, that was excellent."

Emeline frowned. "I'm glad you enjoyed that, because I won't be doing it again. I have to run a respectable campaign, and that means not being associated with people like *you*."

"They're outside waiting," Rosie said gently.

Rising slowly from her chair, Emeline smoothed her skirts and straightened her shoulders before opening the door of the small room they'd rented for this broadcast. "Hello," she said.

"Emmy!" her little sister Lucy shouted, flinging her arms around Emeline's waist. "I missed you so much!"

"You got so tall! Look at you, you're a giant!"

"I can't wait for you to come live with us, Emmy! There's plenty of food, and Mama gets help for her lungs, and—"

"I can't come live with you, Luce. I have to work to make that possible for everyone, not just us."

Lucy's face fell. "I know. I understand, I guess—but I'm really going to miss you."

"I'll miss you too, Honey Bee. We'll see each other again, I promise."

Her mother wheeled closer, apprehensive. "You changed your name."

"I had to."

"I understand. Just... just don't forget where your roots are, Em."

"I won't ever forget that, Ma." Emeline examined the chair. "Nice wheels."

"They've changed my life. I work at the... well, I guess I shouldn't say, really, but I work helping people. I'm going to get married soon. You'd like him. Very pragmatic."

"That's really good, Ma."

"I've missed you something fierce."

Emeline brushed a tear from her cheek. "I missed you, too. No one makes corn bread like you, not even Rosie."

"You should talk to your sister, you know. To Georgie."

"I have nothing to say to her, and she knows exactly why."

"She did what she had to do, Em."

"We disagree on that point. Besides, I'm sure she's far too busy disrupting trade routes to care."

"She spent years looking for you. She didn't do much else. She's the only reason Carmen got sent out to Turas-Mara Station, the only reason we were able to get you out of there."

"Is that what she told you? The reality is much less favorable. I was kidnapped, held prisoner on three different ships. I just... I need time and space, and to be able to decide my own fate for a while."

"Don't forget about us, you hear?"

Emeline bent over and hugged her mother. "I could never." With that, she hugged Lucy one more time, and boarded a vessel bound for Skelm just two bays away.

"We'd better get a move on," Delia said. "It won't be long before they figure out that we pirated their antennae."

Rosie rested her chin on Delia's shoulder. "It will be at least three days back to Bradach on the Dry Barrel."

"Two if we get a move on," Captain Tansy said. "Let's go. I already have a hit out on this ship from a merchant I pissed off last year."

"You steal his stuff?"

"No, I never showed up for the second date."

"Ouch."

"Tell William and the rest of them to hurry up. I want to get gone in the next ten minutes."

"I'll get them," Carmen said, the yellow fabric of her dress flouncing prettily even in the dim light of the travel beacon.

Captain Tansy sighed. "We're going to have a hell of a time on our hands, you know. Now the Coalition knows that thing is missing, we're going to be in for the fight of our lives."

"You think so?" Rosie asked.

"I know so. Everything up until now has just been the calm before the storm."

Delia glanced up at the departure boards and sighed. She had a freedom she'd not had before, but with it came more danger than she'd accounted for.

* * *

Good morning, I'm Delia Forrest. In today's news, we can announce that the leader of The Scattered, Cassius Calvetti, was captured by Coalition forces at Terringgough Gulch amid tense negotiations with Obsidian Enclave. Reports suggest she has been taken to a maximum-security prison of unknown location.

"How are we doing on getting intel?" Captain Violet asked, leaning against the bar of the Purple Pig. "Cass? What about Barnaby? We know he got pulled in by the Obsidian Enclave ship at Terringgough Gulch."

"Nothing, yet," Thomas answered, scribbling notes on scraps of paper. "We're still working on it."

Overseer Amaranth Allemande of Sector Six has been presented with a commendation from the High Council for her efforts in arresting Calvetti, and is headed back to the Outer Rim to continue assisting General Wilhemina Fineglass with research expeditions.

"Yeah, because that monster really needs more accolades," Evie huffed.

"It's too bad that trip down the elevator shaft didn't take her out," Larkin said, offering Georgie and Henry a smile.

Georgie only stared down at her empty glass. "Yeah. Too bad," she said.

In trade route news, we can announce that new nav maps which include all currently functioning beacons and blockades. They can be collected from your friendly, local black market trader. Remember to tip them for their service!

"That's going to ruffle some feathers in the Capital," Rosie said, drying a glass. "Ned did a fantastic job in getting those out there."

"It will help the smugglers for sure," Evie replied. "Captain Tansy already brought in three transports this week."

Stay tuned for tomorrow's broadcast: everything you need to know about grey market chips and disabling tracking on your Coalition-issued tracking devices. Until then, I'm Delia Forrest. Thank you for listening.

"How is the signal pirating going?" Captain Violet asked.

"No interference yet," Rosie said. "Thanks to Kady's coding."

Delia emerged from the Purple Pig's basement, stretching her arms over her head. "Nice job on the Calvetti information, Will," she said, sitting at the bar. She grabbed Rosie's hand and kissed it. "Hello, my love."

"You saw me an hour ago," Rosie said, laughing. She leaned over the bar and kissed her, their lips brushing gently, and lingering a moment too long.

"No news from any of the main prisons," Will said, holding his side. "Strange. It's like they vanished her into nothing."

"We'll find her," Larkin said. "We always find our people."

"Not Marina," Bailey interjected, setting down a crate in the kitchen doorway. "We haven't found her yet, either."

"We will. If anyone can track them down, it's Evie."

"Any news from The Scattered?" Captain Violet asked, looking at Delia.

Delia sighed. "Nothing yet. They're scrambling. I didn't want to broadcast that, though."

"Understandable."

"Rosie, you finished yet?"

Larkin nudged Rosie with her elbow. "You can go, Eves and I will finish up preparing for the lunch rush. We'll see you later?"

Rosie nodded. "You can't keep me out of that kitchen." She untied her purple apron, hanging it on a hook just inside the swinging kitchen door.

Hand in hand, Rosie and Delia walked the streets of Bradach, feeling the mirrored sun on their skin, and even if for a few moments, it was like they'd never spent a day apart. With a deep breath, Rosie slid the letter to her family into the mail bag at the docks. All she could do now was hope for a reply.

461

* * *

End of Book 5

Keep reading for a sneak peek into the next novel in the series, **Unbound Oath.**

Sign up for my newsletter and get information about convention appearances, book launch parties, new releases, and more! Get bonus content for the Cricket Chronicles series like deleted scenes and extended cuts.

http://eepurl.com/gOQBaP

Unbound Oath preview

Cassius Calvetti was never supposed to be the leader of the rebellion. She certainly hadn't dreamed that she would rise to the top of The Scattered when she stumbled into one of their havens, half dead, less than five years earlier. They'd saved her life, and in return, she threw everything she had into the organization of more raids, more strikes, more refugees being transferred across the Near Systems and out of Coalition control. She smirked. The Coalition hated that.

She stared at the ceiling of her cell, the smooth, unblemished concrete painted white like the floor, the walls, the iron bars that kept her imprisoned, and the metal slab they had the audacity to call a bed. It was like a starvation of the mind, and it was enough to make her doubt her own reality. If fate was fair, she was already dead, paused in death's waiting room for one of the old gods to collect her, or send her back for another round in the Near Systems. She wouldn't mess up again, next time.

"Prisoner four-oh-seven, come to the slot to collect your rations."

Cass sighed, her legs dangling over the side of the bed, the metal biting into her thighs. "I think I'll skip dinner today, actually."

The prison guard pounded on the bars with his metal gloves. "Prisoner four-oh-seven! Now!"

"Fine, fine, gods, keep your uniform on." She frowned at the half molded protein brick that slid through the narrow slot. "Got anything else? I had this yesterday. And the day before that. Every day since I got here, actually."

"Eat it."

"I'm not hungry," she said, glancing between the bars.

"No hunger strikes allowed. Eat it."

"What will you do if I don't?"

The guard narrowed his eyes. "Then I'll be forced to report this up the chain of command, and they will come down here with feeding tubes."

"Do you ever have an answer other than that?"

"No."

So she pinched her nose, chewed twice, and swallowed, just as she had twice a day for nearly six months. "There. Eaten. Are you happy?"

"I don't want to hear a peep out of you the rest of the night."

"Not like there's anyone to talk to, anyway."

The guard disappeared down the long, sterile corridor, and turned the corner at the dead end, no doubt to go and annoy other prisoners.

Six months with no questioning, no news from the outside, no clue as to what had happened after they'd lifted off Terringgough Gulch.

She closed her eyes and counted to three hundred, and almost on the dot of the final number, she heard the guard cross into the adjacent corridor. "Time to get to work," she muttered, her ear to the wall. No movement. Good.

"Three up, two down, left," she repeated under her breath as she reached under the metal frame of the bed to retrieve the makeshift key she had been bending into place for nearly a month. The last two had failed to work in the lock, but this time she just knew it was going to work.

It wasn't easy, memorizing the shape of a key as it hung on the belt of a guard, but it was her only chance at escape. They wouldn't let her have anything inside her cell, not even a paper and a pencil, for fear she would find some way to get out. She wasn't a master con artist, but she had patience and reserve, and thick calluses on her hands that allowed her to slowly nudge the metal into shape, metal that had been snapped from one of the bed's supports. That alone had taken nearly two weeks of careful work.

The makeshift key was cold and heavy in her hands, and it carried the weight of thousands, all desperate to escape Coalition control. If The Scattered was smart, they'd have replaced her the moment she was taken. After all, that's how she had ended up as leader in the first place. They needed a leader, especially now.

Slowly, painfully, she pressed at the metal, first with her hands, and then her feet, given only socks to wear and no boots made for a sluggish pace, but it was better than no pace at all. There was a ventilation duct on the opposite wall. If she could spring herself from her cell, then she could escape into the shaft, find her way out of the building... and then what?

It didn't matter.

Cass was resourceful and determined; if she could make it out of this cell, then she could figure out the rest on the fly. If she stayed trapped in this cell, there was no telling what might kill her first - the Coalition, with a public execution, or the creeping boredom that was already rotting the edges of her mind.

About the Author

Ryann Fletcher is a writer who lives with her wife and too many craft supplies. She writes sapphic science fiction and fantasy, and likes to cook.

You can connect with me on:

- https://ryannfletcher.com
- https://twitter.com/IMRyannFletcher
- https://facebook.com/RyannFletcherWrites
- https://instagram.com/RyannFletcherWrites
- https://www.tiktok.com/@ryannfletcherwrites

Subscribe to my newsletter:

- http://eepurl.com/gOQBaP

Also by Ryann Fletcher

Unbound Oath

Cassius Calvetti was never supposed to be the leader of The Scattered. Awaiting trial in a Coalition prison, she makes one more desperate attempt at escape.

It's been eight years since Olivia Guisette took on the job of being the right hand to High Councilor Tarand. When she's given an ultimatum, she winds up facing down death.

In book 6 of The Cricket Chronicles, alliances unravel and new adversaries creep towards victory.